RACE
for the
FLASH
STONE

K. PATRICK DONOGHUE

Published by Leaping Leopard Enterprises, LLC

RACE FOR THE FLASH STONE
eISBN: 978-0-9973164-3-8
ISBN: 978-0-9973164-2-1 (paperback)
ISBN: 978-0-9973164-4-5 (hardcover)

Published by Leaping Leopard Enterprises, LLC
www.leapingleopard.com

First edition: April 2017
Cover art and design by Asha Hossain Design LLC
Author photograph by Down Owens Photography

DEDICATION

To my mother and father,
Phyllis and Kevin
For your lifelong gifts of love, guidance and encouragement

Contents

Acknowledgements

I would like to extend my thanks to the extraordinary group of people who helped me create *Race for the Flash Stone*.

First and foremost, I would like to thank my wife, Bryson, and my two sons, Michael and Stephen. I am humbled by your encouragement, support and understanding. During the nine months it took to write the book, you were thoughtful sounding boards, constructive critics and enthusiastic cheerleaders (as you always are). I couldn't have published the story without your love and support!

Next, I would like to thank my super-fans, fans and other *Shadows of the Stone Benders* readers. Many of you wrote to share your views about the story, the characters and my writing style. Your constructive feedback inspired a number of enhancements in *Race for the Flash Stone*, and your encouragement made the story a joy to write!

In addition, I would like to thank the team of people who helped shape and polish the presentation of *Race for the Flash Stone*: to my editor, Katherine Pickett of POP Editorial Services, for your guidance, suggestions and for challenging me when necessary; to my proofreaders, Cheryl Hollenbeck and Lisa Weinberg, for your eye for detail and genuine interest in my stories; to Asha Hossain, for crafting a cover design that brings the story's mysterious elements to life; to Amber Morena, for the fresh and eye-catching look of the hardback and paperback interiors; to Donna Owens, for your photographic artistry; and last but not least, to James Lee and Kevin Maines of JML Design, for your sleek design of my author web site.

Finally, I would like to thank my mom and dad, Phyllis and Kevin, to whom this book is dedicated. It never ceases to amaze me how many ways you show your love. Thank you for being the best super-fans a son could ask for!

Preface

Thank you for choosing to read *Race for the Flash Stone*, the second book in The Anlon Cully Chronicles series.

For fans of the first book in the series, *Shadows of the Stone Benders*, welcome back! I'm pleased you've decided to join Anlon, Pebbles and Jennifer for the next leg of their ongoing adventures.

For those who are new to The Anlon Cully Chronicles, greetings! Given "*Race*" is a continuation of the mystery first explored in "*Shadows*," I encourage you to tackle the series in order. While it's possible to read *Race* as a stand-alone mystery, your enjoyment of the story will be enhanced with a deeper understanding of the storyline and character relationships portrayed in *Shadows*.

With those salutations made, I offer a prefacing remark to all readers—those who approach *Race* with a healthy willingness to suspend disbelief will enjoy the story the most!

While *Race* is an archaeology-based murder mystery about the search to prove the existence of a long-forgotten civilization, there is a strong element of fantasy in the story (more so than in *Shadows*).

The heightened element of fantasy in *Race* is a direct outgrowth of feedback I received from thousands of *Shadows* readers. Among these readers, there was a pronounced desire for more focus on the magnetic stones featured in *Shadows* and the ancient people who created them. Therefore, a greater proportion of *Race* is devoted to the fantastical stones and fictional civilization.

If you consider yourself a purist when it comes to mystery/thriller/suspense novels, fear not! So long as you can handle an Indiana Jones-style/level of fantasy, you'll find plenty of action, treachery, twists and turns to hold your interest all the way through.

To help all readers with the fantasy elements of the book, I've included a glossary of fictional terms used in the story, as well as an illustration of the *Sinethal* (Master Stone). eBook readers can quickly access these sections by clicking on the links for each in the table of contents.

Regarding the story itself, the initial chapters of *Race* are designed to bridge the gap between the state of affairs at the end of *Shadows* and the onset of the core action of *Race*. As a result, readers will notice a small crossover in timeline between the two stories.

Shadows readers will recall most of the story occurs over a week's time in early May, while the Epilogue scene takes place in mid-July. In *Race*, the early chapters focus on the activities of the various villains involved in the story between mid-May and mid-July, with Anlon, Pebbles and Jennifer joining the storyline in early August (Chapter 4, Minds Over Matters).

With those prefacing comments in mind, I hope you enjoy the adventure depicted in *Race for the Flash Stone* and that the story leaves you yearning to know what happens next in the series' third installment, *Curse of the Painted Lady*.

Prologue:
In the News

May 16–May 31

MAN KILLED, ANOTHER INJURED, IN FAILED KIDNAPPING ATTEMPT
Authorities believe the incident may be related to two unsolved murders

STOCKBRIDGE–May 16–A 60-year-old Great Barrington man was shot and killed by police Saturday during a botched kidnapping attempt that also left a 42-year-old Nevada man clinging to life.

According to authorities, the incident began when Mr. Pacal Flores, a resident of Great Barrington, allegedly kidnapped Ms. Anabel Simpson, 58, from her home in Bennington, Vermont, and then drove to the abandoned Stillwater Quarry outside of Stockbridge.

Once there, Flores contacted Dr. Anlon Cully, a Nevada resident visiting Stockbridge, and demanded certain rare artifacts as ransom. Cully alerted police and then went to the quarry. Before police arrived, a confrontation erupted between the two men and Cully was gravely injured.

Law enforcement officials were tight-lipped when questioned about Cully's injuries, but an anonymous source close to the investigation said he was brutally beaten with a stone.

Det. Lt. Jennifer Stevens, 32, from the Massachusetts State Police's Berkshire Detective Unit, arrived on scene during the confrontation. According to the police report, Flores attacked Stevens, at which time the detective fired three shots. A police spokesman said Flores was struck twice in the upper torso and died before EMTs arrived.

In a bizarre twist, the anonymous source indicated Flores might have played a role in the recent murders of two Stockbridge-area archaeologists, Dr. Devlin Wilson and Dr. Matthew Dobson. According to the source, Flores and Dobson worked for Wilson, and the artifacts demanded as ransom belonged to the deceased Wilson.

During a brief press conference on Sunday, law enforcement officials identified two others as persons of interest in connection with the crimes: Dr. Thatcher Reynolds, age 64, a New York resident, and Ms. Margaret Corchran, age 38, a Florida resident.

Authorities seek the assistance of the community in establishing Reynolds' and Corchran's whereabouts. Anyone with information is asked to call the Massachusetts State Police tip line.

NEW DETAILS EMERGE IN DEVLIN WILSON MURDER INVESTIGATION
Police formally charge Margaret Corchran with murder of archaeologist Devlin Wilson. Corchran's brother, Kyle, named co-conspirator.

CONCORD–May 24–New Hampshire Assistant Attorney General James Dooley announced Margaret Corchran has been charged with first-degree murder in the death of the archaeologist Devlin Wilson earlier this month. Dooley also announced Corchran's brother, Kyle Corchran, has been charged with conspiracy to murder for his role in the plot to kill Wilson.

According to police officials present at the announcement, the Corchrans lured Wilson to a treacherous White Mountains hiking trail where Ms. Corchran caused Wilson to fall to his death while Mr. Corchran served as lookout.

Authorities said Mr. Corchran has confessed to his participation in Wilson's death and is cooperating with police to help apprehend Ms. Corchran, who remains a fugitive at this writing.

Dooley indicated the motive for the murder stemmed from Wilson's discovery of thefts from his private art collection. The Corchrans acted to prevent the archaeologist from contacting police about the missing artifacts.

The thefts occurred at Wilson's home in Stockbridge, Massachusetts, and are the focus of a separate investigation by Massachusetts State Police. Dooley stated the two jurisdictions are collaborating in the collection of evidence and apprehension of Ms. Corchran.

Massachusetts officials have charged the Corchrans with multiple counts of grand theft, trafficking of stolen goods and unlawful entry. Ms. Corchran received an additional charge for felony assault for injuries inflicted on Mr. Corchran during a failed robbery attempt.

Dooley said Mr. Corchran is currently being held at Massachusetts' Cedar Junction prison hospital, where he is recovering from injuries sustained during Ms. Corchran's assault. He indicated Mr. Corchran will be transferred to a New Hampshire prison facility once doctors approve the move.

The assistant attorney general finished his announcement by making a plea for any information regarding

Ms. Corchran's whereabouts. He said the fugitive is considered armed and dangerous and a threat to the community. Those with information are encouraged to contact the New Hampshire State Police or Massachusetts State Police.

MISSING NEW YORK MAN SOUGHT FOR QUESTIONING IN MASSACHUSETTS MURDER INVESTIGATION
Dr. Thatcher Reynolds implicated in murder
of archaeologist Matthew Dobson

PITTSFIELD–May 25–Dr. Thatcher Reynolds, 64, a professor of archaeology at New York's Hamilton College, remains missing as Massachusetts State Police officials continue to investigate his possible involvement in the murder of Matthew Dobson, 74, of Stockbridge.

Dobson was the research partner of the archaeologist Devlin Wilson, 85, who was murdered in a separate incident several days before Dobson's killing. Police believe both men's murders shared a common motive—theft of rare artifacts from Wilson's private art collection.

It is in this context police seek Reynolds for questioning. Police believe the professor was involved in a scheme to steal from Wilson. Reynolds' possible involvement came to light after the main suspect in Dobson's murder, Pacal Flores, of Great Barrington, was killed in a confrontation with police.

According to authorities, evidence collected from the homes and offices of Flores and Reynolds indicates both men conspired to snatch artifacts from Wilson, with the intention of selling the stolen goods to black-market foreign collectors whom police have yet to identify.

Flores and Reynolds reportedly killed Dobson after they discovered that he had designs on stealing the same artifacts in Wilson's collection.

Police believe Reynolds fled the upstate New York area shortly after Flores was killed by police, and his whereabouts remain unknown. They speculate Reynolds may have fled the country with the assistance of the unidentified black-market collectors. Those with information regarding Reynolds' whereabouts or the murder of Matthew Dobson are encouraged to contact the Massachusetts State Police.

ARGENTINIAN MINING MOGUL UNDER HOUSE ARREST AS U.S. AUTHORITIES SEEK EXTRADITION FOR GRAND THEFT

Klaus Navarro vehemently denies allegations,
vows to fight extradition attempts

WASHINGTON, D.C.–May 31–U.S. State Department officials, in conjunction with the Department of Justice, are engaged in contentious extradition discussions with Argentinian government representatives regarding alleged crimes committed by Argentinian citizen Klaus Navarro, age 47.

Navarro, a businessman who controls several South American mining companies, is a well-known collector and trader of Mesoamerican art. He gained national prominence nearly two weeks ago when the Massachusetts State Police named him as the ring leader of a group that plundered valuable art pieces owned by the murdered archaeologist, Devlin Wilson.

According to Justice officials, Wilson was killed because he discovered the thefts and threatened to expose the thieves. One of Navarro's alleged co-conspirators, Kyle Corchran, of Dallas, Texas, was captured by police and fingered Navarro as the "head of the snake."

Mr. Corchran indicated that he and his sister, Margaret Corchran, of Miami, Florida, acted as brokers between their uncle, Matthew Dobson, and Navarro in orchestrating several thefts from Wilson's art collection. Dobson, an employee of Wilson's, had unsupervised access to the art collection.

Navarro's attorneys deny their client's involvement in any crime. They claim Navarro entered into legal purchase agreements of several pieces from Wilson's collection under the belief the transactions were authorized by Wilson. Navarro issued a statement echoing this position and vowed to fight to clear his name.

Thus far, Argentinian officials have rebuffed State Department demands for extradition. A spokesman for the South American country's diplomatic corps told reporters U.S. officials have provided no concrete evidence of Navarro's involvement other than the dubious claims of a man facing murder charges. An anonymous U.S. law enforcement officer called the Argentinian position "laughable."

1

Garden of Evil

Pézenas, France
June 2

Tightening his robe against the chill, Jacques Foucault followed the Painted Lady as it danced its way through the garden. With great interest, he watched the spotted butterfly bob and weave over and around the blossoms in search of a satisfying meal. Several times the insect landed on floret clusters. Each time, it stayed just long enough to sample the flowers' nectar before darting off again into the sea of pink. All the while, Foucault trailed behind in stealthy pursuit.

Foucault was surprised by the butterfly's movements. He had expected the intrepid migrator to quickly zero in on the beacon, but its actions thus far were erratic and hesitant. Perhaps he was trailing too closely, causing the Painted Lady unwelcome stress. Or maybe, he thought, the medallion bouncing against his chest interfered with its ability to detect the beacon.

He backed off and let the butterfly dart ahead. Once it disappeared, Foucault popped out of the bushes and strolled along the cobblestone path bisecting the garden. When he arrived at the center courtyard, he lowered onto a stone bench, lit a cigarette and waited for the Painted Lady to flutter back into view. Sure enough, its beating wings soon emerged from behind flowering bushes at the edge of the courtyard.

Unlike its earlier meandering, the butterfly now flew with purpose and conviction as it headed straight for a group of bushes encircled by black, glittering rocks. When it came to rest on the tallest bush inside the ring, it began to dine on a blossom's juice. Foucault exhaled a wisp of smoke and said, "If only it were that easy, *mon amie*."

The comment was followed by a heavy sigh. After so many years of searching, he finally had Malinyah's map within his reach. With it came the promise of finding the remaining *Tuliskaeras*, cone-shaped stones with the power to slice through any object its user chose. Wood, rock, metal, people—it didn't matter. The *Tuliskaera* could cut through all four at once if necessary. The fearsome Stones were the last pieces Foucault needed to complete his preparations, but once again his hopes were dashed.

It had happened in a blink of stupidity, and now a new plan was needed. A plan complicated by the possibility the map was no longer in Anlon Cully's possession. If Foucault's suspicion was accurate, it meant the map had most likely found its way to Klaus Navarro. From what he knew of Navarro, the Argentinian would pose a formidable competitor in the hunt for the *Tuliskaeras*.

Making matters worse, Cully still had Malinyah's *Sinethal*. The black tablet held many secrets, including the information necessary to recreate the map. If Cully learned to extract those secrets, he too would be tempted to search for at least one of the *Tuliskaeras*. To Foucault, one in Cully's hands was one too many.

Together, the risks posed by Navarro and Cully were concerning, but they paled in comparison to the one foremost on his mind—all this trouble because Thatcher Reynolds had been reckless.

With a shake of his head, Foucault whispered, "*Imbécile.*"

At that moment, the distant chime of the chateau doorbell filtered outside, rousing Foucault from the disheartening thoughts. Rising from the bench, he extinguished the cigarette in a nearby snuffer and headed toward the chateau. As he mounted the terrace steps, an impeccably dressed man appeared through the drawing room door and greeted Foucault. With a bearing as formal as his attire, the ebony-skinned man spoke with a crisp British accent. "Good morning, Monsieur."

"Christian! *Allô!*" beamed Foucault, his gloom vanquished by the arrival of his longtime associate, Christian Hunte. "How was the flight across the pond? Henri did not bump you around too much, I hope."

"Henri was skilled as usual. We enjoyed a smooth ride."

"*Bon!* Do you bring me good news?"

Christian paused, then said, "I am afraid not."

"Ah, that is unfortunate, but not unexpected. Reynolds is with you?"

"Yes, he is waiting in the vestibule."

Foucault gestured for Christian to join him at the patio table. While Christian unbuttoned his suit jacket and delicately lowered himself onto a chair, Foucault poured two glasses of a pink-tinted juice. Handing one to Christian, he toasted Christian's continued good health and said, "Very well. I will deal with him momentarily. But first, tell me what you learned of the map."

"I could not confirm its whereabouts," Christian said. "Reynolds believes Cully retains the map and the *Sinethal*, but he has no proof to support the claim."

"What of this Corchran woman and her brother? The papers say they ransacked Devlin Wilson's home. Could they have taken the map?"

"I am sorry, Monsieur. I was unable to discover much about the Corchrans. I was rather occupied managing Reynolds' paranoia whilst sneaking him out of the country."

"He gave you trouble?"

"He was tiresome, but nothing I couldn't handle. I believe you will find his attitude unchanged."

Foucault frowned. "*Pourquoi?*"

"I told him Li Wu was a ruse. He is unhappy we lied to him. He says the pressure we applied led to his current situation. He thinks the press is treating him unfairly, calling him a thief and murderer. He sees police at every turn. His list of complaints is unending," Christian said.

"Then it is good we have brought him here," Foucault said. "Did you learn anything new about Klaus Navarro?"

"Beyond what's in the press reports? Not yet."

Foucault's face turned grim. "His presence in this *comédie* worries me more than the others, Christian. If he is as greedy a profiteer as rumors suggest, *The Betrayer* could easily manipulate him. Either way, the map in Navarro's hands would be very dangerous."

"Agreed. Given that Cully is hospitalized, and Margaret Corchran missing, shall I prioritize Navarro, then?"

"Possibly. We will talk more when I am done with Reynolds."

"Very well, Monsieur."

For a moment, they sat in silence. Foucault fingered the medallion hanging from his neck and thought again of how close they'd come. He uttered a deep sigh and then said, "Ah, well, let's get this over with. Have him meet me in the garden."

Without further discussion, Foucault rose from the table and descended the terrace stairs. As he walked along the cobblestone path, he gazed lovingly upon his treasured garden. In truth, it was more than a garden to him. It was a place of worship and sacrifice. A cathedral.

The walls of Foucault's cathedral were formed by a dozen towering ceiba trees arranged in a horseshoe pattern. Their sprawling roots weaved over and under each other to form a bocage-like wall that stood nearly three feet high around the inner garden. When sunlight glowed into the garden from behind the trees' crisscrossing branches, the gaps between limbs sparkled like panes of stained glass.

The core of the garden was devoted to a single subspecies of flower, the fragrant *Nerium oleander*. Planted in an unearthly, inky soil, the pink-blossomed flowers dotted thousands of tall bushes arrayed in arching rows. With branches that reached for the sky like outstretched arms, the oleanders served as Foucault's flock.

At the terminus of the cobblestone path was the small oval courtyard with several stone benches positioned around its edges. In the center of the courtyard sat a stand-alone plot of oleanders ringed by black rocks. Here, at Foucault's altar, the Painted Lady still feasted.

Relaxing onto a bench, Foucault lit another cigarette and awaited his guest.

A moment later, Foucault heard a sharp rebuke echo from the terrace. He turned to see Christian and Reynolds standing at the top of the terrace steps. As Christian pointed in the direction of the garden, Reynolds grumbled something and shook his fist. A thin smile crossed Foucault's face as Christian bowed politely and returned to the chateau, leaving the rotund professor stewing on the terrace.

Adjusting his crimson silk robe, Foucault puffed on the cigarette and retrained his gaze on the Painted Lady while Reynolds stomped toward the garden, muttering all the way.

When Reynolds reached the courtyard, he pushed his crooked glasses up on his nose and stared down at the seated man with a mix of anger and confusion. Foucault met his stare and motioned for him to sit on an opposing bench.

Reynolds remained standing and gruffly said, "See here! What's the meaning of all this? Who are you?"

Foucault removed the cigarette, glared at the light-skinned African American and flicked ashes onto the cobblestones. As the buffoon hovered above him, Foucault admonished himself once more for his choice of marionette. Alone, the man's rumpled suit and partially untucked shirt spoke volumes. When combined with wild shocks of snow-white hair and the scruffy layer of white stubble upon his face, Thatcher Reynolds looked more like a hobo than a tenured archaeology professor.

Dropping the half-smoked cigarette to the ground, Foucault crushed it beneath his foot and exhaled the last of its fumes. With a slight bow, he softly said, "My name is Jacques Foucault. Please be seated, Dr. Reynolds."

Reynolds stomped a foot. "I want to know what's going on! Why the canard about Li Wu?"

"Calm yourself and sit, *s'il vous plaît.*" Foucault's voice was suddenly stern.

As Reynolds slunk onto a bench opposing his host, Foucault said, "*Merci.* Li Wu was a small deception to shield my involvement. I am the man who hired you, not the fictional Li Wu."

Foucault watched his guest absorb the totality of the admission.

The man's eyes darted back and forth and beadlets of sweat formed on his brow. Reynolds slapped his thighs and said, "Do you understand the trouble I'm in? Do you?"

The question was met by a stony response: "Your *situation difficile* is minuscule next to the *problèmes* your failure has created for me."

"I don't understand. Who are you, then? What's your interest in the map? The Flash Stone?"

"None of your concern."

"Of course, it's my concern! I know nothing about you. For all I know you're an outright criminal."

"Come now, Doctor. How much did you know of Li Wu? Eh? Did you bother to ask for credentials? Did you demand a face-to-face meeting? *Non.* You cared only about payment . . . and the chance to usurp Devlin Wilson's discovery. To take credit for his labors. Is this not so?"

"How . . . how dare you!" Reynolds sputtered.

"Did you ever question why Li Wu sought Devlin's map? Or the *Tuliskaera*?"

"The what?"

"*Tuliskaera*, the Flash Stone, as you call it."

Reynolds rose off the bench and jabbed a finger at Foucault. "Look, I wasn't hired for any of that. I was hired to recruit Pacal Flores. Which I did. I knew nothing of the map or Stones until then."

"Your memory is selective, *mon ami*," Foucault coolly answered. "But it is irrelevant. We are not here to argue over the past."

Stalking closer to Foucault, Reynolds said, "Irrelevant? My reputation is ruined! Kaput. The media, they're calling me a murderer! I killed no one! They say I'm a thief. I stole nothing!"

"Bah!" spat Foucault, rising to face the man. "If you are innocent, why did you run? It was *stupide*—it made you look *coupable*."

The comment shook Reynolds. He staggered backward and slumped onto the bench. He bowed his head. "I didn't know what else to do."

Foucault considered the man in front of him. His display was pathetic. He was so full of indignant bluster, he could not see his own culpability. And he was a liar. Once Reynolds was paid for the introduction to Pacal, he willingly, enthusiastically, inserted himself deeper into the plot to steal the map.

At the heart of it, however, Foucault realized the whole fiasco was his own fault. As soon as Devlin started making inquiries about the Stones, Foucault should have snuffed out his interest by any means necessary. But, he had been too worried such an action would draw the attention of *The Betrayer*. So, he opted for a subtler approach — an approach that backfired spectacularly.

Foucault slid his hands into his robe pockets and curled his fingers around two cookie-sized stones. Stepping close to the altar of flowering shrubs, he stooped to inhale the oleander's light aroma and casually withdrew his hands from his pockets. In each palm, he cupped a stone.

"Tell me, did you see the map yourself?" he asked.

Reynolds, clutching strands of his snarled hair, shook his head.

"Did you speak of it to anyone besides Pacal?"

"No, why would I?" said Reynolds.

"You told Christian you believe Cully has the map. Is this true?"

The despondent man nodded.

"Where did Cully get it?"

Reynolds peered up. "Excuse me?"

"Where did Cully get the map? It went missing after Devlin died."

"I don't remember."

Turning his back to Reynolds, Foucault began to slowly rub the stones together in a circular motion. They made a scratching sound, like sandpaper smoothing a rough surface, though it was barely detectible from where Reynolds sat.

"Think harder. Where did Cully get the map?"

Foucault continued to grind the stones. Soon, their etchings began to glow and their heat rose in his palms. Reynolds stared at the ground and mumbled, "Why does it matter? Cully has the Master Stone. That's where Devlin got the map."

Foucault wasn't listening. His concentration was focused on the stones. When they glowed a bright red, he ceased grinding and tapped them together. A spark leapt to a nearby bush, instantly withering an unsuspecting blossom.

Reynolds saw the flash and flinched. He said, "Look, I did the best I could! I can't help it if I don't remember."

Spinning around, Foucault advanced toward the seated man, the stones now searing his palms. Reynolds rose to his feet, then edged from shadow into sunlight and held up his hands. "What are you—"

Without further warning, Foucault flung his arms wide, palms facing Reynolds. The flustered archaeologist cowered when he saw the glowing discs clutched in Foucault's hands. He screamed in protest just as Foucault crashed the throbbing stones together. A flaming bolt surged forward into Reynolds' chest. He writhed uncontrollably as the bolt pierced deep into his body.

With a wild sneer carved on his face, Foucault pounded the stones again, this time with more intensity. Another bolt, brighter than the last, flared at Reynolds. He convulsed as it sliced a second trail through his chest.

Terror filled the stricken man's eyes. He teetered, clutching his chest, and toppled to the ground, his shirt and jacket afire. A sickening odor quickly filled the air, overwhelming the sweet scent of oleander all around the two men.

Releasing the crackling stones, Foucault grimaced and stared down at his singed, swollen hands. He backed away and collapsed on a bench just as the Painted Lady drifted back into view. It hovered briefly over the burning, motionless body before flitting off again toward the altar. Foucault watched its snaking path until it vanished into the bushes.

Rapid footsteps sounded from the terrace. A moment later, they came to an abrupt halt and Christian called out, "Monsieur! Are you injured?"

"I am fine, Christian. Get some ice, *s'il vous plaît.*"

"Right away, Monsieur."

As Christian scurried away, Foucault turned his back on Reynolds and left the cathedral. Through clenched teeth, he seethed once more, "*Imbécile!*"

2

From Under the Rock

San Carlos de Bariloche, Argentina
June 10

Klaus Navarro hovered over the worn volume of Olmec legends and once again scanned the *Rivers of Gold* excerpt. It read like a fairy tale—a godlike figure who melted rock into a bubbling stream of gold.

As a third-generation miner, Navarro had been fascinated by the story since childhood. On many occasions, his grandfather would lead him down the stepped bowl of the family's original copper mine to act out the legend.

The patriarch's eyes would narrow to mere slits as he bent low. In hushed tones, he'd prowl the mine floor and arrange the scene—the natives cowering at the canyon's precipice, the god in elaborate headdress surrounded by raging torches and the wall of glittering rocks awaiting transformation.

Suddenly, his grandfather would rise up, utter an incantation and slam his hands together with a thundering clap. Navarro still recalled the echoes reverberating around the bowl. Flashing his hands all about, his grandfather would animate the rocks exploding into colorful tendrils that arced through the sky before splashing to the ground and pooling into a molten river. Then his grandfather would grow wild-eyed, seize Navarro's arm and dash up the stepped walls.

"Quickly!" he'd blurt. "Run before the river burns you alive!"

Navarro smiled. No matter how many times his grandfather retold the legend, each portrayal was so convincing, he truly expected the mine walls to burst into a river of gold.

Flipping through the Olmec tome to read other versions of the tale, the child within Navarro thanked the old man for diluting the myth's scarier elements. For none of the translated excerpts contained the wondrous fireworks display his grandfather described. Instead, they depicted a ferocious battle between a serpent and snakes.

The fish man stood atop the rocky mound and touched the teeth together. A serpent leapt forth and bit the rocks until they woke. They moaned and their hearts glowed. The serpent bit again and the rocks turned to snakes. Hissing smoke, they slithered around the serpent and bit back. The serpent danced among them and ate every snake it touched. Soon, smoke filled the sky. The hissing stopped and the fish man opened the teeth. When the smoke cleared, the serpent and the snakes were gone and the hill flowed with golden water.

Navarro closed the book and pondered the possibility, a simple tool that could melt rock. If true, the Flash Stone might forever change how precious metals and gems were mined. No more would it take months of drilling and blasting to uncover rich deposits. Gone would be the hordes of day laborers sifting and chipping to find small nuggets. Costs would plummet and profits would soar. A new world, one that Navarro would dominate.

Stroking the long strands of his ponytail, Navarro stared out the parlor's floor-to-ceiling windows. Surveying the panoramic view of the Andes, he thought, "Once it is mine, even mountains will kneel before me."

Savoring the fantasy, Navarro imagined the stunned faces among the world's diamond cartel when he cut stone like butter before their eyes. Gold diggers? Ruby miners? It wouldn't matter. He'd make them all bow. They would have no choice. They would pay him to gain access to his rock-melting stone, or his "serpent" would drive them out of business. Either way, Navarro would win.

Eight months ago, the Olmec legend was just a favorite childhood story. Then, out of the blue, came an unexpected whisper of Devlin Wilson's discovery . . . a set of curious stones . . . stones with unusual magnetic characteristics . . . powers unlike anything ever seen. Navarro was still surprised at how quickly that whisper led to the possibility the story was more than myth—and by how quickly he found himself mired in intrigue.

He thought back to when Matthew Dobson and Margaret Corchran first described the discovery to him. He remembered listening with passive interest when they told him one person could lift and move heavy objects simply by humming on one of the stones. They claimed another stone could turn the flowers of poisonous plants into fountain-of-youth nectars. They even described a stone that held audio and video recordings made by an ancient civilization. Navarro recalled scoffing at such notions.

But then they described a stone that cut through rock using a beam of light and the childhood tale suddenly leapt to his mind. He demanded to know more and was shown a statuette of a man using the device. It looked strikingly like a stone relief Navarro had acquired years before that depicted the mythical serpent's tooth in use.

He recalled offering Dobson and his niece, Margaret, an obscene sum for the Flash Stone's procurement, but he was told Devlin didn't possess it. Instead, they said, Devlin had a map, a map that led to caches of all the stones. They offered to sell him a copy of the map.

Navarro had been skeptical. He demanded proof of the map's authenticity before committing to its purchase. Dobson came through with that proof—a stash of gold coins found at one of the map sites. That sealed it for Navarro. He wanted everything: the map, the gold, the statues and all the magical Stones in Devlin's collection.

Dobson and Margaret readily agreed to purloin the artifacts, and an alliance was formed. But Devlin caught Dobson with his hand in the till before the fool delivered the treasure or the map. Then Margaret panicked and stupidly killed Devlin and suddenly, Navarro's fantasy turned to nightmare. Instead of netting the prized relics, he found himself in a Buenos Aires jail, charged with grand theft. Extradition to the U.S. hung over him.

Navarro gritted his teeth thinking about that Buenos Aires jail cell. But he'd gotten lucky. His attorney struck a deal with the Argentinian government and Navarro was placed under house arrest while the two governments bickered over the Americans' extradition demand. So long as Navarro kept his cool and no new evidence came to light, his attorney was confident he'd walk free.

"Don't do anything stupid," the attorney had said. "Another week, two at the most, and the Americans will fold. Your house arrest will be over and the matter will be closed."

During his confinement, Navarro had been consumed by despair. He had lost his chance to acquire the Waterland Map. Without it, there was no hope of finding the Flash Stone. He spent several days mourning the lost opportunity, but then an anonymous text message from a Miami-area phone number reawakened the opportunity to turn his fantasy into reality.

It had been almost midnight when the blunt text arrived: "dear rat bastard, let's talk waterland. mwah, warrior princess."

When he first viewed the message, Navarro debated whether to respond. In fact, his first inclination was to delete it. It smelled like a trap, a feeble ploy by the Americans to trick him into a compromising exchange. With the extradition case against him crumbling, he suspected the Americans were desperate to fortify their hands.

However, the language and the attitude conveyed in the message was pure Margaret Corchran. No one besides Margaret dared to call him such names, in texts or otherwise, and he doubted anyone else knew her as "warrior princess."

Then he remembered the little bitch had used the same venomous salutation in front of Kyle on more than one occasion. So, Navarro returned to the view that the text was a setup, possibly one involving Kyle masquerading as his sister. The two-faced Corchran had already demonstrated his willingness to roll over on Navarro. What did Kyle have to lose by doubling down and participating in a police sting designed to nab Navarro?

But, after he had slept on it, the chance to acquire the Flash Stone proved too great a lure. He felt confident he could navigate a benign text exchange to at least discover whether Margaret or someone else hid behind the anonymous message.

Now, as he stood by the parlor windows caressing his ponytail, Navarro typed his response.

NAVARRO: I'm listening

For an hour, he paced the window bank waiting for a reply. With each minute that passed, his thoughts turned increasingly sinister. He imagined a bank of American agents, huddled around a computer, triangulating his cell phone signal. Meanwhile, a group of police officers sat with Kyle, feeding him instructions on how to coax Navarro into a conversation. He imagined a polished government attorney joining the conversation to help craft the response, and then Kyle massaging the response to reflect Margaret's voice. These suspicions cycled over and over while he waited for the anonymous texter's reply. When it finally arrived, Navarro's skepticism was at full alert:

(305): good. you still want it?

Navarro refrained from making a compromising statement.

NAVARRO: Want what?

Three replies followed in quick succession:

(305): Ha! we both know what IT is!
(305): and we both know you want it BAD
(305): it'll cost ya, though. BIG TIME

Navarro paused to consider a response. So far, there was nothing in the conversation to dispel the notion of a setup. Rattling in the back of his mind was the voice of his attorney cautioning him to lay low. Time to see what's crawling under the rock, thought Navarro.

NAVARRO: Call me
(305): seriously?????
NAVARRO: Yes
(305): TOO risky
NAVARRO: Understood. Adios

When he pressed send, Navarro was fully convinced the anonymous texter was not Margaret Corchran. More frustrated than disappointed, he shoved the phone in his pocket and retrieved the book of Olmec legends. Replacing the volume on the parlor bookshelf, Navarro sighed and turned his thoughts to other matters.

Less than a minute later, his phone buzzed. He ignored it. Two minutes after that, another buzz. Enough of this foolishness, he thought. Whisking out the phone, he prepared to delete the entire conversation. Then he saw the notification screen. It indicated the two new texts were images.

Curious, Navarro opened the conversation box and his eyes met two photographs. The first was a picture of Margaret's weapon of choice, the Sound Stone. It sat at the foot of a chaise lounge. In the background beyond the chaise, the photo showed a beach and a tiny sliver of crashing waves. The photo carried no caption.

The second photo changed everything. In the selfie, a woman wearing a wide-brimmed hat and sunglasses blew a kiss to the camera. Though her raven hair was now blond and much shorter, there was no mistaking the smirk on her face. The caption read, "Toodles. Hope the feds fry your pansy-ass."

NAVARRO: Hold on
(305): ooh? reconsidering, are we?
NAVARRO: Where are you? I will come to you
(305): shhh, it's a secret!
NAVARRO: Then come visit me
(305): haaaa . . . freakin . . . haaa!!!
NAVARRO: What then?
(305): i talk, you do as you're told

NAVARRO: Careful, warrior princess. Remember your place.

(305): yawn . . .

(305): simple rules . . .

(305): i give you bank info . . .

(305): you send $ . . .

(305): you get prize . . .

(305): everyone goes home happy

NAVARRO: Call me

(305): any funny business, prize goes bye-bye

NAVARRO: Understood

(305): k, call in a sec

A moment later, his phone began to ring. He immediately answered.

"Well, hello there, Klausie. Enjoying house arrest?" Margaret said.

"Do you really have it?" he asked.

"Uh-huh. It's pretty. Lots of colors."

"How much?"

"Half mil."

He scoffed. Cheeky little bitch, he thought. She wanted the originally agreed fee . . . for only a portion of the promised take. And after all the trouble she and her brother caused him?

"That's the deal," she said. "Take it or I'll find someone else. Who knows, maybe I'll use it myself."

"You've already been paid a sizeable deposit, why should I pay more?"

"That was then, this is now," Margaret said, yawning. "Besides, life as a fugitive is *expensive*! You have a pen to write down the wire information?"

Navarro spat an unflattering stream of expletives.

"The bank name for the wire is First Bank of Grand Cayman."

"Even if I agree to the price, what assurance do I have you'll deliver?" railed Navarro.

"The name on the account is Victoria Bradley. That's Bradley with an 'ey.' Did you get that?"

"Answer me!"

A sigh echoed from Margaret's end of the line. "I'll email it to you as soon as the wire clears. Now, are you ready for the account number?"

"Email? No, for that price I want the original!"

"Don't have the original, sweetie. Anyway, my copy's better than the original."

"What does that mean?"

"My copy comes along with a special file that will help you read it," Margaret said. "Now, do we have a deal or not?"

3

Out of the Frying Pan

Pézenas, France
July 15

With a smile and a wave, Jacques Foucault watched the Daimler Consort depart with the last of his dinner guests. As the classic car rumbled its way down the gravel driveway, Foucault reflected on the pleasant evening.

It had been a small gathering, just a handful of fellow Société Astronomique de France members whose company Foucault enjoyed. Their conversation had been lively, with debates flowing as generously as the Carignan. Foucault's cheery mood had been further enhanced by an unexpected text from Christian midway through dinner.

"Found her!" read the message.

Foucault could barely contain his excitement. He excused himself from the table, nearly knocking over his wine, and scurried outside to send a quick reply: "Where?"

"You won't believe it."

"Where, Christian?!"

"Barbados."

"*Mon Dieu!* Returned to the scene of the crime, has she?"

"It would seem so."

"Very well. Will call you in one hour."

With the Daimler gone from sight, Foucault walked around the side of the chateau and followed a path to the observatory. As he strolled along, he glanced up at the night sky and greeted the familiar stars. They were like old friends by now, keeping watch over his lonely crusade.

Once inside, Foucault flipped the switch to open the dome doors and settled into a chair aside the telescope. Eyeballing Cassiopeia's position through the open gap, Foucault trained the telescope on the constellation and peered through the lens. Adjusting the scope, he searched beyond the western tip of the W-shaped constellation until he found tonight's target, the Bubble Nebula. Fine-tuning the focus on the colorful formation, he smiled and mumbled, "*Magnifique.*"

He admired the nebula for several minutes before he dialed Christian. When the call connected, Foucault said, "*Allô,* Christian?"

"Good evening, Monsieur Foucault. How was the dinner?"

"Excellent! Though Laval and Girard droned on about Perseids again. Every July when the date approaches, they act like children at Christmas," Foucault said with a laugh. "Where are you tonight?"

"Barbados," Christian said.

"Ah, so you are there already. Have you seen her?"

"Yes, she looks like she hasn't a care in the world."

"How did you find her?"

"I went to see her brother, Kyle. It took some incentives to get in to see him, but he was very open when we met," Christian said. "Then I just followed the crumbs he gave me."

"He knew where she was?"

"No, sir. But they shared a private bank account in the Caymans."

"He told you this?"

"Yes."

"Surely, he shared the same information with the police?"

"No, sir. He said he didn't. He claims the district attorney reneged on part of his plea bargain. Once that happened, he 'clammed up,' as he put it."

"How did you convince him to talk?"

"Ahem . . . I made a small promise."

"Money?"

"No. I'd rather not say over the phone."

"Very well, you can tell me later. I congratulate you, *mon ami*. I am most appreciative," said Foucault.

"Thank you, sir. She was careless, that helped. She's been using a debit card attached to the joint account."

Foucault gazed back through the telescope lens and asked, "How long has she been there?"

"I spoke with the housekeeper assigned to her room. She's been here nearly a month. Seems to be keeping to herself, but she's definitely up to something. The housekeeper says she's taken several day trips off island."

"*Putain!* Dominica?" Foucault asked.

There was a pause on the other end of the line. Foucault stood and paced around the small room. "Christian? Has she gone to Dominica?"

"Yes. The housekeeper is as nosy as Miss Corchran is careless. Says Margaret's been tossing her used airline tickets and customs receipts in the bathroom trash. She tears them up, but not well enough," Christian said.

"She's using an alias, of course?" Foucault asked.

"Yes. Victoria Bradley."

"Has she found anything?"

"Hard to say. Housekeeper says she's using the room safe, and I noticed she carries a backpack with her at all times."

"What about the map? Did the housekeeper see a map?"

"I didn't specifically ask about a map. I asked if she's left any papers lying around; the housekeeper said no."

Foucault closed the observatory dome and powered down the telescope. As he descended the silo's spiral staircase, he pondered Christian's information. If Margaret was still at the resort, it seemed unlikely she'd found the entrance again. Unless, of course, she was raiding the vault piece by piece.

"Monsieur," Christian said, "I should mention that Kyle denied taking the *Sulataers*. He could be lying. He said he'd seen them, so had Margaret, but said it was their uncle who found them. Matthew Dobson."

"Dobson? Ah, so that's the connection!" remarked Foucault. So, it was possible Margaret was in the dark, he thought. That would explain the repeated trips. That meant there was still time to intervene. He asked, "Do you think she has the map? Did her brother say?"

"I'm not sure. Kyle did say he gave her an electronic copy, but . . . "

"But what?"

"You're not going to like it," Christian said.

"Christian! We don't have time for games," snapped Foucault.

"Kyle said she was supposed to give it to Klaus Navarro."

"*Jésus!*" Foucault swore. "Hopefully, she has not yet handed it over."

"Could be," Christian said. "If she's searching Dominica, she may have decided to keep it to herself."

Foucault cursed the name Devlin Wilson. The meddlesome archaeologist had shoved his hand in the hive and shaken it until it burst. Now the little bees were everywhere! Anlon Cully, Margaret Corchran, Klaus Navarro. And Navarro was a noisy bee. His indiscretions would surely cause other bees to gather. Sooner or later *The Betrayer* would sniff the bees and swoop in.

"You are to watch her every step! If she leaves the resort, you follow her. Do *not* let her out of your sight, do you understand?" Foucault said.

"Yes, Monsieur."

"I will be there tomorrow. Make the arrangements."

Krystal Waters Resort
St. James Parish, Barbados
July 16

Swirling a cherry-adorned skewer, Victoria Bradley gazed at the hues cast by the fading light and uttered a contented sigh. She raised a nutmeg-spiced concoction to her lips, lowered her eyelids and let its tangy flavor slide over her tongue. In the background, light calypso tones masked the gurgle of low tide.

Exhaling with satisfaction, "Vickie" burrowed her toes deeper into the cool comfort of the powdery sand and stared out once more at the clouds floating just above the water's surface.

"Ah," she purred, "I was meant for this."

Reclining on the cushioned chaise lounge, Vickie curled under a coral-and-white-striped beach towel and listened absently to carefree banter from the poolside bar.

Behind her, a cool breeze tickled the leaves of a sprawling mahogany tree, obscuring the approaching sound of a resort attendant. After politely clearing his throat to announce his presence, the attendant spoke with a British accent: "Good evening, Miss Bradley."

The unexpected salutation caused Vickie to flinch. Instinctively, she uncoiled from beneath the towel and made a quick grab for the backpack by the chaise. Her elbow caught the fluted glass resting on the table beside her and tipped it over. She uttered an expletive and glared at the attendant. "You shouldn't sneak up on people like that! What do you want?"

The slim, ebony-toned man bowed apologetically. Attired in a freshly pressed white camp shirt, rose-colored Bermuda shorts, and equally bright white knee-high socks and sneakers, the attendant said, "Pardon me if I surprised you, miss. A gentleman has requested to dine with you this evening. I was asked to deliver his invitation."

Vickie grasped the empty glass and said, "Look what you've done! Go bring a fresh rum punch. With extra cherries. Quickly."

Hands folded behind his back, the attendant stuttered, "The . . . the . . . gentleman was most insistent."

"Do I look like I give a f——?" she spat. Waving the glass toward his face, Vickie said, "Rum punch. Now! And tell the *gentleman* no."

"Very well, miss," he said as he bowed.

While the attendant traipsed away, Vickie stretched out beneath the towel just as the trailing tip of the sun disappeared beneath the ocean. Closing her eyes again, she listened to the soft calypso melody amid rustling from the overhead mahogany leaves.

While she waited for her refill, Vickie pondered the odd dinner request. Over the past month, she'd received more than a dozen dining invitations, but they were all delivered in person. Some were rude solicitations for more than dinner. Others were nothing more than al-cohol-influenced dares. But a few had been sincere. It pained her to turn this final lot aside, but at the time it had been more important to maintain a low profile.

When Christian Hunte returned across the beach with tray in hand, he noticed Vickie was again nestled beneath the towel. Careful to avoid another mishap, he cleared his throat several steps away from the chaise and announced, "Your drink, Miss Bradley."

He leaned forward and presented the tray. Vickie propped an arm against the beach chair and raised her head to verify the extra cher-ries. Satisfied her demand had been honored, she whisked the cock-tail to her lips and said, "There better not be a charge for this!"

Christian resisted the temptation to bludgeon her with the tray. He assured her the drink was on the house and then withdrew a small envelope from his pocket. Placing it on the tray, he bent for-ward to present the envelope. "The gentleman asked that I give you this. He requested I wait to hear your reply."

Vickie slurped the cocktail through the provided straw and peered at the envelope. She cast a dubious eye at Christian and said, "How pushy! I said no. Does the *gentleman* not understand the word *no?*"

Her attention shifted to the patio where two attendants, garbed as voodoo witch doctors, began the nightly ritual of igniting the re-sort's tiki lamps. She loved to watch the dots of light turn into blaz-ing torches. From the beach, it looked like hell arising in the dark-ness. Hoping Christian would take the hint, she ignored his presence and continued to watch the witch doctor ceremony. Absently, she moved her hand to the backpack.

With clenched jaw, Christian lifted the envelope and placed it on the side table. He cleared his throat again and prodded, "I believe, Miss Bradley, it would be in your very best interests to read the note."

What balls, Vickie thought. The rich don't like to take no for an answer! She was half-tempted to demand the attendant lead her to the sender. There, she could tear the note in half in front of him and tell him to pound sand. But . . . such a display would attract undue attention. And it was still too soon for that.

She stared down at the gilded envelope. The front was embossed with the sender's initials. The gold "JMF" glittered in the torch light. She flipped it over and lifted the unsealed lip. Inside was a simple folded card:

Chère Margaret,

A pleasure to run into you so far away from home. I had the good fortune to meet with your brother, Kyle, recently. He sends his love.

I am anxious to speak with you about the map, a matter of importance to both of us. Won't you kindly accept my offer to dine this evening? It would sadden me to miss the opportunity to chat and instead inform the authorities of your presence here.

Chaleureusement,
Jacques Foucault

Mouth agape, Margaret flushed with perspiration. A small gasp escaped as she fought to maintain her composure under Christian's watchful eyes. Crushing the note in her hand, she stared into the growing darkness and said, "Please tell the gentleman I accept his invitation."

Christian bowed and said, "As you wish, Miss Bradley. I will meet you at your suite at eight sharp and escort you to dinner."

Still in a daze, Margaret laid a hand atop her backpack and groused, "I don't need an escort, I know how to find the dining room."

"Monsieur Foucault wishes to dine in a more private setting. He expressly requested that I escort you. Eight sharp, Miss Bradley."

From the patio lounge, Foucault observed the exchange while enjoying the flavor of a thin cigar. Per usual, Christian had accomplished his task with discretion. There had been a moment when it seemed Margaret might make a spectacle of herself, but Christian's level-headed responses kept the situation from escalating.

While Christian tramped once again toward the patio, Foucault could see Margaret peer over the back of the chaise to follow his re-treat. The fear in her eyes was unmistakable. Foucault wondered, would she run? If emotion trumped reason, it was a distinct possibility.

When Christian reached the patio, he moved toward the main lobby as previously instructed. If Margaret did make a run for it, there was one lonely road leading from the resort to the main road through St. James Parish. With Christian posted at the resort's gated entrance, she would not make it far.

Once his confederate was out of sight, Foucault watched as Margaret lowered her gaze and quickly lifted the backpack from the sand. From his vantage point, Foucault could not see what she was doing, but it was clear she was rummaging for something. He feared the target of her search might be a cell phone. It would alter his plan if she alerted Navarro before their dinner.

His attention was distracted by a text from Christian: "In position."

"Good," he answered. "Hold there for now."

"Has she moved?" came the reply message.

Foucault glanced up to see Margaret perched on the seat's edge, phone to her ear. He cursed and extinguished the cigar. He pounded a terse text to Christian. "She's making a call. Plan B may be necessary."

However, when Foucault looked up again, Margaret was scowling and she yanked the phone from her ear. Muttering to herself, she rapidly tapped the screen and cupped her ear to the phone once again.

Christian texted, "On my way."

"No, stay in place!" Foucault typed in reply. A moment later, he followed with, "Get ready, she's on the move."

Foucault slapped down payment for his drink and rose from the table. He wedged his way through the crowded cocktail hour with one eye glued to Margaret. She stormed across the sand, backpack anchored to her shoulder. The gauzy wrap covering her bikini-clad figure flailed in the ocean breeze. As she neared the patio, she veered sharply to the right, phone clamped to her ear.

Pausing behind the frame of the tiki-hut bar, Foucault watched Margaret head for a winding path leading to the eastern wing of the resort. He exited the lounge and followed her at a safe distance. Suddenly, she halted on the dimly lit path. Foucault hopped into a nook in the shrub garden lining the path.

He reached into his trouser pockets and cupped his hands around the stones. Peeking around a shrub, he saw Margaret shove the phone in the backpack and punch her thigh. Then, she briefly fumbled in the backpack for another item before resuming her march.

Foucault eased his hands from the stones and retrieved his cell phone. He quickly typed a message to Christian: "All is well. Wait another fifteen minutes to be sure. Then prep for dinner."

Slamming the door shut, Margaret heaved the backpack onto the sofa with a flurry of expletives and made her way to the bedroom. She tossed off the sheer wrap and collapsed onto the plush ivory duvet. Covering her face with both hands, she struggled to settle her mind. Who the f—— was Jacques Foucault? How did he find her? Had he really talked with Kyle? What did he want? Why didn't Navarro answer his damn phone?

"What a mess!" she said.

Margaret had been convinced her new persona was rock solid. Complete with a new hairstyle and touristy wardrobe, she breezed through security in Miami and then through customs in Barbados. They'd barely looked at her Bermudan passport. Since then, she'd moved about Barbados and the surrounding West Indies islands without a single moment of concern. How, then, did Foucault find her?

Had Navarro sent him? Maybe that's why he wouldn't answer her calls. Navarro had said he would contact her when he needed her help, but he didn't say how he would establish contact. She could understand why he might want to reach out through a third party, but why go through the dinner invitation theatrics?

Was it Kyle? Margaret considered the note's reference to Kyle a strange inclusion. Was it meant to signal something to her, or had Foucault included it solely to unsettle her? It seemed impossible he could have met with her brother. Strangers don't just walk into prison hospitals and talk with inmates. Besides, Kyle had no clue of her whereabouts. Even if he did, he'd surely tip the cops before anyone else. She was certain he was thirsty for revenge.

Maybe Foucault was a bounty hunter, Margaret thought. She was keenly aware that both the FBI and Interpol were hunting for her. Had they established a reward for her capture? Or maybe it was Cully. Had he hired a private investigator to track her down? The more she thought of these possibilities, the less feasible they seemed. If Foucault was a bounty hunter, why not take her into custody immediately? Again, why the dinner invitation?

One thing was certain, the mention of the map implied Foucault knew about the Stones.

An hour later, the attendant arrived to escort Margaret. After introducing himself as Christian Hunte, Foucault's private secretary, the two left to meet the French aristocrat. Their path led first through the resort's main lobby and then out onto the marble rear patio abutting the beach. By now it was fully dark and the patio seemed afire with two dozen tiki torches snaking along its perimeter.

Reaching the beach, Christian retrieved a large lantern hidden in a pool box at the patio's edge. He opened the lantern's glass door and lit the thick candle inside. Then he motioned Margaret to follow him down a wood-plank walkway that cut across the sand and disappeared into a thick stand of palm trees.

Margaret warily eyed the dark trees as they approached. Was it a trap? She slid a hand into the purse dangling by her hip. When they reached the tree line, she gripped the Sound Stone and closely surveyed the dancing fronds for hidden assailants.

The wind whipped suddenly, causing the taller palm trees to sway and creak, their fronds raking the air with howling hisses in every direction. Senses heightened and heart racing, Margaret tugged the Sound Stone from her purse and guided it to her chest. Christian never spoke as he led her along the path. He seemed unconcerned by the sounds and darkness and maintained a leisurely pace while the candle inside the lantern furiously fluttered.

Margaret prepared to raise the Stone to her mouth, fearful of an ambush, when she noticed faint but growing light through the rustling underbrush. With a sigh of relief, she lowered the Stone back to her purse and widened her distance from Christian.

She was close enough now to see a well-lit beach beyond the stand of trees. Tiki torches surrounded a large, open-air tent featuring a stagelike platform upon which rested a formally arrayed dining table. Pressed white linen, sterling silver flatware and crystal stemware sparkled from the light cast by the torches.

At the end of the plank walkway, Christian turned and said, "We have arrived, Miss Bradley. There is a small bench beside you where you can remove your sandals to walk across the beach. I will return to escort you after dinner. I hope you enjoy a wonderful meal."

Margaret nodded her thanks and sat to slide off her sandals. As she stepped beyond the plank, her toes met the cool cushion of the fine-grain sand. Gripping her slinky black-and-gold cocktail dress by its flared hem to avoid a sudden gust revealing more than she intended, Margaret approached the tent.

Underneath the tent canopy three tuxedoed attendants stood at attention, but no one was seated at the dining table itself. Scanning the secluded cove, Margaret spied two white Adirondack-style chairs close to the rippling surf. In between the chairs a small table was set with an ice bucket and an open bottle of champagne. On one of the chairs sat a man with cigar in hand staring idly at the Moon's reflection on the ocean's surface.

Margaret could see the man's thick, silvery hair ruffling in the sea breeze. She stepped cautiously toward him and clutched the purse tightly against her ribs. She briefly considered projecting the troublesome stranger out into the ocean. But that would mean killing the dining porters as well—not exactly the way to maintain a low profile.

The sound of Margaret's feet kicking sand caught the man's attention and he rose to greet her. The erudite Frenchman stood, adorned in traditional evening attire—black tuxedo, white shirt and black satin bow tie—and smiled politely as she reached the chairs. A gold medallion draped around his neck swayed as he bowed slightly. "*Enchanté*, Mademoiselle Corchran. Allow me to introduce myself. I am Jacques Foucault."

Though the lilt of his voice was cheerful and inviting, the use of her real name pierced like an unexpected stab. A sharp reminder, despite the relaxed ambience, that this meeting would be all business. Unconsciously shifting the purse pressed against her torso, she said, "The name's Victoria Bradley."

Strands of her hair fanned in the wind and blocked her view of the subtle smile upon Foucault's face. "*Mais oui*, Mademoiselle Bradley. Will you join me for a glass of Cristal?"

"No, thank you," Margaret quickly answered.

"*Quelle déception, mon amie*," Foucault whispered to himself. To Margaret he said, "Please, Mademoiselle, let us sit and talk."

Margaret swiped the hair from her eyes and stepped past Foucault to the Adirondack chair on the left. Shifting the book-sized Prada purse to her right hip, she sat and clamped the wispy hem of her dress underneath her crossed legs.

Foucault retrieved a flute from the table and slowly filled the stemware halfway. Placing it back on the table, he lifted a second glass and did the same. Margaret watched his motions and clenched her jaw when he filled the second flute.

Reposing in the chair next to her, he raised a glass and said, "*À la vôtre*."

Margaret ignored the toast and stared out at the dark reflection of clouds on the ocean's surface. Maintaining her vision on the sliding shadows, she brusquely asked, "Can we just get on with this?"

Foucault savored the light flavor of the champagne's varietal blend and followed her gaze out to sea. He was disappointed at her gruff, almost childish disposition thus far. She didn't realize it yet, but there was much he could offer that the unctuous Klaus Navarro could not. Yet Foucault was a patient man, with years of experience cultivating collaborators. This one, he realized after their brief exchange, would involve a greater measure of taming than others.

Casually brushing grains of sands from his slacks, Foucault asked, "Do you like shrimp, Mademoiselle? One of our courses tonight will be an exquisite curry made with succulent Guyana shrimp."

With a roll of her eyes, Margaret thought, I don't give a f—— what you serve, I'm not touching a speck of it! She turned to Foucault and, ignoring his question, said, "Look, I've had a long day. Tell me what you want so I can get out of here."

He lifted the glass again for another sip and sighed. A cloud passed in front of the quarter Moon and the beach momentarily descended into darkness. Returning the glass again to the table he softly said, "*Se calmer.*"

The remark and the paternal tone of his voice was maddening. Screw this, she thought. This conversation is going nowhere. Reaching into the opening of her purse, Margaret cupped the Sound Stone and snapped, "Calm down? Quit toying with me. Get to the point or I'm out of here."

The relaxed Foucault smiled. "*Tu fais le bébé.* Come now, it is such a beautiful evening. Let us enjoy each other's company. There will be time after dinner to discuss matters."

Her fingers tensed around the Sound Stone and her temper flared. She jumped out of the chair and pulled it from within the purse. Retreating a few steps, Margaret dropped the purse onto the sand and said, "Do you know what this is? If you really did talk to my brother, then you know what I can do with it."

Foucault, shaking his head in amusement, raised himself out of the chair, straightened the cuffed sleeves of his shirt, readjusted the medallion hanging between the buttoned dinner jacket's lapels and stepped back into the wet sand behind him. He extended arms on each side of his body and politely said, "*Oui*, Mademoiselle. I know what you hold in your hand, though you know only *un peu* of its powers. By all means, demonstrate your *prouesses.*"

Margaret's face contorted into a mongrel snarl as she raised the Sound Stone to her mouth. A gust of wind pushed against her and she wobbled slightly. Eyes riveted on Foucault, she inhaled deeply, unconcerned that her dress hem ballooned upward and flapped above her waist. Lips crushed against the back of the curved stone, she huffed a fierce tone.

Expecting Foucault to soar through the night sky and into the water, Margaret was confounded by the smiling Foucault's unwavering stance—and by the fact that the Sound Stone quivered in her hand. She squatted lower to align with Foucault's center of gravity and hummed harshly on the bowl-shaped rock again.

While his jacket rippled from the sound waves emanating from the stone, and a pile of sand plopped over his dress shoes, Foucault remained anchored where he stood. This time, the vibration of the stone nearly caused it to slip from her grip.

The Moon reappeared from behind the masking cloud and bathed Foucault in bright white light. "You may try one hundred times, *madame*, and the result will be the same."

He watched with pleasure as the expression on Margaret's face shifted from hate to fear. Lowering his extended arms back to his side, he nodded toward the chair and requested she sit.

Margaret backed away, darting a panicked look at the chairs, while the lower half of her dress was still pasted against her midsection. Acting quickly, she trained the Stone on one of the chairs and hummed urgently. The chair violently jerked out of the sand and spun rapidly in the air toward Foucault. With his hands cupped in the direction of the spinning chair, he swiftly clapped his inner wrists together. The chair exploded with an ear-splitting snap into hundreds of jagged strips.

Margaret momentarily gaped with unbelieving eyes before she turned to flee. On her third, stumbling stride, Foucault aimed his cupped hands at her retreating figure and slapped his wrists together again.

The colliding blow felt like a baseball bat pounding against the flesh between her shoulders. She staggered forward and splayed face-first onto the beach, her dress shredded by the rending blast of air. Gasping for breath, her nostrils caked with sand, Margaret curled onto her side and coughed to expel the gritty mixture of sand and saliva.

Foucault motioned to the porters still positioned on the dining platform to leave. Without a word, the porters turned and headed for the plank walkway bisecting the palms. Adjusting his shirt cuffs, he quietly stepped toward Margaret's sprawled and retching body.

He knelt next to Margaret and gallantly covered her torn dress with his dinner jacket. Her eyelids fluttered uncontrollably in a futile effort to clear sand from her vision. Gently patting her shoulder, Foucault whispered reassuringly, "There, there, *mon enfant*. Lie still and I will get a wet cloth for your eyes. Now that you understand the limitations of your *Breylofte*, we will start our conversation over."

Beneath the dining canopy, Foucault poured Margaret a glass of Cristal. Still wiping her red, stinging eyes with a damp linen napkin, she struggled to regain command of her senses. Beside her place at the dinner table rested the *Breylofte* and her purse. Across the table, Foucault lazily inhaled on a thin cigar and watched her furtive efforts to compose herself. Her cell phone and room key sat on his plate.

Unable to persuade herself to look at him, Margaret stared down at her lap and pulled his jacket tightly across her chest. The inescapable coarse, sticky feel of sand and salt air layered her arms, legs, neck and hair.

Tenderly he said, "There is no need to be ashamed. Each of the *Lifintyls* have countervailing powers. Unless you studied them as long as I have, you would not know this about the *Breylofte*."

Through milky eyes Margaret faced Foucault and tried to suppress a quizzical look. *Lifintyls? Breylofte?* What was he talking about? Snuffling involuntarily, she asked, "Who are you?"

"Less a threat to you than you think. Possibly an *allié*—if you can lower your defenses long enough to find out." While Foucault spoke, he typed out a message on his own cell phone and placed it on the table.

"Ally?" she questioned.

"*Oui*. I sought to meet you in the hopes we might form an alliance." Foucault nodded as he flicked ashes onto the platform by his chair.

"Why would I want an alliance with you?"

"Simple, Mademoiselle. Because I can offer you much more than your Klaus Navarro."

"What makes you think I'm in an alliance with this Klaus person?"

Foucault shook his head with disapproval and said, "Come now, Margaret, do not be coy. I found you. I know your true identity. I demonstrated my ability to neuter the *Breylofte*—and I showed you *Dreylaeks* can do more than just defend. Do you really believe I am not aware of who pulls your strings?"

Mustering a small measure of bravado, she said, "*No one* pulls my strings! You didn't answer my question. Who are you?"

Smoke poured from his mouth as he answered, "I told you my name."

"You know what I mean! You obviously know about the Stones. Are you a collector? Or a smuggler like Navarro?"

Foucault considered her question while sipping champagne. "*Non*. I am not a collector in the classical sense. I don't gather trinkets to admire or display, but I am interested in the Munuorians and their *Tyls*."

"Moon what?"

"Moon-war-E-uns. They made the *Lifintyls*, the 'Stones' as you call them."

"What did you call this?" she asked, lifting the Sound Stone.

A pleased smile stretched across Foucault's face. "It is known as a *Breylofte*."

"Is that French?"

"No. The Munuorians gave the device its name. It means 'air mover' in their language."

"How do you know that?" she asked.

He shrugged. "Didn't your Uncle Matthew teach you about the Munuorians?"

"A little. But he didn't know their name. He called them Stone Benders. What did you do to block the Sound Stone?"

Foucault nodded appreciatively. At least she is curious, he thought. He unclasped a golden cufflink fastening his left sleeve and withdrew a cookie-sized, deep-emerald-colored stone. Gripping the stone between his finger and thumb, he said, "With this. Well, two of these. One for each wrist."

Squinting across the table at the thin, shiny rock, Margaret said, "More Stones? What did you call them?"

"*Dreylaeks.* The name has a dual meaning. One is 'defender,' the other 'healer,'" he said.

Over Foucault's shoulder, Margaret saw Christian approaching the platform. Foucault noticed her body tense. He reached out a hand. "*Calmer*, Mademoiselle. He will not hurt you."

When Christian stepped up to the table, Foucault handed him Margaret's room key and cell phone. He instructed him to search her room. Turning to Margaret, he said, "Please tell Christian the passcode to your phone. Then, we can finally eat."

Margaret's face reddened. "Why should I?"

"Also, if you have anything in the room safe, we need that code as well," Foucault said.

She hesitated. Foucault pressed on. "I need to know who you called on the beach. That is all. As for the safe, Christian will not take anything that isn't mine."

"Yours? What's that supposed to mean?"

"It means we know you have been snooping around Dominica. Just like your uncle. If your brother is to be believed, Monsieur Dobson stole my *Sulataers*. They were of great value to me and now they are lost. I aim to ensure you've removed nothing else from the Maerlif."

"I don't know what you're talking about," she said.

"The gold, *mon chère*. It was mine," he said. Foucault watched the shock spread over her face. "Yes, you know of what I speak. It was hidden in a place I have guarded for many years. The *miscreant* blew it open with explosives and took my *Sulataers*."

"I've found nothing," said Margaret.

"That is good to hear, and it doesn't surprise me," Foucault said. "After the intrusion, I took measures to ensure it would not be discovered again. Still, I need to be sure. After all, you have the map, do you not? And you have a *Breylofte*."

Margaret looked at him quizzically but provided Christian with the passcodes nonetheless. "The room safe is empty."

As Christian hustled away, Foucault said, "I believe you. Now . . . what have you done with the map? Your brother guessed you gave it to Navarro. Is that true?"

She nodded. There was no reason to lie at this point.

"Most unfortunate," he said. "How long has he had it?"

"A month, maybe more."

"Do you know his purpose? Why he wanted the map?"

She shrugged. "To find more of the Stones, I guess."

Foucault's concentration was interrupted by a text from Christian confirming Margaret's calls were placed to an Argentinian phone number. He also confirmed the calls went unanswered. Foucault looked up at Margaret and said, "*Bon*. I'm pleased you didn't lie to me. It is fortunate you did not connect with Señor Navarro." While he rubbed a *Dreylaek* between his fingers, he added, "You say Klaus wants more of the *Lifíntyls*. Do you know which ones?"

"If you've talked with Kyle, you know what he wanted."

"One likes to be sure the truth has been shared."

Margaret said, "Navarro wanted anything and everything Devlin had."

While she spoke, another text from Christian arrived. He validated the room safe was empty. Foucault read the message and then asked, "Did he mention any of the Stones using the Munuorian names. For example, did he say the word *Sinethal* instead of Master Stone?"

She shook her head.

"Did he mention the name Malinyah? Or the name Muran?"

"Nope. Who are they?"

Foucault massaged his temples and thanked the heavens. Maybe Navarro was blind to the *Tuliskaera* after all. As he considered the possibility further, he realized it was irrelevant. The man had the map. He still had to be dealt with, or he would eventually learn of the fire cutter.

For a few minutes, Foucault sat with hands folded, deep in thought. Christian returned with a train of porters carrying their dinner. While they served the meal, Christian handed the phone and keys back to Margaret. Foucault seemed not to notice the buzz of activity around him.

Once the porters retreated, he quietly asked, "Did you retain a copy of the map?"

As Margaret sampled the curried shrimp, she nodded.

"*Dieu Merci!*" Foucault exclaimed, clapping both hands together. "Let us eat then . . . and discuss our alliance!"

4

Minds Over Matters

Incline Village, Nevada
August 5

re they gone yet?" Pebbles asked.

Jennifer Stevens gunned the engine of her Jet Ski and zipped past the secluded cove's entrance. She looked left and right, and then turned to signal all clear.

After acknowledging the signal, Eleanor "Pebbles" McCarver stepped into the icy water and cupped the *Breylofte* with both hands. Placing the scratchy underside of the bowl-shaped stone against her lips, she pointed the bowl's open end at her Jet Ski drifting ten feet away.

As she started to hum on the Stone, the water between Pebbles and the watercraft rippled from the burst of sound waves, pushing the Jet Ski a little farther away. She frowned and lowered the Stone.

Squatting a bit lower to concentrate the Stone's energy on the heavier, lower section of the watercraft, Pebbles repositioned the *Breylofte* against her mouth and resumed humming. Immediately, the Jet Ski began to jiggle. She increased the intensity of the hum and felt the *Breylofte* vibrate in her hands, an indication the Stone was ready to do its voodoo. Pebbles lifted her head an inch and the Jet Ski lifted two feet out of the water.

At the entrance of the cove, Jennifer kept one eye on Pebbles' maneuver while watching for unsuspecting passersby. On more than one occasion over the past two weeks, a boater or fellow Jet Skier had happened along while they practiced levitating objects in mid-air. When they practiced with rocks or logs, they could quickly fling the objects into the water before anyone noticed. But a Jet Ski floating in the air?

Pebbles raised her head slowly and the swaying watercraft climbed higher. When it reached twenty feet above the lake's surface, Pebbles steadied her humming until the swaying ceased. She turned left and ever-so-gently moved the Jet Ski thirty feet in the same direction. Then, running low on oxygen, she delicately lowered it. When it splashed down without incident, Pebbles raised the *Breylofte* above her head and shouted, "Woohoo! New record! Beat that, copper!"

"Big deal. You have an unfair advantage, anyway!" Jennifer called back.

"Ah, you're just a sore loser," bellowed Pebbles.

Jennifer zoomed back toward the beach and pulled up next to Pebbles. Cutting the engine, she crossed her arms and said, "Seriously, with all the jabbering you do, your lungs are more developed. That's the *only* reason you won."

"Ha!" Pebbles said. "You're just jealous."

"Oh, am I? And who was all 'boo hoo' an hour ago?"

The jab was a reference to an earlier competition where the two women endeavored to determine which of them could shoot the other the farthest with the assistance of the *Breylofte*.

Pebbles pushed the empty Jet Ski toward shore and said, "That was entirely luck on your part. The wind interfered with my shots."

"All six of them?"

"Care to go again?"

"I don't know, we're running kinda late as it is."

"So, in other words, you're chicken?" Pebbles taunted. "Come on, one turn each, winner takes all."

"Fine, what distance?"

"Hmmm, fifteen feet. Or, is that too far for you?"

"Let's get it on."

Jennifer hopped off and together they slowly guided both Jet Skis onto the beach. While Jennifer paced off a rough fifteen feet from the water's edge, Pebbles stood back and waited impatiently. When Jennifer arrived in front of Pebbles, she dragged her foot to create a line in the sand . . . making sure to kick the excess sand atop Pebbles' toes.

"That'll cost ya, copper," Pebbles said.

Jennifer yawned in her face and retreated to the water's edge.

Pebbles readied the Sound Stone and called, "Okay, make like a starfish."

Jennifer extended her arms and widened her stance. She closed her eyes and clenched her teeth just as Pebbles huffed on the Stone. The blow caught Jennifer's right shoulder and spun her two feet back, but she remained standing. She turned around and grinned at Pebbles.

Pebbles said, "Do over. I wasn't ready."

"Uh-uh," Jennifer said. "One round. You made the rules. My turn."

She marched up the sand with hand extended. Pebbles frowned when she passed over the *Breylofte*. "I'm toast."

"Yes, you are."

When both were in position, Jennifer asked, "Any last words?"

"Be gentle?"

Jennifer focused her aim between Pebbles' hips and took a deep breath. The hum that followed was short and sharp. The sound waves caught Pebbles square in the midsection and sent her flying ten feet back. With arms and legs flailing, she hit the water with a scream.

Shivering, she emerged from the lake and adjusted her bikini top. As she waded back to shore, she maintained a quiet, yet undefeated expression. Jennifer teased her by displaying Pebbles' signature victory pose—finger pointing at a flexed bicep.

"What can I say," Pebbles said. "Lucky again."

Jennifer tossed her a towel and said, "Luck has nothing to do with it. I just aim better."

"Oh, here we go again. Five years in the army, five years as a cop, yada, yada." Pebbles wrapped herself in the towel.

"Exactly, I've had a lot of practice aiming at things," Jennifer said, pulling a hoodie over her string bikini.

While Pebbles clutched the towel around her neck with one hand, she bent down to load up her daypack with the other. Tossing sandals, sunglasses and bottled water in the sack, she asked, "Tell me, what military exercise requires you to hum on a stone? Hmmm?"

"None, but the principle is the same," Jennifer said. While she waited for Pebbles to finish packing, she pulled out her cell phone and checked for messages.

Pebbles mocked, "Principle, schminzaple. You just got lucky."

"Call it what you will, I still won. By the way, Anlon texted. Wants to know where we are. Should I tell him we're waiting for your bruised ego to heal?"

"I'll answer myself, thank you very much." Pebbles retrieved her own phone and tapped a quick message: "Heya! On our way back now!"

Anlon replied within seconds: "Good, I'm hungry. Sydney's?"

Pebbles turned to Jennifer. "A.C. wants to go to Sydney's. You in?"

"Sure, but it'll be crowded. You think he's ready for that?"

"He wants so bad to get back to a normal routine. I think we can manage. We should try, at least," Pebbles said while she typed an affirmative reply to Anlon.

Shortly after, Anlon responded, "Great, I'll call Syd and set it up. Tell Jen I'd like her there too. We have Stones to talk about!"

A gasp escaped from Pebbles and she covered her mouth. "Oh, my God. It's official."

"What? What did he say?" asked Jennifer.

"See for yourself," said Pebbles, tossing the phone to Jennifer. Gathering the last of her things, including the *Breylofte*, she prodded Jennifer. "Hurry, we need to get back before he changes his mind!"

Anlon Cully grasped the iron railing with one hand and leaned on a walking stick with the other. Gingerly, he extended his good leg over the landing's edge and proclaimed, "One small step for man . . ."

Down below, Pebbles and Jennifer stood side by side on the driveway and watched Anlon sidle down the first step. Pausing to rebalance, Anlon inhaled the pine-scented air and smiled at his two companions. "See, told you I could do it by myself."

"Looking good!" said Jennifer, while filming the descent on her phone.

Pebbles, nibbling on a fingernail, edged toward the staircase and cautioned, "Don't get cocky, Doctor Cully! And keep away from the pine needles."

"I see them, I'm fine," he said.

Pebbles kicked off her sandals and perched on the bottom step. When he teetered slightly, she clutched the railing and readied to dash upward. Anlon steadied himself and motioned for her to move back. "Quit staring at me like I'm going to keel over! I'm forty-two, not eighty-two, for goodness sakes!"

When he reached the driveway surface, Pebbles leaned forward to kiss his cheek. "I'm sorry, A.C. You did great."

Anlon returned the kiss and wrapped an arm around her waist. "Thank you. Now, let's get going. I need to eat some *real* food . . . fast!"

"What? No more protein-gruel?" Jennifer asked.

Rubbing his jaw, Anlon said, "Never again. It ruins the taste of tequila."

"Are you sure you're up for this?" Pebbles asked.

"Probably not, but I'm doing it anyway," Anlon said.

"Will you at least ride with Jen in the Jeep?" pleaded Pebbles.

"Nope. I have a rain check for a scooter ride, and I'm cashing it in."

"Well, okay, if you say so," came Pebbles' solemn reply. After a short pause, her face brightened. "I can't believe you're finally going to ride with me!"

Garbed in black tank top and cut-off denim shorts, Pebbles scooped up her sandals and joyfully skipped to the sparkling, hot-pink scooter. She leaned on the seat to slide on the sandals and then ran her fingers lovingly over the shiny surface of the moped's frame.

Jennifer locked an arm through Anlon's and escorted him across the driveway. As they neared the scooter, she asked, "Nervous?"

"Nah," Anlon said.

"I would be if I were you. I've seen her on a Jet Ski!" Jennifer whispered.

Safely aboard the bike, Anlon handed the walking stick to Jennifer. He strapped on a black-and-white-checkered helmet and waited for Pebbles to slide in front of him.

"Take it nice and slow," Anlon said.

"Oh, please. What fun is that? Wrap your arms around my waist and hold tight," Pebbles said. She lowered a black helmet atop her pink, pixie-cut hair and pressed the ignition button. The scooter puttered awake and Pebbles revved the engine. A happy scream sounded above the whir of the moped motor.

Behind them, Jennifer leaned under the Jeep's roll bars to stow a jacket and Anlon's walking stick on the back bench. She then hopped into the driver's seat, fashioned her honey tresses into a quick ponytail, slid aviator sunglasses into place and gave Pebbles a thumbs-up.

Pebbles revved the engine again and lurched forward onto Lakeshore Boulevard. The unexpected motion nearly bucked Anlon off the bike, but he managed to right himself before she zoomed off.

With ragged enthusiasm, Pebbles put the scooter through its paces as they snaked up the side streets of Incline Village. During the ride, Anlon marveled at Pebbles' instant transformation from mother hen to reckless driver. Twice he succumbed to the overpowering urge to shut his eyes—once at a sharp bend in the road, and the other when she jerked around a car backing out of a parking spot. He burst out laughing when she silenced the engine outside Sydney's Bistro and said, "Careful getting off."

It was on the early side for dinner when they arrived, but the bistro was already packed. As they approached the crowd mingling outside the entrance, Pebbles and Jennifer extended arms to clear a path for Anlon.

His unsteady movements and frail appearance drew odd stares as they wound their way through small groups of people waiting for tables inside the restaurant. Anlon couldn't help but notice a toddler pointing at him as he shuffled past. He smiled in return, but wished for the day when people would once again concentrate their stares on Pebbles' array of tattoos and piercings instead of him.

Upon wedging their way through the front door, Sydney Armstrong spotted Pebbles immediately. Taller than average, she stood out in most crowds. When combined with her colorful, spiky hair, she was unmistakable. He waved to her and pushed through the throng to greet them.

When he got to Anlon, he called above the din, "Anlon! I'm so happy to see you!"

"Likewise, Syd," Anlon said with a smile. "It's good to be back."

"We'll fatten you up, don't you worry!" Sydney assured him. "Come, let's get you out of this melee. I've blocked off the entire courtyard for you."

The "courtyard," as Sydney deemed it, was a small deck attached to the bar that accommodated four tables. It was quiet when the leading door was closed, and there was a gap between the surrounding pines to catch a glimpse of the lake a thousand feet down the mountainside. Reserved normally for cozy, romantic gatherings, it afforded diners the chance to chat without the need to shout.

Settled around a table, they placed drink orders and chatted about Anlon's new neighbor, Griffin Taylor. Known to the rest of the world as "Bones," Griffin was the lead guitarist for the popular metal band Ice Zombies. He had moved into the lodge abutting Anlon's property the month prior. Anlon expressed surprise that Griffin had yet to throw an all-out bash. "Isn't that what rockers do?"

"Not this one," Jennifer said with a shake of her head. "He's into his privacy more than you are!"

She explained that Griffin purchased the home to escape the craziness of "La La Land," and that he favored the comparative tranquility of Tahoe's north shore. Pebbles teased her for the insider tidbit and prodded Jennifer to share more revelations gleaned from her "private" chats with their famous neighbor. Anlon sputtered, "What? Did I miss something?"

Jennifer truncated Pebbles' inquisition. "Okay! Enough about me! Besides, aren't we here to talk about the Stones?"

"Yeah, you're right," said Pebbles. Turning to Anlon, she nudged his shoulder and said, "You've been all shushy since Devlin's stuff arrived. We're dying to know what you've been up to!"

"Hey, there's a lot to sort out, you know!" he said.

Just then, the waiter appeared through the bar's side door with their drinks. Once distributed, he asked if they were ready to order dinner. Anlon started to speak, but Pebbles cut him off. "You don't eat until you start talking."

"You're . . . evil," he said, laughing. "Can I at least have a sip of my beer first?"

Turning to Jennifer, Pebbles asked, "Should we allow it?"

"Hmmm . . . I don't know . . . "

Before they could object, Anlon smiled and whisked down a few hearty gulps. Plunking the half-empty glass on the table, he stared off toward the lake and gathered his thoughts.

"I'm sorry. It's been frustrating," he said. "Guess I should have brought you both in earlier, but there are just so many damn threads. I thought I could put some of them together before I asked for your help. But, honestly, I've gone about as far as I can on my own."

Pebbles said, "Well, we are ready to help. More than ready, right, Jen?"

Jennifer nodded. "Absolutely."

"So, tell us about your threads, and let's start knocking 'em out," said Pebbles.

He paused for a moment and then said, "I guess the hardest part's been trying to figure out where to concentrate first. I know we're all fascinated by the Stones, and I want to learn more about them too, but there are other things at play."

"Such as?" Pebbles asked.

"Well, first and foremost, I want to honor Devlin's legacy. He devoted a decade of his life to prove the mythical 'fish men' truly existed. And as far as I'm concerned, prove it he did. But, to the rest of the world, the evidence is incomplete."

"What do you mean?" Pebbles asked. "Aren't the Stones all the proof necessary? Especially, the Master Stone . . . I mean . . . *Sinethal*?

Who could meet Malinyah and not come away believing the Munuorians existed?"

"I don't disagree. But that's not how other archaeologists will see it. Sure, they'll be bowled over when they view the Stone, but they'll want more than that," Anlon said.

"Like what?" Jennifer asked.

"Well, I'm sure they'll ask many questions. Annoying, but necessary questions. Such as, where did the Master Stone come from?"

"*Sinethal*, Anlon. It's called the *Sinethal*," Pebbles corrected.

Anlon swirled the remaining IPA in his glass. "Fine. *Sinethal*. Where did it come from?"

"Devlin found it in a museum, right?" Jennifer asked.

He shook his head and set the glass down.

Pebbles leaned in. "Wait, I thought they found all the Stones in museums?"

"So did I," Anlon said.

"I don't understand." Pebbles looked at Jennifer and then back at Anlon.

"Me neither. I've been through every box of his records and every file on his computer. There is no mention of the *Sinethal* or any description of an artifact fitting its description. The other Stones all came from museums. I found detailed inventory records for each in Devlin's artifact catalogue file, but zippo for the *Sinethal*," he said.

"How bizarre," Jennifer said. "I thought Pacal told us it was found in a museum."

"Nope. My memory might be hazy, or maybe the beating he gave me knocked it out of me, but I don't think he ever said that." Anlon stretched out his stiff legs. "We don't even know for sure *when* Devlin found it. All we know is, several days before he was killed he begged George Grant to hold it in his office safe.

"The more I've thought about it, I think it's a reason, if not *the* reason, Devlin didn't go public with his discovery. Imagine if he stood before the world and revealed the *Sinethal* and Malinyah without documenting the Stone's origin. They'd call it a hoax and laugh him out of the room.

"I think Devlin wanted more evidence. Maybe Malinyah can provide us with that evidence, but I don't think the academic and scientific world will accept Malinyah's word. They'll want more proof. Physical proof, if possible."

Pebbles was about to speak when the waiter returned for their dinner orders. At the same time, Sydney stepped outside to check on them. He suggested they let him craft several dishes for them. They enthusiastically agreed and returned to their conversation.

Pebbles went first. "So, how are we going to get proof? The Waterland Map?"

Anlon rolled his eyes and put his head between his hands. "Gah! Don't get me started on that damn map!"

"Why? What's wrong with it?" asked Jennifer.

"It's impossible to read. I've tried several different approaches. So far I've struck out on every one," he said.

"But, the longitude and latitude grid?" Pebbles asked. "I thought all we had to do was layer the Waterland Map over a current world map?"

"Tried that. All the marked sites end up in the oceans," Anlon said. "Then, I thought, well, if the world turned upside down like the great flood myths say, maybe we just need to turn the map upside down. That did result in a few of the marks ending up on land, but most were still in the oceans. Mind you, it's entirely plausible that some of the sites are under water now."

Pebbles reflected on the story Malinyah shared about the asteroid's brush with Earth. "I see what you mean," she said. "Malinyah said the Stones were stashed before the flood, so you're right, some might have been wiped out."

Anlon nodded. "Exactly. Then, I went fishing through Devlin's papers and computers again and found the three notebooks you two discovered at Dobson's house. When I first looked through them, I was sure they would help. They are clearly field journals of sites Devlin searched for more of the Stones, but I don't know why he picked them. They're all islands. There's no mention of the map in the notes, just coordinates he searched. I tried several ways to maneuver the Waterland Map in order to line up the three sites, but no combination worked."

"How odd," Pebbles mumbled.

"What's that?" Anlon asked.

"Oh, I was just trying to remember what Malinyah said about the map, and I just realized I never asked her about it. We talked about the asteroid, and the flood, and going to help the survivors, but I don't think we ever discussed the map," she said.

"Well, maybe she can help us, I don't know. It's one topic, among many, we should talk to her about," Anlon said.

Pebbles' ears perked up at Anlon's comment. "You mean you're finally going to get the *Sinethal* out of storage?"

"Yeah, it's time. I'm sure Antonio will be happy to get the last of Devlin's things out of his hair. I don't think we can go much further without Malinyah's feedback."

There was a break in the conversation as Sydney emerged through the bar door with two waiters bearing their dinner: grilled coho salmon topped with a blueberry compote, steamed red king crab, asparagus sautéed with crumbled bacon, loaded baked potatoes and crispy sourdough rolls served with rock-salt-infused butter.

When the family-style platters landed on the table, Anlon stared at the dishes with lusty eyes. "Mmmm . . . bacon."

Jennifer laughed. "Really? Bacon? What about the salmon? The crab?"

"You don't understand," Anlon said. "It's a cruel fate to smell bacon and know you can't eat it."

Without further banter, they disappeared into the meal's varied flavors. Sydney returned to uncork a vintage California Chardonnay and joined them for a toast to Anlon's revived health. Outside of that interruption, they dined in silence. Anlon ate slowly, savoring each bite. It wasn't his first solid-food meal since regaining the use of his jaws, but his teeth reveled in every crunch.

After dinner, it was Jennifer who restarted the conversation. She said, "So, we have two threads to pursue: the origin of the *Sinethal*, and sorting out how to read the map. Is that it?"

"Um, no. Not by a long shot," Anlon said.

"What? Wait. There's more?" Pebbles asked.

"Heck, yeah. You know those notebooks I mentioned? Well, in one of them, there's a very strange passage . . . and an out-of-context drawing. I don't know if they're related, but it sure feels that way when I look at the pages."

"Well . . . ?" Jennifer prompted, her fork and knife poised in the air.

"You remember Devlin's statues? The ones Dobson stole, and the ones Navarro came looking for?"

"Yeah, the Easter Island–looking dude and the oriental one," Pebbles said.

"Exactly! Devlin drew a picture of the oriental statue next to a frantic passage about time running out," said Anlon.

"Why?" Jennifer asked.

"You tell me," said Anlon.

Sydney reappeared to ignite a fire tower beside their table while the waitstaff cleared the dishes. The guests extolled praise for the excellent dinner, which caused the humble restauranteur to blush bright red. A moment later, another attendant appeared bearing the bistro's signature dessert, Baked Sierra. The attendant handed the dessert tray to Sydney, who proudly placed it in the center of the table.

Armed with spoons, the three took turns dipping through the meringue shell to extract scoops of cinnamon ice cream and gingerbread cake.

Sydney peeked outside and asked, "How is it?"

Pebbles thrust a thumbs-up while Anlon said, "Amazing, Syd! All of it."

Sydney smiled and bowed. "It's great to have you back, Doc!"

"It's better to *be* back, Syd," said Anlon.

Anlon and Jennifer exchanged silent smiles while Pebbles attacked the melting concoction with ferocious intensity. Anlon teased, "Easy there, kiddo. You'll get brain freeze!"

Pebbles looked up from the plate long enough to mumble an unintelligible retort. Meringue dotted her chin, cheeks and the tip of her nose. Jennifer whisked out her phone and snapped a memorializing pic. A muffled "not fair" sounded from Pebbles' full mouth.

Jennifer pushed back from the table and sipped her wine. Holding up three fingers of her free hand, she said, "So, find the *Sinethal* origin, decode the map, sort out the statue. What's next?"

"The Flash Stone," said Anlon. "If Pacal wasn't lying, Thatcher Reynolds was after the Flash Stone."

"*Tuliskaera*," mumbled Pebbles through the last of the Baked Sierra. "Malinyah called the Flash Stone the *Tuliskaera*. She said it means 'fire cutter' in their language."

"Right," said Anlon. "Pacal said it was a weapon that makes the Sound Stone look like a twig."

Pebbles corrected Anlon again: "*Breylofte*. The Sound Stone is called the *Breylofte*."

"Yada, yada," Anlon said. "We need to find the *Tuliskaera* before Thatcher."

"But, we need the map for that, right?" Jennifer said.

"Yes. See, I told you, lots of threads," Anlon said.

"What about Navarro? Margaret Corchran? She got away with a copy of the map," reminded Pebbles.

"Two more threads," Anlon said with a nod. "Gotta tell you, though, I find it hard to believe they'll figure out the map before we do."

He turned to Jennifer. "By the way, any news from your colleagues about Thatcher, Navarro or Margaret?"

She shook her head. "No, I spoke to Dan Nickerson a couple days ago. Margaret and Thatcher are still missing. Navarro's been quiet since he beat out extradition."

With the Baked Sierra conquered, Anlon divvied the last of the Chardonnay and said, "Well, on the bright side, I've made some progress figuring out how the Munuorians developed their power to manipulate magnetism and how they made the Stones. I've been hoping to test the theories out, but I need a willing test subject."

His eyes were glued to Pebbles as she sipped her wine. Lowering the glass, she said, "Is this about the blood sample you wanted?"

He nodded. "Partially."

"No way, I don't like needles!" she said.

Anlon frowned and pointed to her nose stud, eyebrow rings and the hummingbird tattoo on her neck. He said, "Should I go on?"

She said, "They're different, and you know it."

"I hoped you might make an exception in the name of science," he said. "But I'll withdraw the request if you help me with a different experiment . . . one that doesn't involve needles."

"What kind of experiment?" Pebbles warily asked.

"A memory exercise," said Anlon.

5

Maps and Mysteries

Incline Village, Nevada
August 6

Anlon stretched his legs and lowered the notebook to his lap. Hoping to push yet another of Devlin's riddles from his thoughts, he closed his eyes and focused on the tune echoing from Incline Beach. He smiled with surprise as a group of teenagers began to sing along with a sixties classic: "Hey, hey, hey . . . that's what I say . . ."

With cascading effect, the young crooners inspired others to add their voices. First came fellow sun worshipers on the beach. Then, patrons milling at the dockside bar. Soon, the infectious melody spread to a scattering of boats floating in the bay, and the recorded song was drowned out by the collection of live performers.

Caught up in the spontaneous revelry, Anlon bobbed his head and tapped the notebook in rhythm. By the time Mick Jagger bemoaned his lack of satisfaction, Anlon had joined in as well. It felt surprisingly good to hear his own voice sing again.

When it ended, all around celebrated with hoots and applause. Anlon clapped too and took an anonymous bow for his participation. It was a nice change to sit on the patio and enjoy Tahoe's charms without carrying the full burden of unraveling Devlin's research. Now that Pebbles and Jennifer were diving in to help, Anlon looked forward to spending more time reacclimating to the life he enjoyed prior to Devlin's death.

First though, there were two problems to solve. Problem number one was the Waterland Map. The document remained undeciphered. Problem number two was the matter of Devlin's erratic actions in the months leading up to his death. From the incomplete clues Devlin left behind, it was evident he was trying to find something very specific. Something to do with the Munuorians and their Stones. And whatever it was, it troubled Devlin. Deeply. Anlon was determined to discover the source of Devlin's angst.

Anlon gazed down at the pocket-sized notebook in his lap. Its scribbled title read, *Dominica*. On the table next to him sat two other notebooks, *Guadeloupe* and *Martinique*. Anlon was convinced the notebooks held the clues to interpret the Waterland Map and Devlin's peculiar actions.

His uncle had used the notebooks to detail his observations from field trips to the three Caribbean islands in the months prior to his May death. Devlin had first visited Martinique in January. Then came Guadeloupe in February and finally Dominica in March.

For the most part, the three journals were alike. On each island, Devlin surveyed different geographic locations and landmarks and then recorded his findings. At first glance, it appeared the island visits were expeditions to find a cache of Munuorian Stones. But, then Anlon found confusing entries in the Dominica book that seemed at odds with that conclusion. Given the confusing entries and the fact that Dominica was the last island Devlin searched before his murder, Anlon considered it the most important of the three.

However, before diving into the Dominica journal, there were several overarching questions about the Caribbean expeditions that demanded Anlon's attention. What led Devlin to focus on the three islands? Was there a connection between them? Was there a reason for the order in which they were searched? While Anlon had yet to arrive at definitive answers, he had developed a theory that seemed to tie together a solution for all three questions.

He initially focused on Devlin's choice of the three islands. It seemed a reasonable assumption that Devlin selected the sites from the Waterland Map, but until Anlon deciphered the map, it was impossible to prove whether his assumption was correct. Yet, there were some clues to support the assumption based on what Anlon knew of the map already . . .

The night before, Anlon had pulled out the Waterland Map to take another stab at deciphering Devlin's cryptic drawing. As he mulled the unusual topography and color-coded markings, he had to remind himself it was really two separate maps that Devlin merged into one.

The first of the merged maps was the source of the color-coded markings. Devlin had seen the map during visions with Malinyah's *Sinethal*. From those visions, he learned the markings represented sites where the Munuorians cached their special Stones in advance of a near-Earth asteroid encounter. The Munuorians feared the asteroid would devastate the planet and stashed the Stones as a precaution. A prehistoric example of man hiding acorns ahead of a winter storm, Anlon thought.

The second map merged by Devlin was copied from a wall drawing found in an Egyptian pyramid at Giza. This map supposedly showed the topography of the mythical Egyptian underworld known as the Duat. Devlin's interest in the Duat map was driven by a practical consideration. Its topography was similar to that of the map he viewed during visions shared by Malinyah. Instead of trying to draw Malinyah's map from memory, Devlin simply traced the pyramid's Duat map and then inserted the Stone cache locations shared by Malinyah.

Shortly after Devlin's death, Anlon had learned that Devlin was originally drawn to the Duat map early in his search for the Munuorians, long before he found the *Sinethal* and met Malinyah. Subsequently, he learned the reason for Devlin's interest in the map from Devlin's friend and fellow archaeologist, Cesar Perez. According to Cesar, the catalyst was an obscure academic article penned by a contrarian scholar.

Anlon recalled how excited Cesar had become when he realized the connection between Devlin's map and the article. The man had jumped out of a chair, pounded a fist against his open hand and exclaimed, "Of course! The Waterland Map."

In the article, Cesar had explained, the scholar offered an unconventional explanation for a curious feature of the Duat. Wherever the Duat was discussed in Egyptian texts or murals, it was always described in inordinate topographical detail. Cesar had said the ancient Egyptians didn't view the Duat as an ethereal vacuum filled with clouds. They viewed the Duat as a physical place with mountains, rivers, valleys and the like. Not only did the Egyptians describe these geographic features, they also named many of them.

Anlon had since read the article himself. In it, the scholar suggested the Duat was, in fact, a physical place. It was Earth as it existed prior to the mythical great flood. Only, the scholar didn't believe the flood was mythical. Based on other cultures' mythologies of the event, he believed a planet-sized asteroid passed close to Earth. In the process, it caused vast changes to the face of the planet, including a great flood that washed over Earth, destroying everything in its path. It caused new mountains to rise and other lands to be submerged beneath the sea. Water became land and vice versa.

The heretical academic suggested the ancient Egyptians carried a memory of this event and baked it into their theology. They saw the Duat as the face of the Earth before the flood—a world that was submerged by the great flood. Hence, when the sun set on the new world, it rose in their underworld . . . or the world they knew before the flood. The scholar dubbed the previous world the "Waterland." Devlin just borrowed the name for his merged map.

With the article circulating in his mind, Anlon had studied Devlin's merged map late into the night in the hopes some new clue would pop out. When none did, he had headed for bed. Careful to avoid waking Pebbles, Anlon had tiptoed into the bedroom and slid under the covers. She had stirred and then nuzzled up against him, but she never awoke. For another hour, Anlon had stared into the darkness while reflecting on the Waterland tale.

Although Anlon's specialty was biomechanics, not geology, his scientific background offered enough of a grounding to imagine the implications of a close encounter with a planet-sized asteroid, especially one with a magnetic polarity different from Earth's.

As the asteroid neared Earth, its gravitational field would have caused the oceans to rise up in huge swells. Given Earth's current waves and winds are dictated by the Moon, a body in space that sits nearly two hundred and forty thousand miles away with a mass equivalent to just one percent of Earth's, Anlon wondered what would have happened if an asteroid with fifteen percent of Earth's mass, the same as Mars, passed halfway between the Moon and Earth.

Would not Earth's waves and winds have gone crazy driven by the gravitational pull of a body with fifteen times the Moon's mass at half its distance? Wouldn't the stronger waves and winds have swamped the lands and given the appearance of a great flood to those on the ground?

Anlon had envisioned the intense gravitational pull also triggering volcanic eruptions and earthquakes on a global scale. Such a pull might have been strong enough to disrupt the Earth's crust, causing portions of the crust to buckle in places and rise up in others. Astronomers point to such effects when moons get too close to their host planets, Anlon had thought. Why not a passing asteroid?

Combined with the monster waves, the stresses on the Earth's crust would have caused water to flow differently around the changed landscape. To the people on the ground, Anlon imagined it would have appeared as if new mountains had sprung from nowhere while other lands disappeared beneath the oceans.

If that wasn't terrifying enough, Anlon had contemplated the implications of a passing asteroid with a strong, oppositely polarized magnetic field. Electrical storms the likes of which no living person had ever seen. Huge caverns riven by tremendous bolts of lightning. Raging fires everywhere.

Eyes closed, Anlon had imagined the oppositely-polarized asteroid reaching out and grabbing hold with one gravitational hand and one magnetic hand and ravaging the planet. Then, as it moved past, he envisioned the asteroid inflicting a final indignity. When all the forces, gravitational and magnetic, released, the Earth flipped upside down like a spinning ball dropped in water.

At an average speed of sixty thousand miles per hour, equivalent to high-end speeds of modern-day near-Earth asteroids, the prehistoric asteroid would have terrorized Earth's inhabitants for far more than a week. The worst of it would have lasted half a day, but it would have seemed a slow-motion train wreck for three days beforehand. And its physical aftershocks would have persisted for months, if not years, as the planet tried to adjust to its new orientation and topography.

All that assumed not a single piece of the asteroid broke off due to Earth's gravitational pull. If one included the effects of chunks breaking off the asteroid and pummeling the planet, the landscape changes would have been amplified further.

Prehistoric Armageddon. If it really happened, Anlon had thought, it was stunning to believe anything survived it. Devlin had believed it happened. And he believed there were survivors. And these survivors set their memories of it on stones, on paper, in songs and in tales told by fireside. And in those tales, they spoke of strange men who arrived by sea, bearing curious stones. Men who rescued the survivors from the brink of extinction and helped them build a new world.

Too wired to sleep, Anlon had tossed off the covers and returned to his office to study the map some more.

As another chorus of beachgoers began to belt out a Bruno Mars tune, Anlon stifled a yawn and sipped from a glass of lemonade. The urge to lean back and go to sleep fought with his desire to crack Devlin's map and the riddles posed by the journals.

Setting the glass down, he lifted the Dominica journal and stared once again at its cover. As Anlon saw it, the primary challenge reading Devlin's map was the lack of a key or legend. While Devlin had inserted color-coded dots on the map in various spots near or along coastlines of the preflood land masses, he inconsistently applied the dots. In some locations, there were five, in others two. Some places had green, red and black dots. Others green and brown or other combinations. But, Devlin left no explanation as to what the dots signified!

Compounding matters, there was a second challenge to interpreting the map. Devlin had inserted longitude and latitude grid markings, but to Anlon, the coordinate grid appeared to be inaccurate.

When Anlon had first viewed the map, the grid led him to believe it would be a simple matter to layer a current world map atop Devlin's drawing and align the respective longitudes and latitudes. However, that didn't work. Nearly all the color-coded dots were ocean bound.

It didn't take long before Anlon considered flipping the Waterland Map upside down—a la the planet flip described in the great flood legends. But, when he inverted Devlin's map and again lined up the grid with a current world map, many of the dots were still positioned far from any land mass. While it seemed reasonable to assume some of the preflood caches were submerged after the asteroid passed, Anlon had expected more marked points to appear on land. Further, inverted or not, he had expected at least one of the map's points to line up with Dominica, Guadeloupe or Martinique. None did.

Yet, Devlin found one of the Munuorian caches on Dominica.

This fact had led Anlon to consider a chilling possibility. Devlin wasn't able to read the map either! At least, he hadn't been able to until he went to Dominica. The map was a work in progress, which explained why Devlin didn't provide a key. It also explained why he went to Guadeloupe and Martinique in addition to Dominica. The brilliant SOB had used the three islands as directional finders to fine-tune the map.

Anlon had reached this conclusion after plotting the coordinates of each island. This exercise showed the southernmost tip of Guadeloupe was almost exactly one degree of latitude north of Martinique's northernmost point with Dominica nearly dead-center between the two.

When he realized how closely the three islands were positioned, Anlon reexamined the Waterland Map and the latitude and longitude markings. Given the map's small, hand-drawn scale, Anlon finally had understood Devlin's difficulty reading his own map. A misplacement of a given latitude or longitude line by a solitary degree could result in a seventy-mile miss in estimating a cache's location . . . a distance equivalent to the span between the three islands!

That told Anlon *why* Devlin chose to visit the three islands. Somehow, Devlin had lined up the map in a way that placed one of the cache sites somewhere in the Caribbean near those three islands, but Devlin wasn't able to tell which island was closest to the site given the scale of his own map. So, he had gone to all three to sort it out.

Unfortunately, Anlon had no idea what led Devlin to conclude one of the map's sites was located in the West Indies. Devlin left no explanation in the notebooks or otherwise. In order for Anlon to line up the map in the same way, he needed another reference point. He wondered if Malinyah had given Devlin a clue to figure it out. Anlon made a mental note to add that question to the list of queries for Pebbles to probe with Malinyah.

While the Dominica book contributed to Anlon's solution for Devlin's choice of the islands, it presented other puzzles that continued to bedevil Anlon. The first was a confounding passage toward the rear of the journal:

> *Finally! Found Sound Stone glyph on western slope of Morne Trois Pitons, approx. GPS coord. = 15°20'28"N / 61°19'38"W. Unusual spike on magnetometer seemed to confirm site, but could not locate entry. Used GPR in grid search around glyph, found two possible cavities, but readings faint. Tried Sound Stone per M, but no judder. Disappointing! Need to find one fast! Running out of time!*

The passage indicated Devlin found one of the Munuorian's Stone caches, but his uncle's concern about time didn't make sense to Anlon. Although Devlin did exhibit a sense of panic in the week leading up to his death that May, causing him to hide the map and Stones in different places, the Dominica trip had occurred two months before he was killed. So, what was the urgency in March? Was he already aware of Matthew Dobson's thefts at that point? Did he already fear others were after his map?

Equally exasperating was the sketch that appeared on the opposing page. The proximity of the sketch in relation to the passage implied a connection, but Anlon could find no explicit link described in the journal.

The sketch closely resembled one of two statuettes that Dobson had stolen from Devlin's artifact collection. The figurine in question had an ornate dragonlike head and a human body with a face that displayed a menacing snarl. It crouched with legs spread and gripped a swordlike object in one hand. To Anlon, it gave the impression of a soldier preparing for battle. A mythical warrior from some dynastic Chinese period, he supposed.

In the notebook, Devlin's drawing showed the dragon-man's features from an offset, rear angle and seemed intended to depict the fine details of the dragon's head. A spiked mane ran down the center line until it reached the man's shoulders. Curled flourishes bordered the visible brow, ear and shoulder. Where the mane crested atop the head, a last feature stood out—a small circle drawn around a fish. The same fish symbol was among the six etched on Malinyah's *Sinethal* . . . and was also stamped into each side of the gold coins discovered by Dobson.

If not for the fish symbol, Anlon would have deemed the dragon-man statuette an unrelated relic, but its appearance in the notebook—particularly given its proximity to Devlin's urgent reference—warranted deeper consideration. After all, if the statuette was valuable enough for Dobson to steal, and for Devlin to commemorate in the notebook, it must be somehow connected to the Stones. But in what way? And what did the statuette have to do with the island of Dominica?

Another conundrum was the figurine's oriental-styling. In Anlon's opinion, it just didn't fit in with the bulk of Devlin's artifacts. Roughly half of Devlin's collection was pre-Columbian, including pieces of Mayan, Incan, Olmec and Toltec descent. The other half originated from lands abutting the Mediterranean, including Egyptian, Sumerian, Babylonian and Greco-Roman pieces. To the best of Anlon's knowledge, Devlin's inventory held no artifacts of Sino origin.

If the sculpture wasn't from the Orient, where did it come from? Devlin's inventory records provided no information about the dragon warrior. It was one of the missing pieces of information Anlon hoped Jennifer could track down. Setting aside the urgent reference about time and the out-of-context drawing, Anlon was puzzled by two remaining features in the journal.

The first oddity appeared on several pages in the journal. Someone had used a yellow marker to highlight a number of Devlin's penciled observations. Anlon suspected the highlights were added by Dobson, not Devlin, but at this point it was only conjecture. Since the notebooks had been recovered from Dobson's home in the same search where Jennifer and Pebbles found the horde of Munuorian gold coins, Anlon speculated Dobson had used the Dominica journal to find and open the stone vault that had eluded Devlin.

The second oddity was more baffling. Toward the end of the book, at the bottom of a blank page, Devlin had scribbled two names as questions: *Ometepe? Isabela?* When Anlon first found the scrawled names, neither rang a bell, but a quick Internet search revealed both as islands. He discovered Isabela is the largest island in the Galápagos archipelago, while Ometepe sits in Lake Nicaragua on the Pacific Ocean side of Nicaragua. After a bit more research, he discovered an interesting feature of both islands: they are home to prominent volcanos, as are Guadeloupe, Dominica and Martinique.

For some reason, Devlin was interested in volcanic islands, and Anlon had an inkling why, but it meant Devlin was looking for something besides the Stones.

Jennifer slowed to a walk and wiped her brow. Panting heavily, she stopped at the entrance to Incline Beach and bent over. With hands on knees, she checked her time for the five-mile run and grumbled.

Rising up, she cupped her hands atop the knot of her ponytail and slowly walked back to Anlon's house. As her breathing steadied, Jennifer inhaled the clean mountain air and wondered how hot it was back home in western Massachusetts. August usually meant hot and sticky, quite a contrast to Tahoe's dry, cool climate.

The change in scenery was just as stark. Western Massachusetts was pastoral. Rolling hills and colonial architecture dominated the landscape with the low-rise Berkshire Mountains in the background. North Tahoe, she'd discovered, was alpine all the way—tall mountains, towering pines and architecture that ranged in style from lodges to chalets.

Yet, despite the alpine atmosphere, the vibe of summer in north Tahoe felt more like Cape Cod than a mountain resort area. It was Jennifer's third week staying with Anlon and Pebbles and every day had been a beach bonanza. When she and Pebbles weren't beach hopping around the lake in Anlon's open-top Jeep, they were riding his Jet Skis or relaxing on his boat. When they went out to eat or shopped, everyone was in board shorts, bathing suits and flip-flops. And Jennifer noticed there were a surprising number of people immersed in the surfer culture, a surprise given the conspicuous lack of waves on the lake. Pebbles said they were holdovers from the winter season when skiers and snowboarders ruled the area.

To Jennifer, hanging out in Tahoe was certainly a much better way to serve her suspension than moping around Pittsfield. And the change in scenery helped to distract her from stewing about the suspension . . . most of the time. However, when the unpleasant memory managed to surface in quiet moments, Jennifer found it hard to suppress her anger. She had solved one murder, stopped another in progress, but got busted for destroying the weapon Pacal had used to pulverize Anlon's body. The punishment just didn't seem fair to Jennifer given the outcome of the case.

But Jennifer had to admit, with each fun-filled day that passed in Tahoe, it was getting easier to let it go. Anlon and Pebbles had seen to that! Pebbles had become the sister she never had, and Anlon had been a gracious and inviting host. As a result, Jennifer had quickly fallen in love with the area and now understood why Anlon had settled there and lured Pebbles into staying too. If only she could adapt to the altitude!

Arriving at Anlon's, she walked across the driveway and passed around the large, lodge-style home to reach the back patio. There, she spied Anlon lounging on a chaise under the shade of two dozen pine trees.

"Hey there!" she said with a wave of her hand.

Anlon waved back. "Hey. How was the run?"

She stuck out her tongue. "Awful. The altitude is still killing me."

"Don't worry, you'll get used to it soon enough," he said.

Jennifer plopped onto a chair facing Anlon. "I've been here for three weeks now. Shouldn't that be enough?"

"Nah, takes most people a bit longer than that."

"God, every time I finish a run I sound like a barking seal!"

"So that's what I heard! I thought it was a dying fox!"

"Haha," Jennifer said.

Anlon smiled and pointed toward the kitchen door. "There's some fresh lemonade in the fridge if you're thirsty."

Jennifer kicked off her shoes and peeled off her socks. Rubbing a foot while gazing out at the lake, she said, "Okay, thanks. I'll get some in a sec. How's your leg feeling today?"

Anlon raised the spindly limb and adjusted the straps of the elongated brace before replying. "Pretty sore," he said. "Lots of leg lifts in physical therapy this morning."

"Well, you're moving around a lot better than you were last week. I know the PT is painful, but it's paying off."

"Yeah, can't wait to lose the brace, though . . . and the walking stick."

"Hey, it's better than the cast and wheelchair, right? At least you can take the brace off when you're chilling."

"Yeah, I guess that's true," Anlon said, massaging his thigh.

"Pebbles already head out?" Jennifer asked, now rubbing the other foot.

"Yep. She wasn't in a good mood when she left, so fair warning."

"Why? What happened?"

"I had a few packages delivered when I was at PT. She wasn't happy *at all* about the 'early' wake-up doorbell."

"That's funny, I didn't hear anyone ring the doorbell early this morning."

"He came at ten-thirty."

"Ah. Well, I bet she's stoked to go pick up the *Sinethal*. What time was she meeting with Antonio?"

"Um, that's another thorn in her side. Antonio hasn't returned her call yet."

"I'm sure he'll call back sometime today," Jennifer said. "You taking the boat out?"

"Nah, I'm enjoying relaxing right here. You can take it out if you want," said Anlon.

"Hmmm . . . it's tempting, but I'd rather get my assignments," Jennifer said with a smile.

"Ah, so you're eager to start, are you?"

"I'll go grab my notebook and be right back," said Jennifer. She stuffed her socks in her running shoes, jogged up the slate steps and disappeared through the kitchen door. A few minutes later, she poked her head out the door and asked, "I'm getting some lemonade, you want another glass?"

"Sure, thanks," Anlon said.

Jennifer reappeared through the door with pen clutched in her teeth, notepad crooked beneath one arm and a full glass in each hand. She padded down the steps, handed one of the drinks to Anlon and repositioned herself across from him.

With pen poised, Jennifer said, "Okay, fire away. What do you need?"

"I need your sleuthing skills to help find some pieces of information that are missing from Devlin's records," Anlon said.

"The *Sinethal*, right?"

"Yep, that's the most important one."

Jennifer rattled the pen in her hand. "Do you think he found it on a dig?"

"Certainly possible, but I've been through all his expedition notebooks and didn't find anything. You're welcome to look through them yourself. A second pair of eyes wouldn't hurt."

"Okay, I will. What about a private collector?"

"That's another possibility, but tracking down a collector might be tough. I'm afraid there's not much to go on in Devlin's records."

"And you said last night we don't know when Devlin found it, right?"

"Exactly. Best guess is five to six months before he died."

"How'd you come up with that?"

Anlon pointed at the table with the three expedition books. "The earliest of his expeditions to hunt for the Stones, at least the earliest one I can find any record of, was a trip to Guadeloupe in January," he said. "And I'm certain he went there looking for something to do with the Stones. It's possible he went on expeditions before then, but like I said, I haven't found a record of any."

"Right," Jennifer said, scribbling down a note. "So, I'll start with the idea he somehow acquired the *Sinethal* in the December–January time frame."

"I'm not sure I can help you much on where to begin."

"That's okay, I'll figure out a strategy," Jennifer assured him.

"Great, thank you. One less loose string for me! You have carte blanche for whatever you need. Travel, money, whatever. The sooner you can find out the answer, the better."

"Sounds good. I'll get cracking as soon as I take a shower."

The assignment excited her. It was exactly the kind of detective work she enjoyed—finding the missing link. Already, ideas were flowing into her mind. Go through Devlin's inventory records, look for any artifact loans, purchases or sales within the last year. Contact the parties involved in the transactions. It seemed reasonable to assume Devlin might have stumbled across the *Sinethal* while in discussions about other items.

Anlon watched Jennifer jot down a flurry of notes and smiled. "Something tells me you've already nailed a strategy."

"Not yet, just thought of a couple ideas," she replied as she continued to write.

"I do have two suggestions, for what they're worth."

"Great. What are they?"

"George Grant," Anlon said. "Devlin left the *Sinethal* with him before he was killed. Maybe he told Grant where he got it?"

Jennifer nodded. Devlin's attorney was a decent possibility. Devlin might have said something in passing when he asked Grant to hold the *Sinethal* for him, something that didn't seem important to Grant at the time. In her experience, the biggest breakthroughs often came from the smallest detail.

"I'd also check with Anabel Simpson. She told me she didn't know anything about the Stones, but who knows. Maybe I didn't ask the right questions," he said.

That reminded Jennifer about the pictures of Anabel and Devlin she found at Devlin's house in Stockbridge. She jotted down Anabel's name in her notepad and said, "Sounds like a trip back east is called for. It's too bad Dobson's and Pacal's laptops were impounded. Maybe while I'm back in Mass, I can get Nickerson to take a look at them. Want me to try?"

Dan Nickerson was a detective lieutenant for the same Massachusetts State Police detective unit as Jennifer. She and Nickerson had worked on several cases together when Nickerson was just a detective-trainee and they had formed a good friendship.

"Think he'll talk to you given your suspension?" asked Anlon.

"Who, Dan? We talk all the time. He knows I got a bullshit slap on the wrist. It might cost you some Patriots tickets, but I think I can persuade him," she said, grinning.

"Say the word, I'll make it happen," he said.

Jennifer flipped to a new page. "That's a good start. Lots to chew on. Anything else?"

"The statues," said Anlon. "Same drill. I want to know where they came from, especially the dragon-head statue that Devlin drew in here." He lifted the Dominica book, flipped to the page with the dragon-man drawing and handed it to Jennifer. "There's no reason I can figure to explain why this drawing is in this notebook. If we knew where Devlin acquired it, that would give us a lead to follow."

"Okay, that's on the list now too."

"The only other thing I'd love to know is where Margaret Corchran is hiding. She killed Devlin and I want her ass to pay for it. Navarro and Thatcher are of less concern. If you can find out anything about where she is, that would be helpful. I can't do anything about it personally unless I meet her face to face . . . which seems unlikely to happen. But I'll spend any amount necessary to help capture her. Reward money, whatever," Anlon said.

Jennifer added that to her list. It would be a little dicey trying to nose in on Devlin's murder investigation given her suspension, but maybe Nickerson would be willing to give her a glimpse at the latest inside scoop.

"Sounds good, I'll see what I can do," she said. "Well, I've got a full plate. Better get started."

She rose from the chair and headed for the stairs. On the second step up, she heard Anlon call, "Oh, by the way, 'Bones' dropped off a little something for you. It's in a bag on your bed."

Jennifer froze in midstep. "Excuse me?"

"Yeah, he stopped by a little while ago. Nice guy, we had a good chat. He said you left something at his place a couple nights ago. Wanted to return it," Anlon said with a wink.

Red-faced, Jennifer dashed in the house without a word. She was certain she hadn't left anything at Griffin's, but, then again, she had been a little tipsy . . .

When she entered the guest room, she spied the shopping bag sitting near the foot of the bed. With one eye closed, she spread open the handles and pulled the garment out.

Anlon heard a happy squeal echo from inside the house.

In Jennifer's hands was an autographed Ice Zombies limited edition T-shirt from the *Frozen Dreams* tour. The autograph read, "Book 'em, Jenno."

6

Seybalrosa

Incline Village, Nevada
August 7

nlon and Pebbles lounged on the aft bench and watched the last glint of sun pass behind the mountains. When it dipped below the horizon, Pebbles nuzzled up to Anlon and said, "Mmmm, that was a good one."

"Sure was," he replied. "The colors were awesome tonight."

Pebbles raised herself up briefly to adjust the blanket covering their legs, and then reclined back against Anlon's chest. He wrapped his arms around her shoulders and kissed her cheek. Together, they looked upward and waited for the sky to fill with stars.

It was a clear night and already dots of light began to twinkle above. At Tahoe's altitude, there was always a spectacular array of visible stars and constellations, even when the Moon was full. But tonight, it appeared as a thin crescent, and it was already edging toward the western horizon. Once the Moon set, there would be no competing light to obscure the heavens, and that meant tonight's sky would be chocked with more stars than usual.

The setting pleased Pebbles greatly. She had become an avid stargazer after Malinyah's telling of the great flood saga. In fact, it was now one of her favorite rituals. She would come out on the lake, with or without company, and stare up at the constellations.

She would first orient herself to Cassiopeia and then watch the other constellations wheel around it, just as the Munuorians had done for thousands of years. Though Cassiopeia appeared in different places in the night sky throughout a year's time, Malinyah had said it rarely disappeared from view. To Pebbles, it felt comforting to know it was always there.

Pebbles pointed to it and said to Anlon, "There she is, Cassiopeia."

"Yep," he said. "What did Malinyah call it?"

"Breylif," Pebbles said. "It's their word for 'butterfly.'"

She held up her hands with palms facing the sky. Then she touched the tips of her thumbs together and said, "If you hold your hands like this, it makes the shape of a *W*."

With her thumbs acting as a fulcrum, Pebbles rotated her hands so that the palms touched each other. Then, she reversed the rotation outward. As she repeated the motion, she said, "See, it's a butterfly flapping its wings."

"That makes a lot more sense than naming it Cassiopeia. Somehow, a big *W* doesn't look like a woman sitting in a chair to me," Anlon said.

"No kidding."

After a moment's silence, Anlon asked, "Speaking of Malinyah, did Antonio call back yet?"

"No, his assistant said he's traveling," Pebbles sighed. "But she promised to give him my message."

"I'll email him," said Anlon.

"Nah, don't bother. I can deal with a few more days' waiting," said Pebbles. "Besides, you said you wanted to do your 'experiment' before I talk with Malinyah again. That gives us some time."

"You want to do it now? Won't take very long."

"Hmmm . . . Depends. What's involved?" Pebbles asked.

"It's simple. I ask you some questions, you answer them. Easy as pie."

"Sounds too easy. Is it some kind of trick?"

"No tricks, I promise," Anlon said, crossing his heart.

"What's the experiment supposed to prove?" she asked.

Scratching his head, he said, "If I tell you that, it will skew the results."

"A.C., if you want me to be your lab rat, I want to know what the test is about," Pebbles said, crossing her arms and legs.

"'Lab rat' sounds a little harsh. How about we say you're my test partner?"

"You can call me anything you like, but I ain't doing any experiment unless you tell me more!"

"Okay, okay. Take it easy. I'll explain." Anlon said with a laugh. After a brief pause to gather his thoughts, his demeanor turned serious. "So, among the many things I've been thinking about, I've been wondering how the Munuorians stored their memories on the Master Stone, er, *Sinethal*. At the same time, I've been trying to understand how it's possible for us to interact with Malinyah's memories. And why the memories seem so real."

"Go on, I'm listening . . ."

"Well, figuring out the 'how they did it' part is still murky, but I think I understand the other two pieces."

"So . . . ?"

Anlon stroked her hair and gazed at the glittering lights from homes along the shoreline. "I think the *Sinethal* experiences were designed to achieve something very important to them."

"Like what?"

"I think they wanted to ensure the most important memories were never forgotten. That their people, and anyone who used the *Sinethal*, would retain the core of important memories in a way that was less likely to be forgotten.

"Think about it. Paper decays, stone weathers, oral stories get changed with each telling. Think about how hard it is to retain important cultural memories in the context they occurred. Take a story about an important event in our history, say, man walking on the Moon. How would you learn about that today?"

"Hmmm . . . I guess I'd go on the Internet," Pebbles said.

"Good starting point. What would you do?"

Pebbles sat up and turned to face Anlon. "Well, I'd do a search, get a bunch of hits. Read some articles, watch some videos, look at some pictures, stuff like that."

"How long do you think you'd retain what you saw and heard?"

Tossing aside the blanket, she stretched out her legs along the bench. "I don't know. Some parts I'd remember for a long time. Like the famous photo of Neil Armstrong's footprint on the Moon, that's the first thing that pops in my mind when I think of the story. And the scratchy recording of him saying, 'One small step . . . ,' but other parts would probably fade pretty quickly. Facts and figures, those kinds of things."

Anlon said, "Okay, so, now imagine Neil Armstrong was a Munuorian, and he saved his memories of walking on the Moon on a *Sinethal*, and you interacted with his memories. Imagine asking him to show you what it felt like to step on the Moon? To not just hear his words, but to feel your foot touch the Moon's surface just as his did. To know the odor of space and the sound of your own breathing inside the helmet. To know how cold it was inside the capsule, or how dark space really is. To see little blue Earth over the horizon. To feel his elation, pride and wonder. Would you ever forget that experience?"

Pebbles shook her head. "No way."

"Even if you forgot parts of it, don't you think you'd remember more of the story from experiencing his memories than you would from web research?"

"Absolutely," she said.

By now, Anlon was up and limping around the deck. He laced his fingers through his hair and said, "I think it was done purposely. The Munuorians intentionally embedded multiple cues, sensory cues, along with stored memories. I think they did it to improve the odds the memories would endure over time."

"Okay, I'm sold," said Pebbles. "What do you want me to do?"

"I want to test your memory. I ask you some questions, you answer them. The first questions are aimed at quick recall."

"Sounds easy. Let's do it," she said.

"Great, hold on a sec. Let me get a piece of paper and a pen."

Anlon limped to the stairs leading below-deck. He poked his head in the small chamber and grabbed a pen and paper from the galley counter. Returning to the bench, he asked, "You have your cell phone handy? Good, turn the flashlight on and give it to me. Great, now take the paper and pen. Okay, now draw me the *Sinethal* etching."

"Easy peasy," said Pebbles.

She drew a circle with six rays. Two of the rays were placed on a horizontal plane opposite each other. With even spacing, or as best as she could approximate, she drew the two lines above the horizontal plane, one at eleven o'clock, the other at one o'clock. She did the same for the two lines below the horizontal plane, one at five o'clock and the last one at seven o'clock.

Next, she filled in the various symbols. Starting with eleven o'clock, she moved clockwise and inserted each of the symbols: the leaf, followed by the sound waves, followed by the star. Then came the two hands, the rhombus, and finally the fish symbol. As a bonus, she included the names of the Stones associated with each symbol, the names Devlin gave them and the original Munuorian names.*

Pebbles smiled and handed the paper back to Anlon. "There you go."

He scanned the drawing and nodded. After turning off the flashlight app, he leaned over and handed back her cell phone. "Nice touch adding the names."

"Like I said, easy peasy."

"Okay, hot shot, what was the name the Munuorians attached to the flood story?"

"Munirvo. It means 'star washer' in their language. It's the name they gave the asteroid, not the flood, per se."

Anlon lowered onto the center island bench and faced Pebbles. "Okay, Munirvo. Got it. Now, give me a snapshot of the story. A minute, maybe two minutes long."

"Um, that might be a little tough," she said.

"Why?"

"To get everything right, I need to think about it for a few minutes."

---

*For a diagram of the Sinethal etching, see page 342.

"Nope, no time. Start talking, tell me what happened."

Pebbles crisscrossed her legs and massaged her wrists. "Hmmm . . . Okay, I'll try. So, there was this asteroid. I'm talking *huge* asteroid. It passed super close to Earth and pretty much destroyed the planet. The gravitational pull of the asteroid was crazy intense. When it got near Earth, it pushed the Moon further back and flipped the Earth. That caused a monster tidal wave that seriously crushed everything in its path. There were fires, volcano eruptions, earthquakes, you name it.

"Almost nothing was left. Most people were killed. Same with plants and animals. But, there were some people who survived. Barely. That's where the Munuorians came in. They knew the asteroid was coming long before anyone else, and they knew what it might do. So, they hunkered down and waited out the worst. When it was over, they went out to look for survivors. To help them. Well, some of the Munuorians went out to help. There were others who weren't thrilled about it, but enough went out that it made a difference."

"And the Stones?" asked Anlon.

"Right, well, the Munuorians were special. They were different from other people on Earth at the time. They had a sixth sense; they could interact with the Earth's magnetic field. It allowed them to create magnetic tools that helped them do a bunch of stuff. Build, farm, heal injuries, move things.

"They used the tools to protect themselves when the asteroid came, and then they went out and shared their tools with survivors, people who didn't have their sixth sense. Without their help, the survivors would have been hosed. The Munuorians saved them. If they hadn't helped, pretty much everyone would have died. That last part's my opinion; Malinyah doesn't say it that way."

"It's been, what, three months since you've been with Malinyah?" Anlon asked.

Embarrassed to give Anlon the precise day count, Pebbles nonchalantly said, "A little less, but close enough."

"A minute ago, you said the Munuorians knew Munirvo was coming, right?"

"Yep."

"How did they know?"

Pebbles patted Anlon's knee. "You know that, I've told you before. Malinyah said the asteroid came from Cassiopeia. She said they were watching Cassiopeia and saw it."

Looking up at the sky, Anlon asked, "Why were they looking at Cassiopeia?"

"Again, I've told you this already. Because other asteroids had come from there before." Pebbles frowned.

"Don't get frustrated with me, there's a method to my madness."

"Sorry."

Anlon pointed in the direction of Cassiopeia. "Did she say whether they could see Cassiopeia year-round?"

"She said it was visible most of the time."

"Do you remember if she showed you a vision of the constellation when she told you the story?"

"Yeah, that's how I know about the *W* butterfly thing," Pebbles said.

Leaning forward, Anlon said, "All right, let's see how good your memory is. Try to remember where Cassiopeia was in the sky in the vision she showed you. Was the asteroid inside the *W* or outside it?"

"What? There's no way I can remember that." Pebbles said.

"Ah, I think you're wrong. I think you can pull it out of your memory," Anlon said, tapping his forehead. "Concentrate on sensations you associate with her telling of the story. A smell, a sight, a sound. Anything. Take your time, there's no rush."

"Hmmm . . . I'll try, but I'm not sure it will work."

"That's all I ask."

Pebbles closed her eyes and tried to recall her last session with Malinyah's *Sinethal*. It was a few days after the Stillwater Quarry incident, that much she remembered. Anlon was in the hospital and Pebbles was staying at Devlin's house. She and Jennifer had spent most of that day cleaning up the mess left by the Corchrans when they trashed the house while hunting for the *Sinethal*. After Jennifer had left for the evening, Pebbles had poured a generous goblet of Cabernet and settled on the study's sofa with the black Stone. She remembered sipping the wine and running her fingers over the etchings before lying back on the sofa and activating the Stone and Malinyah's memories . . .

The first thing that popped into Pebbles' mind about the "visit" was Malinyah's cheerful greeting as she approached from across the marble hall. She could still visualize the wide strands of sunlight filtering between the hall's columns. Then, she remembered the sound of the trickling fountain outside the hall and the pungent aroma of the flower gardens beyond. Malinyah reached for Pebbles' hand and led her outside. Together they walked up a hilly path of red clay.

Pebbles opened her eyes and wiggled her toes. Looking at Anlon, she said, "It's so weird, but my feet feel clammy again just thinking about it."

Anlon said, "Thinking about the asteroid makes your feet clammy?"

"No, silly, the red clay does," she answered.

"What red clay?"

"The clay on the path," she said.

"What path?"

"Forget it," she said. "It's not important."

Pebbles closed her eyes again and wiggled her toes.

Back into the memory, she recalled Malinyah leading her to a massive, wide-branching tree with bright pink foliage and dozens of long, ribbonlike roots jutting two to three feet above the ground in every direction. Gaping at the canopy of pink above her head, she exclaimed, "That's a cool-looking tree!"

Malinyah turned and smiled. "It is beautiful. We call it Seybalrosa."

In the background, beyond the hill crest where Seybalrosa anchored its snaking roots, Pebbles could hear crashing waves. Peering left and right, she noticed rows upon rows of tall cacti curved around the tree. To Pebbles, the collection of prickly plants did not appear to be a natural formation but rather a designed garden. The limbs of the cacti looked like outstretched arms reaching toward the Seybalrosa's drooping leaves.

Arriving at the tree's base, Malinyah motioned for Pebbles to sit on a curled root. Sliding beside her, Malinyah patted her thigh while inhaling the Seybalrosa's pleasing aroma. Pebbles recalled asking Malinyah why they had come to the tree. Malinyah told her she wanted to share the Munirvo saga so that Pebbles could understand their purpose in sharing the Stones with the asteroid survivors. Malinyah said it was customary to tell important tales about their history at the shrine.

The sights, sounds and aromas of the *Sinethal* experience always stretched believability to Pebbles, but every time Malinyah physically *touched* her it seemed a sensation beyond possibility. Yet, there could be no mistaking the feel of Malinyah's hand gently tapping her knee. She could feel its warmth and the light pressure of her fingertips rapping against her skin. Even now.

Pebbles' eyes opened and she said to Anlon, "Ugh! It's happening again. When we sat by the tree, she touched me. I can literally feel her fingers on my leg right now."

"Tree?"

"Yeah, the Seybalrosa tree," she said.

"Say-ball-rosa?" Anlon scratched his head. "You've never mentioned that before."

"Really? I'm sure I must have. It's a shrine."

"Shrine?"

"Yeah, they had this big tree with gnarly roots. It had pink leaves and a bunch of cacti around it. Malinyah said it was the place where they tell important stories. Now, be quiet!" Covering her face with both hands, Pebbles searched her mind for the beginning of the Munirvo tale. It was a struggle to drop back into the conversation. She chided Anlon, "Now you've made me forget!"

"Remember what I suggested," Anlon said. "Focus on the sensations you remember, not the story. Her hand on your leg, the clay on your feet, the pink leaves, any scents or sounds."

Pebbles peeked from behind her hands and hissed, "Shhh!"

She took a deep breath and tried Anlon's suggestion. She concentrated her focus on the Seybalrosa's pink leaves and suddenly remembered a light wind tickling the leaves. Then the sound of the waves filtered back into the memory and she recalled the butterfly . . . a golden butterfly with black dots that came to rest on Malinyah's shoulder.

When it landed, Malinyah didn't even notice. Then several others touched down on her shoulders and head. They both laughed when one tried to land on the bridge of her nose. Malinyah wriggled her nose and it fluttered away. It circled the two of them before descending onto Pebbles' shoulder. Malinyah smiled. "The Breylif, he wants to hear the story too!"

Anlon watched with fascination as Pebbles' hands slid from her face. Her eyes remained closed, but her head moved about as if watching something. She reached to her shoulder and softly giggled. Then she nodded her head and clasped her hands in her lap. Her face adopted a grave expression.

Pebbles listened intently as Malinyah commenced the Munirvo tale: "We call ourselves Munuorians. The name means 'star watchers.' We have watched the stars for years beyond count and have learned many secrets from them. Over the ages, they've fed our powers, fostered wisdom, brought new life . . . and reawakened terrors."

One night, she told Pebbles, a new star appeared in the sky. It was faint at first but still drew the attention of their astronomers, people Malinyah called the Fandis. She said the Fandis had been expecting the new star to appear.

Pebbles interrupted to ask, "Wait, why were they expecting it?"

"Because, it has happened many times before," she said.

Malinyah bent down and used her finger to draw a pinwheel design in the red clay. Pressing a finger into the clay, Malinyah made a mark on a thin inner spiral. She said, "Terra is here." She then pressed her finger at a spot slightly ahead of Earth on an outer spiral of the pinwheel. She said, "The trouble always comes from here."

Malinyah motioned her hand to imitate the pinwheel spinning. She said, "As we move around the sun, so does the sun around the wheel . . . and the wheel, in turn, spins through the black.

"The Fandis believe that as the wheel turns, its path crosses stones that sit in the black. When the crossings happen, the Fandis say the stones hit stars and planets in the outer spiral. Some of the pieces fall into the path of Terra's spiral. Sometimes the pieces fly close to Terra, sometimes not. Sometimes they are small, other times very large."

"How did they know where to look?" Pebbles asked.

Malinyah drew a *W* in the clay and then took Pebbles by the hands. She filled her mind with a vision showing a sky full of stars and a small-but-bright Munirvo. She said, "Can you see the shape I drew?"

"Yes, I see it."

"The pieces always come from the sky around this. We call it Breylif."

"You call it a butterfly?" asked Pebbles.

"Yes, does it not look like one?" Malinyah asked in return.

"Hmmm . . . maybe," said Pebbles.

Exiting the constellation vision, Malinyah lifted a butterfly with the tip of her finger. "What do these creatures do? They go from one flower to another, taking food from one to give it to others. We view Breylif in the sky the same. Sometimes it gives, other times it takes."

Returning to the story, Malinyah told Pebbles the Fandis watched Munirvo for a year. As it grew brighter and larger, they measured its path and speed and assured the Munuorian elders, including Malinyah, it would not come near Terra. She gripped Pebbles' hands again and showed her a vision of Munirvo approaching in the night sky.

Malinyah said, "They said it would come close to Rosa, but not Terra. Then, the unspeakable happened. The star clashed with Rosa. For three nights, the night sky flashed with lights brighter than Manā. When the light faded, Rosa throbbed in the night sky . . . and the star veered toward Terra . . . with many smaller lights trailing behind.

"It was then the Fandis foresaw the catastrophe to come. They said Munirvo and the stars trailing it would pass close to Terra in less than six months. We began preparations immediately."

Malinyah paused and bowed her head. A terrible ache rippled through Pebbles' body. The butterfly lifted off her shoulder and drifted toward the cactus garden.

Anlon watched the rapid changes in Pebbles' body language and facial expressions. Her face suddenly twisted in anguish. She clenched her arms across her abdomen and rocked forward. She uttered a low moan.

Malinyah described to Pebbles the preparations her people took to protect themselves from the chaos that was to come. Using their special Stones, she explained, they burrowed safe havens in the mountains. In these chambers, they stockpiled food and other supplies. For water, they tunneled through the rock and channeled a mountain waterfall into a carved streambed. Around the base of the mountains, the Munuorians piled massive boulders into a makeshift breakwater.

"All the while, Munirvo drew closer," Malinyah said. "Soon, it was visible during daylight and grew as large as the Sulā. Unlike the golden rays from Sulā, however, the star-washer was bright white. At night, its flickering tail spread across the horizon and dwarfed Manā's light."

The Munuorians sent out their trading ships to acquire a final round of provisions. Upon returning, the ships' captains reported unrest among the civilizations in the foreign lands across the seas.

Malinyah described the civilizations as primitive tribes with disparate cultures. "They possessed only a rudimentary understanding of the stars," she told Pebbles. "For some, the constellations served primarily as mystical deities. For others, Terra and the stars were of one world."

Although the Munuorians built friendly relationships with many of these civilizations, the foreigners were universally skeptical of the more advanced Munuorians. Understanding this, the Munuorian elders, the Andaers, forbade the use of the Stones in the presence of foreigners.

Malinyah looked intently at Pebbles. "Upon returning from the trading voyage, the greatest of our captains, Mereau, met with the Andaers. He told them the nations were completely unprepared for what was coming. He begged us to let him disperse the fleet to the closest nations and warn them, help them prepare.

"Some of the Andaers, including me, supported Mereau. Others did not. One voice was stronger than all. Muran. Muran said it was too late to help them. Already the seas had begun to roil. Muran said the ships would be destroyed before they reached them. Mereau called Muran heartless. I was there when he screamed, 'We have the power to save them. We have to help!' But Muran's argument swayed the Andaers . . . all except me."

Malinyah's face flushed crimson and Pebbles felt the Munuorian's emotions surge through her own body. Malinyah unfurled her hand and one of the butterflies danced off her shoulder, circled down and landed on her open palm. A tear trickled down Malinyah's cheek. She whispered, "It was unforgiveable."

To Pebbles, it felt like someone clawing her insides. She tightened her hands into fists and slammed them on the boat bench. "Why? Why wouldn't they help?"

The sudden gesture startled Anlon. He watched with concern as tears streamed down Pebbles' face. She barked deep, guttural cries. Sweat coated her face and neck. She pounded the bench over and over. Anlon had watched long enough. He leaned over and grasped her wrist. He called out sharply, "Pebbles! Stop! Snap out of it!"

She fought against him, eyes still closed. Anlon grasped her other wrist and lifted her off the bench. He pulled her against his body and quickly wrapped his arms around her. Pebbles' whole body shuddered and she tried to squirm away. Anlon placed his lips against her ear and whispered soothingly.

Her body suddenly slumped against him and her eyes fluttered open. She panted heavily for a short time. When her breathing settled, she wrapped her arms around Anlon's waist and lowered her head to rest on his shoulder.

Huddled inside the folds of the blanket, Pebbles leaned back against the aft bench and rested her feet on the center island. Still in a daze, she closed her eyes and struggled to understand what triggered the intense experience. After all, tonight wasn't the first time she had revisited a conversation with Malinyah. In fact, during Anlon's long recuperation, Pebbles had thought of Malinyah constantly. There were certainly emotions that arose when reminiscing about their past conversations, but nothing like tonight's explosion.

Pebbles was also surprised by the new details that rushed forth during tonight's replay of the Munirvo tale. Given the time that had passed since Malinyah first shared the saga, she expected the opposite.

In the background, footsteps stuttered across the deck. A moment later came the unmistakable plunk of a cork stopper, followed by two extended trickles. Then Pebbles felt Anlon cup her hand around a chilled shot glass. She smiled and took two small sips.

Anlon gulped down his shot and flopped onto the bench next to Pebbles. They sat in silence for several minutes. The lake was perfectly still.

It was Pebbles who spoke first. "I don't know what to say."

Anlon remained silent, unsure what to say himself. He was dying to know what transpired during her trance, but he felt it was too soon to ask her to talk about it.

Pebbles stirred in the seat, opened her eyes and looked at Anlon. "That was some crazy you-know-what!" He smiled and took hold of her hand. She said, "How did that happen? I never touched the Stone."

"Beats me. Are you okay?" Anlon asked.

"Yeah, I think so. I'm exhausted, though."

"I'm not surprised; it was exhausting watching you."

"I just did what you said: think of the sensations. And, wham, I was *so* sucked in. I didn't react like that when Malinyah told me the story."

"Sorry, I thought focusing on the sensations would make it easier to reconnect with the memory. I didn't think it would cause you to relive it," Anlon said.

"Oh, you were right. I definitely reconnected," she said. "How is it possible?"

"You sure you want to know? It's kinda geeky."

"I can handle it. Hit me with some science."

"Okay. Answer me this, how does memory work? How do you think the brain stores memories?"

"I haven't had enough tequila to answer that, just tell me," said Pebbles, pouring another shot.

Anlon laughed and held out his glass for a refill too. After a sip, he said, "So, the hippocampus is a tiny little organ in the brain. It helps the brain organize memories."

"Do tell," said Pebbles, earnestly interested.

"Well, during a memorable event," Anlon explained, "the brain records sights, sounds, thoughts, emotions and other senses associated with the event. But, all those pieces of input are captured and stored in different parts of the brain. Sights are recorded one place, sounds another, and so on.

"In order to create a full memory, one that includes all the pieces, there has to be some kind of gatekeeper that knows where all the individual pieces were first captured and stored. The gatekeeper not only has to know where they're stored, it must know how to organize the pieces into a one, all-encompassing memory.

"The hippocampus is the gatekeeper. Every bit of a memory passes through the hippocampus on its way to be stored, and every time we want to recall something, our brain goes back through the hippocampus to find all the memory's individual pieces. Essentially, the hippocampus is responsible for both breaking memories apart and putting them back together."

Pebbles considered his description and said, "So, by focusing on a single sensation, my hippocampus used that bit to go find the rest of the memory? I thought of the tree and that made me remember the wind and the waves, and then, boom—the whole thing came back. Every little detail. A lot of them I totally forgot until now. Like the butterflies."

"Butterflies? There were butterflies? Hmmm . . . I want to hear all about them. They're packed with cryptochromes," Anlon said.

"Cryptochromes? What the heck are those?"

"A story for another night; we don't have enough tequila to go there!" said Anlon. "But, your analogy is right on. One sensory memory leads to another and then the whole thing comes together.

"In my opinion, it suggests that when you interact with the *Sinethal*, the electrical signals exchanged back and forth between you and the Stone are essentially conversations between your hippocampus and a hippocampus-like device or component inside the Stone that organizes Malinyah's memories.

"You ask Malinyah a question, you don't just get a flat answer. No, you get the sounds, smells and other sensations associated with the answer. You get how she feels about the answer. What she wants *you* to feel about the answer. It's contextual memory. It's honestly astonishing to consider."

Pebbles reflected on the feelings that stirred inside when she recalled Malinyah's sadness and anger. Anlon was right, once the sensory cues built up, there was no stopping the memory from rushing forth. But it surprised her that she could literally *feel* Malinyah's emotions. She said, "I get the whole 'senses' thing, but how does the hippocampus include feelings?"

Anlon raised his glass. "Aha! Ready for another geek-term?"

She smiled and licked her lips. "Ooh . . . give it to me."

"Amygdala."

"Eh-McDonald's?"

"Haha. *eh-mig-duh-lah.* It's a little organ, about the size of an almond, that sits right next to . . . ?"

"Our friend hippo?"

"Exactly," said Anlon. "Most emotional responses in our brains happen in the amygdala. Not all, but most. Others occur in the hypothalamus. Guess where that sits?"

"A.C., seriously, stop with all the erotic words. My amygdala's getting wet."

Anlon laughed and then answered his own question. "Also right next to the hippocampus." He paused for a moment while staring at the stars, and then said, "Now, I'm no neuroscientist, but . . . if you were designing a brain and you wanted to make sure emotional context was included in memories, wouldn't you make it just as easy for the hippocampus to store and retrieve emotions as it does with sights, sounds and so on?

"The amygdala and hypothalamus sit closer to the hippocampus than any other sensory organs in the brain, so it seems logical to assume the hippocampus also interacts with them when storing and retrieving memories."

Pebbles considered Anlon's explanation while she sipped her drink. There was no denying her recall of Malinyah's tale included vivid emotions. In fact, the emotions eventually overwhelmed all the other senses.

"So, coming full circle," said Anlon, "I think the Munuorians ensured important memories like the Munirvo tale are deeply engrained in anyone who experiences the story through a *Sinethal*. They did this by exchanging bits of sensory and emotional context, cues if you will, that help a person reconstruct the memory from those bits.

"It's incredibly imaginative and *very* sophisticated technology. *Way* beyond anything we can do today. It shows how advanced the Munuorians really were."

"Hold up, though. You asked me a pretty minor detail in the so-called important story," challenged Pebbles.

"Right, I know. It may seem like a small detail, but sometimes small details are the most important things in a memory. And a lot of the time, we forget small details, or we recall them selectively. By the way, did you see Cassiopeia again?"

"Yep, I remembered asking Malinyah where the asteroid came from. She showed me a sky with stars and Munirvo. It was in a very different place in the sky than it is here," said Pebbles.

"Interesting. Where on the horizon was it? Can you remember?"

"Why are you so interested?"

"Just a hunch. Humor me," Anlon replied.

"Um, let me think." Pebbles pointed at the stars above and said, "Right now, it's pretty high up. But, in the vision, it was low in the sky. Like, if the horizon was at three o'clock, Cassiopeia was around two o'clock."

"Was Munirvo inside or outside the *W*?"

"Inside, definitely inside."

A smile spread across Anlon's face.

"What?" Pebbles asked. "Why are you making that face?"

7

The Prospector

San Carlos de Bariloche, Argentina
August 7

Niles Drummond ambled into the parlor with Stetson clenched in both hands. Across the room, Klaus Navarro rose to greet the grizzled, bowlegged man while suppressing the urge to laugh. Though Drummond was a respected geologist, he looked more like a cartoon character with his bushy mustache, steel-toed cowboy boots, bolo tie and enormous belt buckle.

Despite his comical appearance, however, Drummond was an exceptional prospector. His early reputation was built as a North Sea wildcat oil driller. As he gained renown for his ability to locate pockets of Brent Crude beneath mountains of undersea rock, he attracted the attention of the mining industry. After his discovery of new diamond deposits off the Namibian coast and then a new kimberlite vein in the Sakha Jubilee mine, he became a rock star among prospectors.

As Navarro's mining enterprise expanded beyond copper, he'd sought Drummond's assistance on a few excavation projects. Although the Scotsman's fees were exorbitant, he was discreet and didn't mind bending the rules on his clients' behalf—traits that endeared him to Navarro.

Along the way, Navarro discovered they shared a taste for pre-Columbian artifacts and this led to a secondary relationship. A relationship where Navarro "acquired" relics of interest to Drummond in return for undefined preferential courtesies. Navarro had lured him to his mountain home for just such a courtesy.

Decked out in all-black Armani, Navarro sashayed across the room to greet the ruddy Anglo. In his hand he carried a small wooden case. After exchanging pleasantries, Navarro presented Drummond with the case. The visitor's eyes gleamed as he inspected the Aztec dagger inside. The blade, made of pounded flint, was not especially unique. The handle, however, showed exceptional craftsmanship. Carved into the shape of a jaguar's head, it was inlaid with a mosaic of gold and jade.

"There are only two other Aztec blades of similar beauty in the world," Navarro proclaimed.

"A fine piece, indeed." Drummond said. "How did you convince the owner to part with it?"

"It wasn't easy, my friend," said Navarro. A lie. The knife had been in his collection for some years, payment from a Colombian drug lord for his "export" assistance—a side business that netted many of the rare treasures Navarro possessed.

"Well, you have my attention," said Drummond. "What's on your mind this time?"

If you only knew! Navarro thought.

Navarro was still irked that Margaret had oversold the "special file" that accompanied the Waterland Map. She claimed her brother Kyle had discovered the encrypted file when searching for the map on Devlin's stolen laptop. She told Navarro the file contained a key that would help him read the map.

But all the file contained was a listing of thirty locations. On the list, two locations were marked with an *X*, Guadeloupe and Martinique. A third location, Dominica, was marked by an asterisk. Next to the asterisk was a set of coordinates. That was it.

When Navarro had first eyeballed the map, before he even tried to line up the three islands, he could see there were no marked sites grouped so closely together. It hadn't taken long to realize the implication of the "special file"—Devlin Wilson hadn't known how to read his own map.

Without a second point of reference, the map was useless. With his Rivers of Gold stone at his side, Navarro had spent long hours hovering over the map trying to make sense of the confusing topography and nonsensical longitude and latitude markings. When he first plotted the marked sites at their given longitude and latitude, many of the points were far from any land. There was one in the Tasman Sea, another in the Sula Sea, a third in the Andaman Sea and so on. Of the dozen sites marked, only a few were on land. And none of those agreed with any of the sites on Devlin's itemized list.

Navarro, a student of ancient mythologies, understood the significance of the "Waterland" reference and so he had turned the map upside down, shifted the meridian and plotted new points. This approach had seemed more promising. More of the points were on land, including a few in South America . . . a key point in Navarro's mind. For the *Rivers of Gold* story was an Olmec legend, and the core of Olmec archaeological sites were situated in southern Mexico. But none of the newly plotted points were located in Mexico, and none were in the Caribbean.

He had scanned Devlin's list and found several Central and Latin American locations, but there was no telling if they were anything more than guesses on Devlin's part, as he suspected Guadeloupe and Martinique turned out to be for Devlin.

Nevertheless, when his house arrest was finally rescinded in mid-July, Navarro had rushed out to visit Dominica. He was not optimistic about finding any of the Stones; he figured Devlin had plundered whatever cache was hidden there. However, he thought he might learn what the cache site looked like, an important detail given Navarro was unsure of how to identify a site even if he found a way to read the map.

Using the coordinates on Devlin's list, he had trekked up the slope of Morne Trois Pitons. Unaware of what to look for once he got there, Navarro searched in vain. Some part of him had hoped for an ancient ruin or some obvious landmark to guide him to the right spot. As he sat on a rock on the volcano's slope, he realized the folly of a visual search. After all, he was a miner and as such was experienced in seeking buried treasure, treasure with magnetic properties.

Navarro had returned to Argentina to formulate a new approach, one that relied on his expertise as a miner. The first step he took was to examine the magnetic characteristics of his Rivers of Gold relief in more depth. Although he had owned the Stone for many years, he thought of it only as a piece of art depicting the ancient serpent's-tooth legend. That view had changed when he learned of the Stone's magnetic properties from Dobson and Margaret, but he'd only performed a cursory Gauss meter check at that time to confirm the relief's authenticity.

This time, he took a more studious approach. He scraped a sliver from the Stone and sent it to one of his mining company labs for analysis. He tested the Stone with a magnetometer in addition to revisiting the Gauss meter readings. He also brought in magnets of varying strength to evaluate the Stone's reactions. From these efforts, Navarro had discovered three interesting attributes about his prized relief.

The lab analysis had shown the Stone contained olivine basalt peppered with kimberlite. That, in and of itself, hadn't surprised Navarro. Diamond deposits are often encased in volcanic rock such as olivine basalt. And the diamonds in those deposits are almost always embedded in "pipes" of kimberlite ore. And olivine basalt, diamond and kimberlite are all magnetic rocks. However, the lab pointed out the sliver's composition was unusual in one striking respect—the kimberlite was uniformly distributed throughout the basalt.

Beyond the lab analysis, Navarro found the magnetometer and Gauss readings showed strong and unusual magnetic signatures, something Navarro had neglected to realize when he first tested the Stone's magnetism. And the last finding, most curious of all, was that the Stone didn't react with any of the magnets he tried.

With this additional perspective in mind, Navarro had returned to Dominica with a better sense of what to seek. Along with a magnetometer, he brought a small ground-penetrating radar device. Whether the Stones were cached in a small cavity, such as a time capsule vault, or something more elaborate, the radar would help him narrow his search area if the magnetometer picked up an unusual magnetic signature.

Navarro had scoured the volcano's slope around Devlin's coordinates once again. To his delight, he detected the same signature exhibited by the Rivers of Gold stone. The reading was faint but definitely there. To his dismay, the ground-penetrating radar found no cavity.

He weighed blasting open the stone face of the volcano at the strongest point of the signal, but ultimately decided against it. The volcano was a popular eco-tourism destination and it teemed with hiking groups. Some were interested in the Boiling Lake, a bubbling brew that formed in one of Morne Trois Pitons' steam vents. Others were there for the geysers, waterfalls and lakes in the Valley of Desolation at the base of the volcano. Navarro realized an explosive charge would attract the attention of the tourists and their guides, and the smoke and sound would have made him easy to locate. There would have been little time to do a search, and less time to escape before the national park's caretakers arrived. The last thing Navarro needed was to find himself under arrest again. It was better to take the knowledge he'd gained and reconcentrate on deciphering the map. So, he had returned empty-handed to Argentina to once again examine the map and Devlin's list.

Then, one afternoon, he sat at the parlor desk with the map, Devlin's list and the Rivers of Gold stone. Also on the desk was the Gauss meter and a compass. While Navarro puzzled over the map, he twirled the compass in his hand. Frustrated, he slapped the compass down next to the Stone. His eye caught the compass' sudden shift.

Navarro frowned. His desk was situated along the window bank at the far end of the room. He had built the home so he would have an unobstructed view of the Andes, located dead west of the bank of windows. That meant dead north was somewhere along the wall facing the desk. Yet, the compass wasn't pointing north. Navarro lifted the compass and aimed the "N" at the opposing wall. The needle followed his movements and settled where it was aimed.

He placed the compass back down next to the Stone and it immediately shifted to a southwest position. Navarro stared and stared at the needle. And then it hit him. He estimated the needle's degree difference from dead south and shifted the map an approximate amount while keeping Dominica centered on the map. Once accomplished, he looked for points in Central and South America. There were a few. One in particular drew his interest—an area he knew very well. He quickly compared the site to Devlin's listing and cursed. "No wonder I missed it. The idiot wrote down the wrong river!"

Navarro's eyes twinkled as he relived the discovery. Leaning forward, he offered Drummond a cigar. "I need your help to find some stones."

Drummond crunched the cigar in the corner of his mouth. "Huh? Stones, you say?"

"Yes, there are some stone relics that interest me," Navarro said. "I need your help to find them."

The prospector's mustache twitched as he replied, "Why me? I'm a driller, not a bone digger."

"True. But you know rocks . . . and magnetism. The pieces I seek have unusual magnetic properties. For a man of your skill, they should be easy to find."

Drummond snorted. "You give me too much credit, Klaus."

"You use magnets to find diamond pipes, don't you?"

"Well, yes. But finding a pipe isn't easy."

"I realize—"

Drummond interrupted. "And keep in mind, diamond pipes are massive structures, tons and tons of material. If you were after gold, that's easier to find with magnets, but stone trinkets?"

"Niles, I know. Please, let me finish," Navarro said. "Under normal circumstances, I realize sniffing out a small cache of stones seems impossible. But these stones are not normal."

"What type of stone are we talking about?"

Navarro paused before answering.

"You don't know, do you?" asked Drummond.

"Of course, I know. I have a piece made by the same culture. It's made from volcanic basalt. It also has some kimberlite."

Waving the cigar about, Drummond laughed. "Basalt? You might as well be looking for a spec of gray sand on a black beach."

Navarro said, "The odds are somewhat better than that. I have a sense of where to look, and I don't think they're buried too deeply."

"Where? Are we talking previous dig sites? Ruins?"

Navarro again paused. The truth was he didn't know for sure, though he had a solid hunch. If his reading of the map was accurate, the site he had in mind was, in fact, a ruin. An obscure ruin. An ancient structure near caverns well known to prospectors. Caverns with a mystical reputation for their "waterfall of jewels."

Whether the stones were hidden in an exposed section of the ruin, entombed in an unearthed chamber or buried in the caverns was unknown. Therefore, Navarro shaded his answer. "If not at ruins, then close by."

Drummond ground his cigar butt into the tray resting on the table between them. "If they're concentrated in a small area that's close to the surface, you're right, the odds are better. But, Klaus, basalt? There is nothing unusual about basalt's magnetism. Yes, some types of basalt are more magnetic than others, but not remarkable enough in small quantities to stand out unless you're literally standing on the rocks themselves."

"I understand your skepticism," Navarro said. Rising from his chair, he added, "Wait here, I have something to show you that might change your mind."

He left the parlor through a side entrance and snaked down a circular stone staircase. At the bottom of the stairs was a vaulted door. After punching in the required code to open the door, he entered the gallery holding his most prized artifacts. He passed illuminated displays of pottery, jewelry, statues and other relics. Some were Incan, others Mayan, and still others were of Olmec or Toltec ancestry.

At the rear of the vaulted room stood a bank of locked drawers holding smaller pieces. Navarro snagged two pairs of latex gloves from a wall dispenser. He shoved one pair in his blazer pocket and the other he donned.

He unlocked the top drawer and slowly lifted a greenish, square, dinner-plate-sized tile from within. He carried it reverently from the room until he gingerly set it down on the table in front of Drummond. While the prospector leaned forward to study the tile, Navarro quickly stepped to the nearby desk and removed three items from a side drawer: a small magnet, a compass and a Gauss meter.

Returning to his seat, he handed the spare latex gloves to Drummond and placed the items next to the stone. He chose his next words carefully. He wanted to tempt his guest enough to help, but not so much that he created a competitor.

"This stone was made by the same people who created the pieces I'm after. Have you seen a stone like this before? In a museum, perhaps?"

Drummond stroked his mustache and frowned. "No, I don't think so."

"You can find stones like this in museums all over the world. Hundreds of them. That is how I came across this one years ago. They have different etchings and come in different colors, but they're all the same shape and size."

"Are they Mesoamerican?"

"Their origin is unknown. They've been found at sites in the Americas, Europe, Africa and Asia."

Drummond peered at the pictograph etched on the surface of the stone—a man holding a cone and tube together. At the cone's tip was a starlike flash. From the flash, a wavy line extended across the stone's face. He said, "I don't understand. If there are many in circulation, why do you want to dig for more?"

The man was insightful. That might prove to be an issue later, but right now Navarro needed his help. He said, "I've heard rumors there are other stones made by the same people that are different in shape and size. From what I've been told, these other stones are extremely hard to find, even from private collectors. I like rare things, so they interest me."

The intrigued look on Drummond's face was transparent, but he held his tongue. He asked for permission to lift the stone. Navarro assented. Drummond tugged on the gloves and examined the tile closely. The surface was coarse but the edging precise. He flipped the stone over and discovered a bored cavity in the center. On opposite sides of the center circle, two semicircular cuts arced inward from the tile's edges.

Returning the tile to its face, he studied the stone itself. Basalt is not naturally green, he knew, but the weight and grain of the stone was consistent with the volcanic rock type. He also studied the etching itself. It wasn't haphazard or rudimentary. The cuts were even and precise. They looked like they'd been tooled by modern means.

He placed it back on the table, pointed at the items next to the stone and asked, "What's special about its magnetism?"

Navarro handed him the compass. "Go stand by the windows. Tell me which way is north."

Drummond squinted at him and pulled at the corners of his mustache.

"Go ahead, do it. Show me where north is," Navarro prodded.

The prospector tromped to the windows and held the compass steady in his palm. He waited for the needle to settle before pointing a finger toward the main parlor door.

Motioning him back to the sofa, Navarro said, "Line up north again on the compass, and then place it on the stone."

When he did, the compass reversed direction. Drummond shrugged. "Big deal, so the tile was cut from a rock with different polarity. That's not unique."

"True," Navarro said, "but it *is* unusual for such a rock to point twenty-three degrees west from due south. Magnetic north shifts from time to time, but not that much. Wouldn't you agree?"

His guest gave a slight nod. Navarro pointed to the Gauss meter and said, "Turn it on. Hold it against the stone."

Drummond flipped the switch and watched the meter flicker to life. He slid out the device's stylus and touched it to the stone. The needle trembled violently. Drummond frowned. He moved the stylus away for a moment and the needle settled back to center. He guided it back against the stone and the wild movements resumed.

"Don't just touch it. Hold it steady against the rock," Navarro encouraged. "Tell me what you see."

To Drummond's amazement, the needle jumped back and forth in a steady, rhythmic pattern. He said, "What the hell?"

Easing back on the chair, Navarro smiled. "You see, not so common after all."

"To say the least!" said Drummond. He repeated the experiment several times before setting the meter aside. "The signature is similar to kimberlite, but kimberlite doesn't pulse like that."

Navarro reached for the small magnet on the table. Navarro hovered the magnet an inch over the stone. His hand was steady — there was no sign of attraction or repulsion. He flipped the magnet over. Again no reaction. He turned the tile facedown and repeated the same movements with the magnet. Given the Gauss meter's intense readings, there should have been some reaction with the small magnet. It should have ripped from Navarro's hand and either cemented to the tile or shot across the room.

"Impossible!" Drummond said.

"Yes," Navarro agreed. "Have you ever seen a magnetic pulse like that from a static object?"

"Never."

"If I told you where to look, do you think you could detect it?"

Drummond eased back against the sofa and crossed his arms. "If it's close to the surface, possibly. If it's buried deep, I don't think so. Even though the signal's very strong . . . and unique . . . a small object like this would be hard to pick up under tons of rock."

"Understood. What if there were more than one of these buried together? Say, a dozen of them or more?"

Drummond edged his head from side to side and said, "A cache of stones with similar properties? Yes, that would make the Stones easier to detect, but they'd still need to be close to the surface. Too much rock in between would distort the signal."

"Will you do it? I will pay you well."

"I'll admit, you've got me interested. You said you know where to look?"

"There are several possibilities. One stands out above others. How soon can you start?"

Once Drummond departed, Navarro returned his prized serpent-tooth relief to the vault. He was most pleased the Scot had agreed to lead an expedition. If Drummond found a trove of the magnetic relics, the Flash Stone might very well be among them and then Navarro's Rivers of Gold fantasy would finally become reality.

Even if his coveted prize wasn't part of a discovered trove, Navarro would at least know his reading of the map was on target . . . and that meant he could confidently search other marked sites. One way or the other, he was one step closer to finding the mythical stone-melter.

With that pleasant thought in mind, Navarro reclimbed the stairs to the parlor and contemplated next steps. Drummond was available to start in three days, so there was little time to plan the expedition. It would be an arduous trek; the site was deep in the Amazon jungle. It would be dangerous; the ruins sat squarely in Cinta-Larga territory. The reclusive tribe was not fond of trespassers . . . particularly prospecting trespassers.

Navarro paced the breadth of the parlor's wall of windows and weighed the merit of joining Drummond's party. The esthete within him argued in favor of deferring the treasure hunting to the expert. Navarro was, after all, a collector, not a bloodhound.

Yet, the thought of entrusting such an important mission to a man who could be easily bought troubled him. It would be so simple for Drummond to abscond with the relics and claim the site was barren.

How could Navarro possibly contest the claim, unless he was there when Drummond scoured the ruins?

And then an idea struck Navarro. There was a way to ensure his personal safety *and* keep tabs on Drummond. He would recall the tenacious Margaret Corchran to service. In a near whisper, he said, "Ah, Margaret. You have caused me much trouble. Time to repay your debt."

In fact, the longer Navarro considered his idea, the more he realized it might help him kill two birds with one stone.

8

Special Delivery

The Embarcadero
San Francisco, California
August 11

When the Lincoln came to a stop, Pebbles thanked the driver and exited the Town Car. Adjusting the tote slung over her shoulder, she paused on the sidewalk to look up at the towering granite edifice and was nearly toppled by a throng headed for the adjacent BART station.

"Sorry," she mumbled repeatedly as she wedged a path through a crisscross of pedestrians. Reaching the revolving doors, she fell into line and awaited her turn to push into the lobby. Once inside the soaring atrium, she spied the security kiosk and strode in its direction. The echoes of her high heels clicking against the marble were lost in the competing clatter of footsteps, conversations and beeping turnstiles.

A waif of a man darted in front and bumped against her arm. Eyes glued to his cell phone, he grumbled at her to watch her step. Pebbles halted to offer a comeback and was jostled yet again. This time she drew a cross glare from a woman reattaching the lid of her "Venti" coffee cup.

"Geez," Pebbles said, "this is worse than happy hour at Sydney's!"

When she arrived at the security checkpoint, the chiseled guard rose and spied her warily. Pebbles smiled in return and said with cheer, "Hi, good morning."

The blank-faced attendant, easily a foot shorter than Pebbles, crossed his arms and said, "Name?"

Resting her tote on the countertop, Pebbles straightened the lapels of her suit jacket. "Oh, sure. I'm Eleanor, Eleanor McCarver. I'm here to see Antonio Wallace. Is it always so busy here?"

The guard leaned forward to consult his computer. He scrolled through the list of the day's scheduled visitors and found her name. Without looking up, he said, "ID."

"No prob. Hold on a sec," she said as she dug in the tote for her wallet. Extracting her driver's license, she passed it to the guard and girded for the inevitable reaction. Although she'd been living in Tahoe for over a year, Pebbles had yet to declare Nevada residency. So, her Georgia driver's license remained her primary form of identification. The frumpy license picture, taken shortly before she graduated from law school, didn't exactly jibe with her current look.

The security officer studied the license, gazed up at Pebbles, then looked back at the identification. She maintained a friendly smile and placed a hand over her heart. "I know, it's kinda an old picture, but it's me. I promise."

The guard didn't respond, but continued to eye her up and down. Pebbles prayed for him to look past the pink pixie-cut hair, neck tattoo, metallic-blue lip gloss and diamond stud in her nostril. Given his chilly demeanor, she fully expected him to reject the ID at any moment and send her packing. Instead, he handed the license back, punched a few keystrokes and printed out a visitor's sticker.

While Pebbles pressed the sticker to her suit jacket, the security guard pointed toward the bank of elevators and said, "Thirty-fifth floor. Use the visitor's gate."

"Okay, thank you!" she said with a smile. "Hope you have a nice day!"

The ride up the packed elevator was unremarkable, save for the prodigious yawns emanating from a pudgy, unkempt man in jeans and flip-flops standing a little too close beside her. The yawns themselves didn't bother Pebbles, but the invasion of personal space was a little unnerving.

The elevator made several stops, allowing Pebbles the opportunity to move farther and farther away from zombie-man as the car thinned out. She was most surprised when the lift arrived at the thirty-fifth floor and they both moved to exit. The curly-haired man paused at the door and gestured for Pebbles to go first.

As the man broke into another gaping yawn, Pebbles mumbled her thanks and scooted past him into sleek confines of Whave Technologies' corporate headquarters. Standing by the elevators was a smiling blonde clad in a mauve dress accented by a short strand of pearls. Before the woman introduced herself, she waved to zombie-man and said, "Good morning, Dr. Hollingsworth."

As he strolled by both women, Dylan Hollingsworth flashed a peace sign and replied, "Morning, 2K."

Turning toward Pebbles, the woman said, "Miss McCarver? I'm Dr. Wallace's assistant, Kathleen Kierney. How was your flight in?"

"Good, thanks. Appreciate you sending the car to pick me up," said Pebbles.

"My pleasure." Kathleen gestured to the right with her head and said, "Follow me and we'll get you settled. Dr. Wallace is running a bit late this morning."

Once inside the suite's secure entry doors, Kathleen led Pebbles through a labyrinth of chrome and glass hallways. Along the way, Antonio's polished assistant greeted a dozen coworkers with the same mix of cheerful formality she had bestowed on Pebbles.

Although Kathleen appeared to be barely thirty, a few years older than Pebbles, she carried herself with the poise of a boarding school matron. Yet, she didn't strike Pebbles as stuffy. In fact, she seemed to possess a warm rapport with the eclectic group of engineers and technologists they encountered.

And *eclectic* barely did justice to Antonio's assortment of employees. A bearded man with dreadlocks stepped barefoot from a copier nook wearing board shorts and a T-shirt that read "Hang Loose." When Kathleen said hello, he winked and replied, "Whaz up, 2K?"

Then, they passed a young Asian woman kneeling on the chair in her cubicle. Pebbles couldn't be certain, but it appeared as if the woman was wearing pajamas. Spongebob pajamas, at that. In a chair beside her sat a balding man in his midsixties adorned in suit and tie.

The two were intensely discussing a CAD-CAM image on her computer screen.

In every direction, Pebbles saw people engrossed in their work or in conversation, and no two looked alike. Under her breath, she said, "This is my kinda place!"

When they finally arrived outside Antonio's office suite, Kathleen offered Pebbles coffee and led her into a lounge that served as a gallery of sorts to wait for Antonio. In the center of the room was a long, leather-cushioned bench. From this bench one could sit and view framed, poster-sized photographs of the company's inventions mounted on the surrounding four walls. Beneath each photograph stood a stand-alone glass case that housed a miniature model and brief description of the corresponding creation.

Pebbles sipped coffee and perused the displays. She was drawn to the wall opposing the entrance where a solitary exhibit stood. Larger than all the others, it was emblazoned across its base with the phrase, "The Whave That Started It All." The exhibit was a shrine to the Whave engine, a revolutionary adaptation of the combustion engine that promised dramatic improvements in fuel efficiency and emissions.

When Pebbles reached the Whave display case, she peered inside and broke into a huge smile. Next to the sleek, whale-shaped miniature model was a snapshot of four men huddled arm-in-arm around a life-sized prototype of the engine. She immediately recognized Anlon. Although his sandy hair in the picture was longer than it was these days, and without the gray that dominated his locks now, there was no mistaking his smile and penetrating eyes.

Anlon stood next to Antonio in the center of the photograph. To Pebbles, Antonio looked as if he'd barely aged. His clothes and eyeglasses in the photo were a bit dated, but otherwise he was the same trim African American with the boyish grin. Pebbles' eyes fluttered when she focused on the man on the other side of Antonio. It was her sleepy elevator companion. He'd certainly gained some weight since the picture was taken, but he had maintained the same scruffy look. Pebbles thought it interesting that Anlon had never mentioned a Dr. Hollingsworth. Nor had he ever mentioned the last person in the photo, a slight Asian man whom the caption identified as Corky Tamura.

In many ways, it didn't surprise Pebbles. Though Anlon and his three Whave engine colleagues became mega-millionaires by selling the patent for their invention, Anlon left Whave Technologies to lead a simple, quiet life. He didn't talk much about his past, didn't boast about his accomplishments and rarely entertained visitors. Pebbles had made progress coaxing him out of his reclusive shell, but he still tended to shut himself off from time to time.

As Pebbles turned her attention to the next display, Antonio emerged from his office and strode toward the lounge. With a deep voice, he called, "Pebbles! Thank you for waiting. Sorry my call ran over."

"No sweat, Antonio. It's all good. I know you're very busy." Pebbles smiled as they embraced. When they separated, she pointed at the Whave engine display and said, "That's so cool! Anlon's talked about it a few times, but I've never seen it."

Antonio adjusted his bow tie and ceremoniously bowed. "You're too kind. I'll take credit for the 'cool' design, but Anlon's the one who deserves credit for the inspiration."

Motioning toward his office, he asked, "Speaking of the good Dr. Cully, how's he coming along?"

"Getting stronger every day," she replied as she stepped through the door. "Still gets a little cranky now and then, but his rehab's going well. You shoulda seen him when he got his first taste of real food again. One nibble of a burrito and he almost levitated!"

From behind, Antonio's booming laugh filled the room. "I can imagine! Sipping soup through wired jaws loses its charm fast."

As Pebbles followed him into the cavernous office, she said, "No kidding, I don't know how he did it. It'll still be a while before he can full-out chow down, but at least he's finally off a protein-paste diet."

They arrived at a conference table tucked in the far corner of the room. Pebbles stood by the window and leaned forward to observe the bustling Embarcadero below. She then panned Antonio's view of the bay. To her right, cars streamed along the upper deck of the Bay

Bridge. Dead ahead, a loaded container ship chugged toward the Port of Oakland. On her left, a dozen sailboats floated aimlessly around Alcatraz Island. She said, "Wow, you have quite a view!"

Antonio joined her at the window. "Yeah, it's pretty sweet. I don't stop to enjoy it as much as I should, but it's hard to take my eyes away when I do."

After several more minutes of chitchat, Antonio cleared his throat and asked, "So, Anlon's determined to start up again?"

Pebbles nodded. "Oh, he's been back at it for a few weeks. As soon as you sent over all of Devlin's papers, he disappeared into his office and locked the door."

"Honestly, I'm surprised he held off as long as he did," Antonio said.

"Now he's barking out orders left and right! Well, more murmuring orders . . . still can't open his mouth wide enough to bark yet." She smiled.

"Really? He's not the order-barking type."

"I know, right? Jen and I were pretty shocked. He's not nasty or anything, just super-intense," Pebbles clarified. "You should see his office at the house. There've been nonstop deliveries the last week. Piles of rocks and all kinds of weird, smelly stuff. Keeps mumbling about crypto-whatnots and kimber-somethings."

"Kimberlites?" Antonio ventured.

"Yes! Exactly. Kimberlites. What are they?"

"Diamonds. Well, more like a diamond-rock mix."

"Huh . . . why not just mumble 'diamonds' instead?" she asked idly.

Antonio shrugged and then said, "I have the pieces you wanted."

From behind his desk, he retrieved a steel case and carried it to the conference table. Pebbles popped out of her seat while Antonio entered the electronic combination and bobbed on her toes. Waving a hand over the open case, he said, "These are the last of them."

Two objects were nestled in black foam cushioning. One was a black tile with an etched design. The tile's shape was reminiscent of a smart tablet, although it was three times as thick. Next to the tile was a squat, grayish cylinder the size of a hockey puck.

Pebbles' heart raced as she laid eyes on the *Sinethal* for the first time in three months. A hard three months. She absently ran her fingers over the etchings and thought of Malinyah. She ached to visit with her, but she promised Anlon to wait until she returned to Tahoe. She lifted the cylinder, a device Malinyah called a *Naetir*. It still had Anlon's Sharpie-drawn "X" on one side.

"Kept 'em safe and sound as promised," said Antonio.

"I can't thank you enough. I know it was a big ask," Pebbles said.

"Nah, not really. We do a lot of military work, so finding a secure spot was a breeze. Honestly, the harder part was resisting the urge to take a peek!" Antonio said. Wagging a finger, he added, "Anlon still owes me an explanation, you know. About these stones. About everything."

"Hey, I offered to fill you in back in May!" she said.

"Yeah, I should have taken you up on that. I won't tell you how often I've thought about Anlon and the whole fiasco. Two people dead? Two others damn near killed? Fugitives on the loose? There's gotta be one helluva story behind these stones to cause all that mayhem."

"Trust me, it'll blow your mind," Pebbles confided.

"So you've said before." Antonio pointed at the case and sheepishly asked, "How about a quick preview now? I know I'll get the full download from Anlon in a few days, but . . ."

"Are you kidding? After all you've done for Anlon? Tell me what you want to know," said Pebbles.

Just then, Kathleen knocked on the office door and ducked into the room. Closing the door behind her, she politely reminded Antonio that his next meeting was due to start in five minutes. He grimaced and said, "Gonna need more time, Katie. Please tell Dylan I need to reschedule. Same for my eleven a.m."

"Very well. Dr. Hollingsworth thought you might want to reschedule." Darting a curious look at the open case, she added, "He asked if he could come in for a moment."

"Why? Something urgent?"

Kathleen hesitated before answering. "No, I don't think so. He seemed very interested to meet Miss McCarver."

Antonio asked Pebbles, "You mind? Dylan's our chief technology officer. He worked on the Whave team and knows Anlon."

"No problem. I saw his picture in your hall-of-fame room. We rode up on the elevator together. I feel bad I didn't know who he was or I would have said hello," Pebbles said.

Kathleen left and returned with Dylan.

"I'm embarrassed," said Dylan as he reached to shake Pebbles' hand. "I didn't recognize you in the business suit."

The comment was unexpected, and Pebbles' reaction must have shown it, because Dylan quickly added, "On Anlon's Instagram account, he's got lots of pictures of you."

"Ohhh, right!" said Pebbles. "It's nice to meet you, Dylan. I'm Eleanor. Well, most people call me Pebbles."

As she spoke, Dylan looked past her at the open case. "Are those the infamous stones?"

"Um, yeah, I guess," she said. Pebbles wasn't sure she liked the "infamous" characterization, especially about Malinyah's Stone, but she didn't make an issue of it.

Dylan headed for the table, but Antonio stepped in front. "Hey, buddy, we're kinda in the middle of something here. I'll catch you later, okay?"

"Those are strange symbols on the black one," said Dylan. "Is it some kind of voodoo spell or something?"

Pebbles frowned. "Uh, no."

"Seriously, Dylan. I'll stop by later this afternoon," said Antonio. He motioned for Kathleen to escort Dylan from the office, but Dylan scooted around the opposite side of the table to get a closer look.

Pointing at the smallish cylinder, Dylan asked, "Is this the one that busted Anlon up?"

"Okay, that's enough," said Antonio in a sharp tone. Together with Kathleen, he escorted Dylan out of the office. When they reached the doorway, Dylan shouted back, "Nice to meet you!"

Antonio closed the door and returned to the table. "Sorry about that," he said. "He meant no offense, just doesn't have much of a filter."

Pebbles was beginning to understand why Anlon never mentioned Dylan. She said, "Don't sweat it. It's okay."

"You still up to talk about the Stones?"

"Yeah, sure. Of course. Where do you want to start?"

He crossed his arms and shrugged. "You tell me. Where should I start?"

Pebbles knew exactly where he should start, but wondered how to describe the *Sinethal* without sounding touched in the head. She said, "Hmmm . . . that depends on how much of an open mind you have."

"Hey, you walked through our little gallery, didn't you?" he teased. "Thinking outside the box is what I do."

Pebbles massaged her wrists and stared at the *Sinethal*. Hands shaking, she gently lifted the black tile from the case. The gritty feel of the Stone's surface was oddly comforting. She closed her eyes, inhaled deeply and slid her hands along the edges. When her fingers slipped into the notched depressions on the *Sinethal*'s back side, she shivered and opened her eyes. Bowing her head, she said, "Anlon's going to be angry with me."

"What? Why?" Antonio frowned.

She delicately placed the *Sinethal* on the conference table and massaged her wrists again. "Gah! I can't believe how nervous I am!"

Looking around the room, she spied the sofa in the corner near the office door. She looked at Antonio and placed a hand on his shoulder. "Promise you won't tell Anlon."

"Uh, tell Anlon what?"

She lifted the *Sinethal* and motioned toward the sofa. "Grab the *Naetir* and follow me."

"Excuse me? The what?"

Pebbles was already halfway across the room when she turned to say, "Oh, sorry. The stone with the X on it. Bring it over."

"Okay. Why?"

She perched on the sofa's edge, placed the *Sinethal* on the small oval coffee table and waved for him to join her. "Just bring it over."

He shrugged, grabbed the squat, gray cylinder and traipsed to the sofa. She held out a hand to receive the *Naetir*. She set it on the table next to the *Sinethal*, the X side facedown, and then patted the sofa. "Here. Sit right here."

Once Antonio had settled next to her, she pointed at the black tile and said, "This is a *Sinethal.* The name means 'mind keeper.' The little hockey puck there is known as a *Naetir.* The rough translation is 'spark.' In a minute, you're going to pick up the *Sinethal* like this."

She lifted the tile and gripped it on its sides. She twisted her torso to face Antonio and showed him the backside of the stone. "You'll eventually put your fingers in these little half-moon cuts on the sides. They're like handholds. But first, you take the *Naetir* and move it close to the round slot in the middle."

Antonio's brow furrowed. "Are you going to tell me why?"

"In a sec," she said. "Now, this is important. You hold the *Naetir* with the X-side pointed toward the slot. When your hand gets close, the *Naetir*'s going to yank out of your hand and snap into the slot. It's a little scary the first time you do it. It's kinda loud and it happens super-fast."

The furrow on Antonio's forehead spread into a full-scale frown. "Um, come again?"

She nudged him with her elbow and smiled. "Open mind, remember?"

Lacing his fingers together, Antonio leaned forward and rested his elbows on his knees. He considered her instructions for a moment and then said, "I take it the hockey puck is a magnet."

With a nod, Pebbles said, "Yep. Actually, they're both magnets. Want to see something cool?"

Before Antonio could answer, Pebbles placed the *Sinethal* face-down on the table next to the *Naetir.* She pushed them close together. Triumphantly, she looked back up at Antonio. "Now watch."

She pushed the *Sinethal* about a foot away from the *Naetir* and then turned the gray cylinder to reveal its X-marked side. The *Sinethal* rattled on the table and then slowly shimmied in the direction of the *Naetir.* Pebbles quickly flipped the *Naetir* back over and the *Sinethal* silenced its movements. Then, she guided the *Sinethal* toward the *Naetir* until they touched sides. The two stones sat inert on the table.

Curiosity aroused, Antonio said, "Okay, I get it. That shouldn't have happened. If they're magnets, one side should attract and the other repel. There was a definite attraction when you flipped the puck, a pretty strong one to cause the bigger one to move from that distance.

But, they should have repelled with equal force when the puck was turned to the unmarked side."

"Cool, right?" She smiled.

"Very," he said, nodding. Picking up the *Naetir* again, Antonio examined the Stone closely. "Feels almost hollow. Are you sure it's a stone?"

"Yeah, why?"

"I was just thinking . . ." he said. "There's an easy answer why the opposite side didn't show a magnetic reaction, but it'd only be possible if this wasn't just a magnetized stone."

"What do you mean?"

Antonio didn't answer immediately. Instead, he continued to examine the *Naetir*. He shook it while holding it close to his ear, then tapped on it. He asked, "You think Anlon would let me scan it? See if there's anything inside?"

"Inside?"

"Yeah, it feels hollow. I'll bet you it isn't a stone. Well, it might have an outer shell of cast stone, but I bet you there's something inside it. Like a magnet with some kind of backing that deadens the polarity of one side."

"I'm pretty sure it's a stone," Pebbles said.

Antonio asked, "Where did this supposedly come from?"

"You mean, originally? Or where Anlon's uncle found it?"

"Both."

"Hmmm . . . we don't know where Devlin found it. But, I do know who made it. The Munuorians."

"The who?"

"The Moon-war-E-uns," she enunciated. "The civilization that made all of the Stones Devlin was researching."

"Well, I don't want to burst your bubble, but I don't think an ancient civilization made this. This looks modern to me. Too bad we shooed Dylan out of the room. He could tell us if it's a hoax pretty quickly. He may be socially awkward, but the dude is brilliant."

"The *Naetir*? A hoax? No way. I'll prove it to you," said a defiant Pebbles.

Antonio asked, "How do you know the names of the Stones?"

Pebbles held up a hand and said, "We'll talk about that later." Pointing back at the *Sinethal*, she said, "Go ahead and pick it up and do what I told you."

"Why? What's going to happen?"

"Just pick it up and snap the *Naetir* on."

"Um, Pebbles. No offense, but I'm not touching two magnets with unstable properties together without knowing more."

"Oh, please. Quit being such a baby."

Pebbles tugged the *Sinethal* off the table. Resting it facedown in her lap, she grabbed the *Naetir* and lowered it toward the carved, circular depression in the center of the *Sinethal*'s back side. When the *Naetir* was within two inches, it flew from Pebbles' grip and locked into the depression with a sharp clap that reverberated through the office.

Antonio flinched and called out, "Whoa!"

The clap was loud enough to prompt a knock on the door. Kathleen edged it open and asked, "Is everything okay? What was that sound?"

Tilting his head in her direction, Antonio waved her off. "It's okay, Katie. Just a little experiment."

"Little? It sounded like a gun went off!" huffed the shaken assistant.

Shifting the two Stones to the far side of the sofa to shield them from Kathleen's view, Pebbles said, "Sorry, it's my fault. Didn't mean to scare you."

Fanning her face, Kathleen said, "Whew! I'm just glad no one's hurt."

After Kathleen departed, Pebbles replaced the joined Stones on her lap and teased, "See? Nothing happened. A hole didn't open in the universe. I didn't explode."

"Uh, I wouldn't call that nothing. I've seen a lot of magnets react, but that right there was a first," said Antonio.

Pebbles reached for his hand and circled her fingers around his left wrist. Guiding his hand to the *Sinethal*, she instructed, "Now put your hand right here. That's right, your fingers need to go in the slot on the back. Good. That's perfect. Now, when you're ready, do the same thing on the other side."

With his right hand, Antonio adjusted his glasses and asked, "For real, Pebbles. What's going to happen?"

"Your mind's still open, right?"

He laughed. "Right now, there's a little voice in my head shouting 'Abort! Abort!' and a bunch of red lights flashing."

How much to say? Pebbles pondered. If she said too little, he'd likely freak out when the tingling commenced. If she said too much, it would ruin the wonder of meeting Malinyah. She stared down at the huddled angel tattoo on the inside of her left wrist, felt the wisp of Malinyah's hand on her cheek and inhaled the aroma from the field of Alynioria flowers. Closing her eyes, Pebbles hovered at the edge of the soothing memory.

Eyes still shut, she squeezed Antonio's wrist and said, "You're going to feel tingling in your fingers. Then you're going to see things. Like, right in front of you. It'll seem like you're in some kind of virtual-reality simulation. You'll see things. Hear things. Feel things. It's like nothing you've ever experienced.

"Then, she'll appear. Her name is Malinyah. You probably won't understand what she says. The Munuorians had their own language. Don't be afraid of her, she's really sweet. She calls me Alynioria."

Pebbles opened her eyes and beheld the stupefied expression on Antonio's face. His mouth hung open as if poised to say something, but he uttered no words. He looked at the two Stones fused together. With his left hand holding the *Sinethal* as Pebbles instructed, he hovered the fingers of his right within reach of the other concave notch. He mumbled, "The mind keeper . . ."

"Uh-huh," Pebbles said as she edged his right hand closer to the notch. "You're about to meet a ten-thousand-year-old woman."

Pulling his right hand away from the Stone, he asked, "What's that supposed to mean?"

"Exactly what I said. Her name is Malinyah."

"And who, pray tell, is Malinyah?"

"One of the Munuorians."

"And these 'Moon-people' are . . . ?"

"They're not from the Moon, silly. They lived on Earth . . . but a very, very long time ago."

Antonio pointed at the *Sinethal*. "You're telling me the mind of this Malinyah is inside this Stone?"

She nodded.

"You're pulling my leg," he said, laughing. "Did Anlon put you up to this?"

"Why're you being such a chicken? Put your other hand on the Stone and see for yourself."

"Uh-huh, sure. What happens? Is it like one of those hand buzzers that shocks?"

Pebbles frowned. "Ugh! Fine, don't do it."

She reached for the fused Stones and said, "I'll put them back in the case."

"Hold on, hold on. Don't get bent out of shape. I'm willing to try it, but I want to know a little more first." Antonio pushed her hands away.

Pebbles folded her arms. "You scientists are all the same. You must *know* everything before you *try* anything! Isn't that kind of backward? When you had your first cookie, did you require a lab analysis before eating, or did you just take a bite?"

With a thunderous laugh, Antonio relented. "All right, you win! I'll bite the cookie."

Still holding the *Sinethal* with his left hand, he took a deep breath and lightly touched the upper right corner of the stone. Expecting a shock, he quickly withdrew his touch. When it didn't occur, he glanced at Pebbles and smiled. "Trust, but verify."

Then, as Pebbles instructed, he slid the fingers of his right hand behind the stone and felt for the notch. When they slipped into the depression, Antonio immediately felt a prickling sensation in the fingers of both hands. It wasn't a shock, but it was electrical. Holding the Stone as if it were a steering wheel, he turned to say as much to Pebbles when the vision kicked in.

Antonio found himself in a marble hall. Tall, white columns lined the outer edges. A gust of wind brushed against his left cheek. Instinctively, he turned toward the sensation. A sheer curtain billowed between two columns and revealed a stunning vista beyond its rippling edges. There was a hillside filled with colorful flowers and plants. In the distance, azure waters shimmered under the glare of bright sunlight.

A golden butterfly floated underneath the curtain. Antonio watched it bob and weave through the hall as if pursued by a relentless foe. From behind, he heard the tap of footsteps approaching. Turning in the direction of the sound, he caught his first glimpse of Malinyah.

Tall, bronzed and proud, the blond Munuorian advanced toward him with a warm smile upon her flawless face. She spoke and touched his shoulder. Antonio trembled and pulled away.

Pebbles watched Antonio's body go rigid when the vision began. Much like Anlon's first experience with the *Sinethal*, his face contorted and he sputtered incoherently. When he flinched and belted out a haunting groan, Pebbles cringed.

Before Pebbles could rise from the couch, Kathleen's urgent raps echoed through the door. Pebbles was one step too late to reach the handle. The door flung inward. Kathleen's bewildered gaze locked on Antonio grappling with the *Sinethal*. He moaned and writhed. Pebbles tried to block Kathleen's entrance, but the smaller woman shoved past her and rushed to Antonio. Pebbles grabbed her by the wrist and tugged her back. Kathleen struggled to break free. She barked, "Let go of me!"

Tightening her grip, Pebbles tried to assure the protective assistant. "Kathleen, he's fine. Let him be."

"Let go!" cried Kathleen. She flailed and kicked at Pebbles. Her cry was loud enough to attract the attention of a passing mailroom clerk, who rushed toward the open door. Pebbles released her hold on Kathleen's arm and backed away. Out of the corner of her eye, Pebbles spied Dylan Hollingsworth approaching.

Kathleen hovered above Antonio, unsure of what to do. She spoke to him, but Antonio didn't respond. Suddenly, the writhing ceased and he slowly rocked backward. The contortions on his face melted and he mumbled softly.

Wheeling back toward Pebbles, Kathleen stomped a foot and demanded, "What's going on? What are you doing to him?"

The mailroom clerk halted in the doorway, observed the scene and said, "I'll call security!"

When he turned for Kathleen's workstation, he plowed into Dylan and they both tumbled to the floor. Pebbles covered her face and shouted, "Everybody calm the f—— down!"

As her voice trailed off, Antonio released the *Sinethal*. The *Naetir* popped off and rolled beneath the couch. The *Sinethal* slid from his hands and plunked onto the floor. Antonio slumped over and passed out. Kathleen rushed to his side. Pebbles stepped forward and said, "He needs water. Go find him water."

Without protest, the assistant dashed from the office in the direction of the nearby kitchenette. On her way, she passed the mailroom clerk, who had recovered his footing and was on the phone. While Pebbles lowered onto hands and knees to corral the *Sinethal* and fish under the sofa for the *Naetir*, Dylan slunk into Antonio's office. Unaware of his presence, Pebbles bumped into him when she stood up. Startled, she spun around and spat, "Out of my way!"

Pebbles stalked around him and made her way to the conference table. She loaded the Stones back in their case and shut the lid. When she looked up, Kathleen was holding a bottle of water to Antonio's lips. He was propped up in the corner of the sofa, his face tinged with red. Pebbles said, "I am so screwed!"

9

Sleuth or Dare

New Haven, Connecticut
August 12

Jennifer closed her eyes and listened to the hypnotic clicks of the anteroom wall clock. Through the room's wooden door, she could hear the din of visitors down the long hallway as they moved between exhibit rooms. Crossing her arms, she arched her back against the creaky chair and yawned.

As she nodded off, the tote bag resting on her lap slipped and landed on the floor with an echoing thud. Jolted awake, Jennifer uttered an expletive and snatched the bag. She slapped it down onto the adjacent chair and spied the clock. With a frown, she lifted her cell phone to check the traffic conditions between New Haven and Bennington.

"Fifteen minutes more and I'm out of here," she groused.

She was three minutes from bolting when Dr. Charles Goodwin finally cracked open the inner office door and said, "Ah, you're still here. I've only got about ten minutes, I'm afraid."

Rising from the chair, Jennifer stepped toward Goodwin's office and sarcastically replied, "Turns out that's about all I have, too."

Once inside his office, Goodwin hung his blazer on a corner coatrack and straightened his cuff links. The forty-something curator guided an errant strand of hair back into place before reposing in his high-back leather chair.

While he continued to primp his tie and hair, Jennifer took in the room. It was very different from the other curators she'd visited over the past two days. Instead of the usual array of artifacts, journals and research tomes, Goodwin's office was adorned with pictures . . . mostly of the man himself. Several showed him in pith helmet and safari shorts at various excavations. A dozen more looked like they were snapped at museum galas. In these he posed with a variety of smiling guests. Jennifer recognized a few celebrities among the photos, but most were elderly husband-and-wife tandems. She presumed these were museum benefactors.

Another group of pictures displayed the lead page of journal articles penned by the archaeologist/anthropologist. Finally, on the wall behind his desk was the shrine to his academic prowess. Half a dozen gilded frames held diplomas from a glamorous array of Ivy League institutions.

Goodwin cleared his throat to draw her attention and asked, "How do you know the late Dr. Wilson, Miss . . . ?"

Oh, please, Jennifer thought, he doesn't remember my name? She'd introduced herself less than an hour ago when she showed up *on time* for the meeting. He'd pulled the same stunt then, and again when she'd spoken with him by phone when arranging the appointment.

Suppressing the urge to flip him off, she politely said, "Stevens. Jennifer Stevens. As I've mentioned previously, I'm assisting Dr. Cully in managing Devlin Wilson's private collection."

The visit to the university museum was a result of Jennifer's dig through Wilson's records. Among them, she discovered three potential leads: a museum in Villahermosa, Mexico, where Devlin first located a *Breylofte*; a private collector in Pézenas, France, who Devlin corresponded with about acquiring additional *Naetirs*; and Goodwin's museum. There, Devlin had purchased an *Aromaegh*. Called Story Stones by Devlin, *Aromaeghs* were Munuorian storage-device tablets similar in size and shape to the *Sinethal*, but they came in different colors and housed different types of information. The one Devlin purchased from Goodwin was reddish in color and contained a documentary-style presentation of the Munirvo story.

That led Jennifer to start with Goodwin. Her initial two calls received no response. Frustrated, Jennifer huddled with Anlon, and he suggested trying a different approach. Curators, he had said, are more apt to respond to a colleague or benefactor than to an unknown caller. He suggested Jennifer pose as Anlon's representative in a minor ruse. She was to leave a message indicating Anlon's interest in making a sizeable donation to the museum in Devlin's name.

Anlon hoped the mention of Dr. Devlin Wilson and the words "sizeable donation" would stimulate a return call. The ruse worked. When Goodwin called back, Jennifer finagled a meeting to deliver the donation . . . and to ask some questions about certain pieces in Devlin's collection.

"So, you didn't know him personally?"

"No."

"Are you an archaeologist yourself?"

"No, I work for—"

"I really don't see how I can help you, Miss . . . Sterns, is it?"

Jennifer rolled her eyes. In a moment like this as a police detective, she would have bitten her tongue and ignored the intentional slight. But the man's act was growing tired.

"Dr. Goodwin, do you suffer from brain damage?"

The curator reared back in the chair and adopted a stunned expression. "Heavens, no."

"Hmmm, then do you suffer from amnesia? Or are you just an a-hole?"

The man grew red-faced. His head bobbed and his mouth sputtered. To Jennifer, he looked like a chicken strutting around a barnyard. Before he could retort, she said, "My name is Stevens. S-T-E-V-E-N-S. Can we stop with the power bullshit, please? Or would you rather I tear up Dr. Cully's check on my way out?"

Goodwin snorted and rose from behind the desk. Straightening his tie, he said, "Good day, Miss *Stevens*."

Jennifer ignored him and reached in her bag and removed a handful of photographs. She arranged them on the desk and said, "I understand you have several stones like these among your Mesoamerican collection."

"Perhaps you didn't hear me. I said, 'good day,'" he said with a satisfied smile and wave.

"One of them, this one right here, Dr. Wilson purchased from your museum about three years ago," she answered, pointing at the red *Aromaegh*. "I'm looking to see if he purchased any other pieces from you. In particular, this black stone and these two statues."

Goodwin clenched his jaw and pointed toward the door. Jennifer sighed, gathered the photos and returned them to the bag. As she rose from her chair, she fished in the bag and extracted an envelope. From the envelope she removed the check from Anlon's charitable foundation.

Waving it in front of him, she said, "Then you don't want the twenty-five thousand dollars?"

The curator lowered his pointer, sighed and motioned for her to sit.

"Thank you. Now, where was I? Oh, yeah. I'm looking for information about these other artifacts. I'd like to know if Dr. Wilson purchased these from you, or if you know where he might have purchased them."

Without looking at the pictures, Goodwin straightened his tie for the umpteenth time and said, "I'm sure I have no idea."

Jennifer thought, Well, you might if you bothered to look at them! She lifted the picture of the *Sinethal* and showed it to him. The snarky SOB actually turned his head away to avoid looking! "Just take a look, please," she said.

Goodwin twirled his head and squinted at the picture for less than a second. "Never seen it."

With a shrug of her shoulders, Jennifer stowed the pictures, picked up the check and sighed. "That's a shame. Dr. Cully said he was considering endowing a research position in addition to the donation. He'll be disappointed to hear you were so uncooperative."

As she rose from the guest chair, the curator's eyes fluttered. Jennifer watched his face cycle through a familiar range of expressions while debating whether to call her bluff. Interrogation techniques *do* have value outside law enforcement, she thought.

When Jennifer reached the hallway, she turned and thanked Goodwin for his time. Four steps down the hallway, he called out, "Miss Stevens!"

Jennifer grumbled. Now he remembers my name!

The sound of his feet racing along the hallway brought a smile to her face—a smile that she hid when he implored, "Stop! Hold up!"

Ten minutes later, Jennifer sat in the museum's ready room in an adjacent annex building. As she waited for Goodwin to appear from the attached storage room, she watched three graduate students clean shards unearthed in a recent field visit. Like them, Goodwin required Jennifer to don a lab coat, latex gloves and face mask.

From the storage room, Goodwin brought forth a container holding three of the Munuorian *Aromaeghs*. He carefully unwrapped each Stone and placed them in a row across the examining table. Although he begrudgingly agreed to let her view the Stones, he forbade her from handling them in any way.

He watched with mild curiosity as Jennifer carefully studied the *Aromaeghs*. Two of the square tiles were green and their etchings illustrated unremarkable scenes. One showed a shepherd with livestock, while the other depicted men crafting a boat. Jennifer knew from conversations with Pebbles that some *Aromaeghs* contained virtual reality-like "how-to" tutorials. From the etchings on the two Stones, Jennifer assumed the green *Aromaeghs* fell into that category. The third *Aromaegh*, however, was distinctive in two respects: it was gray, and its etching portrayed what looked like stars. Among them was a constellation shaped like a *W*.

After Jennifer snapped photos of each, she retrieved her notepad and lowered the face mask. "So, you haven't seen the pieces in the pictures I showed you?"

He twitched slightly and said, "These are the only stones we have like the one Dr. Wilson purchased."

"That's not what I asked, Doctor," said Jennifer. "I asked whether you've seen the pieces."

"Look, Miss Stevens, I don't see the point of your questions. We don't have the pieces in your photographs; therefore, we didn't sell them to Dr. Wilson."

Pointing at the row of *Aromaeghs*, Jennifer asked, "How did each of these come to the museum?"

Goodwin shrugged. "Haven't a clue. Why?"

"Humor me. You catalog all the artifacts in your museum, right? I'd like to see the catalog entries for these pieces."

He darted a look at the graduate students across the room and said, "Out of the question. The catalog is confidential."

"Oh, come on, Doc. I just want to know the bio for each piece. Where and when they were found, who made the discovery, you know, that kind of thing. Why's that such a big deal?" prodded Jennifer.

While he gingerly rewrapped each piece, he said in a hushed tone, "Please keep your voice down. I doubt we have that kind of detail for these pieces."

Jennifer said, "Gonna call bullshit on that one, Chuck."

He sneered through clenched teeth. "You wanted to see the pieces. I've shown them to you. We're done."

"Look, cards on the table," said Jennifer. "This is important. Devlin Wilson was murdered because of the pieces I showed you. His killer is still out there, and we're trying to track her down before she kills anyone else."

It was a lie, but Jennifer was running out of options to nudge Goodwin.

"Shouldn't Dr. Cully leave that to the professionals?" snorted the curator.

The urge to knock the haughty look off his face made Jennifer's hand itch. She said, "You're looking at her."

The man tittered.

"Has your museum ever been the subject of a police investigation?" asked Jennifer.

"Certainly not."

"Would you like one?"

"Is that a threat?"

"Well, Chuck, let's put it this way. We can handle this discreetly, meaning you print out the three records I want and I go away quietly. Or, I tip the police. They'll show up with a search warrant, ask a crap ton more questions than me . . . and before you know it, you'll be on the six o'clock news. Either way, I'm getting those records."

"Why on Earth would the police listen to you?" Goodwin asked.

Jennifer reached in her bag, withdrew a business card and handed it to him. Goodwin's face blanched. Without a look or word, Goodwin walked across the room to a workstation. A few moments later, he returned with the catalog printouts. Jennifer stuffed them in her bag and departed.

Through the annex window, Goodwin watched Jennifer disappear around the corner. Dipping into his pocket, he pulled out a cell phone and typed two quick texts.

The first read, "TROUBLE!!!" The second said, "Call me."

By the time Jennifer reached Bennington, it was late afternoon. Shortly after leaving New Haven, she had called ahead to let Anabel Simpson know she was running thirty minutes late. Anabel hadn't answered the call, so Jennifer left a message on her voicemail.

She tried to reach the retired professor twice more during the three-hour drive before Anabel finally returned her call. She had been busy gardening, Anabel said, and had just stepped inside for a drink when she saw she had messages. She told Jennifer to look for her out back if she didn't answer the door when Jennifer arrived.

It had been three months since Jennifer had seen or talked to Anabel. The middle-aged woman had been Devlin Wilson's "lady friend" for more than thirty years. Originally a student in one of Devlin's archaeology classes, Anabel shared his passion for ancient cultures and they quickly developed a friendship that blossomed into something more intimate not long after.

She had also been the person Devlin Wilson trusted to hold the Waterland Map when he grew paranoid that others were after the Stones and map. Jennifer still remembered the day Anlon returned with the precious document after visiting Anabel. According to Anabel, Devlin had asked that she pass it to Anlon.

The first time Jennifer laid eyes on Anabel was at Stillwater Quarry. When she rounded the bend, there was Anabel, cowering, with arms tied behind her back. Then she saw Anlon's twisted body hovering in the air while Anabel's kidnapper, Pacal Flores, swayed Anlon to and fro under the control of a *Breylofte*. The memory of Anlon's lifeless body dangling in the air still sickened Jennifer.

A few days later, after the shock of confrontation with Pacal had subsided for both Jennifer and Anabel, Jennifer had traveled to Bennington to interview Anabel for the police investigation of the kidnapping. Since then, Anabel had emailed on a couple of occasions to check up on Anlon's recuperation and to ask about the status of Devlin's research. Now Jennifer was happy for the chance to speak with Anabel once again.

When her car came to a stop outside Anabel's modest rambler, Jennifer stepped out of the car and breathed in the air of the surrounding Green Mountains. It was thicker than Tahoe, more humid, but it still was a delightful change from the stuffy atmosphere of Goodwin's office.

There was no answer when she knocked on the door, so she did as Anabel had suggested and walked around the back of the house. When she turned the corner, she said, "Whoa!"

From the front of the house, the garden was not visible, but now Jennifer understood why Anabel hadn't heard her phone. It was a veritable jungle of flowers and plants. Everywhere she looked, there were butterflies of every shape and size flitting about.

There, about thirty yards away with a sack of potting soil by her side, knelt Anabel with trowel in hand. Jennifer called to her. Anabel turned and smiled. Using her hands to steady herself, Anabel slowly rose from the ground. When she finally stood, she pressed back her white hair, wiped her hands on a small rag and greeted Jennifer. "Well, hello! Caught me in the act!"

Jennifer smiled. It was a one-liner often made in the presence of cops. Gazing at Anabel's drawn face, she said, "Good to see you, again. How have you been?"

"Oh, getting on all right, I suppose," said Anabel. "Are you back in the area for long?"

"A few days," Jennifer said. "I have to check up on the repairs to Devlin's, I mean Anlon's, home in Stockbridge, and some other stuff."

"You young people, it's always run, run, run. Sometimes, you have to stop and smell the flowers," Anabel said with a laugh, sweeping her arms toward the garden. She staggered slightly from the quick gesture.

"Well, if I had a garden like yours, I would! It's beautiful," Jennifer said.

"It keeps me busy, plus I like my little friends." Anabel held out a hand for a butterfly to land. The Monarch obediently landed in Anabel's open palm. She whispered a few words and off the butterfly went. Turning her attention back to Jennifer, Anabel asked, "Would you like a cold drink?"

"Um, sure," said Jennifer.

Together, they walked back to the house and then settled in the kitchen. It was a classic New England farmhouse kitchen . . . and Anabel had a thing for Holstein cows. On the walls were painted scenes featuring the black-and-white grazers. On the floor, small rugs emblazoned with the cows rested in front of the refrigerator and kitchen sink.

On the gingham-covered table sat salt and pepper shakers shaped like Holstein eggs. On the counter was a small rack with a half dozen other eggs. Some were marble, others painted wood. Every other one was of the same Holstein pattern of the shakers. She even had a clock hanging above the door leading outside with a Holstein whose tail marked the minutes and whose head marked the hours. At the moment, the cow's head was positioned at an unflattering angle extending from the cow's rear end, while the tail chased closely behind.

Anabel apologized for the mess on the kitchen table. She cleared a bowl and newspaper from the table and set them on the counter. From the refrigerator, she removed a pitcher and poured two glasses.

Handing one to Jennifer, she said, "Try it, it's refreshing."

Jennifer sipped and said, "Mmmm, what is it?"

Anabel sipped some herself. "It's tea, dear," she said. "So, how is Anlon? I saw the video of him eating his solid food. He looked so happy."

The mention brought a smile to Jennifer's face. It had indeed been a fun moment. After seeing Anlon glumly sip his meals through a straw for weeks, the sight of the smile on his face after nibbling on the bean burrito was heartwarming.

"He's doing really good. He asked me to say hello."

"That's nice to hear, please say hello back. Devlin liked Anlon very much. I hated to see him get hurt so badly."

"Yeah, me too," Jennifer said, sighing. If only she'd seen his phone message sooner, Anlon might never have been injured. It was a thought that haunted Jennifer every time she saw him limp.

"And how is his young friend, the giggly one with the funny name and tattoos?"

Jennifer was midsip when Anabel asked the question. She nearly spit the drink out at the description. "Pebbles? Oh, she's great. We've had a lot of fun together in Tahoe."

"Good. And you? Are you back working?"

"Not yet. I still have another two months before I can go back. Gotta tell you, though, I'm seriously considering staying out west," Jennifer said. She turned red-faced. *Did I just say that out loud?* she wondered. It was a private thought, one she hadn't shared with any-one yet . . . not even Pebbles.

"Oh, really?" asked Anabel.

Jennifer waved a hand. "Ah, who knows? Anyway, I have some-thing for you." Reaching into her tote, she pulled out the photos she had shared with Goodwin and set them on the table while she dug deeper in the bag for another set of photos.

Anabel spied the top picture and asked, "Oh. Is that Devlin's prized stone?"

"Yep," Jennifer said. "I was going to ask you about that and the other pictures later. First, I wanted to show you these."

She laid three photographs on the table. Anabel gave a small gasp. "My goodness. Where did you find these?"

The three photographs were of Devlin and Anabel at different ruins. The smiling couple stood arm in arm in front of iconic monuments. On the back of the photographs, Devlin had scribbled the dates and locations of each picture. One was taken in 1987 at the Apollo Temple, in Side, Turkey. The next was labeled "Tiwanaku, Bolivia, 1992" and showed the pair next to a tall, red monolith. The last was taken aside a fallen statue in a jungle, and its inscription read, "Zapatera, 2000."

"I found them while I was cleaning out Devlin's things from the Stockbridge house."

"Oh, my! I didn't know he kept any pictures of our trips," said Anabel. "Where were they?"

"I found them in a box in his bedroom closet," Jennifer said.

Anabel smiled. "Not surprising. Devlin wasn't overly sentimental."

"Anlon thought you might want one of them. He said to let you pick."

"That's sweet. Thank you, dear."

"My pleasure," said Jennifer. While Anabel studied the photos, Jennifer continued. "I was wondering if I might ask you some questions about Devlin."

"Oh?"

"Yes, we've restarted his research and there are some things we don't understand. Anlon asked me to see if you could help."

"I'm not sure I can, dear, but I'll try." Anabel refreshed both their glasses with more of the tea.

Jennifer nodded her thanks. "Can you look at these photos? Do you recognize the stone or statues?"

Anabel flipped through the second set of photos slowly, studying each one carefully. When she finished, she said, "No, dear, I'm afraid not. Why?"

"We're trying to figure out where Devlin found them. We can't find any records about them in his files."

"Why? Is it important?"

Pointing at the picture of the black stone, Jennifer said, "Anlon's concerned that no one will take Devlin's discovery seriously if we can't prove where this Stone originated. It's called the *Sinethal*. He thinks other archaeologists will think it's a hoax if we can't show it was found in some temple or ruin, something like that."

Anabel's eyes fluttered and she nodded her head. "Um, yes, they can be like that. Especially if it's something controversial. What did you call the stone, dear?"

"Oh, sorry, I've gotten used to calling them by their Munuorian names. Devlin called it the Master Stone. Does that ring a bell? Did he talk of it?"

Anabel replaced the *Sinethal* picture on the table and lifted the one of the dragon-headed statue. "No, I don't think so. I'm sorry, I'm a little confused. What kind of names?"

"Moon-war-E-uns," enunciated Jennifer. "It's the name of the civilization that made the Stones."

"Oh, that's curious." Anabel's eyes remained focused on the statue. "What's that?"

Anabel shook her head. "Devlin never mentioned names like that."

"Probably because he didn't understand Malinyah," Jennifer said.

Anabel replaced the statue picture on the table and nodded.

Jennifer stacked the pictures and asked, "When Devlin dropped off the map, when he asked you to keep it, did he say anything about the Stones? Anything at all?"

"What? Oh, hmmm . . . let me think . . . No, no, I don't think so. He was very agitated, he was worried about the map. That's all I remember, I'm sorry."

While Anabel spoke, Jennifer sipped more of the pink tea. It seemed strange to her that Devlin would have left such a valuable document with Anabel without providing some kind of explanation. She tried a different tack. "No worries. Speaking of the map, we're having a hard time figuring out how to use it. When you two talked about it, did he say anything about a key? A legend to read it?"

"Hmmm . . . I remember him being very anxious about it, but I don't think we discussed a key."

"Are you sure?" Jennifer asked.

Anabel pulled at her lips and fiddled with her empty glass. "No, I'm certain I'd remember that."

"Oh, well, it was worth a shot."

For the next half hour, Jennifer chatted with Anabel about Devlin and the adventures the couple shared over their long relationship. Then they returned to the garden and Anabel proudly reviewed the wide assortment of flowers. All the while, butterflies large and small zoomed through the air.

Anabel escorted Jennifer to the car and hugged her good-bye. As she was getting into the driver's seat, Jennifer said, "Oh, I forgot my pictures!"

"No problem, dear, I'll go get them," said Anabel.

The woman walked back inside, teetering a little as she mounted the two front steps. A moment later, she returned with the snapshots of the *Sinethal* and statues. The pictures of Devlin and Anabel were not in the stack. Jennifer took the artifact pictures and thanked her through the open car window. "Oh, yeah, did you decide which of Devlin's pictures you wanted to hold on to?" she asked.

"I completely forgot about that. Can I think on it? I promise I'll send back the others," Anabel said.

"Sure, no rush," Jennifer said. "Anlon wanted to hold onto the others for the museum he's planning to build in Devlin's honor, but that's a ways away."

Jennifer watched Anabel wave good-bye through the rearview mirror as she pulled onto the road. Checking the dashboard clock, she realized there was no way she would make it to Pittsfield in time for her meeting with George Grant. At the first stoplight, she picked up her phone to call Grant and reschedule. As she waited for the call to connect, Jennifer thought of the conversation with Anabel and sighed. "Why did she lie?"

10

Find Your Gensae

Incline Village, Nevada
August 12

When Pebbles arrived in the hall, Malinyah was there already, as if she'd been waiting for Pebbles to return. She smiled broadly and opened her arms. They walked to each other and warmly embraced.

Pebbles closed her eyes as Malinyah's arms wrapped around her. The fresh scent of Malinyah's hair was just as Pebbles remembered. She squeezed Malinyah tightly and said, "I've missed you so much."

There was a healing quality in the embrace, one that quickly chased away the emptiness Pebbles felt during the long separation.

"I am happy you've returned, Alynioria," said Malinyah. While she spoke, she stroked Pebbles' hair. "Your spirit is full of light. It fills me with joy."

"It was so hard to be away from you," answered Pebbles. "You can't believe how good it feels to see you again."

Separating from the embrace, Malinyah peered into Pebbles' eyes and nodded. "Come, let's walk outside in the sunshine."

Hand in hand, they left the great hall and descended the marble steps. Outside, the landscape brimmed with color. In the field sloping away from the hall, deep-blue Alynioria flowers rippled in a light wind. Each time the wind ruffled their petals, dozens of golden butterflies drifted up from the flowers and then slowly floated back down.

Beyond the field, the descending terrain continued until it met a beach bordering shimmering, azure waters. On each side of the beach stood tall cliffs capped with patches of bright orange and green foliage.

Malinyah led Pebbles onto a red clay path, just like the one leading to the Seybalrosa shrine. Only, the Seybalrosa tree was nowhere to be seen. And unlike the wet, clammy feeling that her toes experienced before, this time the path was warm and dusty against her feet. The sensation triggered a thought Pebbles hadn't focused on in her earlier visits with Malinyah: she was barefoot.

This caused her to look down as they walked along the path. Then Pebbles realized she wasn't wearing the tank top and Daisy Dukes that adorned her body outside of the vision. Instead, she was clad in a tunic much like Malinyah's. It was cream in color, with piping of dark blue and gold speckles. Sleeveless and knee-length, the tunic tapered from her shoulders to her waist. From there, it hung loosely around her hips and thighs. Pebbles silently wondered, Have I always been dressed like this when I'm with her?

Rather than question the different attire, Pebbles decided to roll with it. It was kind of fun to think of herself as a Munuorian. She squeezed Malinyah's hand and smiled at her friend as they followed the path on its way to the cliff on the left side of the Alynioria field.

Along the cliff's ridge were hosts of windswept trees and stubby bushes. And there were rocks. Lots and lots of rusty-colored rocks. Pebbles halted on the path and let go of Malinyah's hand. She pushed long, golden locks from her vision and gazed out at the vast ocean. Salt air, whipping in the wind, filled her nostrils. Inhaling deeply, she closed her eyes and felt the tunic fluttering against her thighs and chest and the warm sun on her face. The sensations were so real, so vivid.

When she opened her eyes, Malinyah stood in a gap between the rocks and waved for Pebbles to join her. Leaving the path, Pebbles headed toward Malinyah across spongy grass that tickled her toes. As she neared the gap, her attention was drawn to a massive volcano further down the coastline. Barren and black, the volcano was so tall, its peak was shrouded by clouds.

The gap where Malinyah stood turned out to be a landing for a set of precisely carved steps that led down to a wide ledge upon which tables and chairs were set. As they descended the stairs, Pebbles noticed the ledge was not a natural formation. It had been carved into a bowl-shaped veranda. Into its back wall, the Munuorians had embedded a wide variety of seashells. They were unlike any Pebbles had seen. Some had spots, others were striped, but all glittered with vibrant colors.

The veranda held two other interesting features. One was a doorway that led into the cliff. Through this doorway was a long, well-lit tunnel with murals painted on its walls. The other feature was the most unexpected. There were other people seated at tables on the veranda. They were gaily chatting while eating and drinking under the shade provided by the cliff's shadow.

Malinyah guided Pebbles to an open table where they sat side by side. On the table was a glass pitcher filled with pinkish watery fluid. Next to it sat a bowl with fresh-cut fruit. Malinyah poured two glasses and handed one to Pebbles. The glass was heavy and its lip thick. Pebbles thanked Malinyah and asked about the drink.

"It is called *enjyia*. It is nectar from flowers that grow near the slopes of our volcanos, like Tumaera," said Malinyah, pointing to the volcano Pebbles spotted earlier.

Pebbles sniffed the light floral bouquet and asked, "Will I be able to taste it?"

"Drink and see," Malinyah said with a smile.

Raising the glass to her lips, Pebbles sipped the *enjyia*. The fluid's consistency was thin and silky. The flavor was sweet, yet carried an earthy bite. It reminded Pebbles of herbal tea. As she swallowed the *enjyia*, the back of her throat tingled.

"That's so cool," Pebbles said. "I can't believe I can taste your memories of *enjyia*!"

"Wait until you try the fruit. Especially the purple one. That's my favorite," Malinyah replied.

Pebbles sipped more of the *enjyia* and closed her eyes. With her free hand, she stroked the soft tresses draped over her shoulder and listened to the waves roll onto the beach below. How wonderful it must have been coming here on sunny days like this, she thought. It reminded her of lolling on the aft bench of Anlon's boat, curled in a blanket, listening to water lap against the hull. Suddenly, she felt very sleepy.

A voice inside her head—Anlon's voice—said, "Hey, wake up! We need answers!"

Eyes still closed, Pebbles softly sighed. "Aw, do I have to? Can't I just chill a little longer."

"Alynioria?" said Malinyah, jiggling Pebbles' hand.

The sharply spoken name jolted Pebbles awake. It was then she realized her head was resting on the table. Slowly returning to a sitting position, she yawned. "Oops! Guess I have a low *enjyia* tolerance."

Malinyah laughed. "I'm sorry, I thought coming here would relax you, make it easier for us to talk. Maybe the *enjyia* wasn't a good idea."

"No, no. It's honestly perfect. I'm the one who should apologize," said Pebbles as she stifled another yawn. "I guess we should talk. Anlon will be mad at me if I don't come back with some answers."

"Ah, how is your friend? Is he healed?"

"He's not all the way healed yet, but he's getting there. It's so cool you remember him," Pebbles said. "Do you remember meeting Antonio yesterday?"

"If you mean the black man, yes. He didn't say his name. He was too frightened . . . like your friend Anlon."

Pebbles laughed. "Yeah, I think you shock their analytical minds!"

There was a pause while Pebbles gathered her thoughts. There were so many questions to ask, she was overwhelmed. There were questions about the Stones, the map and Devlin. Questions about the Munuorians, about Munirvo and Malinyah herself. Although she knew there was an urgency to learn about the Flash Stone and the map, Pebbles was reluctant to pepper Malinyah about those upfront. So, she started with a simple question, one that Pebbles had often pondered during the long gap since they last spoke.

"Can you tell time?"

"I don't know what you mean," said Malinyah.

"You know, do you notice how much time goes by? Like, can you tell it's been three months since I've visited?"

"Oh, I see. Hmmm . . . It's not an easy question to answer. For my own memories, the ones saved on the *Sinethal*, yes, I can judge the passage of time. But interactions with visitors like you are stored differently."

"Different how?"

"Visitor memories are stored in sequence, but there is nothing that tells me how much time separates each visit, unless in the exchange of thoughts with a visitor, I am told there has been passage of time or I sense a visitor's perception of time.

"Like our visit now, I could tell from your greeting that there was a gap between our visits. You said you missed me. You hugged me tightly. The tone of your voice was wistful. Your mind shared these perceptions and let me know time had passed. I didn't know how much time, only that *you* perceived it as a long time."

"Does that mean when someone's not visiting you, you're not aware of time?"

"That's right. My consciousness is only active when the *Sinethal* is connected with a visitor," Malinyah said.

"Then, do you know how much time has passed since your memories were moved to the *Sinethal*?"

Malinyah picked a wedge of the purple fruit from the bowl and shook her head. A sense of shame washed over Pebbles. Malinyah said, "Don't feel bad, Alynioria. I can sense it's been longer than three months."

The look in Malinyah's eyes belied the frivolous quip.

Pebbles asked, "Would you like to know?"

"Yes."

"Okay. Well, I don't know the exact amount of time, but it's been several thousand years, at least," said Pebbles.

Malinyah's face flushed and she lowered her head. "Thousands of years?"

"I'm sorry. I didn't mean to upset you."

"No, it is good to know the truth. I'm surprised more than I'm upset."

"By what?" asked Pebbles.

"That my *Sinethal* wasn't found earlier. Much earlier," Malinyah said. She paused to consider the implications, then said, "If you are right, though, it means we were not too late. That our captains were successful. That is comforting to know."

The selfless comment awed Pebbles. The Munuorians had risked all to save the rest of the world, and for their efforts, they vanished as a people. She said, "You and your people saved humans from dying out, Malinyah. You helped the world start over again. At least, that's what legends say."

"What happened to my people? Where are they today?" asked Malinyah.

Pebbles meekly said, "They didn't make it. They disappeared."

A ripple of pain passed through Pebbles, but outwardly Malinyah maintained a poised expression. She said, "I feared it would happen, but it's still devastating to hear."

"Why, Malinyah? Why did you fear it would happen?"

"We were too sheltered; we relied too much on our *gensae*. A painful lesson we quickly learned after Munirvo. I hoped we would find a way to recover."

"What's *gensae*?"

"*Gensae*. The gift. The ability to read Terra's mind," Malinyah answered.

The ability to read Terra's mind . . . Is that how the Munuorians viewed their magnetic sense? Pebbles wondered. As a way to read the planet's mind?

"You have *gensae*, Alynioria. Your mind glows with it," declared Malinyah.

Pebbles thought of Anlon's pestering to test her blood. Shaking her head, she said, "No, no way. I can't read anyone's mind, let alone the planet's! You said you relied too much on *gensae*. That you learned that after Munirvo. What did Munirvo do to change things?"

"Take my hands," Malinyah said.

When Pebbles clasped hers in Malinyah's, a new vision appeared. No longer were they seated comfortably enjoying a beautiful day. Instead, they stood in a mucky slime at the cliff's edge. It coated everything in sight. No flowers, no trees, just miles of gray, noxious slime. The sky was yellow-brown and thick with ashy particles. Pebbles shielded her nose and mouth, but not quickly enough to avoid swallowing several burning embers. Through watery eyes, she saw Tumaera gushing torrents of lava into the ocean. No longer azure blue, the sea below bubbled a blackish sludge.

Malinyah released her hands, and Pebbles gasped for air. Coughing to clear the burning sensation from her throat, she downed the *enjyia* left in her glass and poured another. She wiped at her eyes and fought to steady her breathing.

After another glass of *enjyia*, Pebbles finally felt close to normal . . . physically. However, her mind raced as she sought to grapple with the confusing images. They were very different from the images Malinyah showed her beneath the Seybalrosa tree.

"Is that what happened to this beautiful place?"

Malinyah nodded. "Munirvo changed everything. It killed everything. Even the Stones went silent. Our *gensae* was lost."

"At Seybalrosa, your lands were untouched by Munirvo. Well, maybe not untouched, but nothing like what you just showed me," Pebbles said.

"We managed to protect a small area. The rest was destroyed."

"Why didn't you show me that the first time?"

Malinyah bowed her head and sighed. "Had I known several thousand years had passed, I would have shown you the bitter truth. But, when I first met you, I thought you and your friends were survivors. You would have known the worst already."

Pebbles apologized for questions that caused Malinyah to relive unpleasant memories. The Munuorian smiled and thanked her. Pebbles asked her if she wanted to stop their conversation, but Malinyah said she wanted to continue.

"Okay," said Pebbles, "in that case, can we talk about the Stones?"

"Certainly."

"So, the whole reason I met you is because a man named Devlin Wilson found your *Sinethal*. Do you remember Devlin?"

Malinyah said, "Yes, we did not communicate like this, but we were able to share some thoughts back and forth."

"Was he the first person who visited with you?"

"There was one other, one of my own people who came to say farewell. But, yes, Devlin was the first stranger."

"And you thought he was a Munirvo survivor?" Pebbles asked.

"Yes. His curiosity was very strong. Almost too strong," said Malinyah.

"That's Devlin, all right!" said Pebbles. "I only met him a few times before he died, but from all the stories I've heard about him, he was the kind of man who got hold of an idea and didn't let go until his curiosity was satisfied." She paused, then said, "He's the one who rediscovered your civilization."

Pebbles described Devlin's hunt to find proof of the lost Munuorian civilization. She told Malinyah that it all started with Devlin's interest in ancient legends about strange men who came by sea to help survivors of a great flood. The stories interested Devlin because there were so many of them. They were recorded by different civilizations from every corner of the planet and their details were strikingly similar.

Some of the legends carried more details than others, Pebbles explained. Some described fire from the sky, others said the planet flipped over, but all mentioned a great flood that washed over the planet. Pebbles told Malinyah that many of the stories described the awful conditions after the flood and the arrival of strange people by boat. Most often they were described as tall, bearded men, sometimes with reddish hair, sometimes blondish.

Dubbed the "fish men" in some of the legends, the men were viewed as rescuers. They brought food and other supplies. They taught the survivors how to farm, build shelters and hunt. And, per some versions, the fish men carried strange stone tools. Tools that could do things the survivors had never seen. To many of the survivors, the fish men seemed like sorcerers.

"Most people in my time think the stories are made up," Pebbles said. "They call them myths or 'fairy tales.' But Devlin was fascinated by them. He thought the similarities in the legends were too detailed and consistent to be imaginary. So, he decided to look for evidence that would prove the fish men existed."

Malinyah interjected, "Why did people doubt the stories so much?"

"Well, that's the thing. There was a huge gap in time between when your people lived and the oldest sophisticated civilizations we know about. Like three thousand years. Since there was nothing left of your homes, your art or anything that could prove you were ever here, people don't believe it was possible that a sophisticated civilization existed so long ago.

"Our historians call your era 'the Stone Age,' mostly because the only things left are crude stone tools and cave drawings. So, they think *all* humans from that time were primitive, just small groups of people who lived in caves," Pebbles explained.

"But, our *Tyls*? You've found some of them," said Malinyah.

"Yeah, actually a lot of your *Tyls* have survived. They've been found all over the world. Mostly, *Aromaeghs* and *Breyloftes*. The other *Tyls*, not so much. But, no one knows where they came from, and since they've been found in places where more recent civilizations lived, they get lumped in with those peoples' art. That's the craziest thing—everyone thinks the *Tyls* are pieces of art or pottery. They have no idea of their powers."

Malinyah nodded. "There were many primitive people living in our time as your historians believe, but not all were."

"That's what Devlin wanted to prove. He thought the tools described in the legends were too sophisticated to be made by cavemen. Devlin wondered if there might be an advanced 'lost' civilization.

"Anyway, that's what led him to your Stones. I don't remember which Stone he found first, I think it was the *Breylofte*. From what I was told, Devlin was looking at a fish men legend that described the building of a shelter. The legend said one of the builders hummed on a stone and it caused another stone to move through the air. There was a drawing of the legend which showed a man humming on what looked like a bowl.

"So, Devlin went looking for ancient, bowl-like stones that seemed out of place one way or another. He found something very odd. In the pottery of several cultures, he found stone bowls that looked the same—same size, shape and color. He asked other historians about the bowls, but they didn't seem very interested. They were just simple pieces of pottery to them.

"Some museums gave him a few. He took them home and hummed on one of them . . . and he rediscovered the *Breylofte*."

"Very clever," Malinyah said.

"I know, right?" said Pebbles. "Anyway, in the art pieces of those same cultures, Devlin found square tiles that also didn't fit in. Even though the tiles had different etchings and came in different colors, they were all the same shape and size, just like the bowls. And they all had a center notch carved in the back, with two half-circle notches carved in the sides. So, Devlin bought one of them to study.

"From what Anlon told me, some of the fish men legends described survivors learning to farm by looking at tablets provided by the fish men. Again, there was an ancient diagram that showed a man holding a tablet with something sticking out from behind it. Devlin apparently thought the center notch might be made for another stone.

"Then, he noticed the tablet was magnetic. He started thinking some more about the center notch on the back. Did a magnet go in there too? He tried regular magnets, but they didn't attach to the tablet. So, he went looking for a magnetic stone among the art and pottery of different cultures that would fit in the notch."

"And he found a *Naetir*," Malinyah said.

"Exactly. That's when things got really interesting . . . and troubling," Pebbles said.

"In what way?"

"People started dying."

11

The Flash Stone

Incline Village, Nevada
August 12

Anlon checked his watch once again. Pebbles had been lying on the sofa clutching the *Sinethal* for more than an hour. During that time, her facial expressions and body language changed many times. Sometimes it seemed she was elated, other times scared. On one occasion, she coughed gruffly. On another, it looked as though she had fallen asleep. Throughout the session, she mouthed gibberish. Standard fare for a visit with Malinyah.

When the *Naetir* popped off and plunked on the living room floor, Anlon readied a glass of water and waited for Pebbles to open her eyes. Slowly her lids lifted and she greeted Anlon with a big smile.

He smiled back and handed her the water. "You good?"

She propped up on her elbows and sipped the water. She made a funny face and said, "Not nearly as tasty as *enjyia*."

"What?"

"Oh, nothing. You'll see for yourself in a sec," she answered, handing the glass back to Anlon.

"Huh?"

Pebbles picked up the *Naetir* from the floor, handed it to Anlon and then held out the *Sinethal* with her other hand. "Go ahead, she's expecting you."

Anlon looked at the *Sinethal* skeptically, remembering his one and only experience meeting Malinyah. To say he freaked out would be an understatement. "Hmmm," he said. "I'm not sure I'm ready for this yet."

"Oh, it'll be fun! Just relax and take in the view. It's gorgeous. She'll offer you a drink; try it. It tastes pretty good," said Pebbles.

"But, I can't communicate with her," Anlon said.

"I know, you don't have *gensae*!"

"What's that?"

"Apparently, you were right. I do have a magnetic personality," cracked Pebbles. "But, don't sweat it. Just admire the view and try the drink. You won't have to say anything. But, if you want to say something, say *kaeto*. It means 'thank you.'"

"Kay-toe?"

"Yep, you got it," Pebbles said. "Oh, I asked her to show you how the Flash Stone works, what it can do. Remember to call it *Tuliskaera*. When you're ready, hold out both hands and she'll take them. Just let go when you've seen enough."

He sat unmoved.

"Come on, A.C. I promise, it'll be fun. Make sure to check out the volcano. Oh, and look behind the table at the seashell collection in the wall. They're so colorful!" Pebbles beamed.

"Okay, I'll give it a try. But, first, how did it go? Did you learn anything?"

"Oh, my gosh, it was *way* better than I expected. That's why I want to share it with you. And yes, learned lots. We'll talk afterward. Now, quit stalling and fire it up!"

Anlon reclined in an armchair, took a deep breath and lowered the *Naetir* . . .

The first sensation to hit Anlon was the sound of waves. Then, he felt thick, humid air against his skin. His eyesight faded in slowly, but from the blurred colors at the outset of the *Sinethal* vision he could tell he was seaside. Around him, he heard conversation and laughing. A cool breeze ruffled his hair.

When his eyes cleared, he found himself standing on a rocky ledge overlooking the ocean. White birds circled overhead, and Anlon could see ships on the horizon. He teetered slightly, feeling too close to the edge. An arm reached out and steadied him. He turned to see Malinyah smiling at him.

Although he did flinch when she touched him, this time Anlon didn't scream like a little girl. Feeling a sense of accomplishment, he smiled back and said, "*Kaeto*, Malinyah."

She applauded his first words of Munuorian and gave him a hug. To say it was a weird feeling when her body pressed against his didn't do the sensation justice in Anlon's mind. The floral scent of her hair was so light, it seemed barely detectible, but he could still smell it. He reached to return her hug and could feel the thin fabric of her tunic on his fingertips. It was soft and smooth, almost silky. The details of the experience were so vivid, down to the small black flecks dotting the bright blue of her eyes.

They separated and she pointed to an empty chair. Anlon was about to sit when he noticed the wall of seashells Pebbles had mentioned. From where he stood they looked as if they'd been painted. Holding up a hand, Anlon deferred sitting and paced toward the wall.

The voices he heard when the vision began belonged to other people sitting at other tables on the cliff-side lounge. None of them seemed to notice Anlon, which was just as well. If they interacted with him, Anlon could only smile and bow like some kind of foreign tourist.

When he got up close to the wall, his opinion of the shells changed. Still colorful, there was no paint involved in their appearance. The colors, stripes, swirls and polka dots were all natural features. Some of the patterns Anlon recognized from his study of marine biology, but others were completely unknown to him. He reached out and touched the surface of a few. It amazed him to feel their texture.

When he returned to the table, Malinyah offered him a drink, saying, "*Enjyia*."

Anlon, feeling a tad more relaxed, raised the glass and added a second word to his Munuorian vocabulary: "*Kaeto. Enjyia*."

He raised the glass to his nose and sniffed the pink-hued, watery drink. It had the same floral scent as Anlon had noticed in her hair. He took a sip and swished the slick fluid in his mouth. There was a gritty bite to it, similar to the greens powder he mixed in with his morning orange juice. But the *enjyia*'s bite was far subtler. As he swallowed it, he noticed a sweet aftertaste followed by a tingling in his throat.

Anlon bowed slightly and said *kaeto* again. Suddenly, he felt like the foreign tourist he imagined moments before. Malinyah motioned for him to sit. He nodded his head and lowered onto the chair. Looking out at the vista, Anlon's eyes and mind flitted in every direction, trying to take in as much as possible.

Ahead, Anlon's attention was again drawn to the ships. There were three of them, and in the brief time Anlon had been on the ledge they'd already closed in on the shoreline.

The ships were unlike any Anlon had previously encountered. They were streamlined, almost dolphin-like in their shape. From a rounded nose at the bow, the hulls on each ship swelled outward to form bulbous curves that tapered sharply as they neared the stern. Most conspicuous, there were no sails or masts. In fact, there appeared to be no structures above the deck at all. Nor were there any visible oars. Watching the craft cut effortlessly through the water, Anlon wondered what propelled them.

To his left, he saw the volcano Pebbles had mentioned. The pitch of its slopes was steeper than any Anlon had seen in pictures or in person. Its peak hovered above a thin band of clouds, making it look like it floated in thin air.

To his right, Anlon spied another volcano. This one was shaped more like a mound. It was much shorter than the other volcano but had an elongated base. Brightly colored foliage grew along its slopes.

Returning his gaze to Malinyah, Anlon pointed at his chest and said, "Anlon." Pointing to her, he repeated her name. Then he pointed toward the steep volcano with an expectant look. Malinyah nodded her understanding and said, "Tumaera."

He gestured to the mound-shaped volcano, and she replied, "Artosae."

Anlon was thrilled to realize his Munuorian vocabulary had expanded another one hundred percent. He felt a strong temptation to sit back and enjoy the view, but his curiosity wouldn't allow the notion to take hold. Retrieving the *enjyia*, he took another drink and studied the mixture more closely.

It was definitely plant-based, but it wasn't fruity. Given its watery appearance, Anlon guessed it to be something steeped, like tea, or something juiced, like lemonade. A thought crossed his mind. He reached for the pitcher. It was coated in condensation. With his finger, he drew the *Sinethal*'s etched leaf symbol, the symbol for the Seed Stone, as Devlin had named it. He turned the pitcher for Malinyah to see his drawing.

She smiled and nodded. She held out an open palm and circled a fist against it. She pointed back at Anlon's design. "*Terusael.*"

As Anlon guessed, *enjyia* was the life-extending drink made possible by the *Terusael*, the Seed Stone. He presumed her hand gestures symbolized how the Stone was used. Extending both hands, Malinyah encouraged Anlon to reach out his as well.

When she gripped his hands, a new vision appeared. Malinyah stood at a counter. On the counter was a potted plant. Next to it was a pile of small seeds. Aside the pile of seeds was a *Breylofte*. Next to that, a small egg-shaped Stone. Malinyah pointed from the plant to the seeds. She pinched some of the seeds and dropped them in the bowl of the *Breylofte*. She pointed at the egg-shaped stone and said, "*Terusael.*"

Malinyah lifted the *Terusael* and slowly circled inside the bowl of the *Breylofte*. Anlon could hear the faint scratching of the friction between the two Stones. At that point, two things happened: the *Terusael* began to glow and a soft whine echoed from the *Breylofte*. She never altered the rhythm of her circles, but the *Breylofte*'s whine picked up in intensity the longer Malinyah stroked it with the *Terusael*. The inside of the bowl began to glow as well. Malinyah ceased circling and tapped the pulsating *Terusael* against the inner surface of the bowl. Small sparks leapt out. She did this several times and then returned to circling the egg-shaped stone inside the bowl. Malinyah repeated this cycle a half dozen times before ceasing the demonstration.

The two Stones, seated side by side on the counter, turned pale orange as their glows subsided. When they'd returned to their original colors, Malinyah poured out the seeds from inside the *Breylofte*. They had been blackish before, but now were a light brown. She planted the altered seeds in a new pot.

The vision switched to a fully grown, flowering plant. Malinyah picked its blossoms and crushed them in an ordinary bowl. Soon, a pinkish juice formed among the pulverized petals. She poured the juice into a pitcher of water and stirred. *Enjyia*.

Anlon pondered the demonstration. It appeared Malinyah stimulated the seeds with a combination of magnetically charged sound waves and small electrical shocks. He was most impressed by how precisely, and yet gently, Malinyah had manipulated both forces. It was a good reminder that no matter how powerful the Stones might be, it took a practiced hand to wield them.

He released Malinyah's hands and the vision returned to the cliff ledge. He thanked her for the demonstration and sampled more of the *enjyia*. It was probably an illusion, but Anlon felt a little woozy, almost sleepy. He yawned and lowered the glass.

Malinyah extended her hands again and asked, "*Tuliskaera?*"

Stifling another yawn, Anlon nodded.

When the new vision began, Anlon and Malinyah stood at the base of Tumaera. Anlon stared up at its near vertical walls. With his head bent all the way back, he said, "Looks like something from Dr. Seuss."

Looking around, Anlon saw a variety of flora around the volcano's base. They were all popping with rich colors — red, green, orange and even some blue. Among them, Anlon noticed a plant with the flowers Malinyah had pulverized into *enjyia*.

Malinyah called to Anlon. In her hands, she held two Stones. One he recognized as a *Naetir*. The other was a marbled, gray-green, cone-shaped rock. The Flash Stone.

"*Tuliskaera*," said Malinyah, holding forth the cone-shaped device.

Anlon received it and was surprised by its weight. Unlike the feathery-light *Naetir*, the *Tuliskaera* was dense.

About the length of an average bottle of water, the Stone was about five inches thick at the base of the cone. Surprisingly, however, the Stone was not bottom heavy. In fact, it felt perfectly weighted midway up the cone, which seemed impossible for a natural stone. Anlon examined the *Tuliskaera*'s tip with his index finger. There was no hole leading into the Stone, nor was there any seam at either end or along its side.

The most stunning feature was an etched snake coiled around the body of the Stone. The green snake's open mouth was poised to strike. Anlon wondered about the design's significance. He looked toward Malinyah and pointed at the snake. She made an angry face with teeth bared and raised two fingers like prongs. She bit down and hissed. An interesting analogy, thought Anlon.

Malinyah reached for the *Tuliskaera* and then motioned for Anlon to follow her to a field of lava rocks at least twenty feet tall. When they stood about fifty feet away, Malinyah gestured for Anlon to stand back.

Malinyah moved the *Naetir* close to the base of the *Tuliskaera*. Unlike the *Sinethal*, the *Naetir* didn't clamp onto the underside of the cone. She touched it gently against the *Tuliskaera* and circled in a motion similar to her earlier demonstration of the *Terusael*.

After a few minutes, she lifted the *Naetir* to show Anlon the underside of the *Tuliskaera*. He noticed a small circle in the middle of the cone's base was glowing. Malinyah reapplied the *Naetir* and continued to circle it against the bottom of the *Tuliskaera*.

When the snake began to glow, Malinyah ceased scraping. She turned and looked briefly at Anlon, then focused her attention on the lava wall. She slammed the two Stones together and a bolt of lightning shot forth from the *Tuliskaera*'s tip. The bolt sizzled into the wall of lava, turning the spot it first struck into a molten rivulet.

Malinyah slowly moved the beam upward, across, down and back to her starting position. The beam hissed and crackled as it cut into the rock. In one quick motion, Malinyah pulled the *Naetir* away. The rectangular shape she had etched into the lava glowed, while streams of molten rock slid down its surface.

She paused, looked back at Anlon and then once again directed her gaze at the lava rocks. This time, her movement was swift and violent. She slammed the two Stones together and made a slashing motion with the melded Stones. The lightning bolt leapt toward the top of the wall and cleaved a huge chunk free from its spot. A car-sized boulder tumbled down and crashed on the ground. As soon as it landed, Malinyah slashed again and carved the boulder in two pieces as easy as a knife through paper.

Anlon thought of Pacal's description of the *Tuliskaera*: "It's a weapon. It makes this Sound Stone look like a twig."

Malinyah approached one of the cleaved halves. It still smoked along its carved face. She stood a few feet away and tilted the hockey-puck-shaped *Naetir* on its side. She tapped it against the base of the *Tuliskaera* instead of slamming them together. A beam of lower intensity shot toward the rock. The beam didn't waver and crackle like lightning; it was steady like a laser. With a surgical touch, Malinyah shaped the top half into a sphere.

When Anlon let go of the *Sinethal*, Pebbles was standing by with a glass of water at the ready. She helped him into a sitting position and said, "Didn't I tell you? Was that cool or what?"

After a couple of generous gulps, Anlon smiled. "*Kaeto.*"

"*Aegan*," replied Pebbles, invoking the Munuorian's equivalent of "you're welcome."

"Remember how I was saying archaeologists would want more proof than Malinyah's word?" Anlon said. "Um, I retract that statement. Wow!"

"What did you think of *enjyia*?"

"It made me sleepy, but I liked the taste," said Anlon.

"Oh, my gosh. I literally fell asleep on the table for a little bit. Malinyah had to wake me!" Pebbles said. "What did you think of the view from the cliff?"

"Stunning, no other words needed."

"And the volcano?"

"Which one, Tumaera or Artosae?"

"There were two? I only saw Tumaera," said Pebbles. "Did you see the seashells?"

"I did. I touched them. Such amazing detail in Malinyah's memories." Anlon thought of his earlier Neil Armstrong analogy and shuddered to imagine experiencing the first walk on the Moon in the same level of detail.

"Did you see the *Tuliskaera*?" Pebbles asked.

"Yep, held it in my hand. It's heavy," said Anlon. "How about the glowing snake?"

Pebbles hissed and crooked two fingers. Anlon said, "Hey, she did that for me, too!"

They exchanged stories for several more minutes. Anlon told Pebbles about viewing the *Terusael* demonstration. Pebbles shared the *gensae* conversation in return. He talked of the ships; she told him of Malinyah's stark post-Munirvo vision.

"I wish I'd seen that," Anlon said. "So, Malinyah said they lost their magnetic abilities after Munirvo?"

"Well, that was my interpretation, but she didn't say it like that. She said they lost the ability to read Terra's mind."

Anlon nodded. "I think I'd interpret that the same way as you. It makes sense, really. I imagine the world turning upside down would alter the magnetic field."

"She was very open. She said they relied on their *gensae* too much," Pebbles said. "She said that made it harder to cope after Munirvo, that they were kind of screwed trying to survive on what was left of Munuoria."

"Did you ask her about the map?" Anlon asked.

"No, not yet."

"How about the dragon-head statue?"

"Nope. We were kind of reconnecting more than anything else," Pebbles said. "I can go back and ask right now, if you want."

"It would be helpful to get answers sooner rather than later, if you don't mind. At least we don't need to ask about the other statue. Pretty clear it depicts the *Tuliskaera* in use."

"Any other questions you want me to ask?"

Anlon thought about it and said, "Yeah, while you're at it, I've got two more for you. Ask her if she knows where her *Sinethal* was kept. Who knows, she might give us a clue that will help figure out where Devlin found it."

"Okay. What's the other question?"

"Ask her about Cassiopeia. Ask her if it was visible year-round."

"Really? You're fascinated with Cassiopeia, aren't you?"

"Just ask her, please. I'm interested to know whether it was always visible, or if there were times during the year when they couldn't see it. If it wasn't always visible, it would be great to know how many days a year they couldn't see it."

"Is this another memory test?"

Anlon smiled. "For Malinyah, not you."

Pebbles reengaged the *Sinethal* and greeted Malinyah in the marble hall. Together, they walked outside by the wading pool and sat at its edge. Pebbles dangled her feet in the water. Looking down, she again noticed she wore a tunic. She smiled. She could actually feel the tepid water between her toes.

"So, Anlon has some more questions," started Pebbles.

"If it gives us a chance to talk, Alynioria, I'm always pleased to be with you," Malinyah said.

A warm rush passed through Pebbles. She blushed. "That's sweet. I feel the same way."

Malinyah waited for Pebbles' question and swirled her own toes in the pool. Pebbles said, "Let's get the easy ones out of the way first. Anlon's interested in Breylif. The constellation, not the butterflies.

He asked me if you could see it all the time or if there were times you couldn't see it."

"What an interesting question. Why does he want to know?"

"I have no idea. Every time I ask, he just grins at me."

There was a pause as Malinyah contemplated an answer. During the pause, Pebbles lightly splashed the water with her feet. Then she noticed something odd. The broken chain tattoo that graced her ankle wasn't there. She lifted her wrists and saw the huddled angel and Trinity knot were gone as well. As were the scars beneath them.

Malinyah said, "We could see it most of the year."

The answer stirred Pebbles' attention. "Huh? Oh. Right. Um, I know this seems like a ridiculous question, but do you know how many days a year you couldn't see it?"

"Why?"

"Anlon . . . what can I say? He's geeky."

"Geeky?"

"Oh, sorry. Just an expression. He's a scientist; he likes to 'know' things."

"Let me see. I would say a little more than a month each year."

"Okay, great. Thanks. Next question, do you know what happened to your *Sinethal* after you died? Where it was stored?"

Malinyah bristled. "Why?"

"Um, we're trying to figure out where Devlin found it. Anlon thought he might have found it wherever it was kept after you died," Pebbles said.

Malinyah pulled her feet from the water and abruptly stood. "I don't know."

"Is everything okay?" Pebbles asked. Goose bumps dotted her arms and legs. "If I upset you, I'm sorry."

There was no answer from Malinyah. She just stood staring off toward the field of Alynioria flowers. Pebbles asked, "Should I stop asking questions?"

"It's all right, Alynioria," Malinyah said. "Please continue."

"Are you sure? You look angry." Pebbles reached out a hand toward Malinyah, but the Munuorian Andaer paid no heed.

"I'm not angry, I just don't know the answer to your question."

"Okay, well, I won't ask that one again. Promise." Pebbles smiled.

There was no response from Malinyah. She remained standing, arms folded, looking away. Pebbles briefly considered ending the *Sinethal* session, but she knew Anlon really wanted answers about the map and statue.

"Devlin had this statue," she began. "It looks like a man with the head of a lizard or a dragon. The man is holding a sword in one hand. The dragon's face looks angry.

"When Devlin went looking for more of the *Lifintyls* using the map you showed him, he drew a picture of the statue in his notes. We can't figure out why. Do you know anything about a half-dragon, half-man statue?"

A curious Malinyah finally turned toward Pebbles. "A statue? No." Malinyah paused for a moment and then added, "And we didn't use swords to defend ourselves, we used the *Tyls*. There were foreign tribes that used swords, but not Munuorians."

"Oh, yeah, I guess we should have thought of that. It's just, it has the *Sulataer* symbol on the back of the dragon's head. So, we thought it had something—"

"I told you! I don't know anything about a statue," Malinyah growled.

Session over.

12

Jungle Fever

Rio Teodoro (Roosevelt River)
Amazon Rainforest, Brazil
August 14

How much farther?" panted Navarro.

Up ahead, Margaret wiggled through a narrow gap in the thick underbrush, unconcerned by her companion's entreaty. She craned her head below a drooping branch and listened for rushing water amid the chatter of birds in the trees above. Though it was faint, a definite trickle could be heard in the distance.

Leaning over to catch his breath, Navarro's shiny, black ponytail slid over his shoulder and dangled by his face. Again, he cried out to Margaret. Again, she ignored him.

Over the past two days, Navarro had done nothing but whine. If it wasn't the slippery terrain, it was the humidity or the bugs. When nature's discomforts didn't top his bitch list, he railed about her failures in Stockbridge and her perceived general incompetence. On more than one occasion she considered hauling out the *Breylofte* to fling him atop a kapok tree, but she'd managed to suppress the urge. Foucault was paying her to keep tabs on Navarro, not kill him. The longer they trekked, however, the more she craved to silence the fop.

Why Navarro insisted on tagging along was beyond Margaret. This kind of excursion was definitely not in his wheelhouse. The man lived in a mountainside castle with a staff of twenty, for heaven's sakes! Anytime he traveled, at least three assistants handled his every need, and he almost always was accompanied by two brutish bodyguards. "Roughing it" wasn't exactly his style.

For this reason, Margaret resisted his late demand to join the search team, but Navarro declared the request nonnegotiable. He was funding the expedition, including the party's fees, and he wanted to keep a close eye on his "investment."

"You'll slow us down," Margaret had argued. "There'll be snakes, spiders and God knows what else," she added, but to no avail. He had puffed out his scrawny chest and announced the decision was final. Margaret chirped back, "Won't be any Armani boutiques or cafés . . ."

It was a needless thing to say, but watching his near-orange tan morph to purple was worth the tirade that followed.

Truth be told, Margaret's resistance to his majesty's participation went well beyond inconvenience. When Navarro introduced Drummond and his troupe after arriving in Manaus, she had assumed they'd all go together. But Navarro claimed a large expedition would be noticed by the swarm of prospectors residing in Apuí, their proposed jumping-off point.

Stating he wanted a minimum of prying eyes following their path, Navarro announced the group would split into two teams and follow two different paths to the proposed search area. It seemed paranoid to Margaret, and the feeling was reinforced when Navarro tabbed her to join his team. He said he wanted her and the Sound Stone close to him — a sentiment she didn't understand at the time.

Then there was his choice of site to search. Margaret freely acknowledged she didn't know how to read the map, but she was convinced the coordinates Navarro had selected were too far inland and she'd told him so. But per usual, her opinion was ignored.

It was her own fault, really. Their alliance, once strong, was now beyond shaky. She'd been sloppy in Stockbridge, reckless even, and it had cost them both dearly. So, she acquiesced to his site choice, fully aware that if they failed to find a stash of Stones, Navarro would point the finger at her and not Drummond.

Navarro's voice rang out again. "Wait up! You're going too fast!"

Turning to look back, Margaret did her best to hide a smile. Navarro staggered through the tree gap, nearly falling over from the weight of his pack. Then he tripped on a slick root and tumbled to the ground with a splash. He frantically rocked on the ground like a turtle on its back. When he finally flipped himself over, he blurted several expletives in a bizarre mix of Portuguese and German. Stumbling to his feet, he vainly wiped at the slimy mud coating his shorts and spat, "Do you have *any* idea where we're headed?"

She rolled her eyes and unclipped the GPS tracker from her belt. Foisting the device's screen toward Navarro's dripping face, she asked, "You see the red dot?"

"Yes, yes. You've shown me a dozen times already," he snorted, waving his goo-covered hand dismissively.

"Then why keep asking?" Margaret asked as she reattached the tracker.

"Because it makes no sense!" Navarro said. "We've already passed the ruins! Drummond is probably already there. We will be late!"

Margaret reached into a pocket of her hiking vest and withdrew a scrunched-up bandana. Dabbing her forehead, she said, "We can always swim across the river here if you want."

"Ha!" Navarro scoffed. "Not a chance!"

With a smile, Margaret said, "Thought so."

The Argentinian's face trembled. Margaret yawned and unfurled the red neckerchief. He clenched both fists and glared at her through twitching eyes. Smoothing the wrinkled fabric against her thigh, she glanced up at him and thought, God, he really does look like a weasel!

As Navarro edged toward liftoff, Margaret hoped the rat-bastard would at least toss in a fresh, colorful dig instead of resorting to his usual trilingual "bitch whore" shtick.

During his profane tantrum, Margaret calmly rolled the bandana into a long band and tied it around her neck. When Navarro paused to wipe away spittle from his chin, Margaret said, "It'll be dark soon. We need to keep moving."

Navarro quivered with rage. "Where are you going? I'm not fin—"

"Rehashing this now is useless," Margaret called over her shoulder. "Besides, it's your own damn fault it's taking this long."

Navarro hurled another vile insult and again demanded she halt.

Margaret disappeared into a grove of trees and yelled back, "Shhh! You'll wake the Cinta-Larga!"

The gibe was met with instant silence.

Margaret mumbled, "*Touché!*"

Ah, yes, the Cinta-Larga. She was still furious Navarro waited until the last second before revealing the possibility of meeting the dangerous tribesmen on their own turf. She should have suspected something fishy when he insisted they begin their trek on the east side of the Roosevelt River, while Drummond's group jumped off on the west side.

"Look," Margaret had argued, "this isn't going to be easy, even if we start on the right side of the river, so why complicate it? Let's just stagger our start and follow the same path as Drummond."

Navarro had refused, saying he expected they'd find a shallow place to slop across when they neared their destination. Margaret had ridiculed the notion and warned him there was little chance of an easy crossing point anywhere along the river's four-hundred-mile length. But Navarro valiantly declared he'd wade across if necessary. When she reminded him that piranhas and caimans inhabited the river, Navarro's bravado had quickly fizzled.

Before hopping the rickety charter flight in Manaus to head for Apuí, Margaret had tried another approach. She had lobbied to rent an inflatable raft from a local fishing lodge. But Navarro was unwilling to heft more gear through miles of dense jungle.

Margaret had said, "Fine, let's charter a fishing boat and a couple locals. It'll be much faster, and you won't have to lug anything through the jungle."

Idea rejected. Navarro had seemed suspicious of everyone's motives but his own, and he again stated he wanted no prying eyes or curious minds following their trail.

The night before they started out, she had pushed one last time to begin their journey on the river's west side. He vehemently dismissed the notion. When pressed for a reason, he had said only, "The Cinta-Larga. They don't like miners."

"Huh? Who?" Margaret had asked.

Navarro wouldn't elaborate at first, but Margaret persisted. The Cinta-Larga, he had finally explained, were known to inhabit parts of the rainforest south and west of the river. The reclusive tribe was notoriously hostile toward outsiders, especially prospectors.

"Where we are headed is rich in diamond deposits. The Cinta-Larga consider the land and the diamonds their own," Navarro had said.

For more than fifty years, he had clarified, the Cinta-Larga had battled with "trespassing" miners—including several fatal run-ins with local prospectors contracted by Navarro.

"I intend to steer clear of them as long as possible," he had said.

"Does Drummond know?"

"He is a professional, it's his business to know. There was no need to tell him."

Those words echoed in Margaret's mind as she snaked through another narrow cut in the thick underbrush. When he first uttered them, she wondered if Navarro was using Drummond as bait to lure the Cinta-Larga. It seemed to fit his devious M.O.

She knew Navarro's insatiable desire for rare and shiny objects led him to lie, steal and kill as necessary. He might consider himself a re-fined businessman, a miner and "exporter," but to Margaret he was nothing more than a petty smuggler. Yet, he paid well, so she had swallowed her anger and agreed to start on the east side. Besides, the real money would come from Foucault, and that would only happen if she was with Navarro when he found a Maerlif.

Their initial path led southward along the riverbank, but it wasn't long before the soupy shoreline terrain forced them to shift course inland. Every so often, they curled back toward the river in search of a manageable place to cross. Finding no such place, they mean-dered farther south, past their intended destination and closer to the Cinta-Larga.

Twice a day at predetermined intervals, Navarro went off alone to the riverbank in search of an unobstructed satellite signal to call Drummond for a progress update on his side of the river. Thus far, he was fifty-fifty connecting with the Scotsman.

As they neared the heart of Cinta-Larga territory, Margaret was comforted by the weight of the *Breylofte* bumping against her hip. Nestled in a small pack fastened around her waist, the ancient Stone was within easy reach. In a sudden onset, she might not get off a quick enough blast to kill, but she'd surely scare the hell out of the natives!

Navarro, on the other hand, had turned jumpy. Hanging from his belt was a machete-like knife. Early in the expedition, he occasionally unsheathed it to comically hack at hanging vines in his way. Now, Margaret noticed, he gripped it constantly. Watching him brandish the weapon as if expecting imminent attack, Margaret wondered whether Navarro could wield it in self-defense without mortally wounding himself.

Margaret's musings were cut short by a booming crack of thunder. She turned and strained to spy Navarro's slight figure trailing behind. If not for swaying branches disturbed by his hulking backpack, she may not have picked him out against the darkening backdrop. She called back to him. "Thunder sounds close. Let's stop and set up camp before it cuts loose."

He replied with a faint "hallelujah" and wobbled in her direction.

By the time he reached her, Margaret had already tied a tarp to surrounding trees, creating a lean-to. Beneath the makeshift shelter, Navarro hastily unpacked his pup tent and grumbled once more about Margaret's tracking skills.

They had barely finished erecting their tents before the deluge commenced. Curling into her tent to wait out the downpour, Margaret unzipped the waist pack and slid out the *Breylofte*. Lying back, she caressed the smooth curves of the woofer-shaped stone and imagined how easy it would be to step outside, place the Stone to her lips and send Navarro and his tent airborne. An evil smile crossed her face. "That's one way to get his pansy-ass across the river!"

The rain seemed to go on forever, pounding the tarp until it seemed to sizzle. Margaret closed her eyes and tried to relax, but her mind kept drifting to Navarro's questionable reading of the Waterland Map.

She rested the *Breylofte* against her chest and wondered why the

Munuorians would hide their Stones a thousand miles deep in the Amazon. It also puzzled her why Foucault didn't seem to share her surprise. When she called him to relay the coordinates, Margaret held on the line while he punched the numbers into an online mapping app. When he rejoined the call, there was a hint of admiration in Foucault's voice. What did they know that she didn't?

With these thoughts spinning in her mind, she drifted off to sleep.

When Margaret awoke, the storm had passed. She emerged from her tent and went in search of kindling amid the wet jungle floor. Soon after she stoked a fire to life, Navarro popped out of his tent in dry clothes and a much-improved disposition. He even briefly smiled at her while warming his hands over the fire.

"I've been thinking. We are wasting too much time. I'm going to call the lodge and have them send a boat for us. They can take us back upstream and we can cross close to the ruins," Navarro said.

Geez, why didn't I think of that? she silently mocked. Pointing up at the dense canopy above, she said, "Good luck getting a signal."

Ignoring her pessimism, he said, "It's almost time to talk with Drummond anyway. I'll go to the riverbank. Give me the tracker so I can find my way back." Margaret handed it over and Navarro marched out.

He was gone for more than an hour, far longer than his earlier sojourns to the river. When he returned, Margaret sat by the fire munching on trail mix. He said nothing as he approached, but the look in his eyes signaled the return of his bad mood. Soon the flood of complaints would gush forth.

"No luck?" she asked.

"Bah! Drummond's found the site! And the lodge can't have someone here until the morning," he said. "We can do nothing until then."

Margaret pondered suggesting they pack up and try swimming across but thought better of it. Navarro's head might pop off. Instead she said, "Well, at least we won't have to get any closer to the Cinta-Larga."

The comment drew a sullen sneer. Then, without another word, Navarro disappeared into his tent. Once he was asleep, Margaret thought of sneaking in to borrow the satellite phone. She was sure

Foucault would want to know Navarro's man had found the Maerlif. But it was too risky. She had to hope for a better chance tomorrow.

Seeing no point in lingering by the fire, Margaret retired to her tent and lolled toward sleep. As she drifted off, she remembered Foucault's parting words: "Under no circumstances allow Navarro to leave with a *Tuliskaera*. Use whatever means necessary."

She hadn't said it to Foucault, but once the connection terminated, Margaret had mumbled, "With pleasure."

Two hours later Margaret was awoken by a ruckus outside the tent. She could hear stomping feet and grunts. Above the commotion, she heard Navarro meekly call out, "Margaret! Margaret! The Cinta-Larga! The Cinta-Larga!"

She shook her head to clear the cobwebs and bolted into action. She snatched the *Breylofte* from the waist pouch and raised into a crouch. Quickly, she unzipped the tent and duckwalked through the small opening. Once through, she popped up with the *Breylofte* poised to attack. It was pitch dark; the fire had extinguished long ago. She blinked to adjust her eyes while wheeling around to locate the intruders.

All was suddenly quiet. It was then she realized Navarro's tent was unzipped. Damn! she thought. Did they get him? Unsure whether to call out or not, she spun around once more but could see nothing in or around the surrounding foliage.

Margaret risked a terse whisper. "Navarro!"

There was no response.

"F——!" she spat in a hushed voice.

Something plunked onto the leafy floor beyond the tents. Her head snapped in the direction of the sound and she raised the *Breylofte* to her mouth. So intense was her focus, Margaret was totally unaware of the figure lurking two feet behind her.

The point of the long blade sliced through her back and out through her abdomen in a violent thrust. Margaret staggered forward under the force of the blow. Shocked by the surreal sensation, she dropped the Stone and reached for the searing pain. The figure stepped forward and tugged her back against the blade. An involuntary gasp escaped her mouth as the blade's leading edge pushed further out from her abdomen.

Wild-eyed, Margaret flailed against the attacker's grip and cried out for Navarro. A blow met the back of her head and she slumped forward. As she fell to the ground, the blade slid from within her body.

Instinctively, she covered her hands over the wet gash beneath her ribs while she tried to regain her feet. The only thought racing through her mind was, Run! Run!

Margaret scrambled only a few steps before the attacker grabbed her hair and yanked her head back. Without a word, the blade slashed across her throat. Rabid with fear, Margaret cried for mercy. The appeal was met with a swift kick in the ribs and another to the head. She collapsed in a heap and hovered near unconsciousness.

Aware only of sounds, Margaret heard rustling in the foliage around her. Then she felt hands patting her body and tugging at the empty waist pack. The gashes to her throat and torso burned with pain. She curled into a fetal position and tried to clear her milky eyes. Though she was unable to focus, she could sense the sudden change in light. Before her, an orange glow erupted, followed by crackles and hisses. Soon, the orange glow was all around her.

Through the brain fog came a rush of adrenaline, urged forth by the smell of smoke. Rolling onto her side, Margaret's eyes cleared long enough to see a slim figure sashaying away, ponytail bobbing happily as it disappeared beyond the reach of the inferno.

In her fading moments of consciousness, Margaret made a feeble effort to crawl away from the fire. As she did, her hand bumped against a smooth rock beneath the leaves. Fumbling frantically, she caught the edge of the stone and pulled it free from cover.

Too weak to give chase and gasping from the smoke, Margaret fell onto her back and closed her eyes. In the palm of her bloodied hand, she gripped the *Breylofte*.

The boat zoomed upriver, churning the dark water as it sped along. Navarro, standing near the bow, squinted ahead in the darkness.

Turning to the young Brazilian piloting the craft, Navarro asked, "How much further?"

The man held up two fingers. Navarro wasn't sure if he meant two miles or two minutes, but either way, they were close. Darting a look down, Navarro observed their progress on the GPS device. The site wasn't far from the river. Less than a mile, he reckoned.

Still pumped up on adrenaline, Navarro felt the sweat drip from his face and his hands shook. As he relived the feel of the machete slicing through the little bitch, he inhaled deeply and smiled. Margaret never suspected the setup.

She had been a decent insurance policy in the event they stumbled across the Cinta-Larga, but once Drummond found the cache site, her services were no longer required. Now, all that was left was to find the Flash Stone. He closed his eyes and pictured his grandfather strutting around the copper mine, imaginary fireworks leaping from the rocks.

Earlier, during Navarro's brief call with Drummond, the Scottish cowboy described the discovery. They had arrived at the ruin around midday. There, Drummond and the small band of support crew slashed the vines and other foliage obscuring the decrepit outer walls of a half-buried ancient structure.

Once the undergrowth was cleared, Drummond completed a sweep with the magnetometer. He told Navarro he had found the strange, pulsing kimberlite signal. After zeroing in on the area exhibiting the strongest reading, Drummond had employed a ground-penetrating radar. It hadn't taken long to find a sizeable cavity. Based on the readings, the cavity was not a natural formation. The depth of the image was too uniform and its shape too well defined. Navarro had been ecstatic at the news, and he congratulated Drummond.

Navarro had asked if a doorway existed. According to Drummond, most of the ruin was buried under a thick mound of rocky soil, vines and other foliage. Only a section of outer wall was visible. They could dig the mound away to find an entrance, he said, but it would take considerable time to accomplish—an idea Navarro rejected.

Now, as the boat throttled back and steered toward shore, Navarro saw a small gathering of other boats along the riverbank. A man along the riverbank signaled to Navarro's pilot with the aid of two flashlights. The pilot whistled back and maneuvered the starboard side parallel with the bank.

As they bumped against the bank, Navarro ducked to avoid low-hanging branches. Several of them hit against his shoulders anyway, their leaves raking his face and hair. While the man with the flashlights illuminated the landing area, another man reached out to help Navarro step ashore. A beam from the flashlight washed across Navarro, revealing a splattering of blood across the front of his shirt and shirt sleeve.

Turning quickly away from the light, Navarro beckoned for the boat's pilot to pass over his backpack. While the other men patiently waited, Navarro yanked a safari jacket from inside the pack. He put the jacket on and directed one of the men to carry the pack.

They were less than four hundred yards from the river when Navarro saw the twinkle of lights between the thick branches. His heart rate accelerated with each step closer to the ruin. Once again, he thought of his grandfather and the *Rivers of Gold* tale.

When they arrived at the site, a yawning Drummond stepped from a tent and ambled toward Navarro. They exchanged a vigorous handshake and Navarro said, "Show me."

Built by an unknown civilization at an indeterminate time, the crumbling structure was more than an outpost but less than a citadel. Its walls were formed by precisely cut stone blocks, wedged against each other without mortar of any kind. A trading post, perhaps?

As Navarro scanned its length, he imagined it standing proudly along the banks of the river in the days of its use. But, the Amazon had consumed it over the millennia as the jungle stretched its advancing fingers into the river. Running a hand along the weathered surface, Navarro wondered if the blocks had been cut by a Flash Stone and lifted into place by a Sound Stone.

They maneuvered their way along the wall. Bathed by halogen lanterns set around its perimeter, the wall's slick stones sparkled. Navarro could see an area staked by small surveyor flags. Drummond pointed and said, "The strongest reading is here."

Navarro walked close to the wall and scanned the pocked blocks of stone. He was pleased to see Drummond hadn't tried to chisel or blast the rock yet. "What do you think, Drummond? Where should we try first?"

"Depends on whether you want to dig or blast," answered the prospector.

"We can't blast. The noise will attract the Cinta-Larga," Navarro said.

Drummond nodded. "We haven't seen them yet, but I think you're right. I'd rather not risk waking them. But, the lads are bushed, Klaus. If we're going to chisel, we should wait for daybreak and let them rest now. The wall's thick. It won't be easy."

"No, we start immediately. They can sleep later," said Navarro.

"They won't like it," Drummond said.

Navarro glared at him and turned to walk away. Drummond said, "Where is your guide? The woman? She should pitch in."

Without breaking stride, Navarro called back over his shoulder, "I sent her back to Apuí. You'll have to make due."

During the wee hours, three men with picks chipped away at the edges of a slab chosen by Drummond. A chalky dust circulated around them as they took turns whacking the stone. Navarro impatiently watched their progress, every now and then tossing looks toward the surrounding jungle.

He cringed at the sound of their blows echoing among the trees. He had hoped the buzz of the jungle's living creatures would mask the sounds, but as soon as the men had started whacking the wall, the chirps and croaks silenced. Looking back toward the river, Navarro now questioned the virtue of his earlier decision to set fire to the campsite where Margaret had perished.

In the fervor of the moment, it seemed a prudent action to render Margaret's body unrecognizable and mask evidence of the attack. As the men chipped away at the wall, however, Navarro worried the fire might have produced an unintended result: alerting the Cinta-Larga to their presence in the jungle.

When daybreak came, gray light covered the dig site. While the laborers took a water break, Drummond and Navarro inspected their progress. Drummond flicked away crumbs of stone from the divot hewn into the rock.

"At this rate, it will take the better part of the day to get through," Drummond said.

"Too long," Navarro said, frowning.

"I do have a drill," Drummond offered, "but it's noisy."

Navarro shook his head and cursed his options. It was only a matter of time before they were detected. If he gave Drummond the go-ahead to blast, it would mean they'd have to work quickly to clear debris and inspect the cavity. The boom would not only signal their presence; it would tell the Cinta-Larga what kind of intruders lurked in their lands. The irony of the situation caused him to laugh. If only there was a silent way to slice through the rock . . .

Tired of waiting, Navarro turned to Drummond. "Blast it."

Drummond nodded and convened the men. Using Drummond's drill, they bored three holes in a line down the crevice between the slab bearing their divots and another of the wall's decayed blocks. Spacing the holes about a foot apart, Drummond prepared the explosives and joined the others behind cover.

The explosion was loud but more muffled than Navarro had expected. Before the dust cleared, he was up and moving toward the gap. Drummond paced close behind, urging Navarro to wait to make sure the blocks above didn't crash down. Eyes focused on the gaping hole, Navarro sped toward the wall.

Leaning through the gap with a flashlight, he probed the dark chamber. Dust floated inside the cavity, blocking the torch's view beyond two feet. Navarro reached one leg into the gap and bent the rest of his body through the opening.

A loud crash sounded from inside the hole, followed by a shout. A minute later, Navarro slithered through the hole with a scowl on his face and nothing in his hands.

13

Sixth Sense

Incline Village, Nevada
August 14

With a low, throaty rumble, the bow pierced through the shoreline mist and emerged into the open waters of Lake Tahoe. Aboard the small craft, two silhouettes huddled under the open-air canopy as it made its way across Crystal Bay.

Approaching a secluded cove, Anlon silenced the engine and waited for the forward momentum to abate before lowering the anchor. Antonio Wallace watched him dip the iron chunk into the frigid waters and then retreated to the aft bench. Reaching into his anorak, he retrieved two cigars and offered one to Anlon. "Join me?"

Slowly limping across the teak deck, Anlon laughed and invoked Antonio's nickname in reply. "Are you kidding me, Skipper? It's a little early for me!"

"Suit yourself," Antonio said as he lit the plump Cuban and inhaled with satisfaction.

Flopping on the bench next to Antonio, thermos in hand, Anlon eked out a small yawn. "Coffee?"

"Um, hold on a sec. Gotta take care of a couple emails first," said Antonio, rapidly tapping away on his cell phone. Amid the fog and cigar smoke, the reflection of the phone's screen cast an eerie glow on his face.

During the wait, Anlon filled a mug and gazed out at the still waters. Sipping the coffee, he winced. Its bitter, watery flavor made him ashamed to call himself a scientist. Pouring the cup overboard, Anlon hobbled back to the boat's cabin to fetch a bottled water. He returned to the bench as Antonio stowed his phone. Puffing out a thick cloud of smoke, Antonio said, "Okay, all done. Now where's that java?"

Biting his lip, Anlon hid the bottled water from Antonio's view and poured his friend a cup. He briefly contemplated mentioning the brew's poor quality, but thought, Screw it. Payback for the early wake-up! He passed the steamy mixture to Antonio and asked, "So, why all the cloak and dagger, Skipper?"

"I have my reasons," Antonio answered while raising the cup.

Anlon waited for Antonio to recoil after his first sip, but his friend showed no reaction. Either the tang of the cigar was overwhelming or the man's taste buds were no longer functioning, Anlon decided.

"Just call it a desire for the utmost privacy," Antonio said, happily swigging more of the liquid mud.

A brief gust of wind lifted the sandy-gray strands of Anlon's hair. He shuddered and blew on his hands. Casting a suspicious eye in Antonio's direction, he said, "Pretty sure it would have been just as private—and a helluva lot more comfortable—sitting by the living room hearth!"

Antonio exhaled a long trail of smoke and said, "I met Malinyah."

The water bottle in Anlon's hand crinkled from a sudden squeeze. "Say what?"

"Yep, in my office. Now, don't get all ruffled up. I guilted Pebbles into it," Antonio explained.

With a slap of his thigh, Anlon growled, "The little minx, she didn't tell me!"

Antonio tucked the cigar in the corner of his mouth and extended both hands. "Easy, buddy, easy. She didn't know it would cause such a ruckus."

"What? What ruckus?" asked Anlon, his face scrunched into a puzzled scowl.

"Oh, it was a s-h-o-w, my friend," Antonio said, nodding his head. "When I came out of the trance, there must have been a dozen people in my office. Katie even called an ambulance."

Burying his face in his palm, Anlon shook his head and groaned. "Ugh! Pebbles! Why?"

"Like I said, it wasn't her fault. I pushed her for a demonstration. Anyway, it all calmed down eventually, but I don't think Katie will let Pebbles come back anytime soon." Antonio's deep laugh echoed among the swirls of mist.

"What happened?" asked Anlon, still locked in a face palm.

"Oh, I freaked out a little. Kinda like you did, according to Pebbles. Only, I lasted a bit longer than you did before I broke down," Antonio said with a smile.

Anlon cringed and recalled his first meeting with Malinyah. The intensity of the experience had taken him by surprise. Based on Dobson's description of the *Aromaeghs*, Anlon had expected a holographic experience but thought it would be a simple video and audio presentation. He was completely unprepared for the visceral, interactive experience. In fact, he'd been outright terrified when she reached out and touched him on the wrist.

Raising his head, he turned to Antonio and asked, "Did she touch you?"

The tech mogul nodded and shivered.

Anlon said, "That's what set me off. I thought it was going to be more like a virtual reality kind of thing, you know?" Staring out at the steely lake surface, Anlon added, "God, it was such a rush! The feel of the wind on my face, the smell of her perfume. It seemed impossible. And when she touched me? It was like 'whoa' and I lost it."

While Anlon spoke, Antonio reached for the thermos and refilled his cup. Pinching the nearly spent cigar between finger and thumb, he said, "Totally get you, my brother. She didn't touch my wrist; she put her hand on my shoulder. I swear to you, it felt like a real hand. Honestly, every time I think about it, I can feel her hand there again."

For a moment, they sat in silence. Antonio tossed back the coffee and extinguished the cigar in the cup's murky residue. Anlon fidgeted with the cap of his bottled water and pondered his friend's comments.

"It defies explanation," murmured Anlon.

Antonio nudged Anlon and said, "Oh, I think you have an explanation. Pebbles said you've been locked away doing research. Says you've turned your office into a lab. She's not happy you've been so tight-lipped about it."

A grin washed over Anlon's face. He pointed a finger at Antonio and said, "Aha! So, that's it! You woke me up to come out here and pump me about my research."

"Maybe," Antonio said with a shrug.

"You couldn't wait 'til this afternoon?"

"Anlon, for the last three days, I've had the hand of a ten-thousand-year-old woman pressed against my shoulder. I know it's not actually there, but I can feel its warmth. I can close my eyes and sense her fingers patting my skin. I rub at my shoulder and it goes away for a few minutes at a time, but it keeps coming back. Would you wait for an explanation?"

"Um, probably not," Anlon said.

"So, spill. What's behind all this? What have you found?"

"I don't know, Skipper. I have some theories, but I'm a long way from anything conclusive."

"I don't believe that for a second, but, okay, let's start at square one. The Stones are magnetic, correct?"

Anlon nodded.

"And the Stones are not natural, meaning the Munuorians didn't just find them lying around like magnetite?"

"No, definitely not," Anlon said. "The Munuorians had an ability to manipulate magnetism that was lost to the ages."

"Manipulate how? I mean, it's easy to turn a metallic stone into a magnet, but these Stones are *way* beyond that."

"No doubt," Anlon said. "The scientific knowledge and imagination required to conceive the tools, let alone craft them, is beyond remarkable. And to do it ten thousand years ago? Hell, I did a little research into the evolution of magnets. The first 'modern' magnetic tools didn't appear until after Columbus sailed . . . a little over five *hundred* years ago!"

Antonio scoffed. "That can't be right. What about the lodestone compass?"

"Yeah, I looked at the lodestone. You're right, it was around well before Columbus. The earliest mention I found was around 500 B.C.E. But the lodestone was child's play compared to what the Munuorians created. I'm not even sure I consider the lodestone technically a tool," Anlon said.

"What do you mean? You touch a needle to magnetite and the needle points north. Always. It has guided many a ship home over the centuries. How's that not a tool?" Antonio asked.

Anlon said, "I'm talking about *permanent* magnetic tools. The lodestone isn't permanent. You take away the needle, and magnetite can't guide you home on its own. And the needle itself isn't magnetic. It becomes temporarily magnetized by touching the magnetite. Once separated, the needle quickly loses its magnetic properties. By contrast, the Munuorian Stones have been lying around for millennia, and as you've seen for yourself, they're still incredibly magnetic."

The skeptical engineer edged forward while lighting another cigar. "Okay, point taken. It's a very impressive feat, but how can you be sure about the dating? What's to say the tools weren't made much later?"

"You're joking, right? You know anyone on the planet *today* with the brains to create something like the *Sinethal*?" Anlon asked.

Antonio stared out at the horizon as vibrant colors began to burn away the gray cloak surrounding the lake. Stroking the stubble on his chin, he relented. "No, no way." After a brief pause, he said, "But . . . I don't think the little hockey puck is a stone."

"Why? Because it feels hollow?" asked Anlon.

"That's one reason. The missing polarity on one side for another reason. That's just not possible for a solid magnetized object," said Antonio. "I'll tell you what I think it is. I think it's stone on the outside and it's got two things inside. There's a magnet, might be another stone, and there's some material that blocks the reverse polarity on one side."

"Certainly possible," Anlon said, "but that doesn't mean the Munuorians didn't make it."

"It doesn't mean they did, either," said Antonio.

"Skip, you're not making sense. If the *Sinethal* was made by them, and it only works with the *Naetir*—no other magnet can activate it, I've tried—then it had to have been made at the same time. Right?"

"You've got a point. But, Anlon, to make the kind of tool I'm talking about, you'd have to cut stone, shape it, then split it open, carve out the insides, plunk in the backing and the magnet, close it back up and then heat the bajesus out of it to seal it without any seams. You're trying to tell me these people could do all that?"

"I think so."

Their conversation was interrupted by the rising sound of an approaching engine. Both men glanced over their shoulders to spot a small fishing boat heading for the cove.

When Antonio turned back toward Anlon, he asked, "So, what's your best guess? How'd they do it?"

"Honest answer?"

"Nothing less."

"Well, for starters, I think they were different from humans today," Anlon said.

"Come again?"

"I think they had a highly developed ability to detect the Earth's magnetic field. I think they could literally *see* it."

"Say what?"

"Yeah, pretty cool, isn't it?" Anlon smiled.

"Talk to me. Back it up with some facts," urged Antonio.

Despite his friend's skepticism, Anlon noticed Antonio scoot farther forward on the bench. His eyes locked onto Anlon's and the cigar dangled precariously from his mouth. Anlon asked, "What do you know about cryptochromes?"

Antonio plucked the cigar and pointed it at Anlon. "Ah! Pebbles said you've been blathering about cryptochromes. Haven't the foggiest. Educate me."

"All right, here's the short answer: a cryptochrome is a photosensitive enzyme that detects the blue-light portion of the light spectrum. That's significant because magnetized objects exhibit blue light more prominently than other colors in the light spectrum, and because high concentrations of cryptochromes have been found in the eyes and brains of many organisms that interact with the Earth's magnetic field. In fact, some researchers believe these organisms can *see* the magnetic field."

Leaning back against the boat frame, Anlon added, "By the way, cryptochromes also circulate in eyes and brains of humans, but in tiny amounts relative to organisms that interact with the magnetic field."

"Okay," Antonio said. "So, what's your theory?"

Anlon took a deep breath. "I think it's possible Munuorian brains and eyes contained much higher levels of cryptochromes than found in humans today, allowing them to sense the magnetic field in a way we can't. With that sixth sense, if you will, they learned to control magnetism."

He paused a moment to let that sink in. Hearing no complaints, he continued. "Think of it like wind. We can't see it, but we can feel it. We know what it can do, and over time we've invented ways to control it for our own purposes. Manipulating wind allowed humans to fly. We learned to capture its energy to create electricity. We devised ways to blend wind's properties with other technology to artificially heat, cool and dry. I believe the Munuorians learned to work magnetism like we work wind."

By now, Antonio was pacing back and forth. "Interesting," he said. "So, you're not thinking hocus-pocus kind of stuff?"

"I'm not sure what I think. I'm entirely speculating."

Antonio halted and turned toward Anlon. "No, I think you're on to something. If they lived in an area with a strong magnetic field, it's conceivable they developed an evolutionary adaptation."

"Precisely," agreed Anlon, "but something caused them to lose their magnetic sixth sense. Either the magnetic field weakened dramatically or something leeched cryptochromes from their physiology. If Malinyah can be believed, it was a bit of both."

Folding his arms across his chest, Antonio asked, "What did she say?"

"Well, I'm getting all this secondhand through Pebbles, although there are plenty of ancient legends that tell a similar tale. Malinyah says a giant asteroid passed very close to Earth around ten thousand years ago. Its passing influence, gravitational and magnetic, was so powerful it flipped the planet upside down as it went by. The flip ripped up the Earth, caused a massive tsunami and nearly wiped out all living things."

Standing at the stern, Antonio gazed at the leading edge of the sun poking over the eastern Sierras. He said, "That would definitely alter the magnetic field."

"Hell, yes, it would," agreed Anlon.

"Is it possible, though? Flipping the Earth, I mean. It sounds too sudden."

"I think it's possible. It would take a planet-sized body, one with opposite polarity, but it's possible."

"Jesus, how could anyone survive that?"

Anlon said, "I don't know, but some did. The ones who managed to survive were pretty much screwed. Earthquakes, volcanos and God knows what else rocked the planet. Animal and plant life was annilihated. There was little left in the way of food, drinkable water or shelter.

"But this is the really amazing part. The Munuorians knew the asteroid was coming and knew it would be catastrophic. They took precautions that protected most of their own people from the initial horrors, but afterward the world had changed for them too. Their food supply was decimated and eventually disease overran their population. The irony: before they perished, they sent out ships to help other pockets of survivors start over. They loaded the boats with their bravest men and women, along with their special Stones, and went out to rescue humanity. The 'rescuers' were the only Munuorians to survive."

The doorbell rang a cheery tune, awaking Pebbles from her slumber. Startled, she trembled beneath the heavy flannel blanket and cracked one eye open. Finding only rumpled sheets on Anlon's side of the bed, she smiled and nestled under the warm covers to drift back to sleep. Good! she thought. He can get the doorbell this time.

A moment later, the doorbell chimed again, and this time it didn't strike Pebbles as particularly cheery. Annoyed, she rolled over to spy the bedside clock: 10:18 a.m. That meant the caller was their UPS deliveryman, Reggie. If history was any guide, Reggie would ring the doorbell at least two more times before giving up. Pebbles covered her head with a pillow and prayed, "Come on, Anlon, answer the door."

The doorbell chimed for a third time and was followed immediately by several resounding raps on the door itself. With a huff, Pebbles cast aside the heavy layers and crawled out of bed. Naked and shivering, she tiptoed to the bench at the foot of the four-poster bed to pull on sweatshirt and pajama pants.

Thus clothed, she descended the red oak staircase from the lodge's upper floor, her forearms wrapped across her chest to assist the sweatshirt's heating process, and called out for Anlon, but received no answer. It had been four hours since he left to meet with Antonio. Surely he should be home by now, Pebbles thought in frustration.

On the other side of the door, Reggie timidly moved his finger to ring the bell again. He'd delivered enough packages to Anlon's home by now to know that if more than three rings were required, it would most likely be Pebbles who answered the door. And at this time of morning, that could be dangerous!

He was saved from a fourth attempt when Pebbles wedged open the door. Squinting into the sunlight filtering through surrounding pines, she hoarsely said, "Good morning, Reggie."

Chuckling, Reggie scratched at the back of his head and stared downward at the slate-covered doorstep. He said, "Sorry to wake you again, Pebbles. But you know it's not my fault. Just following the good doctor's instructions. He doesn't like me leaving packages on the doorstep."

"Yeah, yeah," mumbled Pebbles through an extended yawn. "Can't you rearrange your route to come by later in the day? I mean, really. Ten in the morning is a bit early, don't you think?"

Reggie laughed as he reached for his handheld scanner and swiped the optical reader over the package's shipping label. Looking back up at Pebbles, he said, "Wish I had that much control over my route! Can you sign here for me?"

Pebbles stepped out onto the doorstep. As her bare feet met the cold slate, she shuddered. Though it was technically still summer, the temperature at six thousand feet in the Sierra Nevadas often dipped into the forties at this time of morning. After signing for the package, she stepped quickly back into the doorway and asked, "What's it this time? Rocks again? More fungus? Or another pile of books?"

"Um, no," hesitated the friendly deliveryman as he turned to descend the front steps, "it's live fish."

"Huh?"

"The package. It's some kind of live fish."

"What?!"

"You probably want to open 'em up and get 'em in fresh water. They came all the way from India."

Reggie skipped down the rest of the stairs and jogged to his waiting truck, unwilling to look back at the incredulous scowl on Pebbles' face. As he mounted the truck's steps, Pebbles heard him whisper under his breath, "Oh, man, is he gonna pay for this one!"

Carrying the watermelon-sized box into the house, Pebbles slammed the door shut with her heel and headed toward the kitchen. The sound of her feet pounding against the bare floor planks echoed throughout the quiet house.

She plopped the box on the center-island granite countertop and then stomped back up the stairs, muttering all the while. Climbing back under the covers, she grabbed her cell phone from the bedside table and ripped off a terse text to Anlon: "U are in SOOOO much trouble!!!"

After a moment's pause, she added, "Better get home fast or I'm flushing the fish!"

Antonio watched with disapproval as Anlon dragged a strip of bacon through the sea of syrup surrounding his pancakes. Then, looking over his friend's shoulder, he scanned the near-empty dockside diner once again. Confident that no one new had entered after they arrived, he turned back to Anlon and asked, "So you're determined to look for more of the Stones?"

Mouth full, Anlon nodded his answer.

"Even though Devlin's killer is still out there somewhere?"

Anlon nodded again.

"I don't know, buddy. Seems very risky to me."

Pushing his plate away, Anlon stared at Antonio. "You don't think I should continue Devlin's work?"

"Well, I—"

"Did Pebbles put you up to this?"

"Not exactly . . . but she is worried about you," Antonio said.

Anlon shook his head. "I thought you, of all people, would understand."

"Understand what?"

"Seriously? If you were in my shoes, you couldn't walk away."

Antonio sipped his coffee, savoring the cinnamon blend, and considered his response carefully. He said, "If someone beat me like they beat you, just to get the Stones, I'm pretty sure I'd find a new hobby."

"Bull," said Anlon, "and you know it!" He paused and then asked, "You'd walk away from the chance to prove historians are wrong about the rise of man? You wouldn't want to understand the secrets behind the Stones? Learn how they were created? How we might use their technology?"

Raising his hands in surrender, Antonio laughed. "Okay, okay. You got me there. I couldn't walk away."

"Damn right you couldn't! Besides, I don't expect to run into Devlin's killer or the other two yahoos who tried to steal the Stones."

"Oh? Why so?"

"Look, it's been four months and we've not heard nor seen anything about Margaret Corchran, Klaus Navarro or Thatcher Reynolds. They all went to ground. And I'm pretty sure I know why."

"Don't get cocky," Antonio warned. "Just because they're fugitives doesn't mean one of them won't try again."

Anlon said, "Devlin made a map. Well, was in the process of making a map—he didn't finish it before he was murdered. It shows where more Stones were hidden by the Munuorians."

"And?"

"We know two of the bad guys, maybe all three, have a copy."

"So you think they're using the map."

Anlon nodded.

Scratching his head, Antonio frowned at Anlon. "Um, isn't that a bad thing?"

"It would be," Anlon said, "except Devlin's map is impossible to read."

Before Antonio could respond, Pebbles' text pinged on Anlon's phone. He read her terse message and sheepishly smiled. "Uh-oh. Time to go."

"Bad news?" asked Antonio, following Anlon to the cashier.

Limping rapidly, Anlon replied, "News of the worst kind."

"Oh no, what's happened?"

"It seems I woke Pebbles, again, and she's none too happy about it!" Anlon handed the cashier a twenty-dollar bill and they left the diner.

Antonio struggled to keep up with Anlon's choppy pace and called out for him to slow down. "Where are you going? The boat's back that way."

Anlon forged ahead while deep in thought. Without warning, he froze and spun around to scan the dock-front row of shops and restaurants. Antonio, trailing right behind, nearly plowed him over. He reached out and grabbed Anlon's shoulders. "Relax, man. I'm sure it's recoverable."

"Oh, you don't know Pebbles!" Anlon said. As he resumed his race-walk back toward the restaurants, Anlon described his recent onslaught of morning package deliveries—adding in the fact that Pebbles had been prematurely awoken four of the last five days.

Just ahead, Anlon spotted the telltale, dancing-tomato signage and glanced down at his watch. Damn, he thought, the restaurant probably isn't open yet! He motioned for Antonio to follow him to the restaurant's door. True to his speculation, the door boasted a large plastic placard announcing Giuseppe's was closed until eleven a.m.

Anlon cupped his hands against the glass and peered through the restaurant's storefront windows. Inside, he spied a few workers milling about, readying the restaurant for the expected lunch crowd.

"You mind telling me what you're doing?" Antonio asked.

"Damage control."

It took five minutes of obnoxious door pounding before the teen-aged shift manager appeared at the glass door in frayed jean shorts and a faded gray "Obey" T-shirt. He pointed at the placard with a "Can't you read, dumbass?" scowl. Thinking quickly, Anlon turned to Antonio and asked, "You mind if I drop your name?"

Amused and curious, Antonio said, "Be my guest."

Anlon successfully cajoled the surfer-dude-manager-with-man-bun to open the door and then said, "Hey, there. Sorry about banging on the door."

The teen scratched his belly and yawned.

"I know you're not open yet, but I have right here the owner of the NBA World Champion Warriors, Dr. Antonio Wallace. You've seen him on TV before, right? No? Come on, you must have seen him before. You know, he's the guy who always sits courtside next to Nyla Patton?"

It was a stretch, Anlon realized, but he hoped the manager would at least perk up at the mention of Antonio's dazzling girlfriend and pop music icon. The teen simply yawned again, this time scratching the scruffy patch of whiskers beneath his chin.

Undaunted, Anlon continued. "We just want carry-out. We'll sit out here and wait."

"No can do, bra. Like the sign says, we open at eleven. Come back in thirty minutes and we'll hook ya up."

"I'm sure Antonio will pose for a picture with you. Heck, if he likes the pizza he might just bring Nyla by the next time he's up here!"

With a shake of his head and a "hang loose" hand wave on his way back inside the restaurant, the manager said, "Dudes, wish I could. G-Sep finds out I opened early and he'll tombstone my ass. The 'Man' said no goof-troops before eleven. *Comprende?* Shaka, bruddahs!"

As the surfer-dude relocked the door and turned away, Anlon and Antonio exchanged confused looks. "Goof-troop?" Anlon asked. "Did he just insult us?"

Antonio slapped Anlon on the back. "I think he did, bruddah! Looks like we wait."

14

Lichens, Algae and Zebrafish . . . Oh My!

Incline Village, Nevada
August 14

Pebbles spotted a lone boat cutting toward shore and dashed out the kitchen door. Down the slate steps, across the patio and along the winding trail, she ran to the dock. As Anlon maneuvered the boat alongside, she crossed her arms and anchored a position at the pier's edge. Though the sun had blazed away the earlier chill, it wasn't evident in Pebbles' eyes. Above the din of the idling motor, she shouted, "Live fish? Seriously?"

Looping the mooring rope to its bollard, Anlon silenced the engine and replied, "Sorry! Didn't think they'd come today. Good morning, by the way."

The short strands of Pebbles' hair swirled in a torrent. She tapped a bare foot against a weathered plank and stiffened her stance. Anlon said, "At least say good morning to Antonio."

Antonio stepped from the bobbing boat onto the pier and approached Pebbles with a smile. "Don't be mad at Anlon. I'm the one who lobbied for an early start."

She unfolded her arms long enough to receive Antonio's embrace, but maintained an unwavering glare at Anlon. "Don't try to weasel out of this by distracting me, mister! Where have you two been anyway?"

Anlon disappeared into the below-deck cabin and shouted back, "Had a lot of catching up to do."

Pebbles brushed past Antonio and hopped down into the boat.

Turning away, Antonio meandered down the dock and whispered to the heavens, "Praying for you, buddy!"

She stalked toward the cabin and spied Anlon huddled in the galley. As she neared the doorway, Anlon emerged with a lime-green pizza box. She immediately recognized the container and halted in midstalk. He stepped forward and said, "Peace offering?"

Mouth agape, Pebbles blinked several times and ran her fingers over the dancing tomato emblazoned on the box.

"It's still nice and hot, and it's your favorite: pumpernickel crust, jalapeños and double pepperoni," Anlon said.

Opening the lid to sniff the enticing blend of aromas, Pebbles stared at Anlon and said, "You remembered!"

The previous winter, driving home from a Squaw Valley snowboarding trip, Anlon and Pebbles had stopped in Tahoe City for dinner. Famished and exhausted, Pebbles announced a craving for pizza and Anlon introduced her to Giuseppe's Pizzeria. They hadn't been back to the eclectic eatery since, but Pebbles still raved about their pumpernickel crust.

"Forgive me, won't you?" Anlon appealed as he wrapped an arm around her waist and kissed her cheek.

"Hmmm . . . you're still trying to distract me . . . and I'm still angry with you . . . but, I am a little hungry!" Pebbles said, presenting her cheek for a second kiss.

Walking ahead of Anlon and Pebbles toward the house, Antonio whispered, "Nice save, my man!"

A few minutes later, they settled around an oak picnic table on the patio. Under shade provided by surrounding pines, Antonio scrolled through messages on his phone while Pebbles munched on pizza.

Anlon appeared through the kitchen door and sidled down the steps sporting a tray laden with glasses and a pitcher of lemonade. As soon as the tray hit the table, Pebbles snagged the pitcher and filled the glasses. She gulped hers down to cool the sting of the jalapeños and then raised the next slice to devouring position. In between bites, she asked, "Are you sure you guys don't want some? It's super yummy."

Both wisely declined.

"Your loss!" Pebbles said with a smile, enthusiastically chomping away.

Once Antonio finished reviewing his email, he placed the phone on the table and inhaled the crisp mountain air. Stretching his arms, he yawned. "So, what's this about live fish?"

Pebbles froze in midchew and dropped the half-eaten slice back in the open pizza box. "Yeah! What gives?"

With a shake of his head, Anlon shoved at Antonio's shoulder. "Nice. Thanks a bunch!"

"Oh, pah-leazze! I haven't forgotten," Pebbles said. "Your bizarre little fish are sitting on the kitchen counter. Did you think the pizza would make them invisible?"

"Actually, I did hope a carb coma might make you forget."

Laughing, Antonio pushed back at Anlon and said, "Shrewd move, buddy! But didn't you tell me you have another package coming tomorrow morning? Isn't this gonna play out all over again?"

"What?" yelped Pebbles.

Training an evil eye at Antonio, Anlon said, "Dude, loose lips sink ships."

Antonio raised his glass to hide a devilish grin. Through the table, Anlon felt the vibration of the pizza box slamming closed. He cringed and thought, Oh, well. So much for the peace offering.

With her ice-blue eyes boring holes through his body and soul, Pebbles demanded, "Explain. Now."

"Okay, okay." Anlon said. "Relax, will ya? They're zebrafish."

"Um, I can read a packing slip. I meant, why have zebrafish joined your unexplained collection of seaweed, fungus and rocks?"

Antonio asked, "Fungus? Seaweed?"

"Yeah, you should see his office. Looks like the swamp-thing moved in!" Pebbles said.

"Technically, they are not fungi. They're lichens. They bind with fungi, sort of a coexistence," Anlon said.

"Whatever! They stink. The seaweed and the lichens are nasty."

"It's algae, not seaweed."

"Ugh! You're impossible!"

Antonio clapped heartily and cut in. "Round one to Pebbles. Now, return to your corners and regroup!"

Ignoring Antonio's interruption, Anlon said to Pebbles, "All right, all right, don't get your knickers in a twist. Let's go to my office and I'll explain."

Antonio hid behind another sip of lemonade, and thought, Tree shaken, not stirred. Now, let's see what drops out!

Pebbles reached the door to Anlon's office first. Turning to Antonio, she placed her hand on the doorknob, crinkled her nose and cautioned, "Gird yourself. Your eyelashes might fall out."

Leaning her shoulder into the door, Pebbles pushed against boxes partially blocking the entrance. She still couldn't believe Anlon's pristine workspace had been turned into the hoarder's paradise that met her eyes. Boxes of Devlin's research papers and artifacts were stacked three high on every open inch of the floor, save a narrow path leading to Anlon's desk and another that snaked behind it. Atop the desk itself, piles of papers and files balanced precariously next to his laptop. Behind the desk, several fishbowls lined the windowsill while a few others sat on a long credenza. In these tanks, Anlon had assembled a colorful array of lichens, algae and now fish. On the built-in cherrywood shelves along the far wall, rows of baseball-sized rocks teetered in front of neatly arranged books. And to the opposing wall, Anlon had tacked a huge world map adorned with pushpins, sticky notes and other scribbled annotations.

One by one, they squirmed along Anlon's makeshift path until reaching the desk. Anlon removed packages from the two guest chairs and invited them to sit. Stepping cautiously around the desk, he slid into his own chair.

"What in God's name happened in here?" Antonio asked with a laugh, wiping crusty debris from the seat of his chair.

"See, I told you!" Pebbles said.

Anlon ignored the exchange of jibes and glanced at the zebrafish happily circling their bowl. It was a shame some of them would be sacrificed in the name of science. Turning his attention back to his guests, he asked, "Are we ready to talk, or are you two going to bitch some more?"

Pebbles opened her mouth to contest the accusation, but Antonio held out a hand and said, "Let me take this one." To Anlon, he said, "I've known you a long time, my friend. This, right here, is beyond immersion."

With a smile, Anlon replied, "It does look a bit obsessive, doesn't it?"

Antonio and Pebbles nodded in agreement. Pebbles again readied a comeback, but Anlon spoke first. "Call me what you may, I guarantee both of you will feel differently by the time we leave this room."

"Assuming we can *find* a way out!" needled Pebbles.

Ignoring the dig, Anlon said, "So, I've been trying to figure out where Devlin left off, where he was headed with his research. Obviously, he didn't expect to get tossed off a mountain, so he didn't leave much of a trail to guide us. Or so I thought."

He trained his gaze on three pocket-sized notebooks lying next to his laptop. Reaching between the paper stacks on the desk, he handed two of the notebooks to Pebbles. "I'm pretty sure they're important. Maybe more important than the Waterland Map. Take a look."

One cover was labeled *Martinique* and the other *Guadeloupe*. Pebbles passed the Martinique journal to Antonio and then cracked open the Guadeloupe book herself.

Inside, the journals were full of notes and hand-drawn diagrams. In the Martinique volume, most of the notes were made in pencil, but there were others inserted here and there with a blue pen. Toward the back, several pages were exclusively recorded in blue ink. The Guadeloupe journal contained similar recordings.

As they flipped through pages, Anlon said, "Devlin was definitely hunting for something, but the more I've thought about it, the less I'm convinced he was after the Stones."

Pebbles said, "Don't tell me, let me guess. He was looking for seaweed and fungus."

"Very funny," Anlon said. Holding up the third notebook, he

pointed to the word *Dominica* on the cover and said, "This one is the most interesting. Devlin apparently found one of the Stone caches here. I say 'apparently' because he wasn't successful recovering any of the Stones."

"Really?" Pebbles said. She looked up at the wall map. "Where is it?"

Anlon winnowed his way between boxes to reach the map. Antonio and Pebbles rose to join him. "You see the two red pushpins, here and here? And the one with both a black and green one, there?"

Pebbles followed Anlon's finger as it passed first to Guadeloupe and Martinique and then to Dominica. She said, "All in the Caribbean."

"I've been to Dominica," Antonio said. "It's very lush. Like a rainforest. Haven't been to the other two, but if I'm not mistaken, there's a pretty famous volcano on Martinique."

"Yep, Mount Pelée," Anlon said. "In fact, all three have prominent volcanos."

"Volcanos?" Pebbles asked. She thought of Tumaera and asked, "Are volcanos important?"

"I think they might be. Lichens love volcanic rock, by the way," Anlon said.

"Ah! Finally, we get to the lichens," Antonio said.

"Same true for the rest of your bilge collection and little fish? Do they love volcanos, too?" asked Pebbles.

"Eh, not all algae, just the stinky ones percolating in these two bowls," Anlon said, smiling. "And zebrafish like water, not lava."

Pebbles gazed back at the map. There she found six black pins, six green pins and two additional blue ones. The blue pins marked two islands: Isabela and Ometepe. The remaining black and green pins were all situated on continental land masses. She asked, "What's with the different color pins?"

"Good question. The red pins are the two islands where Devlin struck out looking for Stones. The black and green pins show my best guesses of Waterland Map sites. One of the sets, black or green, is correct, but I haven't figured out which yet. I won't know for sure until we go hunting for one of each," said Anlon.

"Why does Dominica have both black and green?" Antonio asked.

"Well, if Devlin did find a cache on Dominica, then we have one reference point on the Waterland Map. But there's no way to figure out how to align the rest of the cache locations from Devlin's map with only one reference point. Yesterday, I found two different ways to align the map where a cache location comes close to Dominica. Just don't know which one is right."

Anlon cleared a space on his desk and then retrieved a steel tube resting on the credenza. He uncorked a plug from one end and slid out the Waterland Map. He laid it out on the desk and then retrieved a second map of equal size from a desk drawer. The second map was made of clear plastic and showed the Earth's current topography. Anlon layered the clear map atop Devlin's Waterland Map and aligned the longitude and latitude lines of both maps.

"Now," he continued, "this positioning shows the relationship between the two maps when aligned as Devlin drew the longitude and latitude. When lined up this way, you can see the color-coded spots where Devlin marked Stone caches are pretty much all in the oceans . . . way far away from any land in most cases. You'll also notice, none of the cache locations are anywhere near Dominica.

"So, let's assume the planet flipped over from the asteroid encounter. I flip the Waterland Map upside down, like this, and now what do you see?"

Antonio quickly scanned the map and said, "Still no Dominica."

"Right . . . and only a few of Devlin's marks are on land," Pebbles said.

"Correct on both counts. So, that only leaves two possibilities," said Anlon. "Either Devlin was a terrible mapmaker, or the Earth didn't make a one-hundred-and-eighty-degree flip. I was leaning toward bad mapping, but it might be a little of both."

Anlon returned the current world map to its original upright position. Then, he slowly rotated it until he found a color-coded site on the underlying Waterland Map that aligned near Dominica. He said, "So, I've tried this multiple times, and only one of Devlin's cache locations comes close to Dominica when I rotate the map starting with Devlin's original coordinate grid."

Pebbles looked at the cockeyed alignment of the two maps. "So, the Earth didn't do a full one eighty?"

With a nod, Anlon said, "That's the implication. But, I'm not sure this is the right way to align the map."

"Why?" Antonio asked.

Anlon again returned the current world map to its original position atop the Waterland Map and pointed at the aligned coordinate grids. "Because the ancient Egyptians didn't know about Greenwich."

"Excuse me?" Pebbles said.

Tapping on the clear world map, Anlon said, "The world map's longitude is based on a prime meridian through Greenwich in England. But the Waterland Map is based on a wall drawing Devlin lifted from a pyramid at the Giza complex."

Pebbles massaged her wrists and leaned over the map. "So, you're thinking the prime meridian on Devlin's map might be aligned through Egypt instead?"

"Exactly. When the thought struck me yesterday afternoon, I mocked up a new world map with the prime meridian through Giza and had the copy center in town print it out." Anlon pulled out a second clear map from the desk drawer and substituted it for the Greenwich oriented map. "Observe that no cache location is near Dominica when the two maps are straight up. Take my word, when you flip it over, none of them line up with Dominica either."

Excited, Pebbles rotated the map slowly. When it was nearly inverted, a cache location crossed the West Indies. "Oh, my God, look at that!"

Anlon leaned back in the desk chair and pointed at the wall map. "Yep. The black pins show the land-based cache locations using the Giza orientation. The green ones are based on Greenwich. Which is correct? My money's on the Giza orientation, but there's no way to know which set is right without finding another cache. Regardless, both orientations suggest the planet flipped less than a full one eighty."

"What about the blue pins?" Antonio asked.

"I found them listed on a blank page near the end of the Dominica book. To me, it looks like Devlin planned to tackle them next, but there may be other reasons he wrote them in. As a point of interest, both have sizeable volcanos. But it's puzzling why he was interested in them other than the fact they are volcanic. Neither island is a Waterland Map site, black or green," Anlon said.

He passed the Dominica journal to Pebbles. "There are two other mysteries in this little book. Look toward the back. A few pages before the island list, Devlin drew a picture. Look familiar?"

Pebbles riffled the pages until she came across the drawing. "Hey, that's the dragon statue!"

"Dragon statue?" Antonio asked.

Pebbles handed Antonio the notebook and pointed to the drawing. At the same time, Anlon stepped behind the desk and opened a box. After rummaging through some packing material, he withdrew a foot-high statuette and placed it on the edge of the desk in front of Antonio.

Antonio approached the desk and compared the two renderings. "Yep, they do look similar."

"What's the other mystery?" Pebbles asked.

"Look at the page opposing the dragon drawing. Toward the bottom of the page, read out the last couple of lines," Anlon said to Antonio.

"Um, let's see. Ah, yes. Here we are," Antonio said. "Tried Sound Stone per M, but no judder. Disappointing! Need to find one fast! Running out of time!"

"*M* for Malinyah?" Pebbles wondered.

"That's my interpretation," said Anlon. "Devlin went to Dominica looking for something very specific. It could be more Stones, but his note doesn't say, 'Need to find *them* fast.' He wrote, 'Need to find *one* fast.' He could have meant he was looking for 'one' of the caches. I don't know, maybe I'm overanalyzing it, but I don't get the time urgency."

Antonio spoke up. "Can we go back a second. You made a point of mentioning the two blue-pin islands have volcanos. What's the significance?"

Rising from his seat, Anlon snaked between boxes and plucked two chunks of rock from the assortment lining the bookshelves. Handing one each to his guests, he said, "You're looking at olivine basalt, a magnetic type of volcanic rock."

Antonio turned the black-green chunk in his hands. "And?"

"I'm pretty sure *all* the Stones were forged from olivine." Anlon turned to Pebbles and said, "We know they lived near volcanos."

"That's right, Tumaera and Artosae," Pebbles said. She lifted the basalt chunk. "What makes you think the Stones are olivine? The texture of this looks and feels very different."

"I scraped off slivers from the *Breylofte* and *Aromaegh*. I had them tested. Both are olivine mixed with kimberlite. So is the dragon statue, by the way. After I do the same with samples from the *Sinethal* and *Naetir*, we'll know for sure."

"Okay," said Antonio. "That connects the Stones with volcanos. Are you thinking Devlin was looking to find where they were made?"

"It crossed my mind." Anlon smiled.

Pebbles slapped the desktop. "You're thinking he went looking for their homeland, aren't you?"

Anlon said, "It makes sense from an archaeology perspective. Remember, Devlin didn't discover *any* of the Stones at a dig site. He found them in museums . . . at least, as far as we know. The archaeologists who did discover them found the Stones among artifacts of later-period cultures.

"I think it's possible Devlin went looking for the Munuorian homeland once he found Dominica. I don't know what led him to consider Isabela and Ometepe versus other possibilities, but I think he might have been on the right track."

"Come again? How'd you get there?" Antonio asked.

"Cassiopeia or cryptochromes?" Anlon asked. "Where should I start?"

"Huh?" asked Pebbles.

"Let's start with Cassiopeia," said Anlon, turning to Pebbles. "Remember our conversation about Cassiopeia? The memory experiment?"

"How could I forget?" joked Pebbles.

Anlon leaned back in the chair once more and clasped his hands behind his head. "Well, Cassiopeia is a northern hemisphere constellation. If you're above thirty-four degrees latitude, it's always visible in the night sky. The farther south you go from there, it's only visible for certain stretches of time during the year. If you go below the southern tropics, it's barely visible at all.

"So, if the Munuorians could see Cassiopeia *before* the asteroid flipped the planet, their homeland had to have been at least north of the southern tropics. How far north is the question. Now, if you're at the north pole itself, Cassiopeia would be almost dead overhead all year round. The farther south you go, the angle of its orbit is sloped at a sharper angle. If you're at thirty degrees, the slope is modest, call it midhorizon. If you're at the equator, the slope is dramatic—it comes close to the horizon at its peak visibility and disappears completely for months of the year for the opposing arc of its orbit."

Anlon leaned toward Pebbles and said, "Now we don't know the time of year in Malinyah's vision, but Malinyah told you Cassiopeia was visible nearly year-round. And you said their astronomers watched Munirvo's full approach, which I take as meaning there never was a moment it wasn't visible. The only way that would have been possible is if Munirvo sat inside Cassiopeia's *W*, a point you confirmed in our experiment.

"See, there's a pretty narrow latitude band where Cassiopeia would be visible nearly the full year, where something inside the *W* would be visible all the time, right around twenty-five to thirty degrees north of the equator. That would put the Munuorian homeland preflood in the same band of latitude as Florida."

Anlon lowered his hands and tapped the map. "If I'm right about the Giza meridian and Munuoria was between twenty-five and thirty degrees north of the equator pre-flip, then Devlin's interest in Isabela and Ometepe as possible sites of their homeland makes sense. The Giza orientation of Dominica implies the planet flipped about a hundred and fifty-six degrees counterclockwise. That means Isabela would have been about twenty-three degrees north pre-flip, and Ometepe about thirteen degrees north.

"I doubt Devlin knew about Cassiopeia, but somehow he figured it out. If you ask me, I think Isabela is the more logical choice."

Pebbles' eyes widened. "You think Isabela was their homeland?"

"Not necessarily Isabela itself, but the Galápagos Islands as a whole. Lots of volcanos, the islands sit on a large undersea plateau that's relatively shallow, implying part of it might have sunk below sea level as a result of Munirvo . . . and the wildlife there is packed with cryptochromes. Everybody knows the Galápagos are unique ala Darwin's study of the islands' wildlife, but I'll bet neither of you know that Darwin was also the first to discover the connection between cryptochromes and magnetism in plants. Not saying there's a direct connection, but it's a tantalizing possibility," said Anlon.

There was a pause as both Pebbles and Antonio waited for Anlon to continue. When he folded his hands across his lap and grinned, Pebbles raised a foot close to the zebrafish bowl and threatened, "Explain crypto-whatever or so help me . . ."

Anlon said, "Okay, okay, back off."

Edging the bowl away from her foot's reach, Anlon described cryptochromes again, this time for Pebbles' benefit. When he finished, he said, "Anyhow, the link with my 'bilge collection' is just a hunch. If the Munuorians had high cryptochrome levels, I assumed their diet must have comprised cryptochrome-rich foods. Not necessarily algae and lichens, but wildlife that feeds on them. But who knows, maybe they had a really tasty lichen stew?"

To this, Pebbles gestured a finger down her throat.

"If they were very sensitive to the magnetic field," Anlon continued, "it seems reasonable to assume they lived in or near a highly magnetic area. How else would they be aware of the sensitivity?

"We know they were mariners, so they obviously had easy access to oceans. They may not have lived on islands, but they at least lived near coastlines. Either way, given their special relationship with magnetism, I think it's almost certain they lived in proximity to one or more *active* volcanos."

Antonio interrupted. "Hold up. I follow you so far, but why 'active' volcanos?"

"Again, just a hunch," said Anlon. "It's possible they invented some other way to shape magnetic rock into the *Lifintyls*, but there are only two ways to do it today. You can touch a metallic object to an existing magnet, just like the pin-lodestone combination we talked about on the boat. However, like we also discussed, once separated from the source magnet, new magnets created this way degrade over time and eventually lose their magnetic properties.

"Or, you can superheat a magnetic rock or precious metal and turn it into a magnet. A permanent magnet. By superheat, I don't mean stick it in an oven. I mean the kind of heat that you'd find in a smelter . . . or better yet, an active volcano."

Pebbles looked down at the basalt chunk in her hand and then lifted her head to spy the zebrafish. "So, you think their *gensae* came from living near volcanos and eating foods with cryptochromes?"

"Their what?" Antonio asked.

"*Gensae.* Their magnetic sixth-sense. Malinyah described it as their ability to read the planet's mind," Pebbles said.

Anlon said, "Short answer is yes, I think both contributed. There is a parallel in animals that suggests elevated cryptochrome levels may play a role in sensing the Earth's rhythms—storms, earthquakes, tsunamis, those sorts of things.

"Take the tsunami caused by the Sumatra earthquake in 2004, for example. There were bunches of stories about animals and birds that hightailed away from the coasts of India and Sri Lanka an hour before the tsunami hit. Most scientists say the animals and birds felt the early vibrations of the tremblor, but I wonder if instead they could *see* ominous ripples in the magnetic field—many of the animals and birds who took off are known to possess high cryptochrome levels in their eyes."

Anlon glanced at the zebrafish and added, "Cryptochromes have one last attribute that's compelling. They are essential in circadian rhythms. Why is that significant? Circadian rhythms in humans are controlled by the hypothalamus. Ring a bell, Pebbles?"

"Emotional memories," Pebbles said, nodding.

"Exactly. See, to me, it all ties together. Cryptochromes are magnetic particles. They circulate in the eyes and brain. They're essential in animals to detect the Earth's magnetic field, and they play a role in how the hypothalamus operates. The hypothalamus works closely with the hippocampus and amygdala to regulate memories.

"I think the Munuorians' brains were drenched with crypto-chromes," Anlon said, "and it gave them astonishing powers. And they got those powers from cryptochrome-rich foods like lichens, algae and zebrafish."

"Oh, my," deadpanned Pebbles.

15

Heating Up

Terminal E, Logan International Airport
Boston, Massachusetts
August 16

Peering into the lounge, Jennifer noticed an empty table wedged in the corner. With her roller-bag trailing behind, she scooted through an obstacle course of backpacks, briefcases and other rollers and snagged the table. A flustered businessman arrived next to her just as Jennifer flopped her tote bag on the table's lone chair to stake a claim, and he briefly stared her down. When Jennifer smiled and slid into the seat, the man shook his head, loosened his tie and lumbered away.

"Whew, that was a close one!" she mumbled.

Standing her tote bag on the table's crooked surface, Jennifer nestled the roller under the table and then scanned a laminated bar menu she found wedged between a napkin dispenser and a ketchup bottle. The choices were limited, but at this point she didn't care. Lunch was a distant memory, and she doubted the redeye would offer a better choice.

A tiny woman with a platinum-blond bouffant hustled through the throng with pen in one hand and scratch pad in the other. Jennifer watched the woman take a flurry of orders on her way to Jennifer's table. Each time the woman nodded to acknowledge an order, the massive hairdo waved back and forth, reminding Jennifer of Captain Gambelli's collection of New England Patriots bobbleheads.

Thinking of the bobblehead image brought back pleasant memories of her visit earlier in the day with Gambelli and the rest of the detective squad. Jennifer hadn't been sure what to expect when she popped by the office to meet up with Dan Nickerson for lunch. She had worried they might escort her from the premises with a scolding: "You're still on suspension. Don't come back until mid-October!" But it hadn't gone that way at all. The squad had welcomed her back as if the suspension had never happened. Gambelli himself had come out of his office and given her a big hug. Later he invited her into his office and they engaged in a wide-ranging, relaxed conversation. Each time he laughed, Gambelli slapped the desk, sending his bobbleheads into a frenzied chorus of nods.

At one point during the conversation, Jennifer's cell phone had buzzed with a call from George Grant. When she excused herself to answer it, Gambelli had graciously surrendered his office so she could take the call in private. The subsequent discussion with Grant proved disappointing. Although Jennifer found him cordial and forthcoming, Grant said he was certain Devlin never mentioned where he acquired the *Sinethal*.

After the call, Gambelli had invited Jennifer to join an impromptu detective's meeting about a baffling murder case. It had been therapeutic to get back in the mix of things. In fact, the whole visit had been good therapy. When Jennifer was forced to hand in her badge and weapon, she had felt ashamed. Walking through the detective unit on her way out the door that day, she was unable to bring herself to look at any of her comrades. They had told her to hang in there, that the suspension would zip by, and then teased her to come back with a tan. Yet, despite their fraternal encouragement, Jennifer left feeling as if she'd been kicked out of a family.

She was still reminiscing the "long walk" when Dixie, the living bobblehead, arrived at her table. Caught by surprise, Jennifer quickly scanned the placard and opted for a draft Mexican beer and nachos. As Dixie jotted down the order, Jennifer said, "Might as well get a head start!"

Dixie's pen stopped in midstroke. "What's that, honey?"

"Sorry," Jennifer said with a smile. "Just blabbering to myself."

The middle-aged waitress patted her on the shoulder and walked back to the kitchen. Meanwhile, Jennifer noticed a bank of arrival/ departure monitors hanging over the bar. Unwilling to risk losing her table, she leaned forward and squinted at the screen to check the status of her flight to Mexico City. She was relieved to see her redeye flight was still scheduled to depart at eleven-thirty. Jennifer wasn't thrilled about the two-hour layover thereafter, but it was the only option to reach Villahermosa. She was glad now that Anlon had insisted she book first-class tickets for the round-trip. It had been a more exhausting day than Jennifer expected, and she looked forward to the more comfortable seating for the six-hour overnight flight.

While she waited for her order, Jennifer pulled out her notebook and reviewed the key findings from the last few days.

The museum records provided by the pompous Charles Goodwin turned out to provide little insight. The two green *Aromaeghs* had been discovered during the excavation of a Chorotega site in a place called Zapatera some thirty years prior, while the gray one was donated by the estate of a then museum benefactor. Jennifer planned to follow up with the deceased benefactor's family, but since the donation was made in 2000, she expected it would take some digging to find living family members.

The trip to meet Anabel had been equally unsatisfying. Although it had been a pleasant visit, Jennifer was still puzzled by a few of Anabel's comments. When the first slip happened, Jennifer thought it might have been a misinterpretation on her part. But, later in the conversation, Jennifer had intentionally returned to the subject and Anabel made the same mistake. Either Anlon's memory was indeed affected by Pacal's beating, or Anabel had lied to him.

The question was, why? What did Anabel have to lose by telling Anlon she knew of Devlin's "prized stone" prior to his death? Why had Anabel told Anlon she'd never seen the map before she and Anlon viewed it together? Were they honest mistakes or something else?

If it hadn't been for two other odd reactions on Anabel's part, Jennifer might have written the slips off as simple misunderstandings between Anlon and Anabel. But combined with the other missteps, she was starting to feel ill at ease.

One concern was Anabel's strange response, or lack of response, when Jennifer mentioned Malinyah. Anabel had questioned Jennifer's use of the words "*Sinethal*" and "Munuorians." In fact, Anabel went out of her way to say Devlin hadn't used the names. Yet when Jennifer said the name Malinyah, Anabel just nodded. At first Jennifer thought Anabel might have been so absorbed in her review of the dragon-head statue photo, she missed the name and nodded to be polite. But the nod didn't strike Jennifer as a vacant gesture. It came across as an act of recognition, as if Anabel recognized Malinyah's name.

The other unusual reaction reminded Jennifer of something that occurred way back in May at Stillwater Quarry. After Jennifer shot and killed Pacal Flores, Anabel had picked up the *Naetir* that Anlon had tried to use to fend off the *Breylofte*'s sound waves. She picked it up and put it in her pocket. Had Jennifer not noticed her take it, Anabel might have left the quarry with the hockey-puck-shaped Stone. Jennifer still remembered the bashful look on Anabel's face when Jennifer demanded the *Naetir*'s return. In the craziness of the shooting's aftermath, with EMTs furiously working to save Anlon's life, Jennifer didn't stop to question Anabel and soon forgot about the incident.

However, the memory resurfaced at the end of the Bennington visit, when Jennifer realized she had left her pictures inside the house. The embarrassed look on Anabel's face was the same as it had been that awful day in May when Jennifer asked her to hand over the *Naetir*. It seemed clear Anabel knew more about Devlin's research than she wanted to admit. Jennifer would need to circle back to find out why.

As Jennifer made a note to that effect, Dixie bobbed by and delivered her beer. Before she could take a sip from the pint glass, her cell phone buzzed. The screen showed a picture of the dapper junior detective Dan Nickerson.

"Hi, Dan, miss me already?" she said.

"Hey, Jen. You know it! Everybody loved seeing you today. Can't wait 'til you get back."

"Aw, thanks. It *was* great! Especially hearing about your promotion, Detective Lieutenant."

"Oh, yeah! My new cube's a full square foot bigger and I scored a parking space. Living large!" Nickerson said with a laugh. After a brief pause, his voice took on a serious tone. "Hey, the reason for my call—I thought you'd like to know, we got a hit on Margaret Corchran right after you left."

"Oh? That's great!"

There was an extended pause before Nickerson said, "Well, yes and no. Sometime yesterday she was admitted to a Brazilian hospital as a Jane Doe. She was hurt pretty bad. Given the nature of her injuries, they ran her fingerprints through Interpol and got a match. Interpol let us know this afternoon."

"I don't understand. That's good, right?"

"Um, it would be except she vanished before the positive ID came back."

"What?"

"Crazy, right? Not the hospital's fault or the local police. She knocked a nurse unconscious, took her uniform and disappeared. They have video of her leaving the hospital. I'll email it to you."

"Okay, that's great. Thanks." Jennifer looked up to see Dixie approaching with her nachos. She smiled her thanks when Dixie handed her the plate and then returned to the conversation. "You said she was hurt. What happened to her?"

Nickerson lowered his voice. "Honestly, I don't know how she survived. According to Interpol, the surgeon who worked on her said she was run through with a wide blade. He guessed a machete. Her throat had been cut as well. He said it was a miracle she didn't bleed out."

In between chews, Jennifer asked, "Jesus. Do they know who did it?"

"No, she was too loopy after surgery to talk, and she bolted be-

fore the local PD got a chance to question her. But the Apuí police — that's the town in Brazil where she was taken — think she was
ambushed in the Amazon rainforest, of all places."

"The Amazon rainforest?"

"Yeah, seems like a strange place to hide out," Nickerson said.

Jennifer turned to a clean page in her notebook. "What's the name
of the town again?"

"Apuí. A-P-U-I."

"Great, thanks. What made the locals suspect an ambush?"

"Well, she was brought by boat to a fishing lodge on the Roosevelt
River by some natives that live in the jungle, the Kinta-something,
don't ask me to spell it. The natives apparently dislike outsiders. The
cops think she must have trespassed into their territory and got cut
up for it."

"God, Dan, the whole thing sounds bizarre!"

"Oh, I haven't gotten to the bizarre part yet! I talked to the lodge
manager about an hour ago, a guy named Billy Dubois. He's Cajun
and, damn, was he hard to understand! Anyway, Billy doesn't agree
with the Apuí PD. He said the natives tended her wounds with some
black goop and patched her up before they dropped her off. When
they lifted her from the boat, Billy said the natives treated her like
royalty. He told me he's never seen them act like that before."

Jennifer dipped a chip into the clot of neon-green guacamole atop
her nachos. "What do you mean treated her like royalty?"

"I thought that might catch your attention. Billy said four of the
natives accompanied her upriver. She was unconscious when they arrived. Before they lifted her from the boat, they held a little ceremony.
Three of the men chanted while the fourth washed her feet, hands
and forehead. Billy said they covered her with a golden cloak — his
words — and cupped her hands around a stone bowl. And now for the
bizarre part. The native leading the ceremony painted a symbol on
her forehead. A symbol I have a feeling you'll recognize."

Jennifer's eyes widened. She was just about to ask a question when
someone jostled her table and spilled her beer on her open notebook.

Jennifer vaulted up to avoid the stream pouring over the edge of the table. She cursed and grabbed the notebook. Dangling the dripping pages, she said, "Hold on, Dan. Got a mini-crisis here."

Dixie came shooting over to sop up the mess while Jennifer checked to make sure her tote and roller-bag were unscathed. While Dixie ran to get another dry towel, Jennifer slapped the drenched notebook back on the table and sat down. "A symbol, you said?"

"Yeah, Billy took a picture of her laid out in the boat, and another one of her face. I'm texting both to you right now."

The jpeg files were large enough that it took a couple of minutes for them to appear in her text app. She went right to the one of Margaret's face. Sure enough, Dan was right. She recognized the symbol instantly. In the center of Margaret's forehead, the native had painted three wavy lines.

"Wow. Looks *very* familiar."

"Yeah, thought so. Makes it seem like she went into the jungle on purpose."

"Agreed. Anything else?"

Nickerson paused before answering. "Not officially. Interpol's leading the follow-up. I'll let you know if they pass any more info along."

"Anything unofficial?"

Another pause. This time he whispered, "Promise to keep it on the down low?"

Though he couldn't see her gesture over the phone, Jennifer raised a hand and solemnly replied, "Scout's honor."

"I got a bit more out of Billy than he shared with the Apuí PD and Interpol," Nickerson said.

Jennifer smiled. Dan was the kind of cop who didn't walk away from open-ended clues. "Did you now? Like what?"

"Billy said Margaret came into the fishing lodge a few days beforehand. She was interested in renting an inflatable raft. Billy quoted her a price and she put down a deposit, but she never came back."

As Dixie arrived with a fresh beer, Jennifer said, "Please tell me she used a credit card for the deposit."

"She did. Victoria Bradley's the name on Billy's copy of the card receipt."

"Sweet. Why didn't the fish lodge guy tell the locals or Interpol about it?"

"He said they didn't ask about the deposit."

"Unbelievable."

"Yeah, I don't buy it. I think Billy's lying. I think he just didn't want to get involved. I passed the info on, so everybody's got it now."

"Did you ping the credit card company?"

"Uh-huh. Guess what."

"She's used the card since she left the hospital, hasn't she?" Jennifer pounded the table, nearly spilling the replacement pint.

"No, we didn't get that lucky," Nickerson said, sighing, "but we do know now where she spent the last two months. She ran up one helluva hotel bill at a resort on Barbados. There were also airline charges. Seems 'Vickie' went back and forth between Barbados and a nearby island called Dominica a dozen times."

Apuí, Brazil

It was approaching midnight when Christian Hunte cracked open the bedroom door to check on Margaret. After several fitful hours, the fever had broken and she'd finally fallen asleep. He had done all he could for her; now it was up to Foucault.

Christian stepped out onto the hotel balcony and immediately broke into a sweat. The oppressive air held down the Earth's heat like the lid of a pot, even at this time of night. Wiping his brow, he dipped into his pocket and plucked out his cell phone. He pressed the preset for Foucault's number and waited for the international call to connect.

A moment later, Foucault answered. *"Allô?* Christian?"

"Good morning, Monsieur. Hopefully, I did not wake you."

"*Non.* I am awake," Foucault said. "Did you find the site? Do you have the *Tuliskaera?*"

"Navarro's party got there before me," Christian said. "He blasted it open and came out empty-handed."

A heavy sigh sounded on the other end of the line. "Well, at least Navarro did not take it. There was nothing else?"

"Navarro came out with nothing. He was quite angry. I don't blame him. It definitely was a Maerlif, but it was almost completely buried and well back from the river. They did go back inside and cut out the beacon. The diamond was much larger than I expected. It barely fit in Navarro's hand."

"Was Margaret with him?"

Through the phone, Christian heard the familiar sound of the chateau's creaky patio door opening and the chirping of birds. "No, Navarro was alone when he joined the rest of the party."

"How is our patient?"

"Stable, for the moment. I can probably keep her alive for another day, maybe two if I use all the *enjyia.*" Christian wiped more sweat from his dripping brow.

"*Bon.* I will leave from Béziers tonight. I will bring more *enjyia* with me. Tell me of her injuries."

Pacing the balcony, Christian chronicled the damage. "It is a miracle she's still alive. She has a gash through the abdomen. Entry wound midway down her back on the right side. Exit wound just beneath her right front rib cage. It must have been a very long blade.

"She has an uneven slash across her neck, just above the line of her shoulders. I cannot tell the internal damage, although she's having difficulty breathing. I'd say a punctured lung at a minimum. Her abdomen and back are sutured. The hospital must have provided her with some blood and fluids. There are some other defensive cuts to her hands, but they're minor by comparison. She's been feverish and pale."

After a brief pause, Foucault said, "The prognosis does not sound promising, Christian. Has she spoken?"

"A little. She can only gasp two to three words at a time, but she's been able to answer other questions with her fingers. One for yes, two for no. As I mentioned, she did not make it to the Maerlif; the attack happened before. I know Navarro did it, and they were alone."

"Coward! Attacking her from behind," sneered Foucault. "What else have you learned?"

"She said the Cinta-Larga found her. It must have been shortly after the attack; otherwise she would be dead. I didn't fully understand what she was trying to tell me, but it sounded as if they brought her to the hospital. The Cinta-Larga did a bit of triage on their own. I found traces of *terra preta* and beeswax on the neck wound. They have a long memory."

"So it seems. What of Navarro? Where is he?"

"I don't know. As soon as he came out with the diamond, they left in a hurry. I think they were afraid the Cinta-Larga heard the explosion. Navarro kept looking over his shoulder."

"Hmmm. Do you think Navarro suspects Margaret survived?"

"I couldn't say, Monsieur."

There was another pause as Foucault pondered the new information. At last, he said, "He is shrewder than I thought. I didn't expect he would decode the map so quickly. Now Navarro is a step ahead of us, Christian. He will make for the next closest Maerlif."

"Where?"

"If only I knew," Foucault said.

"Monsieur, there is one other thing I should mention."

"Yes?"

Unable to bear the heat any longer, Christian left the balcony. "I think it's possible the Cinta-Larga have a *Tuliskaera*. Or, did at one time. I passed several channels carved into hillsides that looked unnatural."

"You think they looted the Maerlif?"

Inside the room, Christian hovered his face above the vents of the window air conditioner. "There have always been questions about their never-ending supply of diamonds, Monsieur. And, if rumors are true, they guard their largest deposit with unusually heavy security."

"We will pay them a visit, I think. But, not now. Even Muran would find it a challenge to take on the Cinta-Larga."

"Very well. Unless there is something else, I will go and tend to Margaret."

"One moment, Christian. I have news to share as well. When I arrived home this afternoon, there was a most interesting voice message from a woman working for Anlon Cully."

Logan Airport, Boston

The boarding area was packed. Jennifer curled her feet under the bench seat so a family of five could pass through. A couple of them sniffed the air around her and frowned with disapproval. Jennifer resisted the temptation to jump and say, "It's not me, it's the damn notepad!"

She loathed the idea of parting with the digest-sized booklet, but it did reek. Pulling the warped book from her bag, she flipped through the pages and frowned. Most of her notes had been obliterated and the remaining blank pages were soiled. She briefly considered holding onto it, but the thought of the stale beer odor percolating in her bag for six hours was enough to push Jennifer over the edge. Once the family passed, she tossed the book in a nearby trash bin.

Resettling on the bench, she checked the gate monitor. A half hour to go until boarding. She closed her eyes and wondered if she should call Anlon tonight or wait until she arrived in Villahermosa. She had just resolved to call him, when her phone buzzed.

"Hello," she answered.

"Miss Jennifer Stevens?"

When Jennifer heard the British accent, she looked at her phone screen. It read "Unknown Caller."

"Yes, who is this?"

"I'm sorry to disturb you, Miss Stevens. Am I calling at an inconvenient time?"

Overhead, a loudspeaker announced the commencement of boarding for the gate next to Jennifer's. She wedged a finger in her ear while she depressed the phone tightly against the other. "No, it's fine. Who is this, please?"

"Excuse me, how rude of me. My name is Christian Hunte. I am the private secretary for Count Foucault. I understand you left a message for him."

"Yes, that's right. Thank you for returning my call," Jennifer said. "I'm sorry for the background noise. I'm getting ready to board a flight."

"Oh?" said Christian. "Where are you headed?"

"Mexico."

"Business or pleasure?"

"Business."

"Should we schedule another time to talk?"

"No, no. I'm fine. Now is good."

"How may I be of assistance?"

"Um, well, I work for Dr. Anlon Cully. He's the nephew of the late Devlin Wilson, the archaeologist," said Jennifer.

"Yes?"

Jennifer repeated the explanation she had left on Foucault's voicemail: "We've had a difficult time tracking down some of the purchase records for some pieces in Dr. Wilson's art collection. We need them to appraise the artifacts for probate. Dr. Cully is Dr. Wilson's executor. Anyway, I found correspondence between Dr. Wilson and Count Foucault discussing one of the items and I wondered if I might speak with him about it."

"I see. Can you describe the item? I can ask my employer and phone you back with an answer."

Jennifer contemplated how to describe the *Naetir*. She wondered if "Count" Foucault would know what a hockey puck looked like. "Um, it's a cylinder. About two inches tall, about five inches in diameter. Gray in color. It's a stone."

"Hmmm . . . it doesn't sound familiar. When did this correspondence occur? I handle nearly all of the count's letters, and I don't remember a note from Dr. Wilson."

"About nine months ago, between Thanksgiving and New Year's if

I remember correctly," said Jennifer, ruing the loss of her notebook. "It was an email exchange. I think Devlin, excuse me, Dr. Wilson wrote to him directly."

"Very well. I will be happy to check our records. Will you be gone for long?"

"Thank you, I appreciate it. Um, no. I should be back in the States within a day or two. You can reach me on this number," Jennifer said.

"I will call you as soon as I can," Christian replied.

Incline Village, Nevada

The kitchen door shut with a thud. Pebbles froze in mid-tiptoe and cringed. "Sorry!" With uncorked Cabernet bottle in one hand and two glasses in the other, she continued down the slate steps. "Light the fire, A.C."

"Okay, hold onto your britches!"

While Anlon fumbled along the fire pit's base in search of the starter switch, Pebbles began to hop in place. "Hurry! My feet are cold."

He swung around and reprimanded, "Well, put on shoes next time!" Finally, Anlon's hand found the switch and ignited the fire. "There? That better?"

Clad in a white tank top and black-and-blue polka-dot pajama pants, Pebbles nodded and scurried toward Anlon and the warmth of the fire pit. As she neared the blaze, her pink hair took on a rosy glow. Anlon smiled and relieved her of the bottle and glasses. Placing them on the table between their chairs, he wrapped his arms around her waist.

Pebbles cooed and snuggled against his shoulder. Anlon raised a hand to stroke her soft hair and guided her face to his. He stared into her eyes and kissed her deeply. Pebbles snaked her hands around his neck and closed her eyes as their tongues danced. Pulling away slightly, Pebbles whispered, "Hold on a sec."

Creeping forward, she maneuvered her icy toes atop Anlon's bare feet and sighed, "Ah . . . much better."

Anlon shivered and grimaced before breaking into a thin smile. Pebbles smiled in return and they resumed kissing. The intermittent crackle of flames and the occasional chirp of lonely insects were the only sounds around them. Above, the moonless sky was filled with thousands of stars. Among the glittering white dots, a solitary orange star flickered brightly.

Just as Anlon leaned to nibble Pebbles' neck, his cell phone blared a heavy metal ringtone. He paused, his lips hovering just beneath her ear. Pebbles turned away and clamped her hand against her mouth to muffle a laugh. "Oh my God! You have an Ice Zombies' ringtone?"

With a sigh, Anlon plopped onto a cushioned deck chair and reached for the phone. "Yeah, just added it."

"What? Are you a groupie for our new neighbor?"

"It's Jen's ringtone," Anlon said, smiling.

"Ahh . . ."

Anlon answered the phone.

"So much for romance!" Pebbles said, frowning. She curled onto the chair next to him and poured a glass of wine.

"Hey, Anlon," Jennifer whispered. "Can't talk long. Plane's about to go."

"No problem. What's up?" he asked.

"Are you sitting down?"

"Yeah. Why?"

"Margaret Corchran surfaced. In Brazil, somewhere in the Amazon."

"What? Where exactly?"

Anlon heard muffled noises over the phone, followed by the sound of Jennifer negotiating with the flight attendant. When she returned to the call, Jennifer whispered, "Gotta go. A place called Apuí. Oh, and she'd been to Dominica, too. I'll explain later."

"Okay, thanks for the call. Safe flight," said Anlon. He disconnected the call and turned to Pebbles. "Be back in a sec."

"Hey, where are you going?"

Anlon slowly mounted the back steps. "Margaret Corchran is in Brazil."

"What?" Pebbles stood and followed on his heels.

When they reached the kitchen door, Anlon held it open for Pebbles while saying, "According to Jen, Margaret showed up in Brazil, and she's been to Dominica."

Once inside, they headed for his office and gathered around the map. Anlon found the black pin in the lower left corner of Brazil. Turning to face Pebbles, he kissed her on the cheek and said, "Do me a favor. Hop on my laptop and search for a town called Apuí in Brazil."

"Sure." After a dozen keystrokes, she said, "It's a mining town."

"Where's it located?"

Pebbles clicked on an Apuí map link and up popped a map of Brazil with Apuí marked by a red dot. "Take a look."

Anlon moved behind her to look at the screen, then returned to the wall map. "Well, I guess I can take out the green pins now."

16

Healing Hands

Apuí, Brazil
August 17

Margaret moaned as she curled forward. Behind her, Christian positioned a pillow against the wall and said, "Lean back slowly. Not so fast. Slowly. Slowly."

Relaxing her weight against the pillow, Margaret sighed and ran a hand across the bandage covering her neck. Through bleary eyes, she scanned the room. For most of the past forty-eight hours, her view had been confined to the squeaky ceiling fan wobbling above the bed.

Next to the bed sat a small bureau that doubled as a nightstand. Painted turquoise, the table surface held a battered alarm clock, a phone and a lamp shaped like a toucan. In the far corner of the room sat a lumpy armchair. Once a bright shade of banana yellow, the chair now was mottled with greasy stains.

Upon this chair, Jacques Foucault perched uncomfortably in a tan suit and observed Margaret as she gained her bearings. At the foot of the bed was the only other piece of furniture in the room, a caned-back chair that loudly creaked each time Christian shifted his posture.

"Are you thirsty?" Foucault asked.

She nodded and Christian fetched a bottled water from the adjoining room. Margaret cautiously sipped the water and grimaced as she swallowed. Resting the bottle by her side, she closed her eyes and willed the throbbing in her throat to fade.

"I know it hurts," Foucault said. "In a little while, we will give you something to ease the pain."

Margaret opened her mouth to speak and a sharp sting radiated on her right side. Foucault said, "Do not try to speak. Not yet. Just listen and use your fingers to answer as you did with Christian. *Comprende?*"

She instinctively nodded and was rewarded with a burning twinge in her throat. She groaned and raised an index finger to signal "yes."

Rising from the armchair, Foucault paced across the room's wooden floor and eased down on the bed's edge. The flimsy frame squeaked and shivered under the added weight. He placed a hand atop her sheet-covered thigh. "You are very fortunate to be alive."

Margaret lifted a solitary finger again. Her memories of all that transpired after Navarro's attack were spotty, but she remembered enough to concur with Foucault's assessment.

Once Navarro set their campsite ablaze, she had watched him prance away without a care in the world while she floundered on the ground. She remembered being roused by two dark figures hovering in the glow of the fire. Their faces were stern and their words unintelligible. Convinced it was the Cinta-Larga come to finish her off, Margaret had closed her eyes and waited for the end.

Later, she stirred briefly and found she was on a wide canoe with several natives. One chanted above her while the others oared with the swift current. The chanting native smiled down at her and nodded reassuringly. When she awoke again, she was in a hospital ward. Unable to speak and heavily sedated, Margaret vaguely recalled a parade of doctors and nurses with concerned looks.

And then a policeman had arrived at her bedside and questioned her in broken English. When he took her fingerprints, Margaret realized she was in jeopardy. When he displayed the *Breylofte* and posed further questions, she recalled flashes of the trek through the jungle and Navarro's surprise attack. Mind spinning, she had felt an overwhelming need to flee.

She didn't recall beating the nurse or the escape from the hospital. She did remember lying in wait in a nearby parking lot for an unsuspecting victim. When the elderly man approached his car, she leapt from the shadows and tackled him to the ground. He struggled as she pounded his head against the pavement.

When he went limp, she riffled his pockets and relieved him of his car keys, cell phone and wallet. Still worked up by a combination of pain medication and adrenaline, Margaret drove several blocks away and called Christian. The conversation was brief. Find a hotel and then call him back. The next thing she knew, Christian was prodding her to sip fragrant water.

Margaret was roused from her thoughts by the sound of Foucault's voice. "I am anxious to learn more of your ordeal, but first you are in need of medical care. Christian has done his best to tend your wounds, but we fear you are bleeding inside. If we don't stop the bleeding quickly, you will die. Do you understand?"

She reached down and weakly tapped his hand with her index finger.

He gently squeezed her thigh. "*Bon*. I can stop the bleeding, Margaret, but I will need your help. Do you remember these?"

Foucault held out the *Dreylaeks*. Margaret held up a finger.

"You saw only a glimpse of their powers; they have many beyond self-defense. I can use them to stop the bleeding. *Comprende?*"

She tapped out another affirmative response on his hand.

Foucault said, "Christian will give you something to drink. It is gritty and tastes unpleasant. It will hurt to swallow, but you must drink it all. There is a sedative mixed in. You will become woozy and fall asleep. When you wake, you will be in much less pain. Then we will talk."

Christian handed her a small bottle containing a sludgy mixture of bright orange. She took a whiff of the concoction and flinched. Foucault said, "It smells worse than it tastes."

Unconvinced, Margaret took a small sip and gagged as the thick liquid coated her tongue. The initial flavor had an earthy-briny quality and was followed by a metallic aftertaste. When she swallowed, the grainy mixture scratched her already raw throat. She shook her head and tried to hand the bottle back.

"It is necessary, Margaret. Drink it," Foucault commanded.

With a heavy sigh, she closed her eyes and downed the contents. Christian held out his hand to receive the empty bottle and then guided her into a prone position on the bed. In less than a minute, she was out cold.

Turning to Christian, Foucault said, "Now we wait for her to digest the lichens."

During the wait, Foucault stepped out onto the hotel's small balcony. He lit a cigarette and watched a pair of men on motorbikes pass by and park in front of a small cantina across the street. A group of other men stood on the street outside the cantina and conversed over the clamor of an up-tempo reggae tune.

Evening had descended on Apuí, and the sprawling jungle town was stirring to life. Once a tiny community, the town's population had exploded in recent years thanks to a modern-day gold rush labeled Eldorado de Juma by fellow Brazilians. At the outset, the rush had been an international phenomenon, drawing upwards of ten thousand wildcat prospectors from all over the world. Though the mania peaked within a few years of the initial discovery, prospectors still made up nearly half of Apuí's population.

By day, Apuí was relatively quiet. Most of its working population pushed into the outlying fields, rivers and rainforest early in the morning. Ranchers, farmers, fishermen and prospectors worked long hours extracting nature's bountiful resources in the area. At night, however, when several thousand workers returned from their labors, the sleepy town buzzed with the sounds of a modern city.

While some residents welcomed the influx of commerce created by the gold rush, many others were appalled by the surge of deforestation of the surrounding lands and harsh changes to the tranquil rivers running near the town. Many viewed the prospectors as carpetbaggers who cared for little besides chewing the land for their glittering fortunes.

In turn, Apuí's longtime residents became increasingly distrustful of foreigners—a circumstance that had not escaped Foucault's notice from the moment he deplaned at the town's airstrip. Glowering eyes had followed him across the tarmac and into a taxi. The same was true when he arrived at the hotel, and even now Foucault felt stares among the men outside the cantina. He took a long drag on the cigarette and returned the stares.

The sound of the balcony door sliding open and quickly closing was followed by an update from Christian. "She is still asleep."

"Keep your voice down, *mon ami*," hushed Foucault.

Christian followed Foucault's eyes to the group outside the cantina. "My apologies, Monsieur."

"We need to leave here as soon as possible. Have Henri ready the plane for tomorrow morning," whispered Foucault.

"But she is in no condition to travel."

"We have no choice. The police must be searching for her, and there are too many eyes and ears around us."

The answer emboldened Christian. "Forgive me for asking, Monsieur, but do we really need her any longer?"

Foucault turned and glared at him. He inhaled deeply on the cigarette before flicking it onto the balcony floor. As he crushed it with his foot, he growled, "Inside."

Once Foucault closed the balcony door, he instructed Christian to close the connecting door to Margaret's room. Foucault then sat on the edge of one of the room's two double beds with Christian facing him from the other. In a low voice, Foucault firmly stated, "For now, Margaret's assistance is necessary."

Christian bristled. "May I speak freely?"

"Of course, *mon ami*."

"Her injuries, even with your help, will take time to fully heal. What assistance can she provide?"

"We don't need her fully healed," Foucault said. "Tell me, Christian, why do you think Navarro wanted to kill her?"

"For the same reasons we must. She is a fugitive, she draws too much attention . . . and, she knows too much."

Foucault frowned. "How long was she on Barbados?"

"Two months, give or take."

"Did she draw attention there?"

"No, but she went to Domin—"

"Did she not hand over the map freely? Was she not *un agent infil-tré* for us? For Navarro, did she not guide him to the Maerlif?"

Christian slumped and nodded.

"I ask you again, why did Navarro want to kill her?"

"I don't know," Christian said.

Foucault lit another cigarette and rose to pace the room. "*Précisé-ment!* It is possible he thought she knew too much, as you suggest. But, consider this. What if Navarro discovered she had betrayed him? Did he confront her? Did she confess? Is Navarro now aware of us? Should we not seek answers to these questions before deciding her fate?

"Or, if Navarro remains blind to us, did she learn any more about his intentions? Did she discover if he seeks the *Tuliskaera*? What if he is aligned with Muran?"

It was hard for Christian to debate Foucault's points, but there were other considerations. "Monsieur, every second we delay, Nava-rro moves farther ahead of us.

"And now we know Cully is actively looking for the *Tyls*. We don't know how much he has discovered or where his intentions stand. Can we afford to babysit Margaret for more than another day? Should we not wake her, pry what we need and then be done with her?"

"*Non!* I know you promised her brother we'd kill her when we found her, but I have a plan in mind for Margaret. You will need to trust me as you have many times before, Christian." Foucault patted Christian on the shoulder. "I feel the same urgency to act. So much is at stake."

Christian sighed. "Very well, Monsieur. Have you decided what to do about Cully's inquiry?"

Foucault fiddled with the gold medallion. When Christian first relayed the details of his conversation with Cully's associate, Foucault had been relieved. If Cully was simply cataloging Devlin Wilson's possessions for probate, then it might mean he was otherwise unin-terested in the *Tyls*.

On the other hand, the fact that Cully's associate was headed to Mexico on business worried Foucault. It might mean Cully was trying to decipher the map. Foucault had struggled to read it; why not Cully, too? The longer he pondered the possibility, the more it surprised him that Navarro was the first to crack Devlin's cryptic rendition.

When Margaret first gave Foucault an electronic copy on Barbados, he had been baffled by the map's lack of detail. Even the supplemental file she provided was of little help. He knew of Dominica, of course, and several other burial Maerlifs, but none were apparent on Devlin's map.

The same was true when Foucault layered Devlin's drawing over a world map on his computer. None of the volcano crypts he knew of aligned with Devlin's map, with the sole exception of Dominica—and that was only possible when the map was rotated at an odd angle. Though Foucault was intimately familiar with the Egyptian Duat wall drawing that inspired Devlin's map, he was surprised by the angle required to find a point that aligned with Dominica. He wondered whether Devlin had incorrectly interpreted Malinyah's vision.

However, when the map was aligned with Dominica as its focal point, Foucault had noted a few sites that seemed plausible Maerlif locations, even if they weren't situated near volcanos. After all, Foucault had thought, Malinyah might have chosen to stash *Tyls* in places other than volcanos. She might have picked more accessible spots along the Munuorians' trading routes. This latter thought had attracted Foucault to one particular site on the Dominica-oriented map, Parque Natural Los Alcornocales, near Gibraltar, in southern Spain.

When considering the site, Foucault had been drawn to its strategic location. From the many *Tyls* found among Greek, Mesopotamian and Egyptian ruins, Foucault had long ago concluded that some of the ships sent to help Munirvo survivors had made their way to the Mediterranean. Beyond the *Tyls*, there were other signs the Munuorians had visited the area. In Foucault's mind, many of the mysteries surrounding dynastic Egypt hinted at Munuorian influence. There was their fascination with pyramids as burial monuments. One could also point to the unexplained, precise shaping of their stone blocks, sarcophagi linings, spheres and sculptures. Many showed no chisel marks, no evidence of manual tooling of any kind. And, of course, there was the biggest archaeological mystery of all . . . how they moved and placed the massive blocks to construct the pyramids.

Foucault speculated the Munuorians passed the Spanish site on their journey to reach Egypt as well as other locations in southern Europe and northern Africa. So, Foucault sent Christian to Los Alcornocales.

For several days, Christian had traveled around the rocky Spanish park with detecting devices and a *Breylofte* but found nothing. Then, shortly after Christian returned to Pézenas, Navarro had contacted Margaret to request she join him on an expedition to "find more Stones." She, in turn, had alerted Foucault.

When pressed for the expedition's location, Margaret had said Navarro would not reveal his intended target. He only told her to meet him in Manaus, Brazil.

It was a puzzling choice, Foucault thought at the time, for the map showed no site in Brazil when aligned to Dominica. Nevertheless, Foucault decided to send Christian to Manaus to await an update from Margaret. Later, after she finally communicated the coordinates of Navarro's search, Foucault had again rotated Devlin's map atop the world map and discovered it was possible to align with a point deep in the Amazon. The resulting alignment didn't include Dominica as a marked spot, however, leading Foucault to assume Navarro was grasping at straws.

At the same time, Navarro's selection had suggested a troubling thought. The Argentinian had progressed beyond reading the map and was now on the hunt. The question was, whose reading was right, Foucault's or Navarro's?

When he called Christian with Navarro's coordinates, Foucault had told him he thought it was a wild goose chase but asked him to go nonetheless. Christian agreed to the assignment, but he disagreed with Foucault's goose-chase assessment. When asked why, Christian had said, "Monsieur, the Cinta-Larga, surely you remember the Cinta-Larga?"

The mention of the tribe jogged Foucault's memory. He recalled the Amazon denizens and their *terra preta*, the rich soil from which Foucault's oleanders drew their nourishment.

Long before the Cinta-Larga had been chased into the Amazon by invading colonists, they had been farmers, prolific farmers who planted their seeds in "Black Earth," a soil that produced unusually strong yields. *Terra preta* was unlike soil found anywhere else in the world.

After disappearing into the jungle, the Cinta-Larga were forgotten. But in the nineteenth century, whispers of a ruthless tribe spread among Amazon explorers. Rumored to practice dark magic, the tribe was said to possess powers that made rocks cry diamonds. These rumors lured prospectors into the jungle, and ever since, a battle had raged on both sides for the Amazon's gems.

Christian had reminded Foucault of these rumors, adding, "Perhaps Navarro knows something about the map we don't."

"*Oui*. I am missing something, Christian. A detail I should know. I can feel it," Foucault had replied.

It was a sobering thought, one that still weighed on Foucault's mind. In that context, Cully's interest in Mexico was a concern. Might he, too, know something about the map unknown to Foucault?

At present, there was nothing Foucault could do about Navarro. Until Margaret could communicate, he was temporarily blind to Navarro's knowledge and intentions. But . . . he'd be damned to pass the unexpected opportunity to probe the same with Cully.

Emerging from these thoughts, Foucault turned to answer Christian's question. "When we are finished with Margaret, call Cully's associate back. Tell her I've asked you to handle the matter. Answer her questions about the *Naetir*, but for heaven's sake, don't call it that in your conversation. Then, ask her what Cully plans to do with Devlin's *Tyls*. Tell her I might be interested in acquiring one or more pieces if Cully is considering selling them. Let's see what she has to say."

While Christian kept a vigil over Margaret, Foucault disappeared into the adjoining room to rest. An hour later, he returned and announced it was time to begin the procedure. Christian expressed surprise they were starting so soon. "Can she have digested it all already?"

"Not all, but most," Foucault said. "The magnetic particles we need her to digest are bound to sugars in the lichens. They absorb quickly." The puzzled look on Christian's face caused Foucault to further explain. "The conditions are in our favor. She has not eaten for two days, so she is starved for energy. The body will seek the quickest and easiest source of energy available—sugar."

Satisfied with the explanation, Christian peeled away the tape and gauze covering her sutured abdomen. He was pleased to see reduced swelling and discoloration around the stitched wound. Foucault had surprised him when he initially suggested layering Margaret's sutures with gauze soaked in *enjyia*.

In the many years of their association, he'd rarely seen Foucault use it as a topical. When making the recommendation for Margaret, Foucault had explained that it was an effective antibacterial when applied topically. "It is too precious to use on nicks and cuts, but large wounds are another matter."

Christian knew *enjyia* ravaged damaged and diseased cells, but he also knew it worked too slowly to seal a seeping wound. For that, the *Dreylaeks* were necessary.

He was anxious to see the *Dreylaeks* used in this way. Although Christian knew they possessed healing powers, he'd only seen Foucault use them as weapons. He asked Foucault to describe how they would stanch Margaret's bleeding.

"The procedure is not complicated," Foucault said, "but it requires an experienced touch."

If the *Dreylaeks* were heated too quickly, he explained, they would lose their sensitivity to detect the magnetic particles in Margaret's blood. If they were heated too long, they could cause the particles to liquefy and set her internal organs afire. However, if stimulated properly, a heated *Dreylaek* pressed against the skin near the injury would excite the magnetic particles leaking from the rupture. Other magnetic particles circulating in the bloodstream would flow to the injury site and oscillate as Foucault rubbed the second green stone against the first. When enough particles accumulated, the *Dreylaek* pressed against Margaret's skin would vibrate. Then, and only then, Foucault would strike the Stones together, sending a jolt of electricity toward the gathered magnetic bits. Electrified, they would fuse the leak.

"It is the same principle as cauterization, but it does not require an incision to find the rupture," Foucault said.

"But, Monsieur, how can you be sure they gather at the leak and not somewhere else?"

"It is simple, really. Blood vessels have a protective lining. When the lining is intact, it acts as a shield that weakens the *Dreylaeks'* pull on the magnetic material inside the vessel. But, at a tear in the lining, there is nothing to prevent the *Dreylaeks* from attracting their magnetism. It is the only place where a critical mass of the particles can gather," Foucault said.

More fascinated than confused, Christian asked, "What if there is more than one rupture?"

Foucault pressed the *Dreylaeks* between his palms. "That is certainly possible, but if there are multiple leaks, they can only be small ones. Otherwise, she would have died before now. But, to be sure, we will repeat the procedure around each stitched area."

In slow, purposeful circles, Foucault began to grind the *Dreylaeks* against each other. Soon, they began to warm. Closing his eyes, he increased the rhythm of his strokes. As the heat from the Stones rose, he reduced the pressure of the grinding motion but maintained a steady, circular rhythm. Christian noticed a faint glow appear between Foucault's fingers.

Shortly afterward, Foucault opened his eyes and ceased rubbing. Lowering one of the stones to Margaret's abdomen, he said, "It is time."

Villahermosa, Mexico

Jennifer stretched out on the hotel bed and yawned deeply. Kicking off her flats, she wiggled her toes and let the cool air soothe her aching feet. She had been tempted to wear her running shoes to the meeting at Parque-Museo La Venta but decided they might be too informal.

Thus, she had been surprised when the museum curator, Rafael Jimenez, introduced himself wearing sneakers, a Hawaiian shirt and shorts. He had noticed her crestfallen look and said, "As you can see, La Venta is an outdoor museum. It gets too hot to dress up."

In sharp contrast to "Chuck" Goodwin, Rafael had been relaxed, open and quite helpful. He gave her a tour of the Olmec statues displayed around the park and then escorted her to his office. There, he had shown her a map of the La Venta archaeological site, roughly an hour's drive away, where the Olmec statues were originally unearthed. He told her they discovered other artifacts there as well, including a half dozen stone bowls like the one they gave to Devlin.

Handing him a picture of the *Sinethal*, she had asked if they found any comparable stone objects there. Rafael had said no, but then said he'd seen similar tiles in other museums in Central and South America.

Jennifer then showed him the pictures of the statuettes and asked if they looked familiar. He looked long and hard at the dragon-head statue picture and said, "I have seen statues with similar headdresses, but not ones with such an angry face."

"Headdress?" Jennifer had asked.

"Yes, you see here. It's a fish head. The man's head is inside the fish's mouth."

"What? No, it's a dragon's head."

He examined Jennifer's picture again while pulling on his beard. Finally, Rafael had looked up and said, "I don't think so. Here, let me show you."

He banged on his computer keyboard and pulled up a picture of similar statues displayed in a museum. Only, these statues were enormous, much taller than the people gathered around them in the picture. He pointed at one statue which showed a lizard's head with a man's head in his jaws.

In many ways, it looked like the dragon-head statuette in Devlin's collection, except the lizard-headdress man carried a stoic expression.

The figure sat on a bench with arms at his side and stared ahead. Jennifer looked at other statues on the computer screen. One had a headdress of an eagle, another of a jaguar. All of the men beneath the various headdresses exhibited the same blank stare.

A fish head? Jennifer thought. Then she remembered the fish symbol on the back of the statue's head. Of course, that's it!

"Where are these statues?" Jennifer had asked.

"They are in a museum in Granada, Nicaragua."

"Where were they found? Originally?"

"An island close to Granada called Zapatera."

Jennifer's mind raced. She mumbled, "Why does that name sound familiar?"

The answers had followed in quick succession. She gasped and asked Rafael for a printout of the pictures. Noticing the marked change in Jennifer's disposition, he had asked if he'd said something to upset her. She assured him that wasn't the case at all, she was just excited to finally learn the statuette's origin.

When she left the museum, she had called Anlon and Pebbles. They were equally as stunned to hear her news. They were even more stunned when she told them of the connections between the Granada statues and her earlier visits with Anabel and Goodwin.

With the phone call completed, Jennifer had returned to the hotel and collapsed on the bed. Now, lying on her side, she closed her eyes and propped a pillow beneath her head. As she edged toward sleep, a text message alert sounded. It was followed shortly thereafter by another alert.

Stretching across the bed, Jennifer dragged the phone off the nightstand and glanced at the screen with one eye. The messages were both from Griffin. Rolling on her back, she held the phone above her face and read the first text: "You've inspired me to write a new song."

Jennifer beamed when she looked below at the second message. It was an audio file attachment titled "Cuff Me."

17

Ometepe

Incline Village, Nevada
August 25

hould we start with Zapatera?" Jennifer asked.

Gathered in Anlon's office, they stood before the wall map. Anlon said, "I thought about it, especially since it's so close to Ometepe, but neither are marked on the Waterland Map."

Pebbles edged closer to the map. There were two pins dotting Nicaragua, a blue one marking Ometepe on the Pacific side and a black one on the Caribbean side. "So, you're thinking we should start with the black pin here? Hit Ometepe and Zapatera afterwards?"

"Yep, that's where I was leaning. The black pin is in a nature reserve called Indio Maiz," said Anlon. "It's about two hundred and fifty miles by air from Ometepe. But, prepare yourselves. We might end up making multiple trips like Devlin did in the Caribbean."

"What do you mean?" Jennifer asked.

"Well, it's conjecture on my part, but I think Devlin ended up going to Guadeloupe and Martinique before Dominica because his map's longitude and latitude markings were sketchy. Even though the islands are only one degree latitude apart, it still took him three trips to find the Maerlif.

"I've tried to line up Devlin's map the best I can, but it's still imprecise. The scale of the map is so small, one degree off, latitude or longitude, could put us in the wrong place by seventy miles or more,"

Anlon said. "Plus, it'll be rough going, at least for me. Indio Maiz is a dense rainforest."

"Well, maybe we shouldn't try until your leg is back at full strength," Pebbles said. "Or, Jen and I could go without you."

"Not a chance," said Anlon. "I'm going, I'll just have to take it slow."

"Why not start with one of the islands instead?" Jennifer asked.

"We could, but again, neither Ometepe or Zapatera is marked on Devlin's map. Even though we've got some pretty clear signs that one or the other was important to Devlin, we don't know why, we don't know what to look for or where to start. At Indio Maiz, we know all three."

"Just playing devil's advocate," said Jennifer, "we do know Devlin was interested in volcanos, right? Can't we limit our searches on the islands to volcanos? And we know he was looking for something to do with the little fish-man statue. Couldn't we narrow our search further and focus in areas near the volcanos where the life-sized statues were found?"

Anlon folded his hands together and steepled his fingers. "It's a thought. I talked to Cesar Perez yesterday and he said Ometepe is an archaeological playground. He told me there are lots of petroglyphs on Concepción, one of the island's volcanos. We could go there and see if any of the glyphs look Munuorian, but Cesar said it would be hard to get close to the glyphs without permission. He offered to join us in Nicaragua and help us get 'inside the ropes' on Ometepe. Only trouble is, he can't break away for another week."

"Then, let's just wait a week and start with Ometepe," Pebbles said.

Anlon scratched his head and frowned. "I'm cool with waiting for Cesar. If we do find any artifacts, it would be good to have a real, live archaeologist with us. But, I don't know, I feel like we should concentrate on finding the Stones first. The thought of Navarro getting there before us bugs me."

"I hear you," Jennifer said, nodding. "But he may have already gone to Indio Maiz, right? We know he tried Brazil. Wouldn't Indio Maiz be a logical next stop?"

"And don't forget Margaret Corchran. She may be out there some-where, too," Pebbles added. "Not trying to be a buzzkill, but Marga-ret and Navarro probably don't know about Ometepe, right? Wouldn't it be safer to start there or Zapatera?"

Anlon peered at the blue pushpin anchored in the Nicaraguan lake. Ometepe was surely the more prudent option, but it was also the more speculative one. If not for the one-word mention of the island in Dev-lin's journal, Anlon never would have given the place a look.

The fish-man statuette, however, changed all that. Ometepe of-fered a chance to bring clarity to Devlin's odd journal entries, and an opportunity to understand his concern about time. But was that enough to put Ometepe ahead of Indio Maiz? If the priority was to confirm Anlon's reading of the map and find an undisturbed cache of Stones, then Indio Maiz was the place to start.

This was especially true given Malinyah's demonstration of the *Tuliskaera*. It was just as lethal as Pacal had boasted. Such a weapon in the wrong hands would be frightening. And Navarro and Marga-ret seemed the very definition of "wrong hands."

Yet, if Cesar's *Rivers of Gold* hunch was right, Navarro was think-ing like a miner, not a despot. But how long would it take him to go from one to the other? Despite the Argentinian's blustery bravado, he was an adversary to respect . . . and to fear.

And what of Margaret Corchran? Was she still alive? If so, was she in any condition to move about? A machete clear through the ab-domen and a garroted throat? The loss of blood alone should have killed her, but she somehow managed to elude capture *again*. Unless her dead body was discovered, they couldn't count her out. Wounded or no, she had already proven herself a ruthless killer.

And where the hell was Thatcher Reynolds? They hadn't discussed him since Margaret popped up in Brazil. He was the most elusive of the three, and the one with the prime interest in the *Tuliskaera*, al-beit as a middleman. Without knowing who was pushing his buttons, there was no way to know their intentions. At least Thatcher didn't get the Waterland Map, thought Anlon. But who was to say he or his confederates wouldn't try again?

Anlon put an arm around Pebbles and said, "I don't know, Pebbles. My heart says Ometepe, but my head says Indio Maiz. We'll have to keep a sharp eye out, but I think we need to take the risk and try Indio Maiz first. What do you think, Jen?"

"If time is a consideration, I agree Indio Maiz should come first. But, if we run into any of the bad guys, we back off. Agreed? No throwdowns." Jennifer cringed as the pun rolled off her tongue.

With the decision made, Jennifer turned and picked up the fish-man statuette from Anlon's desk. She held it up to Raphael's printout tacked on the wall next to the map and asked, "Why do you think the face is so different from the Zapatera statues?"

"I don't know," said Anlon. "I emailed Cesar a copy of the picture and asked him the same thing. He didn't have an answer."

Pebbles cocked her head to one side. "You know, I'm not sure I'd say it's an angry face. It looks more pained to me."

"I agree," Jennifer said. "But, the sword in the fish-man's hand makes it look like he's ready to attack."

"Yeah, but Malinyah said the Munuorians didn't use swords," Pebbles said. Then she grumbled, "It's the only thing she has to say about it."

"Really?" Jennifer asked.

Pebbles nodded. She'd visited with Malinyah twice since first asking about the dragon-head figurine, and both times Malinyah deflected conversation about the statue. One of those visits occurred prior to Jennifer's discovery.

In the second visit, after Jennifer's trip to Villahermosa, Pebbles revised her description of the statue and told Malinyah it wasn't a dragon-head, but a man wearing a headdress that looked like a fish head. She again mentioned the fish symbol on the back of the headdress and reminded Malinyah that legends about her people referred to the Munuorians as the fish men. Malinyah claimed anew she had no knowledge of the statue, and she repeated the tidbit about the sword.

Jennifer examined the sword. She ran a finger over the long, jagged object and asked, "What if it's not a sword?"

Anlon peeked over her shoulder. "What else could it be?"

She handed the statue to Anlon. "I'm not sure," she said. "Maybe it's a stick on fire, or a snake or maybe—you know, come to think of it, I'd say it looks like a lightning bolt. Maybe he's being electrocuted."

"Hmmm, maybe," Anlon said. The jagged protrusion flared into curls along the length. It was an odd way to depict lightning, but it was conceivable. Pebbles said Malinyah was adamant the Munuorians didn't use swords. But . . . they did use fire. And they surely knew how to produce electricity.

Jennifer asked, "What did Cesar have to say about the Ometepe statues?"

"Not much more than you learned about the Zapatera statues. Most of them are huge, like six to nine feet tall. Cesar said they've been dated to 1500 B.C.E., but he also said the support for the estimate is weak. He said it's possible they are far older. Oh, I did learn one thing new. Guess what they're cut from?"

They looked up in unison. A smile spread across his face. "Olivine basalt."

"But these are reddish. I thought you said olivine was blackish-green?" Pebbles asked.

"That's true, I did say that. But these statues have been sitting out in a hot, humid rainforest for at least thirty-five hundred years. A rainforest that sits damn near the Pacific Ocean. All that salty, moist air can easily turn olivine a red-brown color. It's rust, essentially." Shuffling between the boxes, Anlon reached for a basalt rock on the bookshelf and brought it back to Pebbles. "Like this one here."

"Is the fish-man basalt?" Jennifer asked.

"It is," said Anlon. "Same as the Stones, although it doesn't have kimberlites mixed in."

Jennifer thought of her follow-up phone call with Anabel. "I still don't buy Anabel's explanation."

"What did she say, exactly?" Anlon asked.

"She said she didn't make the connection between the two pictures."

"They do look quite different," Pebbles said. "You didn't notice it either before you showed her the photos."

"I guess that's true," acknowledged Jennifer, "but my gut tells me she knows more than she's saying. I wish I understood why she's holding back."

"Could be lots of reasons," Anlon said.

"Such as?" Jennifer looked at Anlon expectantly.

"Maybe she doesn't want to get involved; maybe it brings back bad memories," Pebbles suggested.

"Hmmm. Maybe, but why didn't she just say that? Instead, when I asked her how she knew the *Sinethal* was Devlin's special stone, she stumbled all over herself. She didn't do any better when I probed her about the map."

"Well, we have to take her at her word for now," Anlon said.

"Yeah, I guess." Trying to shake the gnawing feeling from her mind, Jennifer changed topics. "Can we deal with some logistical matters? When we get to Nicaragua, how are we going to find the vault, and how do we open it?"

"We're definitely going to need Malinyah's help," Anlon said. "Devlin pretty much used the same methods to search each of the Caribbean islands. He obviously got some insight from Malinyah but not enough to make his job easy."

"What do you mean?" Jennifer asked.

"He wasn't able to find a way into the Dominica vault. He found the *Breylofte* petroglyph, and his journal says he tried to use a *Breylofte* to find the entrance, but it didn't work. I'm wondering if he missed something Malinyah tried to share with him, especially since he couldn't understand the Munuorian language."

"But, Anlon, you said you think Dobson found the gold on Dominica, right?" Jennifer asked. "Didn't he follow Devlin's notes?"

"He did. Or, at least I think that's what the yellow highlighter implies. But, I don't know. It is puzzling how he found the entrance and Devlin didn't."

"Well, let's stop guessing," Pebbles said. "I'll ask her right now how to find a vault."

"And how to open it. We need to know that, too," Anlon said.

Anlon and Jennifer stood by the hearth as Pebbles reclined on the living room sofa. She rested the *Sinethal* on her lap and reached for the *Naetir*. Smiling at the two of them, she said, "Hopefully, she doesn't get grouchy like the last couple of times!"

Malinyah was normally expansive in her answers and welcomed follow-up questions. But the questions about her *Sinethal* and the fish-man statue touched some nerve. When Pebbles asked about the artifacts, Malinyah's answers turned curt and dismissive. They were also tinged with a surge of emotion that Pebbles still didn't understand. A cold, stern feeling passed through Pebbles whenever they talked about the objects.

It was so strange. In her last visit, they had a lovely time together until Pebbles raised the subject of the statue. The visit started out with a conversation about the map, and Malinyah was very candid describing why the Stones were cached and why she made the map. She showed Pebbles visions of the map and other bits of the preparations they had made ahead of Munirvo. She even showed a touching vision of her farewell with Mereau.

During the conversation, Malinyah told Pebbles that her role among the Andaers was to safeguard the *Lifintyls*. She said once it became clear Munirvo would be far worse than originally expected, she made the decision to take a portion of their *Lifintyl* inventory and store them along their trade routes. It was a precaution to ensure their precious *Tyls* would survive if Munuoria took a direct hit from a piece of the asteroid.

While Mereau and his captains made their last run for provisions,

Malinyah sent other ships to store sets of the *Tyls* at a dozen locations. She gave them guidance on where to store them, but the ship captains ultimately decided on the final spots. When they returned, she updated the map based on the final placements.

When she showed Pebbles the map, Pebbles noticed it was different from Devlin's landscape. They'd always assumed Devlin used the Waterland Map as a proxy for Malinyah's map, but they weren't identical. For one thing, on Malinyah's map, some locations were well inland, whereas on Devlin's map they were all shown on or near coastlines. Pebbles also asked her about Devlin's color coding because Malinyah's vision of the map showed only one mark at each site. Malinyah was puzzled and could offer no explanation.

Then came the touching vision of her farewell with Mereau. The asteroid had passed and Mereau readied the ships to go help survivors. They stood on the docks while men carried supplies and *Tyls* onto the ships. That was new information as well. Mereau and his captains set forth with their own caches of *Tyls*, but Malinyah gave Mereau a copy of the map to share with his captains in case they needed replacements or there was a demand for more. She told him it would be easier to retrieve needed *Tyls* from the caches instead of coming all the way back to Munuoria. Mereau agreed.

When Malinyah handed him the map, they embraced. Pebbles felt a rush of warmth flow through her, and then a deep sorrow. Malinyah wore a gold medallion on a golden chain. In the middle of the medallion was a black stone that sparkled. In fact, to Pebbles, it seemed to glow. Malinyah removed the necklace and handed it to Mereau, saying, *"Ailta erill, ento ainfa."*

Mereau received the necklace and slid it over his head. He kissed the stone, and then Malinyah, and repeated the parting words. Malinyah cried; Mereau stiffened his jaw and hugged her. As Malinyah sobbed, Mereau held her tight. In his eyes, Pebbles could see tears. Watching the vision, Pebbles felt Malinyah's pain. It was biting, deep sorrow. Yet, although it was sad, the emotions transferred by Malinyah were filled with a tenderness that was hard to describe.

After they separated, Malinyah stood on the dock until the last ship passed from view. Pebbles quietly stood by her side and laced her fingers with Malinyah's. With tears trickling down her face, Malinyah turned and smiled. Pebbles hugged her and they walked from the dock.

When Malinyah exited the vision, Pebbles asked what the parting meant. Malinyah said, "Ever apart, together always."

That's when their conversation had turned to the statue, and Malinyah morphed into a different person. Gone were the affectionate gestures, the smiles and the flowing dialogue. Malinyah wouldn't look at Pebbles; she wouldn't answer questions with more than a word or two. When Pebbles asked what was wrong, Malinyah just stared straight ahead. After that last go-round, Pebbles told Anlon she wouldn't ask any more questions about the statue. She was concerned Malinyah would shut down completely.

So, as she readied to snap the *Naetir* into its slot on the *Sinethal*, Pebbles closed her eyes and hoped for a return of the Malinyah she'd grown to love. With a loud clap, the *Naetir* slammed into place. Pebbles slid her fingers into position and waited for the visions to commence.

When Pebbles arrived in the vision, she found herself alone in the marble hall. It was the first time Malinyah had not been there to greet her. Puzzled, Pebbles circled around the hall and peered out the sheer drapes. Outside, it was cloudy. Another first. She looked toward the Alynioria field and by the wading pool but found both empty. She grew nervous and called out for Malinyah. There was no answer. Pebbles paced the hall more urgently as a cold gust of wind pushed into the room. She shuddered and warmed her arms with her hands.

She walked outside and searched for Malinyah. Her gaze drifted up the hill to the Seybalrosa shrine. It was there she spied Malinyah seated beneath the tree. The branches of the tree whipped in the wind. Pebbles looked up to see a fiery glow filtering through the darkening clouds.

She started up the path, walking at first, but as she drew closer, she broke into a run and called for Malinyah. Her feet sank into the soft clay with every stride. Malinyah had yet to raise her head. It started to rain. Icy blobs of water splattered everywhere. Pebbles could feel the pelting drops trickle through her hair.

When she arrived beneath the tree, she reached out and touched Malinyah on the shoulder. The contact stirred Malinyah from her daze. The Munuorian peered up at Pebbles and said, "You're soaked."

Shivering, Pebbles said, "I called for you, but you didn't come. What's going on, why is it raining?"

Malinyah closed her eyes and the rain stopped. The clouds began to roll back and, soon, there was blue sky above. She reached to touch Pebbles' wrist and suddenly Pebbles felt a warm wave pass over her body. No longer wet, she ceased trembling.

Pebbles lowered herself next to Malinyah. "How did you do that?"

"Not to worry, Alynioria, all is well now." Malinyah smiled.

"Um, no. All is not well. What was that all about?" Pebbles pressed.

The Munuorian patted Pebbles' knee. "You have more questions. Tell me, sweet flower, why have you come?"

For the first time in Malinyah's presence, Pebbles felt anger rise from within. Unwilling to ignore the evasions any longer, Pebbles squeezed Malinyah's hand to quell her pats. "Why won't you talk to me? Have I done something wrong?"

"Why, no. I'm not angry with you."

"Then why do you keep shutting down?"

"I don't know what you mean."

"Malinyah! You're doing it right now!"

Malinyah's sunny smile faded. She pulled her hand from Pebbles' grip and slowly rose. Looking away from Pebbles, she turned and walked from beneath the shade of the Seybalrosa. Pebbles jumped up and trailed her around the cactus garden. With head lowered, Malinyah proceeded to the cliff overlooking the ocean.

A score of orange butterflies leapt from the outstretched cactus arms and fluttered aside her. Confused, Pebbles followed behind. When they arrived at the cliff's edge, Malinyah halted and inhaled the sea breeze. Most of the butterflies settled on her head and shoulders. Others landed on Pebbles, their tiny legs tickled her shoulders.

Pebbles was about to speak when Malinyah softly said, "I am worried, Alynioria. For you, and your friends. Some of what you've told me, some of your questions—they trouble me."

"Why?"

"I misread your intentions."

"My intentions? You think I've lied to you?"

Malinyah turned to face Pebbles. "No. I hear truth in your words and I feel it in your mind. I always have."

"Then I don't understand."

"When you asked for my help, you said you sought the *Lifintyls*."

"That's right."

"Why?"

Pebbles fumbled for an answer. The immediate one that leapt to mind was to prevent the Navarros of the world from using the Stones to hurt others. Then, there was their desire to carry forward Devlin's research. Plus, it was clear Anlon was fascinated by Munuorian technology. And for her own curiosity, Pebbles craved to know more about Malinyah and the Munuorian way of life.

"I guess there are multiple reasons, but they're all about learning more about you and your people," Pebbles said.

"Do you intend to use the *Lifintyls*?"

Thinking of Anlon's interest in the Stones' magnetic properties, Pebbles said, "Well, we'd like to understand them better. Figure out how they work, and how you made them. They're so different from any tools we have today. They could be very helpful."

"Or very hurtful," said Malinyah.

"Oh, I see. You're worried we might misuse them."

Malinyah held out her arm and several of the butterflies took new positions along its length. She blew lightly and the butterflies fluttered upward. They hovered for a few seconds and then descended. She puffed again, this time a bit harder. The butterflies rose higher in the air before landing again on her arm. She mumbled, "Such gentle creatures. Curious. Intelligent. Sensitive. Trusting. Have you seen what happens when they get too close to fire?"

"Okay, I get it. We might have good intentions, but—"

Malinyah interrupted. "Alynioria, I misled you. We did not create our *Tyls* for others. Even among ourselves, they were restricted to those who studied long to master their powers. Then Munirvo came and changed everything. Although we avoided the worst of it, we did not escape unscathed, as I showed you.

"But I didn't show you all. There was great unrest, a feeling among our people that the Andaers failed to protect Munuoria. So many died from the accursed star-washer. There was a rebellion as well as treachery on both sides. It led to bloodshed and chaos. In the end, the very tools we created for our enrichment, the ones that saved us from Munirvo, became weapons that consumed us."

Suddenly, the ocean waves below began to swell. Dark clouds covered the sky. The ground trembled. The butterflies lifted off in unison and rapidly flocked away. Pebbles felt Malinyah's rage shoot through her body. Searing pain stabbed her chest and abdomen. She buckled onto the ground and wretched.

Malinyah screamed, "Deceiver! Murderer! Betrayer! Muran!"

She collapsed next to Pebbles and wailed. Agony, horrifying agony, rippled through Pebbles' mind. She whipped her head from side to side and screamed.

When the convulsions began, Anlon and Jennifer stared in stunned silence. The blood-curdling screams that followed shook them into action. They raced to Pebbles' side and tried to yank the Stone from her grip. Pebbles' back arched off the sofa and her legs flailed. Anlon barked at Jennifer to hold her down while he tried to peel Pebbles' hands from the back of the Stone.

Then the unbelievable happened.

Anlon slid his fingers into the depressions to dig underneath Pebbles' fingertips. At once, he found himself atop the cliff standing above the writhing women. Through wild eyes he looked up to see a flaming chunk of rock barreling toward the water. He staggered as the ground heaved and gusts of wind battered him backward. Behind him, he heard a vicious crack amid the flaming rock's deafening roar. He spun to see the Seybalrosa sheared in two.

Pebbles looked up and saw the top half of the tree flying toward Anlon. She screamed his name and released the *Sinethal*. The *Naetir* rolled into her lap and Anlon crumpled onto the floor. In a stupor, Jennifer stumbled back from the couch and covered her mouth. Eyes blinking to make sense of the scene, she gasped, "Christ almighty!"

Leaning over the sofa's armrest, Jennifer poured tequila into a glass and placed it in Pebbles' hand. Without a word, Pebbles lifted the tumbler to her lips and let its contents slide down. Its burning trail coated her empty stomach. She held out the glass for a refill and murmured her thanks.

In an armchair across the room sat Anlon. His eyes were transfixed on the *Sinethal* resting on the ottoman before him. Jennifer paced over and offered a drink. Anlon accepted the glass with an appreciative smile.

Filling her own tumbler, Jennifer curled into the sofa corner opposite Pebbles and anxiously observed her two friends. She desperately wanted to know what had happened, but she couldn't bring herself to ask. The three sat in silence for several minutes. It was Pebbles who spoke first.

"Are you okay?" she asked Anlon.

"Uh-huh. You?"

"I think so. I ache all over, but the tequila's helping."

Jennifer said, "Um, in case anyone's wondering, I'm not okay. What in the hell just happened?"

Anlon whisked down his drink and grimaced. With a head shake, he said, "These Stones keep dishing out surprises."

His eyes waxed over as he pointed at the *Sinethal*. "When I tried to grab the Stone away, I connected to Pebbles' vision. I have no idea what I walked in on, but it was terrifying. It felt like the world was ending."

They both looked at Pebbles. Her eyes were hollow and her skin pale. A tear trickled down her cheek. "We were talking and then all of a sudden, kaboom! The world *was* ending . . . She's angry. Very angry."

"How did it start, Pebbles? Were you talking about the vaults?" Anlon asked.

"I didn't get that far," she said. "The visit was weird right from the start. Every other time I've met with her, it's always started in the hall or just outside. It's always been warm and sunny. This time, it was dark and rainy. I had to look all over for her. She was up at the Seybalrosa monument. I tried to get her attention several times, but she was zoned out.

"When she finally did snap out of it, I tried to get her to tell me why everything seemed different. She wouldn't answer me. She just dodged my questions again. But then she started to open up . . . and whammo!" Lowering her head, Pebbles massaged her wrists and sighed. "She came right out and said she had lied to me."

"Really? About what?" Jennifer asked.

Pebbles sighed again. "The whole 'we went out to save the world' tale. It wasn't as noble as she led us to believe."

"What really happened then?" Anlon asked.

"I don't know for sure. From what little she said before she popped her lid, there was a revolt after Munirvo passed. People were angry at what had happened. They started fighting each other. She said they used the *Tyls* against each other."

Anlon reflected on her comments while Pebbles and Jennifer discussed other elements of the cliff-side encounter. He thought of the array of ancient myths about the fish men. Regardless of Malinyah's changed story, it seemed indisputable the Munuorians did indeed help survivors of the great flood. How was such a feat possible in the middle of a revolt?

His rumination was interrupted when he heard Pebbles mention butterflies. As he tuned in to the conversation, he heard Pebbles describe Malinyah's moth-to-the-flame allegory. She finished the story by saying, "So, basically, she thinks we'll use the Stones for bad, even

though I've told her before we're trying to stop bad people from finding them."

Anlon's curiosity was piqued. "Why would she think that?"

"I don't know, but I'm pretty sure it has something to do with the
questions about the fish-man statue and her *Sinethal*," Pebbles said.

"What?"

Pebbles marched toward the *Sinethal*. "Yep, and I'm gonna find
out why!"

It was nighttime when Pebbles arrived in the hall. Torches lined
the columns and bathed the white stones in a golden hue. Malinyah
did not greet her, but Pebbles saw her sitting at the edge of the pool,
staring at the sky.

When Pebbles arrived next to her, Malinyah lowered her head and
said, "I am sorry, Alynioria. Please forgive me."

Pebbles looked up and saw Cassiopeia hovering in the sky. Above
it, a small star brightly twinkled. So far away, it looked harmless.

Pebbles sighed and sat next to her. Wrapping her arm around Malinyah's waist, Pebbles asked, "What is going on, Malinyah? There's
something you're not telling me. Something that makes you angry
and sad. Why won't you tell me?"

"It has nothing to do with you, sweet flower. I am sorry I made it
seem as if it did. Your questions caused me to recall painful memories, that's all." Malinyah leaned her head on Pebbles' shoulder and
exhaled deeply.

"It's my fault, Malinyah. I didn't know the questions would hurt
you, but I don't understand why they do. Won't you tell me, please?"

Stroking Pebbles' hair, Malinyah said, "We used to sit here and
watch the stars on nights like this. Every now and then, a star would
streak across the sky. We'd close our eyes and make wishes. Sometimes, we'd walk along the cliff or along the beach. We'd hold hands
and talk of many things. If I could, I would stay in those memories
forever."

A warm sensation washed through Pebbles' mind. It reminded her of the same feeling that passed from Malinyah when she parted with Mereau. Pebbles imagined the two of them strolling at the surf's edge, the foamy water tickling their toes. The Moon glowing overhead, the waves rushing ashore. After surviving all the horror, it must have been devastating to say good-bye. Pebbles hugged her and said, "I understand."

Malinyah, lost in her memories, continued on. "Then, we'd return here and I would braid her hair."

"Huh?" blurted Pebbles. She pulled back and stared at Malinyah. The motion caused Malinyah to let go of her hair. Pebbles looked down and saw blond, curly hair about her shoulders.

"She was a lovely daughter. A sweet flower, my Alynioria."

18

Chessboard

San Carlos de Bariloche, Argentina
August 27

The diamond itself was about the size of a small chicken egg. The surrounding kimberlite added another inch of thickness all the way around, giving the beacon an avocado-like appearance.

Lying on the parlor's white sofa, Klaus Navarro held the beacon up and admired its design. The oblong object was not a natural formation. The outer kimberlite shell had been shaped and polished. The inner diamond was only visible with the aid of an x-ray scan. From this, Navarro could tell it had been cut into a sleek oval with a multitude of facets.

The magnetic resonance of the beacon actually tingled his fingers like a tiny heartbeat. It was an amazing piece of technology, one Navarro surmised was forged with the aid of the Flash Stone. The unique specimen was likely quite valuable on its own, but nothing compared to the riches possible with the serpent-tooth stone.

Navarro was extremely frustrated to find the Rio Teodoro vault empty. The chamber had been looted long ago by people who left curious drawings on the inner walls. He was certain the drawings were not made by the crafters of the Stones. The painted scenes were nothing like the intricate etching of his serpent-tooth relief. Yet, some of the drawings showed barbaric depictions of the Flash Stone in use.

In one scene, sticklike figures lay cut in half while a chieftain in a headdress pointed a triangle-shaped object in their direction. Another image showed a woman lying on a table. Beside her, the plumed chieftain held the triangle to her head. In a third depiction, a group of stickmen ran away with arms raised above their heads. Behind, a dragon-headed warrior stood before a volcano carved in half. Fire coated the triangle-tip object in his hands.

The Cinta-Larga. That was Navarro's bet. They must have discovered the ruin long ago and plundered its treasure. From the drawings inside, he reasoned the Cinta-Larga must have occupied the ancient structure for a time. From the looks of it, the chieftain ruled with a fiery hand.

He wondered if the Amazon natives still possessed the Flash Stone. If they did, it might present an alternative to hunting stone vaults. With enough men and the right weapons, Navarro thought it possible to capture a few of the tribesmen and find out.

Though it seemed desperate, Navarro felt compelled to do something. Anything was better than lying around waiting for Drummond's schedule to free up.

At first, Navarro thought of trying without him. There was another map site in eastern Nicaragua. But, without the experienced diamond hunter, it would take a miracle to find a vault. Navarro knew of no ruins in the jungles of eastern Nicaragua. While that didn't mean none were there, it did mean traversing thousands of square miles of uninhabited terrain similar to the Amazon. Not an appealing prospect, thought Navarro, especially without Margaret Corchran and her Stone.

As a second line of advance, Navarro put out discreet feelers through auction houses and his network of artifact traders for recent news of an artifact bearing similarities to the serpent's tooth. If his reading of the empty Amazon vault was incorrect, it meant someone else beat him to the punch. Cully, perhaps? While the ruin's wall showed no sign of recent entry, it was possible Navarro missed something in the rush to open the vault and clear out before the Cinta-Larga showed up. He never actually examined the wall in broad daylight.

Navarro also briefly considered bringing in another prospector, but the ones he knew who might do the job were far less trustworthy and discreet when measured against Drummond.

No, there was no choice. He must wait. Cursing the delay, Navarro squeezed the beacon to quell its mocking heartbeat.

Pézenas, France
August 28

"*Allô*, Christian. How is our patient today?" Foucault asked when the call connected.

"Doing much better, Monsieur. Much better. Her body responds well to *enjyia*," answered Christian. "I confess, I am amazed at her recovery."

Foucault paced the garden. "She is younger than you and I, *mon vieil ami*. The *enjyia* has greater potency in the young."

"It would appear so."

"When we are done speaking, I wish to speak with her, *comprende*?"

"Of course, sir."

"*Bon*. Now, your message said you have news from Cully's associate?"

"Yes, I spoke with her again this morning. As we suspected, Cully is seeking *Tyls*."

"Tell me." Foucault sat on a courtyard bench and lit a cigarette.

Christian briefly recapped the lead-up to the call. After their initial conversation the prior week, Christian contacted Jennifer again as Foucault had instructed. The second discussion was brief. Jennifer was once again preparing to board a flight. When Christian suggested an alternative time later in the day, Jennifer asked for his email address and promised to get back to him with a couple of appointment options.

From there, they had exchanged two rounds of emails before settling on a date to speak. In the first of the exchanges, Jennifer asked if he'd found any information about the artifact. Christian had replied a day later to say he could find no record of an artifact sold to Devlin Wilson in Foucault's papers. However, Christian told Jennifer he had spoken with the count, and Foucault recalled the dialogue with Wilson. Regrettably the two men never reached an agreement, Christian relayed, but the item was still available if Dr. Cully was interested in rounding out Wilson's collection. Alternatively, Christian's message said, his employer might be interested in purchasing artifacts from the estate.

Two days later, Jennifer sent back a short reply to express her disappointment and to thank him for checking. She told him she didn't think Dr. Cully was interested in purchasing or selling any pieces at this time, but said she would pass the offers along. She then asked if they might still speak by phone. There were some other artifacts in Wilson's collection without purchase documentation, and she wondered if Count Foucault might know anything of their heritage.

"When we did finally speak," Christian told Foucault, "she asked questions about Malinyah's *Sinethal*, though she referred to it as a black tile with etched symbols. Apparently, Devlin purchased the *Tyl* from a private collector, but they can't find the transaction receipt."

Foucault withdrew the cigarette and waved it about. "Pah! Nonsense. Devlin didn't buy the *Sinethal*! What else?"

"She said there were two statues as well."

As smoke circled in the light breeze, Foucault recalled Margaret mentioning Navarro's interest in two of Devlin's statues. "Yes, what of them?"

"She thought they might be too hard to describe on the phone. She said she would email me pictures of them once *they* returned from their trip. She said she would have limited phone and email access while away."

"Trip?"

"Yes, they are headed to Nicaragua."

Foucault stood and began to pace. "You said 'they.' Is Cully going with her?"

"Yes, she said they're going on an expedition . . . into the jungle."

"Where in Nicaragua?" Foucault dropped the cigarette on the cobblestone path and crushed it beneath his loafer.

"A little village called Greytown. It's on the east coast, near the border with Costa Rica."

Foucault lowered the phone and swore. When he returned to the line, he said, "There was no map site in Nicaragua, I am sure of it!"

"I was surprised as well. When she first mentioned Nicaragua, I thought Cully might be interested in Ometepe, but that's nowhere near where they're headed."

"Ometepe is not on the map, either, Christian. I would have noticed that."

"Sir, I think I should go to Greytown, even if it isn't on the map. I know where they'll be staying. She offered me the hotel fax number in case I found anything about the black stone." Christian paused then added, "Margaret is strong enough to fend for herself."

"Are the two of you still in Manaus?"

"Yes, we've moved around between hotels, but we're still near the city. I'm sure if she stays hidden, she'll be fine."

"You said this town is near Costa Rica?" Foucault gripped the medallion bouncing on his chest.

"Yes, I can fly into San Jose and find my way there. Before I go, I will leave *enjyia* and some money for Margaret."

Foucault stalked around the oleander altar while fidgeting with the medallion. "*Non.* I have a different idea. Take Margaret with you to Costa Rica. Find a hotel for her, and then go on to Nicaragua."

"But, Monsieur, it will be difficult to get her out of Brazil."

"Find a way, Christian. It must be done," Foucault said. "When you reach San Jose, call me with the hotel information, *comprende?*"

"Yes, Monsieur."

"Put Margaret on the phone. An opportunity has arisen; it is time we put her to use."

Incline Village, Nevada

Anlon gazed at the book's dust jacket and the pair of smiling men. There was Devlin, garbed like Indiana Jones sans whip. With a cigar clenched in his teeth, he clamped his bear paw of a hand atop the shoulder of Cesar Perez. In the picture, Cesar held a stone tablet in his hands, a prize from the expedition featured in the book—a pre-Mayan calendar the two discovered in a Mexican jungle.

Diminutive by comparison, Cesar was the antithesis of Anlon's swashbuckling uncle. Garbed in a simple white dress shirt and blue jeans, Cesar had a humble, almost apologetic smile. The lines etched in his tanned face, weathered from many years in the field, formed deep furrows. Combined with his gray-streaked black hair, he looked older than he really was. In fact, the picture didn't do the man justice at all, thought Anlon.

They'd spent a harried twenty-four hours together back in May, and Cesar seemed as vibrant as men half his age. And man, did he know his Mesoamerican mythology! It was the reason Anlon had reached out to him again after Jennifer's discovery in Villahermosa. Who better to help them sort out the fish-man statue and its possible connection to Zapatera?

And the call had paid off. Not only did Cesar provide a quick education on the statues of Zapatera and Ometepe, but he volunteered to join them for their Nicaraguan expeditions. His archaeology experience would be invaluable given Anlon's novice status.

In that same call, Cesar had inquired if there'd been any progress tracking down Margaret Corchran, Devlin's killer. Anlon shared the news of her sudden appearance and equally sudden disappearance in the Amazon. This had led to a brief unexpected discussion, one that shed possible light on Margaret's purpose and one that hinted Navarro's involvement: a discussion about the *Rivers of Gold* myth. Though Anlon found the story interesting, it seemed a stretch to connect the legend with Margaret's presence in the Amazon. After all, he had told Cesar, there was nothing to indicate Navarro had been in Brazil with Margaret.

Anlon's opinion changed, however, when Jennifer received an excited call from Dan Nickerson. Interpol had verified Klaus Navarro entered Brazil the same day as Margaret and departed five days later. Nickerson had also told her Interpol discovered Navarro passed through international customs on several other recent occasions, including two trips to Dominica.

So, it now seemed conclusive to Anlon that Navarro had a copy of the Waterland Map and that he was searching for the Munuorian caches. Further, the news seemed to imply Margaret had teamed up with him, which made sense given that Margaret escaped with a copy of the map. With those two things in mind, Anlon reconsidered Cesar's story of the mythical stone-melter. Was it possible Navarro was after a *Tuliskaera*?

After Devlin's death, there had never been any mention of Navarro's interest in the *Tuliskaera*. Margaret's brother, Kyle, told Jennifer that Navarro had hired them to nip the *Sinethal*, Devlin's map, the gold Dobson had found and the two statues he stole.

But, now, Anlon wasn't so sure. With Jennifer positioned on the other side of the desk, Anlon handed her the book and said, "You didn't get to meet Cesar in Stockbridge, did you?"

"Nope," she said.

"He's a good dude, you'll like him."

Jennifer casually flipped through the book's pages. "Pebbles said the same."

"I thought you should hear the story directly from him."

"Absolutely. I doubt Interpol's aware of the possible connection. It might help them locate Margaret's crime scene if Cesar's right." Jennifer put Devlin's book aside and opened a new notepad.

When the call arrived, Anlon put his cell phone on speaker and introduced Jennifer. Once the two had exchanged pleasantries, Anlon said, "So, here's the deal. We just found out Navarro was in Brazil at the same time as Margaret. It caused me to think of your *Rivers of Gold* story and I thought Jen should hear it. She's in touch with the police keeping tabs on Navarro; they might find the story of interest."

"Certainly, I'm happy to help," Cesar said. In fine detail, he shared the Olmec legend. When he finished the tale, he told Jennifer he'd also learned of Navarro's recent inquiries in the art community. To Cesar, the inquiries confirmed his suspicion of a connection between Margaret's appearance in the Amazon and the *Rivers of Gold* story.

Jennifer finished scribbling a note and then leaned toward the cell phone. "Thank you, that's helpful. I've got a couple questions if you don't mind."

"By all means."

"You said the legend is Olmec. Weren't they mostly centered in Mexico, not Brazil?"

"That is correct," Cesar said. "You know your cultures well."

"No, not really," she said lightly. "I just got back from La Venta. I toured the museum."

"Ah. Impressive, isn't it? The Olmecs were artisans with stone."

"Agreed. I wish now that I had made it out to the actual dig site, but I didn't have time." Jennifer sighed. "Anyway, getting back to my question. What makes you think the legend might relate to the Cinta-Larga?"

"Good question. There is no explicit link. Just a suspicion. It's important to understand that many Mesoamerican legends build upon one another. A piece of an Olmec tale shows up in a later Mayan or Aztec story. An artifact from a Zapotec site might share a strong resemblance to a later Toltec or Incan statue discovered hundreds or thousands of miles away.

"Mesoamerican nations and outlying tribes migrated throughout Central and South America. Sometimes the migrations were friendly, other times not. There were exchanges of culture along the way.

"In this case, there is a known ruin in the area where Ms. Corchran resurfaced. It's never been excavated to my knowledge because it sits deep inside the domain of the Cinta-Larga. Most archaeologists are unwilling to take the risk to dip a toe in their lands. Too many have been kidnapped, held for ransom or killed by the tribe.

"The ruin is near a fabled trove of gems called 'the waterfall of jewels'—a place where legends say, 'diamonds flowed like water.' When Anlon told me where Ms. Corchran was found, it reminded me of the myth. Especially after learning of Navarro's 'serpent-tooth' inquiries."

"Okay, got it," said Jennifer. "So, tell me about the serpent-tooth Stone. How did Navarro describe it?"

"Well, I don't know for sure. I've learned of his interest thirdhand. From what I was told, he was seeking a stone artifact with a pointed tip. Navarro said it was an Olmec artifact, one they called the tooth of the serpent."

Thinking back to Malinyah's demonstration, Anlon said, "Sure sounds like the Flash Stone, er, *Tuliskaera*, to me. Especially the connection with snakes."

Manaus, Brazil

Christian took the phone from Margaret. "I am back on the line, Monsieur."

"*Bon*. Did Margaret give you the highlights?"

"She did." Christian left the motel room.

"Any questions?"

Christian walked along the open-air corridor. "A few, sir."

"Very well."

"Why now?"

"Quite simple. We know Navarro did not find what he sought in Brazil. He is sure to try again. With Cully now on the move as well, we have two chess pieces to contend with at one time. If we add in *The Betrayer*, there are three. We should eliminate one as quickly as possible.

"We know Navarro has the map. We know he's used it. We know he's willing to kill to find the Stones, a la Margaret. And yesterday, I learned he's specifically seeking the *Tuliskaera*."

"He is?" Christian paused at a stairwell leading to the parking lot.

"Yes, the *imbécile* is asking around for 'the serpent's tooth.' I heard from two dealers within an hour of each other. If *The Betrayer* has connections, then Navarro is in danger already. I would rather see him dead than have his copy of the map end up in Muran's hands."

"Understood. Do you think he will fall for your trap?"

"I believe he will. If Margaret is right about him, he is impatient."

Standing in the parking lot, Christian looked up and spied Margaret staring at him through the motel room window. "Monsieur, are you sure we can trust her?"

Foucault laughed. "*Mon ami*, she has more motivation than anyone to see Klaus Navarro dead."

Pézenas, France

After the call ended, Foucault milled about in the garden with head bowed and hands clasped behind his back. Strolling through the rows of oleander, he tried to make sense of Cully's trip to eastern Nicaragua. Was it possible Navarro and Cully had decoded the Waterland Map? What had they deduced that Foucault had not?

Frustrated by his failure, he returned inside the chateau to orient the map with the Nicaraguan site. Staring at the computer monitor with cigarette in hand, Foucault first maneuvered Devlin's draft over the interactive world map to line up the Dominica site. As expected, none of the other Maerlif sites appeared in Brazil or Nicaragua. He performed the same exercise using the Brazilian and Nicaraguan sites as his central orientation points and achieved the same result.

Yet, there was something that popped out to him. On the world map, he toggled pins to mark Morne Trois Pitons, Greytown and the Rio Teodoro area searched by Navarro. The three sites formed a scalene triangle. He measured the dimensions, saved the world map and then closed it so that only Devlin's map appeared on the screen. Eyeballing the map, he searched for a triangle pattern of similar dimensions among the dozen marked sites.

As soon as he spotted it, Foucault snuffed out the cigarette, pulled his chair closer to the desk and quickly reloaded the world map. His hand trembled as he shifted Devlin's overlapping map to align the sites making up the triangle pattern with the pins saved on the world map. When they lined up, Foucault stared at the rightward shift of Devlin's map and frowned. Leaning forward, he examined the displaced longitude grid while tapping a finger on the computer mouse.

Thirty seconds later, his hand gripped the mouse and slammed it down. *"Mon Dieu! Je suis un idiot!"*

San Carlos de Bariloche, Argentina
August 31

Klaus Navarro hung up the phone and stepped onto the parlor balcony to clear his mind. Immediately, the frigid air cloaked his body. Shivering, he paced the span of the mountain overlook. Was it possible? he wondered. Could it be that easy?

The call from Julian Van der Berg had arrived while Navarro dined with a Brazilian model. The young woman stood nearly a foot taller than Navarro and possibly outweighed him, but that hadn't dissuaded Navarro from trying to woo her. In fact, it had proved an easy task, for early in their conversation he had learned she loved diamonds.

After Navarro discovered her taste for the shiny gems, he had disappeared into his vault and returned with a necklace fit for a queen. He layered it around her neck and invited her to wear it the rest of the evening. The teenager had giggled and pretended she was a princess of a foreign land. She tapped a spoon against her champagne glass and barked orders to Navarro's servants.

The liveried attendants rushed in and out of the room, rolling their eyes at the end of every round-trip. But, Navarro had found the theatrics amusing. He stoked her portrayal, calling her 'milady' and 'your highness' and plied her with questions about her imaginary kingdom. The more she drank, the more hilarious her performance.

Thus, Navarro had been quite annoyed when a servant entered with news of a phone call. Handing Navarro a note, the servant stood at his shoulder and awaited instructions. When Navarro read the caller's name, he abruptly stood and excused himself. "I will be back in a moment, *Princesita*. Have more champagne."

On the way out of the room, Navarro had cornered the servant and instructed him to make sure the young lady didn't leave with the necklace.

As he rubbed his hands together while pacing the balcony, Navarro reflected on Van der Berg's call. The Dutch art dealer had said an anonymous third party claimed to possess Navarro's prized Olmec artifact and was open to negotiation.

The dealer said the party had shared a photograph of the item, and he emailed the image to Navarro while they talked. Navarro nearly soiled himself when he opened the email. The gray-green marbled Stone was more beautiful than he had imagined, and it featured a surprising design. Coiled around the Stone was an emerald-colored etching of a snake.

He had demanded to know the asking price. Van der Berg hedged. Navarro pressed for an answer. The dealer had said it was a bit unusual, but the third party desired to negotiate directly with Navarro. He said the dealership was only asked to make the introduction. Shortly after ringing off, Van der Berg emailed Navarro the seller's contact information.

Navarro puffed steam into the frigid night air and readied to call the seller. As he entered each digit of the international number, his finger trembled. On the third ring, Christian Hunte answered the phone.

"Yes, hello?" said Christian.

"This is Klaus Navarro. I received your message from Van der Berg."

"Ah, good evening, Mr. Navarro. You are interested, then?"

"I am. Van der Berg said you wished to negotiate directly."

"Yes. My client is very protective of his collection and identity."

"How much?" demanded Navarro.

"It is a rare piece, you understand. Not many Olmec pieces are available these days. But, my client is reasonable in his expectations."

Navarro pounded the balcony railing. "Yes, yes. The price?"

"One million. U.S. In cash," Christian said.

"That is very pricey, my friend." Navarro stepped back from the balcony's edge.

"It is a unique piece, Mr. Navarro. There is no other like it in the world."

Navarro nodded. It was a pittance compared to what the Stone would provide in return. And it would eliminate the hassle of searching for the damn thing. One trip into a jungle was plenty.

"You have the second piece in the set? The one shaped like a tin?" Navarro asked.

"Yes, of course. It isn't ornate like this piece, but it fits well with the other."

"Then it is done. I will wire the funds to Mr. Van der Berg tomorrow morning."

Christian cleared his throat and said, "My client wishes a face-to-face transaction. As I said, cash is preferred."

"What then?" Navarro asked.

"I can meet you in Costa Rica on Monday of next week. Will that be convenient?"

"Costa Rica?"

"Yes, I have other business there to attend. My client desires a discreet transaction, yet prefers the safety of a public place. He suggested we meet at the Las Bolas museum in Palmar Norte. You are familiar with the museum?"

"I know of it. Why not the national museum in San Jose?"

"My client feels it would attract notice to open a briefcase containing such a large amount in the middle of a crowded museum. Las Bolas is less traveled. Hence, more discreet."

"Fine."

"Oh, and, it is preferable that you come alone."

Navarro laughed. "My friend, I'm not walking around with a million in cash without security."

"I understand your hesitation. However, I hope you can appreciate my client's position, Mr. Navarro. It is a rare piece, and, well, to be candid, you have a certain reputation to consider."

Navarro paced the balcony in silence. It was a most irregular proposal. The kind conducted by drug lords and money launderers. A reputable seller would want the assurances of a broker, an insurance bond and an independent escrow agent for this type of trans-action. They wouldn't walk into a park with a priceless artifact and count money on a bench. Yet, how could he pass up such a golden opportunity?

Then, a thought occurred to him. Might it be the Americans? They failed at extradition, but the charges remained in force. Might it be a trap to lure him out of Argentina? But, how would the Americans know of the Flash Stone? And the photo. It seemed genuine to Navarro's trained eye. Plus, Van der Berg wouldn't risk his reputation for the Americans, would he?

Unable to stand the chill any longer, Navarro reentered the parlor.

"Mr. Navarro? Are you still there?" Christian asked.

Navarro grumbled, "Very well. I will come alone."

After the call, Navarro returned to the dining room to find his buxom dinner guest facedown on the table, champagne glass still gripped in her hand. Sighing, Navarro sashayed over, unclasped the diamond necklace and called for servants to carry her to his bedroom.

Incline Village, Nevada

"Look, I know you're spooked by the whole Alynioria thing, but we're leaving tomorrow and we still don't know what to look for or how to open a vault if we find one. Will you please give it another try?" begged Anlon.

Pebbles crossed her arms and sighed. "Okay, I'll try. But if I look down and I'm a teen-aged blonde, I'm cutting out."

"Thank you, that's all I'm asking. Give it a try. Antonio's coming by around four to pick up the *Sinethal* and *Naetir*, so if you could do it soon, that would be great."

"Fine," Pebbles said. "I'll do it right now."

She climbed the oak stairs to their bedroom and retrieved the Stones from the closet safe. Returning to the living room, she re-clined on the couch while Anlon paced by the unlit hearth. Crooking her head in his direction, Pebbles said, "Go away, you're stressing me out."

Once Anlon left, Pebbles connected the two Stones and closed her eyes. When the vision came into focus, Pebbles was in the marble hall. Malinyah appeared from an entrance at the far end of the room. Smiling, she approached. Pebbles took a quick look down and spied her wrist and ankle tattoos. Raising her hands to her head, she felt for her hair. Though she couldn't see its color, it was close-cropped, like her current style. She *was* wearing a tunic, but without the blue-gold piping.

Malinyah sensed Pebbles' demeanor and slowed her approach. Bowing her head, she said, "I upset you."

"Yeah, you did."

"I'm sorry, I didn't mean to hurt you."

"Well, you did," said Pebbles. "I mean, I thought it was cute that you called me Alynioria. I even got a tattoo of the freakin' flower. I thought I was special to you."

Malinyah's face reddened. "Your sunlight is so similar, it was hard not to think of her."

"My sunlight?"

She nodded. "Your spirit, it is bright as the sun. Just like Alynioria's."

Pebbles felt a gentle current flow through her mind. The emotion was genuine, the compliment authentic.

"That's sweet of you, really it is. And, I don't mind talking about Alynioria or you showing me visions of her. I'd really like to know her like I know you. But I can't be Alynioria for you. I'm Eleanor. No, strike that. I'm Pebbles. I want *you* to want to know *me*! I don't want to be a doll you dress up."

Malinyah nodded. "I understand, Pebbles. Forgive me."

Pebbles softened her tone. "I forgive you, of course I do." She paused and then added, "I don't mean to be a bitch, it just hurts. I thought I was special to you; I felt like I was special to you. But, you've been so angry and you won't tell me why. And then you give me a little hint, and, bam, I find out I'm a Barbie doll. It sucks both ways."

There was silence between them. Pebbles' eyes teared. She brusquely wiped the droplets away. "Look, let's talk about this later. Right now, I need your help. We think we've found one of your Maerlifs. Well, the general area where one might be. How do we find it? How do we open it?"

Malinyah's contrite manner shifted abruptly. "So, you still intend to find the *Tyls*?"

Pebbles thrust her jaw forward. "Damn right. And we're going to do it, with or without your help. There are other people looking for them, Malinyah. Bad people. We think they're after a *Tuliskaera*."

Malinyah turned and started to walk away. Pebbles called after her. "Come on, Malinyah, if you really believe I have sunlight like Alynioria, you have to trust me!"

The *Naetir* dropped on the floor. Pebbles blinked and looked around. Rising, she gathered both Stones and walked to Anlon's office. It was empty. She left the Stones on his desk and made for the kitchen. Glancing out the back door, she spotted him seated on the patio, sipping lemonade and tapping his foot in rhythm with an Ice Zombies tune.

Pebbles pushed through the door, clambered down the steps and plopped in a chair next to him. Anlon shut off the song on his phone and looked at her warily. "Um, everything go okay? You look a little ticked."

"Nah, I'll be all right. I think we worked it out. Anyway, I got what we need," she said.

"Then, why are you mad?"

"She called me Pebbles, and, well, I didn't like it."

19

Indio Maiz

Indio Maiz Biological Reserve, Nicaragua
September 5

The zodiac boat left Greytown and traveled up the Rio Indio. At first, the broad expanse of the river offered serene views of the jungle on both banks. The tree line was alive with the steady buzz of insects and the high-pitched chirping of spider monkeys.

Greytown, a sleepy little hamlet bordering the Caribbean Sea, was known locally as San Juan de Nicaragua. In the nineteenth century, it had been a bustling boomtown during the heyday of the California gold rush. For several years, thousands of American and European prospectors had flooded the east coast town seeking a cheaper and faster alternative to reach the west coast. They would board ships in Greytown and travel up the San Juan River until they reached Lake Nicaragua, home of Ometepe and Zapatera. From there, the prospectors made their way to California with dreams of fortune and fame.

But the town's sudden prosperity ended abruptly when the United States navy destroyed the town after disputes with local authorities over tariffs and river access turned ugly. A few years later, with the town struggling to get back on its feet, the San Juan River changed course and flooded the town, destroying it once again. Greytown disappeared from the map and was consumed by the jungle. Eventually, the small town was rebuilt, providing Anlon and his crew the easiest path to reach Indio Maiz.

Already drenched with sweat, Anlon removed his boonie hat and slicked back his sandy-gray hair. Above, dark clouds threatened another downpour. He leaned forward to recheck the seal on the dry bags holding their equipment. So far, they'd managed through two days of intermittent deluges without damage to the magnetometers or ground-penetrating radar.

To his right knelt Pebbles with paddle gripped at the ready. Her eyes anxiously scanned the shoreline for signs of crocodiles drifting stealthily beneath drooping limbs or lurking in the tall reeds. On their first foray of the muddy Cano Negro tributary, Pebbles had nearly tipped the pontoon-shelled boat when a crocodile attacked Jennifer's paddle. Their Rama guide, Hector, had screamed at Jennifer to let the paddle go, but she didn't understand his command.

The croc's powerful jaws had yanked the paddle and Jennifer with it. Cesar Perez grabbed hold of her waist and echoed Hector's urgent plea. Pebbles stood up and raised her paddle to strike the reptile's snout. Jennifer had then let go, and the sudden release caused the boat to rock. Pebbles lost her balance and stumbled backward. Anlon caught her before she went over the side but the motion raised the opposing side of the boat above the water. The dry bag holding their *Breylofte* had slipped over the pontoon and into the brackish current.

As the bright red bag floated away from the boat, they had furiously paddled after it while Hector watched for the reptile's return. When the bag slipped farther way, Hector had reluctantly started the boat's engine. He maneuvered the raftlike craft with great skill and Anlon had snagged the sack containing the precious relic.

Since then, Pebbles had volunteered to serve as lookout, and Anlon transferred the *Breylofte* to a small pack clipped around his waist. Malinyah had been clear: the *Breylofte* was vital to locate and open a Maerlif.

So far, they'd surveyed four landing sites on the south side of Rio Indio without success. They first searched a hilly area near Anlon's best estimate of the Waterland Map's Indio Maiz marking. Using the magnetometers, they had split up into two teams and searched a half-mile radius east and west of the mark.

Moving inward in concentric circles from the outer boundaries of each radius, they had measured for changes in the magnetic field. Specifically, they sought the odd fluctuation pattern associated with kimberlite deposits. Malinyah had said the magnetic-diamond beacon embedded at each Maerlif site was exceptionally powerful.

Although they came up empty, Anlon and Pebbles learned a valuable lesson from the first search. Despite the cloying heat and humidity, long shirts and pants were mandatory in the jungle. Between mosquito bites, cuts and scrapes, Anlon and Pebbles had been a patchwork of welts by the time Hector steered them back to Greytown and their fishing lodge accommodations. It was a mistake they remedied on subsequent forays into the jungle.

Now, as their boat turned west toward the Cano Negro, Anlon's attention was stirred by a light tap on his shoulder. Turning, he beheld Jennifer's outstretched hand displaying an energy bar. Anlon squinted at the package and asked, "Any more of the oatmeal-raisin ones?"

"No, we've only got chocolate–peanut butter left. A certain someone, ahem, ate the last of the oatmeal-raisin *and* cranberry-cashew," she said.

Pebbles pushed back the hood of her slicker. "Ugh! Let it go, woman! I already said I was sorry."

As he peeled the wrapper back, Anlon nudged Pebbles' arm. "What's with you and the sudden case of midnight munchies?"

With an annoyed glare, she barked back, "Don't distract me, I'm working!"

Cesar lifted his head from the map he was studying and laughed. "She's becoming an archaeologist, Anlon. The heat is too much during the day. It kills the appetite. But at night, when the body has cooled down, hunger returns!"

"Thank you, Cesar!" Pebbles said. She slapped Anlon's shoulder. "See, Doctor-Know-It-All. It's *biological*."

Just as Anlon prepared to respond, Hector cut the engine and rattled off a command in a mishmash of Portuguese, English and Rama. Although they didn't understand a word, the same command had been issued enough times that they all knew to start paddling.

They were less than two hundred yards up the Cano Negro when a rain shower let loose, but none of them complained. Although the pounding droplets did little to cool the air around them, the precipitation did temporarily lower the heat trapped beneath their clothing.

The rain continued as they curled through a twist of the river as it wound westward. As they neared their landing site, the rain finally abated. Cesar took advantage of the break in weather to lean forward and tap Anlon on the shoulder. "Before we unpack, can we talk for a moment? I've been thinking of a different search area."

The five of them sat in the anchored boat as Cesar unfolded the map before them. Pointing to the south side of the junction between Rio Indio and Cano Negro, he said, "We've been focused here, near this rise. Now, that makes sense given Devlin's coordinates. But, as you know, Devlin's map is imprecise."

Drifting a finger northward, he pointed at another rise tucked inside the triangle formed by the meeting rivers. "I think we should look here. I was thinking it also matches Malinyah's guidance. A raised, rocky area near the coastline or river. Yes, it's on the opposite side of the river, and further inland, but it's only about three miles from where we've been searching."

"Um, excuse me," Pebbles said. "Hector, didn't you say there are a lot more howlers north of the river?"

Hector nodded. Pebbles turned toward Anlon. She watched him rub at his jaw while considering Cesar's suggestion. Pointing to the rear of the boat, she announced, "If we do it, I'm on Hector's team."

Jennifer tried to hold in a laugh by covering her mouth, but it sputtered out between her fingers.

"Laugh all you want, copper! I'm not going near those monkeys again without a gun!"

"Oh, come on, Pebbles. Just because they're loud and scary looking doesn't mean they'll hurt you," Jennifer teased. "Right, Hector?"

Both turned and looked at Hector. He averted his gaze toward the northern shore.

"See! Hector's on my side," Pebbles said.

"But, Peb—"

"But, nothing! You weren't the one taking a pee when they dropped out of a tree!"

Anlon bit his lip to suppress his own laugh. The visage was one he'd remember for a long time. Pebbles popping from behind the underbrush, pants bunched around her boots, screaming at the top of her lungs as she hopped away from the howlers. Their shrieks were as eerie as they were ear-splitting. At first, Anlon hadn't seen the monkeys, he just heard their shrieks, but then in the trees above, several of them appeared.

As Anlon and Cesar had dashed to aid Pebbles, one of the howlers emerged from the underbrush. His cheeks bulged while he grunted and wailed. Upon spotting Anlon and Cesar, the monkey halted and stomped the ground. Above, his tree-borne brethren bounced on limbs and grunted angrily. Pebbles had stumbled over a tree root and crashed down hard. Cesar then reached under his collar and felt for the thin cord around his neck. A second later, he pulled out the whistle attached to the cord and blew aggressively. The shrill sound had frightened the monkeys and they scattered.

Looking now at Pebbles, Anlon said soothingly, "It's okay, Pebbles. You go with Hector and Cesar. Jen will come with me."

Turning to Cesar, he said, "Look, you're the archaeologist here. If your instincts tell you it's worth a look, I'm not going to argue with you. Hector, is this area accessible?"

"*Si*. Not too bad. But, many *monos*," Hector said.

Looking at Pebbles, Anlon grinned. "Well, monkeys are better than snakes, don't you think?"

Waving his machete, Hector corrected, "Oh, no, señor, plenty of *terciopelo* there too!"

"Tele-what?" asked Pebbles.

"*Terciopelo*. It's a viper. It's venom can be deadly," Cesar said.

Pebbles frowned. "Perfect!"

Decision made, they resumed paddling farther upstream. When they neared their intended coordinates, Hector used the motor briefly to guide the craft to shore. They each sloshed into the water to help Hector tug the boat up onto a shallow portion of the bank. Once the watercraft was secured, Anlon opened the dry bags to test the equipment. Satisfied that each was at full power and operational, he divided the gear between the two teams.

"Everybody's GPS trackers on?" he asked. After a round of nods, he continued, "Good. Put in these coordinates. Latitude 11.046, longitude −83.91. That's about dead center of the hill."

Once they each entered the coordinates, Anlon used Cesar's map to outline their exploration. "Jen and I will head due west and then loop north from the southwest side of the rise. You guys make for the southeast side and loop north. Let's plan to link up at the top unless one of us gets a hit beforehand. Same drill as before. Anyone gets a hit, mark the spot on the tracker and ping the others."

"How far is it from here?" Pebbles asked.

"Mmm, what do you say, Jen? About a mile?" Anlon asked.

Nodding, Jennifer said, "Looks about right if we get a straight shot, but I'd count on some terrain detours."

"Or monkey detours!" exclaimed Pebbles.

Leading the way through the dense foliage, Hector carved a makeshift path with his machete. Cesar followed behind him, alternately darting glances at the magnetometer and the terrain ahead. Bringing up the rear was Pebbles, machete in hand and whistle clenched between her teeth.

About a quarter of a mile inland, their intended path turned more challenging. The ground began to rise and they struggled to gain footholds on mud-slicked roots and stones. Cesar nearly dropped the magnetometer on two occasions, but both times he managed to grab hold of nearby branches to steady himself. Pebbles had to sheath her machete, but she still eyed the trees warily.

Half a mile into their journey, Cesar stopped suddenly. "Now, that's interesting."

Pebbles came up beside him. "Get something?"

"Yes, I think so. Look." He showed Pebbles the magnetometer. "Now look what happens when I turn."

As Cesar turned to his right, the magnetometer registered a low, steady reading. When he waved the meter in front of him toward his left side, the meter's digital reading jumped a modest amount. "It's not much," he said, "but it's more than we've had."

Hector reached behind his gun holster and snagged a canteen clipped to his belt. He uncapped the container, raised it to his mouth and greedily swallowed. Looking back at his companions, he asked, "Which way?"

"Uh, I'd say we need to shift direction to about ten o'clock," Cesar said. "That's where I'm getting the strongest reading."

Hector reclipped his canteen to his belt and then reached for the compass dangling from a lanyard draped around his neck. Noting their present position, he turned sixty degrees as Cesar suggested and started off in the new direction. On her own tracker, Pebbles dropped a pin to mark the spot where they got their first hit and then scampered to catch up with Cesar.

"Shouldn't we give Anlon a heads-up?" she asked.

"Not yet," Cesar said. "The signal's still weak. Could be a blip."

But the signal grew stronger as they trekked farther ahead. They briefly lost the signal when forced to make a circuitous course correction around a swampy depression, but eventually they honed back in on the magnetic trail. Every so often, Pebbles dropped another pin.

When they halted to rest and take water, Pebbles took advantage of the time to study her tracker more closely. Their course had veered toward the southern side of the hill. She could see Anlon and Jennifer's progress on the screen and they too had made a distinct turn in their direction. They were closer to the hill than Pebbles' party, but they hadn't sent a message either.

Pebbles was surprised that Anlon and Jen were ahead of them. Anlon had moved very slowly the preceding day, his weaker leg sore from prolonged exertion. Either Anlon had experienced a rebound in energy or their path was less arduous.

She alerted Cesar and Hector. "Check your trackers. Looks like we're heading right for Anlon and Jen."

Before either could view their devices, three pings rang out. Pebbles looked down at her screen and saw Jennifer's message: "Found it!!!!!"

A second later, Anlon messaged: "We'll wait for you."

Pebbles tapped out a response: "Awesome!!!!!"

While Pebbles and Cesar exchanged high fives, the stoic Hector tapped on his device with one hand while reorienting to Anlon's position with the compass. A moment later they were on their way to meet them.

San Juan de Nicaragua (Greytown), Nicaragua

Christian Hunte was enjoying chorizo and eggs with a dash of hot sauce when his phone buzzed. Between chews, he lifted the smartphone and opened the message: "11.0444, −83.9083." His eyes flickered momentarily as the message sunk in. Thrusting a hand into the backpack on the adjacent chair, he withdrew a GPS tracker. He pressed the power button and scurried from the lodge dining room. Pacing outside on the terra-cotta patio, he grumbled at the device's slow activation process. First came the company's animated logo, followed by a stream of pop-up promotional messages and then a tutorial prompt.

Once he cleared the screen of the annoying fluff, he waited for the tracker's signal strength meter to indicate a connection. Finally, three of five bars appeared and he entered the coordinates. Seconds later, the tracker zeroed in on the spot. Zooming out from the pulsing dot, Christian said, "How did they get all the way over there?"

Christian rushed back in the dining room, grabbed his phone and typed a quick reply: "Have they entered?"

He rattled a fork on the table while awaiting a reply. At one point, a perky waitress stopped by and offered a coffee refill. Christian declined and asked for the check. When she returned with the bill, he quickly paid it and departed.

Christian's vision remained glued to the phone as he stalked back to his room. After another thirty restless minutes, there still was no reply. As he paced the room, he considered the potential reasons for the lack of response. The most likely, he reasoned, was a false alarm. They probably just stumbled across a small diamond deposit and mistook it for a Maerlif.

Alternatively, if they had indeed discovered the vault, they might be having difficulty opening it. Christian recalled his own struggle to find the glyph the first time he visited Dominica with Foucault. Or, perhaps they gained entry and discovered the chamber empty like Navarro in the Amazon.

The only other explanation was distasteful to consider. Had Hector been lured by the riches hidden in the vault? Did his silence suggest a double cross?

Unwilling to wait any longer, he typed a message to Foucault: "Received unconfirmed coordinates. Leaving now to validate. Will contact you later."

Indio Maiz Biological Reserve, Nicaragua

Anlon maneuvered the small GPS rover over the rock with his hand. "Can you see it?"

Standing a few paces behind, Cesar peered at the ground-penetrating radar's display and replied, "Yes, there is definitely a cavity behind the rocks. Where was the strongest magnetic reading?"

Anlon showed Cesar the spot where the magnetometer had gone wild. Meanwhile, Jennifer, Pebbles and Hector prepared to search the hill's stony face for the *Breylofte* glyph. For Hector's benefit, Pebbles bent down and used her finger to draw the *Breylofte* symbol in the mud and described the glyph. "It will be three wavy, evenly spaced horizontal cuts in the stone, one on top of the other, like this."

Cesar overheard Pebbles' description and called back, "It would surprise me if it's intact, Pebbles. These rocks have seen thousands of years of rain, mud and wind since the etching was made. It would be very, very rare to find it untouched by nature." Pointing to the debris scattered around the hill, he added, "Look at how many of the rocks have fallen to the ground. And there, up higher, you can see others have cleaved or shifted. If we do find the glyph, it's likely to be badly weathered. And we may only find bits. It may look nothing like the original carving."

"So, what should we look for?" Pebbles asked.

"Look for any anomalies. A depression that seems too uniform. A shadow that looks like a pattern or design. Anything that doesn't appear natural," he said.

Anlon waited for Pebbles to nod her understanding, then asked, "Where should we start, Cesar? How would you suggest we conduct the search?"

"You will not like the answer, my friend. If we do it right, we need to divide the wall and the surrounding ground into manageable grids, I'd say four-by-four-foot squares given the terrain. Then we will need to examine every stone, fallen or not, with painstaking scrutiny. Any time one of us finds an anomaly, we stop, mark its location and examine it. For an area of this size, it could take several days. If the weather interferes, it might take weeks."

The others in the group joined Anlon as they listened to Cesar's explanation. Pebbles shoved her hands into the back pockets of her cargo pants and frowned. "Well, that sucks." She kicked at a small stone and then piped up, "Why can't we skip all that and just use the *Breylofte* to find it? Malinyah said the Stone will jiggle when it interacts with the entry stone."

"I would advise against it," Cesar said. "A lot of the rocks are loose. You could cause them to fall and make it harder to find the doorway."

Jennifer chimed in. "He's right, Pebbles. The whole damn face looks like it could come tumbling down at any moment."

"Or the wall might cave in on the chamber and destroy everything inside," added Cesar.

Pebbles massaged her wrists and groaned. "But we found the beacon! And you guys just said you can tell there's a hollow space behind the rocks. Can't we at least try the *Breylofte*? Anlon? What do you think?"

Anlon leaned back on a boulder and crossed his arms. Bowing his head, he considered their options. It was easy to see the merit in Cesar's proposed approach. A grid search would minimize the risk of damaging the entry and any artifacts inside the chamber. If they had truly located an intact Munuorian archaeological site, it would be irresponsible to just rip through the wall to see what was inside.

Yet, the time investment to do it right was problematic. Given Navarro's travel to Brazil and Dominica, Anlon considered it likely Navarro would soon turn his attention toward Indio Maiz. And Navarro was all about plundering, not preservation. Anlon shuddered then as he imagined what might happen if Margaret Corchran showed up while they were excavating, or if the sneaky Navarro slipped in overnight and gutted the site.

He said, "My head says go by the book, but my heart says try the *Breylofte.* I'm not sure which to choose." He looked away from the group and sighed. "I want to do this right. That means methodically cataloging everything and anything. On the flip side, I want to stop Navarro et al. from exploiting the Stones. That argues in favor of speed.

"It's honestly maddening. All my training says, 'Take your time.' These secrets have been buried for ten thousand years, what's another few weeks or months? But my conscience is screaming at me to move quickly."

No one spoke for several minutes. Finally, Cesar cleared his throat and said, "Anlon, in archaeology, there is often a pull and tug between speed and rigor. I have faced it myself more than once."

On one occasion, Cesar said, government officials had called him in when an ancient burial site was discovered during the construction of a road through a mountain pass. He had examined the burial mounds and determined the site was far larger than originally suspected.

"I met with the transportation minister. I told him it would take months to properly excavate the site and the road would have to move. Further construction would damage the site. He looked at me and said, 'You have two weeks. Do what you can.' He said the road was too important to delay. So, I had no choice. We did what we could."

He went on to describe another excavation that had been threatened by civil war. The rebel forces swept to the edge of the site. They started to bomb it, intent on its destruction.

"There were two beautifully preserved statues still half-buried in the central structure," he recalled. "The bombs missed hitting them directly, but they were damaged. I had a bitter choice: flee, and let the rebels destroy the statues, or dig them out as fast as possible and get them out before the site was overrun. In the end, I felt it was better to save some rather than none. In both cases, a threat caused me to set aside method. If you feel there are real threats lurking, then every second delay raises the risk to this site."

Uncrossing his arms, Anlon rose from the boulder where he sat. "Very helpful advice, thank you," he said. Then he turned to Pebbles and said, "Let's try the *Breylofte*. If we don't find the door, or if the wall starts to crumble, then we step back and go with the grid search."

Cesar nodded agreement. Pebbles said, "Thanks for siding with me, A.C. I will be super careful with the Stone."

After a brief discussion about where to test the Breylofte, Anlon and Cesar ranged the magnetometers back and forth across the stone face to narrow the potential target zone. Working on the presumption the entry would be somewhere close to the Maerlif beacon, they marked off a twenty-foot area.

Then, using the GPR, they measured for cavity depth and wall thickness at two-foot intervals. From the ten sections, they selected two for the *Breylofte* test — one to the far left of the twenty-foot zone where the cavity wall was thinnest and the other near the zone's center. Here, the magnetic field was strongest but the wall much thicker.

All the while, Hector sat on a log and watched with mild interest, tracker at his side.

20

A Gathering of Snakes

San Jose, Costa Rica
September 5

While a gentle rain dribbled off the café's covered patio, Jacques Foucault sipped a dark roast blend and read Christian's message. He tapped out a quick reply and withdrew a gold case from the inner pocket of his blazer. Selecting a cigarette, he said, "*Enfin!* It's all coming together nicely."

With Christian moving on Cully, and Margaret poised to deal with Navarro, there was a possibility Foucault might eliminate both competitors by sunset. As a bonus, if Cully had indeed found an intact Maerlif, there would be a chance to snatch the *Tuliskaera* and foil *The Betrayer*. Then, it would be a simple matter to lure Muran out of hiding.

Foucault was surprised Muran remained in the shadows, but then again, she was never one to strike until conditions were perfectly aligned in her favor. She was desperate, however, and soon, very soon, she would have no choice but to step into the light.

Sipping the coffee, Foucault allowed himself to imagine the look on *The Betrayer's* face when confronted with the *Tuliskaera*. Would she run? Would she try to bargain? Or would she stand and fight?

Foucault's musings were cut short when a call from Christian arrived.

"*Allô*, Christian, do you have good news for me?"

On the other end of the line, Christian shouted over the high-pitched whine of a boat engine. "Good morning, Monsieur . . . I hope so . . . I believe so . . . but still no confirmation. I'm headed there now to find out."

As Foucault listened, Margaret Corchran crossed the street and entered the café. She was barely recognizable. Her shoulder-length, bleach-blond hair had been replaced by a spiked Mohawk dyed crimson. Around the borders of her eyes, she'd heavily layered a deep purple shade. Two black gauges adorned her earlobes and a studded collar circled her neck. Between her nose and black lips dangled a silver septum ring. To complete the goth-girl look, she was decked out entirely in black: leather jacket, stretch pants and over-the-ankle Doc Marten boots. She slid into a seat across from Foucault and grabbed a menu.

"*Bon, mon ami*," Foucault said to Christian. "When you get there, call me."

"Of course," Christian replied.

With the call completed, Foucault tapped ashes onto the saucer beneath his coffee and studied Margaret's transformation. From the corner of his mouth, he ejected a stream of smoke and said, "*Magnifique!* Klaus will never suspect you."

Through the rasp that now passed for her voice, Margaret said, "It only has to work long enough for me to kill the rat bastard!"

He nodded appreciatively, but then cautioned, "Do not underestimate him, *mon chère*, he is cunning."

Tugging the collar of the jacket to reveal the long scar, she said, "I won't make the same mistake twice."

They discussed the plan one more time. She was to arrive at the Finca 6 museum at two p.m. There she was to proceed to the courtyard and take a position near the museum's largest "Las Bolas" sphere. Navarro had been instructed to occupy a bench facing the sphere. The assassination would be simple. Once Navarro was seated with the briefcase by his feet, Margaret would sneak behind him and slit his throat.

"There will be no time for drama. Your stroke must be swift and decisive. Do *not* revel in the kill," Foucault instructed. From the side pocket of his blazer, he withdrew a slim knife. He pushed it, shining and black as night, across the table to Margaret. "I expect this to be returned. It carries many memories."

Margaret frowned and touched the knife. "Why this instead of the Stone?"

Foucault smiled. He had considered it. It was the very reason he brought Margaret a replacement for the *Breylofte* she left behind in Brazil. Using the Stone to dispatch Navarro would be satisfying irony. He imagined Navarro sitting on a courtyard bench, impatiently scanning the museum foot traffic for Foucault's courier. Hidden from view, Margaret slides a hand into a backpack and withdraws the *Breylofte*. She directs the Stone at one of the smaller ancient balls resting on the grass. Humming on the *Breylofte*, she lifts the one-ton sphere from the ground and guides it over his head.

A few tourists notice the ball moving through the air and gasp. Others spot the hovering sphere and point in its direction. Navarro hears the commotion and whirls around to see people pointing above his head. Just as he looks up, Margaret releases the ball from the *Breylofte*'s hold. The last thing Klaus Navarro sees is the perfectly round orb, carved and shaped by those with a memory of the very Stone he covets, colliding with his face.

"Too risky, too public," Foucault said.

The truth, however, was that he did not trust Margaret to control her emotions. The moment she saw Navarro and grabbed the *Breylofte*, Foucault was convinced bloodlust would rage through her veins. The Stone would sense her emotion and feed it. She would become frenzied. She would not hide in the shadows. She would not notice tourists nearby. She would thirst for a confrontation, for Navarro to know that she was alive and there to seek vengeance. It would be a public spectacle, one that Navarro might escape.

Margaret lifted the blade from the table. "It's very light."

"Yes, and lethal. You will only need one stroke. If the museum has metal detectors, the knife won't be detected, but keep it out of sight," he said.

She nodded her understanding. He was about to provide further instruction when Christian called again. Foucault motioned silence to Margaret while he extinguished the cigarette.

"*Allô?*"

Over the roar of the motorboat, Christian shouted, "Confirmed. They found the Maerlif, but they haven't opened it yet."

Foucault consulted his watch. "Text me the coordinates. I will be there in two hours. If you get there before they open it, hold them and wait for me."

"If it's already open?" Christian asked.

"Do not let them leave with any *Tyls*."

"If they resist?"

"I will be surprised if they resist, but if they do, don't kill Cully. I need to talk to him, learn what he knows. The rest are expendable."

"Understood."

Margaret listened intently to Foucault's half of the conversation. When he finished the call, she asked, "You found Cully?"

Foucault retrieved his gold case and lit another cigarette. He inhaled the rich tobacco deeply and waved away her question. "Concentrate on *your* mission, Margaret."

She tucked the knife in her jacket. "Don't worry about me, it's as good as done."

He frowned and cleared a stray ash from his trousers. How many times, he thought, have I heard such boasts? A hundred? A thousand? More? Many of them came from men and women far more skilled than the peacock before him. He rose to leave the café. In parting, he said, "Once you are in the museum, you are committed. Do not leave until he is spent. *Comprende?*"

Indio Maiz Biological Reserve, Nicaragua

Anlon handed the *Breylofte* to Pebbles. "Okay. You're up. Try the zone on the left first. Go slow. If you get a vibration, don't try moving any stones. Just holler and then we'll figure out next steps. And don't get too close. If you shake something loose, you don't want to get bonked."

"Got it," she said. Taking a deep breath, she cupped her hands around the Stone and prepared to use it. Closing her eyes, she tried to recall Malinyah's Maerlif tutorial.

"Wait!" Jennifer said. "Not yet. Anlon, can I have a word."

She scampered to where Anlon and Pebbles stood and motioned for Cesar to join them. When he arrived, she leaned in close and whispered, "Don't you think we ought to prepare Hector for what might happen? If she starts tossing boulders around, he might bug out."

The question rattled Anlon. "I honestly forgot he was here. Should we send him back to the boat?"

"Yikes, don't do that! What if howlers show up? We need that gun around," whispered Pebbles.

Jennifer rolled her eyes. "Enough with the monkeys already! They're as scared of you as you are of them!"

"And we have the *Breylofte*," Anlon reminded. "But, I don't mind if Hector stays. I'll talk to him."

They broke from the klatch and Anlon headed for Hector. The guide was still resting on the log, munching on a banana while looking at his GPS device. Anlon called, "Hector, need to talk to you. Cesar, can you come over and translate for me?"

The call startled Hector and he dropped the tracker. He cursed while he picked it up and stood to meet Anlon and Cesar. Anlon pointed to the *Breylofte* in Pebbles' hands. "Hector, in a minute, Pebbles is going to put that bowl to her mouth and hum."

Pebbles raised the *Breylofte* to her mouth to simulate Anlon's description while Cesar relayed his comments in Portuguese.

"When she does, it will send out sound waves that will shake the rocks. Some of the rocks may rise up in the air. It may look strange, but please, don't be frightened. It's just a tool that uses sound to move things."

Once Cesar finished the translation, Hector shrugged and returned to finish his banana. Anlon asked Cesar, "He looks a little disinterested. Are you sure he understood?"

"He said he does," said Cesar. Pointing at the *Breylofte*, he added, "I haven't seen it myself. I'm anxious to see it in action."

They all stepped back and watched Pebbles approach the target zone. She closed her eyes again and tried to remember Malinyah's instructions just as the clouds let loose with sheets of pounding rain. A chorus of shrieks echoed through the trees. Pebbles gasped and swung around. "They're here!"

To escape the shower, the group ran under the low-hanging canopy of a mangrove stand. Pebbles darted looks at the taller trees surrounding the hill as the haunting grunts and wails grew louder. Anlon wrapped an arm around her and patted her shoulder. "Relax. They're probably just excited by the rain."

She tucked the *Breylofte* against her pelvis and mumbled, "I'm trying to remember what Malinyah said to do, but I can't concentrate with all the noise."

He smoothed his hand along her back. "Try focusing on a sensation from the memory. Just like we did before. Don't worry about the monkeys. They're not interested in us, I promise."

While the howlers chattered away, Pebbles cast a doubtful look at Anlon before closing her eyes once more. She searched her memory for a sensation associated with Malinyah's demonstration. The first thing that came to mind were the torches.

She remembered the blaze of their heat upon her face and the sound of the flames whipping in the wind. The wind. That's right, she thought. It was windy . . . and dark.

A vision of Malinyah appeared. She stood next to Pebbles with a *Breylofte* in her hands. Malinyah placed a hand on the stone wall and said, "Stand so you can reach out and touch the stone. When you hum, make your voice deep, like this."

The memory made Pebbles smile. Malinyah hummed like a chanting monk: "Ooouuummmhhh."

Pebbles watched the *Breylofte* shake in Malinyah's hand. She lowered the Stone and handed it to Pebbles. "You try."

While Pebbles relived the vision, the rain continued to fall. Soon, the mangrove leaves ceased to provide cover. Rain pelted their edges until they tipped downward and streamed water all over Anlon and his companions. He did his best to shelter Pebbles from the worst, but it was a losing battle. At least the howlers had lost interest in the storm, thought Anlon.

When Pebbles mouthed "Ooouuummmhhh," Anlon shot a surprised look at Jennifer.

Inside the vision, Malinyah praised Pebbles. "Very good. Did you feel the vibration?"

That caused Pebbles to remember the scratchy feel of the *Breylofte* wobbling in her hands. Then came a rush of visions: Malinyah humming at the wall, the rumbling of stones and the whoosh of dust escaping as cracks emerged along the entry stone edges. The dust tickled her nostrils.

"What is she doing?" Jennifer asked as she watched Pebbles swish her hand back and forth beneath her nose.

"Shhh," Anlon whispered. "She's reliving Malinyah's demonstration."

"She has to wipe her nose to make the stone work?" Jennifer asked.

"Be quiet!" he said.

Malinyah stepped to the wall and wedged her fingers into the gap created by the Breylofte. "Once you see the cracks," she said, "point the *Breylofte* on one side or the other. Not on top, not on bottom. Pick one side and hum."

She demonstrated the proper technique. The entry stone trembled and shifted outward several inches. Malinyah stuck her hand into the small opening and said, "When you can fit your hand inside, move to the open side so that the *Breylofte* can push the stone from behind. Hum at the gap, not the rock. It will push it open like a door."

The last thing Pebbles remembered before emerging from the memory was the rush of cold air when they entered the Maerlif. She shivered and opened her eyes.

"Okay, I'm good," Pebbles announced. She uncoiled from Anlon's arm and stepped from beneath the mangroves. In the pouring rain, she splashed toward the stone wall.

Anlon rose to follow her, but stopped when Jennifer said, "Hey, where did Hector go?"

He turned to spot Jennifer stepping into the thicket of mangrove branches. She called out for Hector, but the rain overwhelmed her shouts. She scanned the dense underbrush as the leaves danced back and forth. Several times, Jennifer heard cracking branches, but each time they echoed from different directions.

Planted in the center of the clearing, halfway between Pebbles and the spot where Jennifer had disappeared into the mangroves, Anlon darted looks in both directions. He shouted for Pebbles to hold up, but she continued to the wall without pause. Cesar followed close behind her and turned when he heard Anlon's shout. Although the rain muffled his plea, Cesar could see Anlon's outstretched hands signaling stop. Cesar nodded and scurried to catch up with Pebbles.

Directing his attention back toward the mangroves, Anlon spied Jennifer wending her way back to the clearing. He called out, "Anything?"

"No. Maybe he had to take a bio break," Jennifer yelled back.

"With all his gear?" Anlon asked. "Look, his pack is gone. Everything."

As Jennifer approached Anlon, she unclipped her GPS tracker and wiped away the layer of water obscuring the screen. Cupping the device to shield it from further droplets, she looked for Hector's red dot. The display showed he had walked away from the site on the southeast side and curled westward. Then the trail ceased. She motioned for Anlon to look at the device. "See, he went that way, but then stopped."

They called a few more times before joining Pebbles and Cesar at the base of the wall. Anlon said, "Sorry. Hector took off without saying anything. You ready?"

Shivering, Pebbles nodded. "Ready as I'll ever be. Stand back a bit."

The group retreated a few steps as Pebbles crouched into position. She raised the *Breylofte* to her lips and hummed a steady, low tone against the flat base. The driving rain in front of the Stone pushed outward on both sides. From Anlon's vantage point, it looked like curtains spreading open. He observed no movement in the wall, but in the background the howlers stirred to life once more. This time, however, their shrieks took on a new form.

When the rain had first commenced, their shrieks had varied in pitch and tone. To Anlon, they seemed to be talking with one another through a combination of pig grunts and wails. Some would chatter while others listened. Then answers would resound among the treetops. Dozens of individual conversations simultaneously crossed through the jungle canopy.

But, now, their shrieks arose in unison. The same pitch and tone reverberated all around them as the howlers joined together to form a solitary haunting groan. Eyes closed, Pebbles seemed unaware of the monkeys as she continued to hum on the *Breylofte*, but the rest of the group shot anxious looks at the trees surrounding the clearing.

Not only were the howlers singing as one, but they were rapidly swinging through the trees on their way to the clearing. Dozens of them dropped out of the trees and scurried to the ceiba tree rooted on the hill's crown. In droves, they climbed the tree and continued to moan.

Pebbles ceased humming on the Stone. When she did, the monkeys silenced immediately, startling her. She opened her eyes to see a hundred of the howlers dotting the tree's branches. Upon their faces was an expectant gaze directed at Pebbles. She turned to the others and said, "Whoa! Where did they come from?"

Anlon said, "They came as soon as you started humming."

"That's so weird!"

"Did any stones move?" Jennifer asked.

Cesar leaned in. "I saw nothing, but I confess, the monkeys distracted me."

"I had my eyes closed," Pebbles said, "but the *Breylofte* didn't vibrate at all."

Anlon gestured toward the wall. "Try again."

As soon as Pebbles began to hum, the howlers commenced chanting. The rain showered the swaying monkeys as they wailed in unison. Again, though, the wall remained motionless. Pebbles halted her buzz on the Stone and at once the monkeys hushed.

Anlon nodded at the monkey-filled ceiba tree. "They're tuning into the sound waves from the *Breylofte*."

"How's that possible?" Jennifer cocked her head.

Anlon thought of cryptochromes and the hypothalamus before explaining. "It appears they can detect changes in the magnetic field. It's an odd reaction, though."

"That's an understatement!" Pebbles said.

"Yeah, I suppose so. Normally, animals consider a sudden change in the magnetic field as a threat. They either flee or fight. It's a survival instinct," Anlon said.

Pebbles eyed the monkeys dubiously. "Hopefully they're not gathering for a fight."

"I don't think so," said Anlon. "They seem soothed by the sound waves, attracted to your humming."

Jennifer asked, "If they're picking up the sound waves, why aren't any of the rocks moving?"

From behind, a clear voice with a British accent answered, "The rain, Miss Stevens. It distorts the sound waves."

They spun around to find Christian Hunte standing at the edge of the clearing.

Beside him stood Hector Santos . . . gun in hand.

With hands raised, Anlon stepped forward and barked, "Who the hell are *you*?"

Removing the outback hat sheltering his head from the rain, Christian bowed slightly. "At present, my name is not important, Dr. Cully." To the full group, he said, "Please, everyone, do keep your hands where they can be seen. Young lady, I would be much obliged if you dropped the *Breylofte*."

The British accent tickled Jennifer's memory.

"Please, miss," said Christian. "The *Breylofte*. Release it and move away. Señor Santos, please scatter the monkeys."

The words had barely left Christian's mouth before Hector pointed the gun skyward and ripped off three quick shots. The booming echo circled the clearing. The howlers dispersed in a frenzy, grunting and screeching as they scrambled for the safety of the jungle.

Pebbles dropped the *Breylofte* as instructed and raised her hands.

Jennifer kept her eyes on Hector. The wiry guide seemed quite pleased with himself, she thought. He blew on the smoking barrel and then retrained his aim on the group. The urge to rush him and kick away the gun briefly flowed through her mind, but Cesar stood in the way. She slowly nudged past him and said, "No one is armed here, Hector, you know that. Lower the gun."

Hector spat at Jennifer and uttered an unflattering expletive in his native tongue. Cesar snapped at the guide in Portuguese while Jennifer crept to the front of the group. Directing her gaze toward Christian, she said, "There is no need for him to keep the gun pointed at us. Please tell him to point the gun away."

"A noble request. I would feel better about honoring it if you didn't have a rather large machete hanging from your belt," replied Christian.

In the excitement, Jennifer had completely forgotten the dangling blade, even though she could now feel its weight against her hip. She glanced down and unclipped the snap hook looped through her belt. Together, the hook and machete plunked into a small puddle. Christian motioned to Hector to lower his aim.

That voice, she thought, I've heard that voice somewhere before.

Anlon pushed up next to Jennifer. "What do you want from us? The *Breylofte*? Take it."

"Calm yourself, Dr. Cully. If I was after the *Breylofte*, I would have already seized it," Christian said.

"Then, what do you want?" Pebbles demanded.

Christian looked up at the clouds and squinted as rain spattered his face. Reaching into his pocket for a handkerchief, he lowered his head and wiped his eyes. He adjusted his hat to better shelter his face. "Right now, I want the rain to stop. Until it does, we wait."

"Why?" asked Anlon. "Just take what you want and go."

"This isn't a robbery. I haven't come to steal," Christian said.

"Then, what the hell is this about?" Anlon asked. "You seem to know who we are and why we're here, though I don't know how. If you're not here to steal, what *are* you here for?"

Jennifer added, "And why the gun?"

Christian walked past the group and lifted the *Breylofte* from the muddy turf. As he wiped away debris from the bowl's edges, he said, "My employer wishes to meet with you."

When Christian said the words "my employer," Jennifer's memory clicked.

"Jacques Foucault!" she blurted. As she recalled her last phone conversation with Christian, her stomach twisted.

"What?" Anlon darted a startled look at Jennifer.

"Jacques Foucault is his employer." Pointing at Christian, she added, "His name is Hunte, Christian Hunte."

Christian bowed. "A pleasure to meet you in person, Miss Stevens."

While Hector kept watch over Anlon and crew, Christian strode to the wall. There, he examined the zones marked by Anlon and Cesar, then moved backward several paces. Gazing up at the top of the hill, he spied the ceiba tree at its crest.

Cesar placed a hand on Jennifer's shoulder. "Jacques Foucault? As in Count Foucault? Are you sure?"

"Yes, I'm sure. He's a private collector. He and Devlin traded email about one of the Stones last fall. Why? Do you know him?"

"A little. I've met him on a few occasions. He's more than a collector."

Anlon frowned. "What do you mean?"

"Jacques Foucault is the author of the Duat-Waterland paper," Cesar said.

Anlon's jaw dropped. Before he could say anything, Jennifer said, "It's my fault. I mentioned we were traveling when I talked to Hunte on the phone. He asked me where we were headed . . ."

Christian called over his shoulder, "It's very impressive that you found it. I take it you had difficulty finding the door?" Turning back toward the group, he approached Anlon. When they stood face to face, he asked, "What made you decide to look north of Cano Negro?"

"I'm not answering any questions until you tell me what you're doing here."

"You will see soon enough. He should be here within the hour."

21

The Stoneman Cometh

Indio Maiz Biological Reserve, Nicaragua
September 5

For most of the hour, the rain refused to let up, leading Anlon to appeal to Christian for permission to string a tarp to the branches of the mangrove stand. Under Hector's trigger-happy scrutiny, they erected the makeshift lean-to and then dragged a couple of fallen kapok limbs beneath the tarp. Hector and Christian sat on one limb while their captives crowded on the other.

Anlon tried several times to probe Christian further, but the Brit ignored his entreaties. Meanwhile, Pebbles noticed Cesar rocking unsteadily on the log and asked for clearance to fetch water and food from their backpacks. Christian assented but directed Hector to retrieve the provisions. The sullen guide glared at Christian and did not budge. Christian sternly repeated the order. Hector looked at Pebbles with disgust. "Let the *puta* do it."

"Classy," said Pebbles. "You do well with the ladies, don't you?"

Hector's face contorted and he charged at Pebbles. She mocked his show of machismo with a laugh, leading the enraged guide to smack her across the face with the back of his hand.

Furious, Anlon launched up at Hector. "That's f——ing it!"

He slipped on the wet ground and crashed into Hector's midsection. They grappled briefly before the stronger Hector shoved him to the ground. As he stood over Anlon, readying to whip him with the pistol, Jennifer lunged for Christian.

Christian was focused on the scrap between the two men, but heard the splash of Jennifer's first step. As she stumbled forward to tackle him, Christian wheeled to face her and slapped his inner wrists together. The unexpectedly loud clap startled them all, even Hector.

The *Dreylaeks'* blast pushed Jennifer sideways, causing her to tumble against Hector's legs. The Rama guide fell on top of Anlon and the gun flew out of his hand. It scooted across the trampled foliage until it bumped up against Pebbles' boots.

Before Hector could clamber over Anlon to reach the pistol, Pebbles leapt up and snagged it. She spun to face Christian, while Anlon tripped Hector, who in turn knocked into Cesar.

"Enough!" Christian roared, slamming his wrists together again. The blast of air crashed into Pebbles and sent her tumbling backward. Christian marched to her side and kicked the gun away while the rest of the group lay tangled on the ground.

Brusquely tugging the dark green Stones from inside his shirt cuffs, Christian showed them to the group and bellowed, "The next one of you who does anything foolish gets cut in half! Now, slowly, up on your feet!"

In the distance, the whir of an approaching helicopter announced the impending arrival of Jacques Foucault. While Hector recovered the gun, Christian shoved the Stones in his pocket and walked out into the clearing to signal the helicopter.

Soaked and muddied, Anlon and the others watched the helicopter lower to treetop level. There it hovered, looking for a place to land. The pilot delicately maneuvered the aircraft another ten feet lower. The wash of the propeller blades plastered the vegetation in the open patch as well as the surrounding trees and everyone below.

Squinting through the turbulence, Anlon saw the helicopter door open as the aircraft touched down. A skinny, gray-haired man, dressed in a gold blazer and dress slacks, climbed onto the landing struts and hopped out. He seemed unfazed when he splashed onto the mucky terrain next to Christian. He waved to the pilot and the whirlybird ascended.

As it circled away from the site, Foucault adjusted his shirt cuffs and blazer lapels and then greeted Christian. Together, they walked to the Maerlif wall.

Anlon and the others stood grouped together and craned to get a clear view of Foucault, but Hector stood in their way. Anlon turned to Pebbles. There was a large red welt on her cheek. "Are you okay?"

"I'm fine," she said with a defiant thrust of her jaw. "It stings, but I've had worse."

"What did he use to knock you down? Are those Heal Stones?"

She nodded. "Yeah, Malinyah calls them *Dreylaeks*, but I didn't know they could be used that way."

In the distance, they could see Christian hand Foucault the *Breylofte* while the pair paced between the two marked zones. At the farthest zone, Christian turned briefly and pointed at the huddled group. Foucault turned as well, bringing his face into view.

"That is definitely Foucault," whispered Cesar.

Hector demanded quiet. Straining to get a better look over Hector's shoulder, Pebbles ignored the command and asked, "Is he like Navarro?"

"If you mean, 'is he a scoundrel?' then, no," said Cesar. "He *is* a collector, but to my knowledge, a reputable one."

"I said quiet!" Hector snarled, waving the gun at Cesar. The shout roused Christian and Foucault's attention. After a brief consultation, Christian called, "Señor Santos, bring them here."

Hector herded the group together. As they crossed the clearing, Cesar whispered, "He's also an astronomer. He owns the world's largest private collection of meteorites."

"Meteorites?" said Anlon in a low voice. "Ah, I see."

"See what?" Pebbles asked.

Only a few steps from reaching Foucault and Christian, Anlon leaned close to Pebbles and whispered, "Our mystery man has a magnet fetish."

Until that moment, Pebbles' view of Foucault had been shielded by Hector and the others trudging ahead of her. As the group fanned out before their captors, Pebbles got her first glimpse of the smiling Frenchman. Before her eyes focused on his face, they were attracted to the medallion dangling from a gold chain around his neck. She blinked several times and staggered backward. Raising a hand to her mouth, she gasped.

Her mind flashed with a stream of images. Malinyah seated beneath the Seybalrosa . . . the coming of Munirvo . . . the uprising against the Andaers . . . men on ships . . . Malinyah waving good-bye . . . her last embrace with their captain . . .

The others turned to see her shrink to her knees. Tears filled her eyes as she relived Malinyah's heartbreaking farewell. She hugged her arms across her chest and mumbled in a trancelike tone, *"Ailta erill, ento ainfa."*

The smile slid from Foucault's face and his mouth fell open. His eyes flared and he grasped Christian by the arm. "What did you tell them?" he shouted.

Christian insisted he'd said nothing. Anlon crept to reach Pebbles as she rocked on her knees and blankly stared at Foucault. Anlon knelt beside her. "Pebbles? What's the matter? What's going on?"

With a quivering, outstretched finger, she pointed at Foucault. "Mereau!"

Foucault flinched, then teetered against the wall as Christian moved to steady him. Jennifer seized the moment of confusion to chop down on Hector's wrist and deliver a stiff kick between his legs. The unsuspecting man crumpled instantly and Jennifer yanked the gun from his hand. Before he could groan a syllable, she reared back and let loose another vicious kick to the side of his head.

As Hector collapsed unconscious, Jennifer spun to face Foucault and Christian. Gripping the revolver with both hands, she motioned Cesar out of her line of fire. He dove to the ground as Jennifer squatted, aimed the pistol and shouted, "Down. Get down now! Both of you!"

Christian's head snapped in Jennifer's direction. He spied the gun and released his hold on Foucault. There was never a moment's hesitation. He pushed Foucault aside and whipped his forearms together. Jennifer fired.

The booming gunfire masked the harmless clap of Christian's colliding wrists. Its echo ricocheted off the rock wall and throughout the clearing. The howlers, deep in the jungle, began to whoop and grunt. Christian clutched his chest and fell over.

Jennifer called to Foucault. "On the ground! Hands behind your head."

Foucault hesitated. Pebbles screamed, "Don't shoot!"

Unmoved, Jennifer growled, "Do it! So help me, I will put your ass down if you f——ing blink wrong!"

Sinking to his knees, Foucault raised his hands above his head. He stared down at Christian twisting next to him. "Christian! Be still!" Then, glaring up at Jennifer, he slowly lowered his arms to the ground until he was on all fours. He pleaded, "Let me help him. I can save him."

"Down!" she commanded. Once Foucault lay prone with hands clasped behind his head, she said to Anlon. "Check him; he probably has Stones, too."

"Jen!" Pebbles cried out.

Foucault lifted his mud-caked chin. "They are in my cuffs. I have nothing else. Hurry, take them."

Anlon started with the cuffs and tugged the *Dreylaeks* from their hidden pockets. From Foucault's jacket, Anlon removed a satellite phone, wallet and cigarette case. When he finished patting down Foucault's legs, he said to Jennifer, "That's it. Just the Stones."

Jennifer turned to Cesar. "There's a first aid kit in my backpack."

As Cesar dashed to retrieve the backpack, Pebbles stepped in front of the gun. "Please, Jen! Put the gun down. It's all over."

Clenching her jaw, Jennifer said, "Move out of the way."

Pebbles crossed her arms. "No!"

Anlon came alongside Jennifer and placed a hand on her shoulder. With the other, he slowly edged the gun barrel down. "Come on, Jen. Let's take it down a notch."

Cesar returned with the first aid kit and knelt by Christian. The injured man shivered and continued to gasp. Blood gurgled from his mouth as Foucault pleaded, "Please, it is almost too late!"

Anlon turned to Foucault. "Go! Help him."

"I need the Stones. The ones you took," Foucault reached out his hand.

The rush of adrenaline that fueled Jennifer's quick actions began to taper. Suddenly, she felt weak. As Anlon eased the pistol from her hands, she mumbled, "Don't do it, Anlon. He'll attack."

Anlon passed the pistol to Pebbles as Foucault rose to his feet. Anlon reached into his pocket and handed over the two Stones. "I'm trusting you, don't screw me!"

Foucault snagged the *Dreylaeks* and joined Cesar at Christian's side. Pebbles followed suit, while Anlon wrapped an arm around Jennifer. "Are you okay?" She didn't answer. In a softer tone, Anlon said, "Look, I don't know diddly about battlefield wounds. You do. Why don't you see if you can help."

Jennifer nodded and joined the others. Foucault ripped open Christian's jacket and shirt and surveyed the bubbling entry wound. He directed Jennifer, Pebbles and Cesar to gently turn Christian on his side. Jennifer spied the larger exit wound and said, "Passed through his lung. We need to seal it."

She fished in the first aid kit for field dressing to stanch the exit wound. Foucault waved her off. "There is no time."

"If we don't seal it quickly, he's not going to make it," she said.

"Quickly, roll him facedown!" barked Foucault.

Jennifer stared at him. "Why, what are you going to do?"

"He's going to use the *Dreylaeks*," Pebbles said.

As the group started to roll Christian, Jennifer told them to halt. She tore open the dressing package and yanked out the thick bandage. Pressing it against the bullet's entry hole, she gave them the okay to continue. As they rolled him, Jennifer maintained pressure against the chest wound.

Foucault clasped a *Dreylaek* in each hand and began to grind them in a circular motion. A glow steadily arose between his hands while Christian wheezed and flailed his arms. Pebbles reached down and squeezed his hand.

"Christian? Can you hear me, *mon ami*? There is no time to do this gently. Prepare yourself."

Christian nodded rapidly. Foucault said to Anlon, "We need you too, Dr. Cully. Please, everyone, hold him down . . . *Bon* . . . Mademoiselle, remove your hand now or lose it."

Jennifer quickly slid her hand from beneath Christian. The glow between Foucault's hands was nearly white when he ceased to rotate the Stones. The *Dreylaeks* themselves pulsed a brilliant red. Foucault's hands briefly separated before he slapped them together. A thin, crackling beam shot forth into Christian. The glare caused all but Foucault to avert their eyes. Christian uttered a gurgling wail and writhed against the hands that held him down.

Foucault slowly scraped the Stones to adjust the electrical discharge. Smoke rose from the wound and the smell of burning flesh filled the air. Christian passed out. For ten seconds, Foucault oscillated the beam around the injury before pulling the Stones apart.

Jennifer released her grip on Christian's leg and covered the charred flesh with another dressing. They quickly flipped him over and Foucault repeated the ancient surgical technique. When it was over, Foucault dropped the glowing *Dreylaeks*. Hands seared and swollen, he sighed, "We have bought him time, but he needs more care."

"Without a doubt. Can you recall the chopper? There's no way he'll survive if we try to carry him to the boat," Jennifer said.

"If you permit it, I can. My pilot, Henri, is on standby. He can be here in less than twenty minutes."

"On one condition," Anlon said. "Jennifer, you go with him and get the damn gun out of here."

Jennifer agreed. "I'll take sleeping beauty with me, too. Turn him into the police."

Anlon retrieved Foucault's satellite phone. With Foucault's hands in no shape to handle the phone, Anlon had him recite the number while he punched the dial pad. When the call connected, he held the phone and Foucault relayed instructions to Henri.

The call completed, Jennifer directed her gaze to Foucault and said, "The bigger question is what to do with him."

"I hear you," said Anlon. "But, he's unarmed now. And there'll be three of us and one of him. We'll manage until you get back." Looking at Pebbles and then Foucault, Anlon added, "Besides, we have a lot to talk about. I don't know what just happened between these two, but I want some answers."

Foucault peered into Pebbles' eyes. "As do I."

"He did hold us hostage," Jennifer reminded them. "And he was armed. If you ask me, I don't think he showed up just to chat. I wouldn't trust him."

"It is true," Foucault said with a nod. "I came to discourage your treasure hunt, by force if necessary. But . . ." His voice trailed off and he shook his head. "To hear those words again . . . It changes everything."

Finca 6 Museum
Palmar Norte, Costa Rica

When Margaret Corchran arrived at Finca 6, there were half a dozen cars parked in the grass outside the ranch-style museum. With the appointed time of the meeting still an hour away, she mounted the front steps, endured the mandatory tour and video inside the main building and then trekked outside among Las Bolas.

Hoisting her backpack over one shoulder, Margaret surveyed the perimeter of the converted banana plantation while stopping to admire dozens of the ancient spheres lying in a mix of grass and scrub. She was pleased to see so many tucked close to low-slung trees and bushes. The foliage would provide excellent cover to observe Navarro unseen.

There were fewer benches than she expected, but all were strategically placed in shady areas to provide visitors respite from the sweltering heat. There was one that stood out among the others. It was positioned opposing the largest of the museum's spheres under a stand of tall trees.

The monster orb was easily ten feet around. Though its surface was pocked and coarse, it still inspired a sense of wonder . . . even to

Margaret. Admiring the feat of craftsmanship, she thought back to the museum video's description of the stones' discovery. She imagined the farmers, clearing jungle growth, stumbling across randomly strewn stones. Margaret could picture them gathered around the globes, hands on hips or scratching their heads, while a rush of questions filled their heads. What are they? How did they get here? Who made them?

Standing behind the bench, Margaret scanned the surrounding area and a smile slithered across her face. Foucault had picked the ambush site well. The trees shading the stone and bench were thick with leaves. With the sun slightly beyond its apex, the whole area would remain shaded for some time to come. Further, there were several decent observation points within a short walk, including a small outbuilding less than ten feet behind the bench.

An approach from the rear of the building on either side would be easy and quick, she thought, but it would be hard to get into position unseen. She knew Navarro's paranoia well enough to know he would ignore Foucault's instructions and bring at least one bodyguard.

Alternatively, there was a dense grove of jungle foliage to the left of the building that might serve as a more inconspicuous hiding spot. However, she worried it might be too challenging to sneak out from the copse without rustling fronds and leaves.

Another approach option was the path that snaked between the bench and sphere. It led from a field of smaller spheres beyond the grove and continued in the direction of the main museum building. As it curled around the grove, it briefly passed behind two tree trunks that blocked the view of the path from the bench. It was a more exposed approach, but one that might garner less attention if played right.

She imagined strolling along the path, head buried in a museum brochure, knife gripped inside the folds. Don't mind me, she thought, I'm just a gawking tourist. Nearing the bench, she would look up to see the orb and slow her pace. It would be a natural reaction to step back from the path to get a better view. With one eye on the seated Navarro and the other on the orb, she would loiter behind the bench and slide out the knife. Navarro would likely position his bodyguards far enough away to avoid detection, so even if they grew uncomfortable with her so close behind him, it would take them too long to reach the bench. She closed her eyes and savored the thought of yanking back on the bastard's ponytail and slashing his throat. There would be no time to utter pithy parting words, but that was almost better. She would leave him as he left her—gasping, covered in blood and stricken with panic.

Roused from the dark fantasy by a couple arriving to admire the monolith, Margaret glanced at her watch and departed to quickly scope out egress options.

Once the deed was done, she counted on a moment's shock among the bodyguards at the sight of Navarro flailing to the ground clutching his neck, and then another brief delay as they mulled whether to rush to his aid or chase after her. After all, she doubted Navarro brought his henchmen expecting an attack. He was probably more worried about the money he carried, so their eyes would be glued on the briefcase.

Assuming the worst, she expected one or more to give chase. This made it unappealing to consider an immediate dash for the parking lot. She looked around and reasoned the best course of action was to flee into the grove behind the outbuilding. From there, she could pull the *Breylofte* from her backpack, deal with any pursuers and wind her way through the foliage back to the parking lot.

To test her theory, she disappeared into the grove. Sure enough, it was only one hundred yards between the point where she entered and the edge of the parking lot. She decided to move her rental car close to the grove and position it facing outward so she could escape quickly when the time came.

If she could make it to the junction of Route 34 and Route 2 before any chasing vehicle was in sight, there was little chance of getting caught. There, the junction split in three directions, all of which provided means of returning to San Jose. If one or more cars tailed too close behind on the museum's dirt access road, she could pull over and blast them into the surrounding banana trees.

She smiled with satisfaction; all her bases were covered. Removing the knife from her pack, she once again admired its light weight and said, "Payback time."

Indio Maiz Biological Reserve, Nicaragua

When the helicopter arrived, Anlon roused Hector. The guide, who was tied at the hands and feet, struggled to free himself while regaining his senses. Anlon shouted above the thumping sound of the propellers, pointing at the hovering aircraft. "Settle down and listen. You're going back to Greytown in that. When it touches down, we're going to lift you aboard. Don't squirm, or we might 'accidentally' drop you. Got it?"

The guide glared at Anlon and attempted to spit in his face, but the air turbulence splattered the trail of goo on his own face instead. Cesar came alongside and shouted to Anlon, "Do you need me to translate?"

"Nah, screw him," Anlon called back. To Hector, he shouted, "By the way, you're fired!"

Their agreed plan called for Jennifer to deliver Christian to a waiting ambulance and Hector to the police. Once the handoffs were complete, she would head for the lodge to retrieve dry clothes, food and water for the group. Then, Henri would fly her back. Anlon questioned how she planned to describe the shooting so as not to land in jail herself. Jennifer assured him it wouldn't be a problem, but provided no explanation.

As Jennifer prepared to climb aboard, Foucault approached. "My bag is in the back. In it, there are several bottles filled with pink water. Please feed one to Christian if he wakes during the ride. If you would, please leave two of the bottles with me. For my hands."

Jennifer retrieved the two bottles of *enjyia*, slid on her backpack and shouted to Anlon: "I'll call when I'm on my way back. Don't trust him, Anlon. And don't give him any of the Stones!"

22

Flash Point

Indio Maiz Biological Reserve, Nicaragua
September 5

With the helicopter on its way out of the preserve, Anlon, Pebbles, Cesar and Foucault gathered at the base of the hill. Exhausted, they sat atop fallen rocks in silence. Foucault took advantage of the break to slather his hands with *enjyia*. With Anlon's assistance, Foucault wrapped his hands with gauze and then drank some of the *enjyia*. He offered some to the others. Anlon and Cesar deferred, but Pebbles decided to sample the real thing. She pursed her lips after a sip and said, "Yuk. Malinyah's is much better."

The gray blanket that had covered the sky for much of the day had given way to late-afternoon sun. The rain-drenched foliage surrounding the clearing sparkled under the influence of rays filtering through broken clouds.

Anlon pondered where to start the conversation. When they left Tahoe for Nicaragua, the mission seemed simple: find evidence of a Maerlif to affirm Anlon's reading of the Waterland Map. He knew it was a long shot to discover an intact vault with a cache of *Lifintyls*, but he hoped they'd at least find ruins or some other evidence that pointed to the Munuorians and their Stones.

So, the discovery of what appeared to be an intact Maerlif was an exciting and unexpected development. Yet, presently, opening the vault was the last thing on his mind. Fighting for dominant attention were the sudden appearance of Christian Hunte, the subsequent arrival of Jacques Foucault and Pebbles' reaction when she saw the aristocrat.

Given the whirlwind of events, a good part of Anlon wanted nothing more than to head back to the lodge, enjoy a nice dinner accompanied by a stiff drink and start all over the following day. But that wasn't possible.

His thoughts were interrupted by Foucault. The Frenchman looked between Anlon and Pebbles and said, "The confrontation, it was my fault. I told Christian to prevent you from entering the crypt until I arrived. I am sorry. I worried you might damage the *Tyls* inside.

"I didn't know you knew to use the *Breylofte*. I thought you would blast it open like greedy treasure hunters. However, once I landed, Christian showed me how you marked the wall and he told me you had a *Breylofte*. I realized your intentions were different than I had feared. And then I learned that Señor Perez was in your party, and I told Christian to release you all.

"Dr. Cully, please accept my apologies . . . and please allow me to introduce myself properly. I am Jacques Foucault." He bowed slightly and then turned to Cesar. "It is good to see you, my friend. I am sorry for restraining you and your companions."

Cesar's voice was stoic. "It was very dangerous, Monsieur. It could have escalated into something far worse."

"Damn right, it could have!" growled Anlon. "What's your interest here anyway?"

Until that moment, Pebbles had remained quiet. She was exhausted. The long slog through the jungle, the rain, the monkeys, the sudden onset by Hunte and Hector, the threats and the violent confrontations combined to drain her energy.

But those events paled when stacked against meeting the man Malinyah credited with saving the human race. It was beyond possibility. Yet, there was no mistaking the medallion. If there had been any doubt, it was erased by the images and emotions that rushed forth when she came face to face with Foucault.

In answer to Anlon's question, she said, "He is Mereau."

"*Non*, madam, you are mistaken, I am not Mereau."

"Who in the hell is Mereau?"

The tone in Anlon's voice shook Pebbles. She said, "He's the captain that led the ships to help the survivors, remember?"

Face frozen, Anlon stared at Pebbles. He shook his head. "Come again?"

"He's one of them. A Munuorian. *The* Munuorian. We wouldn't be here without him. We owe him everything," she answered. Turning to Foucault, she repeated Mereau's parting words to Malinyah: *"Ailta erill, ento ainfa."*

Foucault's face reddened as she spoke the phrase. "It is remarkable that you know the words. You understand their meaning?"

She nodded. "Ever apart, together always."

Anlon noted the wistful looks passing between Pebbles and Foucault, then exchanged a disbelieving glance with Cesar.

Pebbles pointed at the medallion dangling from Foucault's neck. "She gave you that. You were wearing that when you said good-bye."

The Frenchman reached for the medallion. "It is true, this was a gift from Malinyah. But she did not give it to me."

"Okay, time out," Anlon said. Pointing a finger at Foucault, he asked Pebbles, "You're trying to tell me he's ten thousand years old?"

Pebbles slowly nodded. Foucault said, *"Non!* I am *not* Mereau."

"Then where did you get the medallion?" Pebbles asked.

"Let me explain, s'*il vous plaît.* I have Mereau's *Sinethal.* I discovered it in a crypt such as this a long time ago."

"And, the medallion?"

Before Foucault answered, Cesar jumped into the conversation. "That is the second time you have used the word 'crypt,' Monsieur. Are we to understand you found the tomb of this Mereau?"

"Précisément!" said Foucault.

"What?" Pebbles exclaimed.

Anlon rose from his stone perch and began to pace. A tomb? The Maerlifs were tombs? He cast a puzzled look at Pebbles. "Did you know these were tombs?"

"No way! Malinyah never said anything about tombs or crypts. She said they were hiding places for the *Tyls.* That's it."

While he continued to pace, Anlon's mind raced. Tombs . . .

Cesar asked Foucault, "I see now you choose your words with purpose. You said you found Mereau's crypt 'a long time ago.' When was this?"

A sly grin stretched across Foucault's face. "I see now you listen more closely than I expected. Perhaps I should have chosen my words more carefully . . . I will answer your question, but, first, I should like to know where Devlin Wilson discovered Malinyah's *Sinethal*. I have searched for it for many years."

Where indeed? thought Anlon. Although he didn't know the answer, he was beginning to understand his uncle's confusing actions more clearly. He wasn't searching for more Stones; he went hunting for something else entirely. What better way to prove the Munuorians' existence than to find the final resting place of one of them. Date the contents of the tomb, the bones, and voilà, prove the timeline. Jesus, why didn't the man just say so!

"I wish I knew," said Anlon. "Devlin left us very few clues about any of this."

Pebbles stood and smoothed her hands against the wall. "Do you think it's here? Have we found Malinyah's tomb? Oh my God, Anlon, is it possible?"

"*Non*," said Foucault. "She is not here."

Anlon spun around. "How do you know that?"

"It is simple, Dr. Cully. There is no volcano here," Foucault said with a nonchalant tenor.

Pebbles gasped. "Ometepe?"

The Nicaraguan volcano crossed Anlon's mind at the same moment. It all made sense. Isabela, Ometepe . . . Devlin's search for the Munuorian homeland was instead a search for Malinyah's tomb!

"What's this you say? Ometepe?" Foucault asked, suddenly interested.

Anlon gazed at Pebbles and wondered if the same thought flowed through her mind. He recalled Malinyah's evasions about the fishman statuette and her *Sinethal*. Was it that simple? Did Malinyah lie to Pebbles to protect the location of her final resting place? Had she lied to Devlin as well?

His thoughts were interrupted by another question from Cesar to Foucault. "You say volcano. Then, you found Mereau's tomb near a volcano?"

Foucault ignored the question. His voice rose with urgency as he demanded an answer from Pebbles. "Ometepe? Why do you say this?"

Pebbles shot an embarrassed look at Anlon. He said, "Don't sweat it. If you hadn't said it first, it was on the way out of my mouth."

Cesar said, "Surely, Monsieur Foucault. This name should not come as a surprise to you. If you believe Malinyah was entombed near a volcano, you must have thought of Ometepe in your 'many years' of searching for her crypt. The petroglyphs? The statues? Are there not logical signs to draw your attention?"

Foucault blinked several times and covered his head with his bandaged hands. "No, no, no! You know of the *Taellin*?"

"The what?" asked Pebbles.

"I knew it! You are *alliés* with her, admit it!" Foucault's face turned red as he yelled at Anlon.

Anlon recoiled. "Huh? Her? You mean Malinyah?"

"Don't be *timide* with me, Doctor! You know of whom I speak. *The Betrayer!*"

The sharp epithet caused Pebbles to wince. She recalled Malinyah screaming the words on the cliff-side. The anger in her voice was as venomous as that which spilled from Foucault's mouth. Pebbles said, "Muran."

"*Précisément!*"

Anlon glared at Pebbles. "What the f—— does Muran have to do with this?"

She started to answer but was cut off by Cesar's raised voice. "Forgive my interruption." He motioned for Anlon and Pebbles to sit again. Then, in a subdued tone, Cesar said, "Come, we are talking past each other. Let us take a deep breath and start over. It is clear, Foucault, you have pieces to the puzzle we seek to solve. The same is true the other way around. But none of us will make progress unless we discuss these matters calmly. Agreed?"

Foucault nodded his assent.

"Good. Now, as the three of us are new to the mysteries of the Munuorians, and you claim many long years of knowledge, it seems to me you should go first, Monsieur. Educate us. We will share what we know in return."

Foucault hesitated and looked down at the medallion. Raising his gaze, he stared deeply into Pebbles' eyes. "Very well. I suppose it is best to start at the beginning. My real name is not Jacques Foucault. It is an alias I adopted some fifty years ago. One of many aliases I have used over the centuries. I was born Mathieu Du Pre, in the year 1619."

San Juan de Nicaragua (Greytown), Nicaragua

Jennifer sat in Greytown's Policía Nacional waiting room while officers questioned Hector Santos. Through the thin walls, she could hear the Rama guide shouting at the officers and a scuffling of chairs. While Jennifer was unable to make out the details of the interrogation, the tone of Hector's voice was all too familiar. First came his sullen indifference. Then, he turned defiant. Finally, she heard him gush indignant cries of innocence.

Her own interrogation had been quick, as the story she told was brief. She and her colleagues went into the nature reserve looking for a possible archaeological site with Hector as their guide. Christian Hunte had suddenly appeared, and together with Hector they held Jennifer and her friends hostage at gunpoint for reasons unknown. Jennifer became concerned about the group's safety after the men physically assaulted them and after repeated threats by the gun-wielding Hector. She told the sergeant she had managed to disable Hector and take the gun. Christian had then rushed at her and she fired one shot in self-defense.

When she handed over the revolver, Jennifer made sure to mention that she, Hector and Christian had handled the weapon, in addition to one other member of her party. "You'll find multiple sets of fingerprints on it."

The sergeant examined the revolver and frowned. "You said you fired one shot. There are four empty chambers."

"Check Hector's hands for gunpowder residue. He fired three shots to scare away some monkeys," said Jennifer.

The sergeant crossed his arms over his chest and leaned back in his chair. "You seem familiar with procedure. Are you *policía*?"

Jennifer's face reddened. She had hoped to avoid revealing she was a detective, as she knew her involvement in a shooting while on suspension would not go over well back in Massachusetts. But, as she walked the sergeant through her story, she realized there was no escaping the revelation. "Yes, I'm a detective with the Massachusetts State Police."

"Are you here on official business?"

"No. I'm on . . . vacation."

The sergeant had relaxed considerably after hearing she was a fellow police officer, but he asked for her captain's contact information to verify her claim. After she provided him with Gambelli's phone number, the sergeant said, "I will call him as soon as I finish with Santos. In the meantime, please do not leave the station."

While Jennifer waited, she pulled her cell phone from her backpack. Looking at the screen, she muttered an expletive. There were three notifications showing two missed calls and a voice message from Dan Nickerson. At first she was surprised she hadn't heard the phone ring, but then remembered there had been no cell signal in Indio Maiz.

Jennifer sighed. There was no way she could call Dan back without also talking to Gambelli, and the captain would be pissed to hear of her predicament. After deliberating, however, Jennifer realized Gambelli would learn of the shooting soon enough. She decided it was better to hear about it first from her rather than the Nicaraguan police.

Dialing Nickerson, she puffed out a sigh and waited for the call to connect.

"Jen, hello! How are you?" answered Nickerson.

Bent over on the waiting room bench, Jennifer massaged her forehead. "I've had better days."

"Oh, no. What's up?"

"I'm in a bit of a spot."

"Nothing serious, I hope."

Jennifer crossed her fingers. "Me too."

"Anything I can do to help?"

"Don't think so, but thanks. What did you call about?"

"Oh, right," Nickerson said. "We got a call from Interpol this morning. Klaus Navarro cleared customs in San Jose, Costa Rica, yesterday."

"Holy shit, you're kidding me!" Jennifer's head snapped up. "I flew in there a few days ago!"

"Really? What are you doing down there?"

"It's a long story," she said. "Did Interpol detain him?"

"Not yet, but they're looking for him. They said customs video footage showed he arrived with several other men. Big guys. Serious-looking guys."

"Uh-oh, that's not good," Jennifer said. Closing her eyes, she tried to remember how long it had taken to reach Greytown from San Jose. She, Anlon and Pebbles had flown into San Jose on their way to Nicaragua to meet up with Cesar. There, Anlon had hired a helicopter charter to transport them and their gear to Greytown. It was less than an hour, she estimated. "Listen, Dan. I need to call you back, but I need a quick favor."

"No problem, what do you need?"

"Can you do a quick Interpol search on two names for me?" She spelled Jacques Foucault's and Christian Hunte's names. In the background, Jennifer could hear Nickerson typing.

"Okay, got it. I'll see what I can do. This have anything to do with your problem?"

"Yeah, unfortunately." Jennifer sighed. "Is the captain around?"

"Yep, want me to patch you through?"

"No, I'll call back in a little bit."

On her way out of the police station, Jennifer hung up and pulled out a slip of paper with Foucault's satellite phone number. The Nicaraguan sergeant wouldn't be happy about her skipping out, she thought, but it couldn't be helped.

Indio Maiz Biological Reserve, Nicaragua

"As a young man, I served in the French navy," said Foucault. "I was assigned to the invasion forces that claimed the West Indies. I was stationed on one of the early colonies, Saint Pierre, or Martinique as it is now known, when the island's native people, the Caribs, attacked our settlement. We repelled them and chased them into the jungle, a jungle dominated by a volcano known today as Pelée."

"One afternoon, I was patrolling the perimeter of our encampment when I happened upon a curious stone which had rolled down the side of the volcano. It was curious because it was shaped like a brick. I asked myself, 'What is a brick doing in the middle of a jungle?'

"My curiosity led me to look around the area. I found two more bricks higher on the volcano. Then, I looked up and spotted a small opening on the slope above. As I neared the opening, I noticed other dislodged bricks. I pulled them away and squeezed inside. I was very excited. Pirates were rampant in the Caribbean in those days and I thought I had stumbled onto a treasure horde. To my surprise, I had . . . but it was a treasure trove of Stones, not gold. All except this here."

Foucault used the back of his gauze-wrapped hand to lift the medallion from his chest.

"This I found draped on the chest of a skeleton. Resting on his chest, below the medallion, was his *Sinethal*, facedown. It was clutched in one hand. The other hand rested at the skeleton's side. In it was a

Naetir. I would not know it for weeks, but I had discovered the final resting place of Mereau—possibly the greatest man to ever walk the Earth."

"Mereau's crypt was on Martinique?" Anlon asked. Staring off toward the jungle, he mumbled, "How did Devlin miss it?"

"I removed the Maerlif beacon long ago," Foucault replied. "Without it, Devlin had no chance of finding Mereau."

Pebbles asked, "So, the Dominica Maerlif is a crypt too?"

"*Non.* The Maerlif there was one of Malinyah's caches. You see, the islands of the West Indies were common stopping points for Munuorian ships heading into the Atlantic. Why she chose Dominica ahead of other islands, I do not know," Foucault said, hoping his lie went unnoticed.

The group listened to the rest of Foucault's story as they rested on rocks at the base of the hill. By now the rain shower had subsided and the temperature and humidity were on the rise. While Foucault spoke, Anlon shed his raincoat and squeezed water from his boonie hat. Pebbles had already removed her slicker and sat fidgeting with the *Breylofte*, while Cesar sipped water from a canteen.

Foucault described how he carefully removed the necklace with the medallion. After layering it over his own neck, he noticed the shape of the *Naetir* would fit nicely in the round depression of the *Sinethal*. In fact, he said, Mereau's body seemed positioned to encourage a discoverer to put one against the other. This led him to pry each Stone from Mereau's grip. When they snapped together, Foucault was so frightened by the explosive clap that he dropped the fused Stones and bolted from the tomb.

But, he said, his curiosity led him to return the next day. The Stones had separated and lay next to one another on the dusty floor of the chamber. He picked them up and snapped them together again. When his hands slipped into the handholds, Mereau appeared. Foucault again dropped the Stones and fled the vault.

"Voodoo" sorcery would not arise in the Caribbean for another two hundred years, Foucault told them, but the natives of Saint Pierre were thought to practice dark magic. When he first saw Mereau, he thought it a trick of the Caribs. A hallucination. Yet, the vision of Mereau seemed to Foucault as beyond the primitives' capabilities. So, he worked up the courage to return again and reconnect with Mereau.

This time, he stayed longer. He realized he could interact with Mereau. Although he did not understand Mereau's speech, the ancient Munuorian was adept at communicating through visions and gestures. The interactions were infectious. Soon, Foucault could not go a day without being with Mereau.

"He encouraged me to surround myself with magnets, eat food grown around the volcano. In time, I found I could communicate with him. Understand his thoughts. He showed me how to use the other *Tyls* stored in the tomb.

"He told me of the Munuorians and of his adventures on the seas. He shared stories of their great works and the tale of the Munirvo catastrophe. He asked for my help. Mereau wanted to know what had happened to his people.

"I could not answer these questions, I was just a young sailor on my first voyage, I told him. He begged me to help him and proposed a trade. Help him learn the fate of the Munuorians and Muran. In exchange, he would teach me how to use the Stones. He would make me rich; he would show me how to live far beyond the life span of other men. It was an easy trade to make for a lowly sailor.

"It took centuries to find the answers. I had no idea when or where the Munuorians lived. There was no Internet or encyclopedias to consult, nor was it easy to travel from place to place in search of clues. Indeed, many of their *Tyls* weren't rediscovered until colonists invaded South America and north Africa and unearthed ancient ruins.

"Mereau was heartbroken when he learned the fate of Munuoria. They were a proud people, a brilliant civilization. It was hard to tell him they simply faded away."

When Foucault finished speaking, Cesar said, "An astounding story, Monsieur."

"I assure you, every word of it is true."

Pebbles listened to Foucault with a mix of wonder, envy and skepticism. It was believable that Foucault found a *Sinethal* and learned to use it. It was possible he learned how to make *enjyia* and slowed his aging. She could even imagine Mereau imploring him to seek out the Munuorians' fate. If Malinyah had made the same request of her, Pebbles would have accepted the challenge without question, although she liked to think she would have done so out of fealty rather than for riches or the promise of youth.

But . . . she didn't understand the connection between Foucault's story and Muran, and why he referred to her earlier in the present tense. She asked, "Why was Mereau so concerned about what happened to Muran? She died in the revolt."

Foucault raised an eyebrow. "What did Malinyah tell you of Muran?"

"Not much. Enough to know Malinyah was angry with her. I mean royally pissed. She blamed Muran for the revolt that killed her children."

"So, she told you the details of the revolt?"

"Yes . . . well, somewhat." Pebbles hedged.

Thinking back to when Malinyah finally revealed the reason for her cliff-side outburst, Pebbles recalled Malinyah saying the revolt after Munirvo cost the lives of many, including Alynioria and her other children. She blamed Muran for leading the revolt and turning the people of Munuoria against one another—and for using *Tyls* in the battle, including the *Tuliskaera*.

Pebbles had asked what happened to Muran after she was defeated. Malinyah said she died. When Pebbles then asked about her children, Malinyah became so distraught she could not speak. There were a hundred other questions Pebbles wanted to ask at the time, but she couldn't bear to hurt Malinyah by digging any deeper.

Anlon interrupted her thoughts. "Look," he said to Foucault, "what does all this have to do with you sending your goon to hold us hostage?"

"To prevent you from finding a *Tuliskaera*," he said. "To prevent you from giving it to Muran, or her taking it from you."

"Pebbles just told you she died . . . ten thousand years ago. You're going to need a better story than that!"

"She did *not* die," said Foucault. "At least, her mind did not."

Before Anlon could respond, Foucault's satellite phone began to ring. He saw Jennifer's number appear on the screen and said to Foucault, "Hold that thought."

Rising from the group, Anlon paced away and answered the call. "Hey, Jen, on your way back?"

"Listen, Anlon. Navarro's in San Jose," she said.

"What?" Anlon halted in midstride.

"Just got off the phone with Dan Nickerson. Navarro arrived yesterday; he has several men with him. I think you better open the Maerlif quick, unless you want another uninvited guest!"

"Yikes, okay. Will do. Thanks for the heads up," Anlon said.

"I'm not sure when I can get back, so don't wait for me," Jennifer said.

"Why? What's wrong?" He turned back to look at the others gathered at the wall.

"It's a little sticky here with the police. I'll try to get there as quick as I can."

When Anlon hung up, he nearly threw the phone into the jungle. Could this day get any worse?

Pebbles saw the look on his face and knew immediately there was a problem. "What's the matter, A.C.?"

"Navarro. He's on his way here. He has men with him," said Anlon. "We need to open the Maerlif *now*."

Foucault frowned and sputtered, "*C'est impossible!*"

Stopping dead in his tracks, Anlon stared at Foucault. "Come again?"

The Frenchman darted a look at his watch. Margaret's call was an hour overdue, but that in and of itself wasn't cause to panic. He could think of several benign reasons for the delay, including the possibility that Navarro had arrived late for the appointment.

However, as Foucault considered a range of alternative explanations, a sickening feeling overwhelmed his optimism. If the worst had happened, it was possible Navarro was indeed on his way to Indio Maiz.

A quick phone call to Margaret would clarify Navarro's status, but how could he explain it to Cully without drawing suspicion?

"I am just surprised, that is all," Foucault said. "Let us open the Maerlif as you suggest."

23

The Maerlif

Indio Maiz Biological Reserve, Nicaragua
September 5

D o you know what to do, Mademoiselle?"

Pebbles faced the wall with the *Breylofte* in her shivering hands. She nodded and crouched into position. "Get ready for the return of the spooky monkey choir."

Foucault stood by Pebbles' side and watched the taller woman with great curiosity. She exhibited passion in her words and body language whenever Malinyah was discussed. It reminded him of his own connection with Mereau.

He found it most interesting that Pebbles seemed to possess the ability to converse freely with Malinyah. It had taken Foucault years to tune the magnetic energy of his mind to communicate as freely with Mereau. He was anxious to see if Pebbles could harness her energy to find and open the Maerlif entrance.

"Here we go again," Pebbles said.

There were five sizeable slabs within the initial target area Anlon and Cesar had suggested, any of which might be the Maerlif door. Pebbles picked the middle one to focus on first. She closed her eyes and hummed against the *Breylofte* in a steady, low tone. Unlike her earlier attempts during the rain, the wall this time responded with a light rumble. The vines drooping down its slope began to lazily sway. Smaller pebbles nesting in crevices, and others teetering on jagged ledges, broke free and scattered down the wall face.

While she hummed, Pebbles tightened her grip, causing an audible change in the tone emanating from the Stone. As soon as Foucault noticed the shift in sound, he looked to see Pebbles' fingertips white with tension.

In the background, the howlers began to gather. Grunting and wailing, they swung from treetop to treetop on their way to the ceiba. The jungle bristled with the swish of swaying branches and the intermittent cracks of broken limbs. Dissonant at first, the shrieking monkeys grew more harmonious as they neared the clearing.

Again, Pebbles' tone on the Stone altered pitch. The howlers responded in kind. Anlon and Cesar exchanged looks as Pebbles' face turned beet red. She tugged the Stone from her lips. "Gah! Nothing!"

The howlers greeted her pause with a cavalcade of hoots reminiscent of rabid sports fans welcoming a disdained opponent. Pebbles lowered the Stone. "Damn monkeys!"

Foucault stepped forward and placed a bandaged hand on her shoulder. In a paternal tone, he leaned close and whispered, "You are trying too hard. Relax your grip. Slow your humming. You can't force the door to respond, you must coax it."

"Are you sure you don't want to do this? I've moved rocks, logs, that kind of thing. I've never tried to pull a boulder from a wall," she said.

"*Non. You* must do this. Remember, there are three diamonds embedded in the back of the entry stone. Before you try to pull any slab, you must make sure you've found all three. If you only find one, it's possible you've found the Maerlif beacon instead of the door's diamonds. If you pull the wrong stone, the chamber may cave in. The door diamonds only will respond if you find their frequency. If your sound waves are too strong or too weak, they will not vibrate."

"Okay, I'll try, but I'm having a hard time concentrating with the noise," Pebbles said, pointing her head toward the hundred or so monkeys gathered around the tree.

"Here, let me calm them for you." Foucault gestured for the *Breylofte.*

When Pebbles handed him the Stone, Foucault turned toward the ceiba. Many of the monkeys hopped angrily on the branches while others pounded their paws on the snaking roots. He winced as he cupped the Stone with his burned hands and then pointed it at the tree. When he started to hum, the howlers' throaty moans converged. The monkeys at the tree's base climbed onto branches next to those already there.

Foucault raised and lowered his pitch on the *Breylofte*. The monkeys followed his example each time. He swayed the *Breylofte* to the left; the howlers leaned in that direction. He raised his head and the monkeys did so too. Like a magician charming a basket of snakes, Foucault willed them to follow his lead.

When he paused to breathe, the monkeys started to chatter just as they had done with Pebbles. Abruptly, Foucault huffed against the Stone. The howlers, stunned by the magnetic surge, silenced. They remained quiet for nearly thirty seconds. A few of the monkeys dropped down from the tree and bounded away, but the rest sat in confused silence. Then, a small group began to grunt again. Foucault waited for several more to chime in and then he sounded another gruff blast. Immediately, the rogue protestors hushed. When he lowered the *Breylofte*, the entire collection of primates stared back in quiet obedience.

Foucault turned to find the open-mouthed group staring at him. He smiled, bowed and returned the *Breylofte* to Pebbles. She nodded her thanks and he stepped back to allow her more room. After taking a deep breath, she crouched and started again. The monkeys slowly began to croon in unison. Pebbles did her best to block out their song and focus on relaxing her fingers as Foucault had suggested.

She tried another slab. Nothing. The rock wall trembled and more loose rubble broke free, but she felt no vibration from the cupped *Tyl*. Finally, on the third of five slabs, Pebbles felt the *Breylofte* rattle in her hands. Maintaining the hum, she slowly raised the *Breylofte* higher on the slab's face. Another rattle. She guided it down toward the rock's base, and the Stone tugged at her fingertips once more. Finally, she'd found the three diamonds.

Triumphantly, Pebbles pulled her lips from the smooth underside of the bowl-shaped tool and turned to the others. She flexed a bicep and a wide smile spread across her face. Anlon couldn't help but laugh as she struck the all-too-familiar pose. His cackle had the unfortunate effect of riling the howlers. Emboldened by her success, Pebbles raised the *Breylofte* in their direction and sharply huffed against the Stone as Foucault had done. Instantly, the monkeys fell quiet. As the hundred pairs of blinking eyes stared down at her from the ceiba, she turned toward Anlon and held up the *Breylofte*. "This could come in real handy during happy hour at Sydney's!"

Before Anlon could offer a pithy retort, Pebbles again faced the wall and directed the *Breylofte's* sound waves at the center of the slab. When the vibration recommenced, she hummed with slightly more intensity and she tightened her grasp. The crusty mixture surrounding the slab puffed dust in the air as the slab quivered. Small fissures then emerged along the entry door's edges.

Foucault nodded appreciatively as he observed Pebbles pull one side of the slab outward. Malinyah had taught her well. Cesar stood to the side and recorded the event with a digital camera. Like the others, he was anxious to see inside, but his professional instincts were still intact. Anlon peered over Pebbles' shoulder as the slab came loose.

She halted and spun around. With double biceps curled, she said, "Oh, yeah!"

Anlon and Cesar celebrated in response, as did the howlers. At that point, though, Pebbles was too stoked to care about the monkeys. She advanced to the slab, and just as Malinyah had instructed, she took a position adjacent to the slab that allowed her to blow on its back side.

Directing the *Breylofte's* sound waves through the foot-sized opening, she stepped forward and hummed more aggressively. This pushed the door further outward. The ground in front of the slab bulged as the outward movement shoved turf out of the way. Larger chunks of rock dropped to the ground across the span of the wall. Dust churned in the opening.

Pebbles, feeling dizzy from her exertion, staggered back a few steps and lowered the *Breylofte*. Dropping to her knees, she panted while waving her free hand to clear the dust floating around her head. Above, at the hill's crest, the monkeys erupted in raucous chatter.

Anlon knelt alongside her, hugged her shoulders and kissed her brow. "That was awesome! Cesar, did you get all that?"

Cesar said, "I did. If I hadn't seen it with my own eyes, I would have believed it a trick of the camera."

They were in the midst of celebration when the first *terciopelo* slithered out. Several feet long, the olive-colored snake with yellowish zig-zagged lines along its sides hissed when it emerged. It was followed by three more, including a brownish one with similar markings that was twice the size of the others. Their hissing, obscured by the jubilant grunts of the monkeys, went unnoticed by Anlon, Cesar and Pebbles. Foucault, standing behind the group, was the first to see them.

"Serpents!" he shouted.

The others froze and looked in his direction, then followed his pointing finger to the snakes closing in. Foucault said to Pebbles, "Quickly, the *Breylofte!*"

She lifted her hand and he snatched the device. Leaning forward, he blew sharply on the Stone. The snakes flailed through the air and crashed against the back of the open door. The attack frightened two of them, and they rapidly slithered for the cover of the jungle.

The other two did not, including the eight-foot female. They coiled briefly and then shot forth with lightning speed. Foucault blasted them again, this time sweeping the *Breylofte* across their path. Both snakes crashed against the rock wall with a thud. Before they could recover, Foucault hummed long and slowly against the Stone. The snakes quivered on the ground and then rose into the air. With the snakes held captive by the Stone's sound waves, Foucault lifted them higher and higher. Soon, they dangled at treetop level, wriggling and hissing in protest.

Foucault spun them around in circles, over and over, before yanking his head forward with a great huff. The sound waves hurled the two snakes against the rock wall once again. Lifeless, they slid down and thumped onto the ground. Anlon cringed as he watched. The plight of the snakes was all too familiar.

Once all had quelled their heartbeats, they turned their attention back to the open Maerlif. Pebbles glanced past the dead snakes and said to Foucault, "You first!"

The group readied to enter the Maerlif. From their backpacks, Anlon and Pebbles withdrew small lanterns and flashlights. Cesar walked around the vault entrance, capturing video footage and still frames from different angles. Foucault managed to light a cigarette with his bandaged hands and then checked his watch. Margaret's call was now long overdue.

"What should we expect inside—besides more snakes?" Anlon asked of Foucault.

Pebbles tested a flashlight and said over her shoulder, "The Maerlif Malinyah showed me had metal chests. The Stones were divided between them. But she didn't say anything about bodies."

"I do not think we will find any bodies here. If we do, it will be a first. Burial Maerlifs were reserved for volcano slopes," Foucault said.

"I meant to ask you earlier, why is that?" Cesar asked, lowering the camera.

"A symbolic gesture," Foucault said. "Their homeland was ringed with volcanos."

Anlon thought of Isabela. He asked, "Galápagos? Was that their homeland?"

Foucault froze in place. "What makes you think this?"

"Volcanos, lots of cryptochrome-rich vegetation on the islands, unique plant and animal biology. Plus, Cassiopeia is visible most of the year there."

Foucault dropped the cigarette and crushed it with his foot. "We have no time to discuss this now, perhaps later. Come, I will lead the way."

The entrance stood about four feet high and four feet wide. Each of them had to crawl through the opening, but once inside, the Maerlif ceiling was high enough for them to stand. The entire inside of the vault, including floor, ceiling and walls, was encased in rock. Rock that had been fused by some means. To Anlon, it looked like lava trails.

Over the millennia, chunks of the fused rock had dislodged in places along the walls and ceiling, leaving scattered debris on the Maerlif floor. Most of the debris was covered by a layer of dust; however, a number of chunks looked fresh, no doubt shaken loose by the *Breylofte's* vibrations against the outer walls. It wasn't immediately apparent how the snakes found a way into the chamber, but a portion of the ceiling and one wall glistened with moisture, presumably from the earlier rain. Also, a handful of vines had chewed their way through the outer wall of the Maerlif, providing additional evidence of cracks in the sealed vault. There were surprisingly few cobwebs and no overt signs of insects; however, Pebbles did spot a hairy spider disappear beneath the vines.

When they arrived in the center of the Maerlif, Pebbles expressed relief the chamber contained no bodies or more snakes. Instead, at the base of the deepest wall of the chamber sat four metal chests arrayed in an arc. They were approximately three feet long, two feet tall and three feet wide. The sides of the chests were covered in a sooty grime, and rocky debris layered around and between their bases, but the tops were clean.

Cesar followed closest behind Foucault, filming the entry while doing his best to avoid bumping his head or tripping over rocks. He noticed the cleared lids and made a comment. Foucault suggested the snakes, drawn to the magnetic Stones inside the chests, chose the lids as roosts.

Anlon was last to join the group gathered around the chests. To him, it was a surreal moment to look upon the ancient cases. For more than ten thousand years, the Stones inside had rested in peace while the history of the outside world raced forward. Forgotten to all, their great powers languished in obscurity. He paused to consider the incredible, and unlikely, chain of events that led to their rediscovery. A sense of exhilaration filled him. Devlin's great folly proved true.

"Which chest should we start with?" Anlon asked Foucault. "They all look the same."

"Any will do," Foucault said.

They decided to start with the chest farthest to their left and then work their way around the arc to open the others. Anlon expressed surprise that the chests had no locks. Foucault said, "They were in a great hurry. The asteroid was coming fast. They prepared the chambers, unloaded the chests, installed the beacon, sealed the vault and then left. There was no time for anything else."

While Cesar recorded the event, the three others took hold of the first chest lid and slowly lifted. It was much heavier than Anlon expected. Thinking of the trek through the jungle, it was hard to imagine how they maneuvered the heavy chest this far inland. Then he recalled the chests were left before the great flood. The area was likely along the coast prior to Munirvo.

Once the lid was lowered to the floor, they all peered inside. The chest was filled with *Aromaeghs*. Foucault explained, "If you have not seen these before, they are step-by-step tutorials on how to use the *Tyls* for many common purposes. How to till a field using the *Dreylaeks*. How to use the *Tuliskaera* to cut trees and stone to build homes. How to use the *Breylofte* to create a dam. And so on."

"Yes, we have one. It's more of a storytelling video, for lack of a better description. It shows the Munirvo tale," said Anlon.

"I have seen it; it is hard to watch. Yes, there were storytelling *Aromaeghs* as well. They were used to preserve the Munuorians' history, to record the most important lessons for the young," Foucault said.

The unmistakable rhythmic thumps of helicopter blades echoed through the Maerlif entrance. Anlon turned toward the opening. "Uh-oh, we've got company."

"Jen?" asked Pebbles.

Anlon hitched his belt. "I hope so."

"Oh, my God, A.C., what if it's Navarro?"

"Then we're screwed."

"What should we do?" Cesar asked.

"Damn it! I left the *Breylofte* outside." Pebbles punched her thigh.

With the others flustered, Foucault took control. "Quickly, open the other cases. Look for *Breyloftes*, *Dreylaeks*."

Pebbles and Anlon sprang into action and tugged off the lid of the second case. It was stacked with nested *Breyloftes*. Pebbles grabbed one for herself and handed one to Anlon. "Just hum on it as hard as you can," she advised.

Cesar, with the help of a grimacing Foucault, hoisted the next lid. Inside, the chest was packed with the mother lode of Munuorian technology. Mixed together were dozens of *Naetirs*, *Terusaels* and *Dreylaeks*. Poking through the mix of stone cylinders, eggs and cookies were three pointed tips.

Foucault reached in and cupped a pair of *Dreylaeks*. He directed Cesar to slide them in the pockets sewn into his shirt cuffs. When done, he nodded to Anlon and the four crept toward the entrance. Anlon peeked around the edge as the helicopter's landing struts touched down.

"What can you see, A.C.?"

"It's on the ground, but I can't tell much else." Poking his head out farther, he tried to make out the shapes through the blacked-out helicopter windows without success. "Get ready," he whispered back. "Someone's coming out."

Pebbles cupped the *Breylofte* and held it near her mouth.

"Wait," Anlon called, holding up a hand. A second later he sighed. "Thank God. It's Jen."

He slumped against the Maerlif wall and exhaled deeply. Pebbles lowered the *Breylofte*. "Why didn't she call first?"

Anlon grumbled. "She probably did. I left the satellite phone outside."

They wiggled through the opening to greet her as Henri piloted the copter away. Jennifer wore a stern look as she headed toward them.

Pebbles waved and smiled. "Look at what we fou—"

The sound wave crushed into Pebbles and flung her through the air. Her legs kicked out as she soared past Jennifer, clipping her in the jaw. Both went down hard. Anlon, stunned by Pebbles' sudden flight, anchored in place. When he realized what had happened, he whipped around. The blow caught him on the upper shoulder and knocked him down. He tried to sit up and was pasted against the ground by another blast. He heard Cesar utter an "oof" as he, too, was hit.

"Still yourselves, *mesdames et messieurs*. I don't wish to kill you, but I will if I must."

Finca 6 Museum
Palmar Norte, Costa Rica

Margaret was still sitting in the car when two blacked-out SUVs came barreling down the access road, swirls of dust following in their wake. They were more than an hour late.

They pulled into spots close to the steps leading to the museum's entrance. Margaret watched from behind the open pages of a museum brochure and waited for Navarro to appear. The two vehicles sat idling for several minutes before four burly men exited wearing matching white guayabera shirts and sunglasses.

Margaret laughed at their effort to blend in as tourists. Well, at least they'll be easy to spot, she thought. The four men ascended the steps and approached the security guard. Two of the men engaged the guard in friendly conversation while the other two slipped inside.

Retraining her gaze on the two SUVs, Margaret noticed the drivers of both vehicles remained in place. Nothing happened for several minutes, until at last one of the white-shirted men poked his head out the museum's front door and signaled the vehicles.

The rear door of the SUV closest to Margaret popped open and a ruddy man with a bushy mustache exited. He wore a panama hat, sunglasses, tan shirt and white slacks. He slowly scanned the parking area. When his eyes swept toward Margaret, she buried her face in the brochure. Unsure when to look up, Margaret continued to stare blankly at the brochure. Then she heard a car door slam shut. Darting her head in the direction of the sound, her eyes picked up two men rapidly ascending the museum steps: panama-hat man and another with a long, black ponytail. Dressed in all black, ponytail man carried a briefcase. His majesty had arrived.

As soon as the men cleared the vehicles, the drivers reversed out of their parking spots and maneuvered the SUVs to face outward as Margaret had done. She waited until Navarro and the other man disappeared into the lobby before she made for the grove. As she stepped out of the car, she thought, "Five men plus two drivers? Man, is he paranoid!"

With the backpack in one hand, she quietly moved through the foliage using the other hand to guide fronds out of her way. When she arrived at the edge of the grove, she surveyed the situation. As expected, Navarro sat alone on the bench. On the ground next to him was the briefcase. He gazed at the massive sphere from behind sunglasses. Looking back toward the museum's main building, Margaret could see two of the bodyguards standing on the back porch scanning the grounds in opposite directions.

The other two bodyguards and the panama-hat man who accompanied Navarro were not visible. It was possible they were stationed on the far side of the outbuilding. She could not see it from her vantage point in the grove. However, it was just as possible they were roaming the grounds or standing on the opposite side of the sphere, or both.

Skittish about approaching Navarro without knowing where the other men were positioned, Margaret backtracked into the grove and turned toward the field where the smaller globes were displayed. After ensuring no eyes were focused on the grove, Margaret stepped out into the open and wandered among the smaller spheres. Several museum visitors milled about, taking pictures and chattering. A couple of them snickered at Margaret's goth-girl getup, but the others took no notice.

She halted at a grouping of spheres and took her phone out of the backpack. Looking up after she snapped a couple quick shots, she spied one of the remaining bodyguards positioned on the far side of the sphere. That left two unaccounted for, but from her position she could tell that no one stood near the outbuilding. Navarro was completely alone.

24

Snake Bite

Indio Maiz Biological Reserve, Nicaragua
September 5

Anlon and the others sat against the Maerlif wall next to the dead snakes. Foucault stood in the clearing with the satellite phone against his ear and his eyes riveted on the group. Though they were scraped up and sore, none had sustained a serious injury in the attack. Anlon propped his arms against his bent knees and buried his head. How could I have been so stupid? he thought.

Foucault angrily disconnected the unanswered call and placed another one. This time, the party on the other end of the line answered. Foucault gruffly rattled instructions in French and abruptly ended the call. He tore the bandages from his hands and advanced to the wall.

"I have no more time for foolishness," he said. "I expect your full cooperation, *comprende? Bon.* Now, I want answers."

Turning to Pebbles, Foucault asked, "You said Ometepe earlier. Why?"

Pebbles looked to Anlon, who motioned her to answer the question. "We think Devlin was interested in Ometepe. We think it has something to do with a statue he had in his collection."

"Statue?" Foucault said. "What kind of statue?"

"Like ones on Ometepe and Zapatera. A man wearing a headdress.

It looks like a fish head. It has the *Sulataer* symbol on the back of the headdress." Pebbles glared at him and rubbed her bruised shoulder.

"*Mon Dieu!*" said Foucault.

"What?" Anlon asked. "What's with the statue?"

Foucault quickly asked Pebbles, "What made you think Devlin was interested in Ometepe?"

Anlon jumped in. "He wrote down the name in one of his journals. We thought he was searching for volcanos, but then we made the connection with the fish-man statue. Why did you get excited when Pebbles described the statue?"

"Volcanos? Devlin was interested in volcanos?" Foucault sounded alarmed. "Then it is for certain, Muran lives."

"Volcanos," Cesar said. "We have returned to the topic of crypts, have we not? I take it one of Ometepe's volcanos holds a crypt."

"*Précisément.*" Foucault paced back and forth in front of the others with his hands clenched at his sides.

"Whose crypt? Muran's? Malinyah's?" Anlon asked.

Foucault paused and turned to face Anlon. "Why did you come here, Dr. Cully?"

"What?"

"Why did you seek a Maerlif? Did someone ask you to come, perhaps? Did someone suggest the idea to you?"

"Of course not. I came because of Devlin. I wanted to finish his work. Prove the Munuorians existed." As Foucault advanced toward him, Anlon balled his hands into fists.

"But, you have Malinyah's *Sinethal*, a *Breylofte*," Foucault said.

"That's not enough, and you know it!" Anlon pounded the ground. "No one will believe the story, believe Malinyah. They'll want physical proof. An archaeological site. One that can't be attached to some other culture."

Hovering above Anlon, Foucault sneered, "And you think *that's* what your uncle wanted?"

"I don't know what Devlin wanted! He left us nothing but riddles," Anlon rose up and confronted Foucault. "Look, it's obvious you know something we don't. It'd be a whole lot simpler for all of us if you just told us what you're digging to find out."

"Careful, Dr. Cully," Foucault warned. Anlon retreated a step but remained standing. Foucault said, "I think Devlin was assisting Muran, wittingly or unwittingly, to find a *Tuliskaera*."

"You're out of your mind," said Anlon. "You're trying to tell me there's a ten-thousand-year-old woman walking around? And my uncle was helping her?"

Foucault nodded.

"And you think she wants a *Tuliskaera*?" Anlon challenged.

"I do not *think*, Dr. Cully, I *know*."

The edge in Foucault's voice was defiant. His eyes burned, his face trembled. Anlon observed Foucault's reaction and realized the man wasn't joking. He really believed Muran was alive and was seeking a *Tuliskaera*. Anlon peered at the medallion swaying over Foucault's chest and wondered, was it possible?

The moment he asked the question, he realized his hypocrisy. Anlon thought of the reaction of the average person if told about Malinyah and her *Sinethal*, or if he showed the person a *Breylofte* and said it could lift a tractor trailer high in the sky.

It was clear Foucault knew the Munuorians and their Stones well. He knew their language; he could wield the *Dreylaeks*; he knew of Malinyah. Why, then, was it so hard to believe Foucault's assertion about Muran?

Anlon asked, "Presuming you are right, and this Muran still lives, why would she want a *Tuliskaera*?"

"She is running out of options. She needs to find one fast."

The skin on Anlon's neck tingled. "What did you just say?"

"Muran is desperate," rephrased Foucault.

Pebbles said, "You said her *mind* did not die. Is she on a *Sinethal* like Malinyah and Mereau? Is that what you mean?"

"A clever deduction, Mademoiselle," said Foucault. "But, no, I am certain she is free of her mind-keeper."

"Okay, you're going to need to explain that," Anlon said.

"How much do you know of the *Sinethal*?" Foucault asked.

"A helluva lot less than you, that's for sure," Anlon said. "I know it stores a person's memories and a portion of their consciousness."

"Do you know how this storage was accomplished?"

Anlon thought of his hippocampus theory and the role of crypto-chromes as a facilitator. "Funny you should ask. I think I understand some of it. Somehow, they stimulated the brain to 'upload' memories onto the Stone. The somehow part is murky. Clearly, it was an elec-tromagnetic exchange, but I don't know how it was done."

"You would say, would you not, that it is much like how a com-puter shares data?" asked Foucault. "One storage device is connected to another. There is a mechanism which commands the first to pass information to the other."

"That's how I see it."

"Then, what does that imply?"

"That it's freaky-deaky?" Anlon quipped. "Sorry, I'm a little punchy. It's been a long day. I'm not sure what you're getting at."

Foucault said, "I have a flash drive, I put it into my laptop. I down-load a file to give to someone else. That person works on the file, saves it on the flash drive again and gives it back to me. What do I do with it?"

Anlon considered Foucault's description, then the implication hit him. "Holy crap! Are you saying the *Sinethal* can be downloaded back into the brain?"

The stone-faced Foucault just stared back at Anlon.

"What?" Pebbles jumped up and stood by Anlon.

Foucault nodded. "I mean exactly that. Muran has done it many times over thousands of years."

Pebbles flashed a startled look at Anlon. "She can change bodies!"

"*Oui*," said Foucault. "It was forbidden by the Andaers, but that mattered not to Muran. She cared little that it meant erasing the mind of another. The first time, she did it out of spite. After that, it suited her needs."

"What do you mean, she did it out of spite?" Anlon asked.

Foucault stared at Pebbles while he answered. "Surely, you know. She did it to hurt Malinyah. Muran killed Alynioria, Malinyah's eldest daughter. She erased her mind and took her body."

Finca 6 Museum
Palmar Norte, Costa Rica

Margaret knelt down to return the phone to the backpack. While there, she withdrew the brochure and the knife. Sauntering across the field, she casually unfolded the map and slipped the knife into her palm.

As she strolled in his direction, Margaret considered Navarro's security detail. It was bold of him to bring so many men. Foucault's instructions, delivered through Christian, had been clear: come alone. She had expected Navarro to ignore the demand, but seven men seemed like overkill.

The closer Margaret crept, the faster her heart pounded. She closed her eyes and recalled the bleary-eyed vision of Navarro prancing away from the burning campsite. He had tossed her aside like a dying animal and left her to burn. When she opened her eyes, Margaret could see his smug outline under the shadow of the tree. He sat like the priss he was, cross-legged with hands in his lap. Rage surged in her veins.

Seven feet away, the idea of casually moving behind him was long forgotten. She veered from the path and quickened her pace. With eyes glued on the ponytail dangling behind the back of the bench, she slid the knife forward in her hand. Two feet away and the fop still had taken no notice.

However, the bodyguard on the porch looking in Navarro's direction had. He screamed out to Navarro to look behind him as he bolted down the museum steps. Navarro, surprised by the shout, whipped his head in the direction of the bodyguard. It was a fatal mistake.

Margaret grabbed hold of the ponytail and yanked it down mercilessly. The man cried aloud as his head snapped back. With vengeful speed, Margaret stroked across his neck, digging as deep as the knife would allow. His howl was cut short by a sickening escape of air from the gaping wound.

Nothing she imagined was as sweet as the tug of the knife through his flesh. Even in the other hand gripping strands of his ponytail, Margaret felt his body shudder. Standing over the mortally wounded man, the one who had struck her down in the dark, she couldn't resist the temptation. Wrenching his ponytail down farther, she sneered with delight as his wild-eyed face came into view. It was then she realized the dying man was not Klaus Navarro.

Margaret was stupefied. Before she could regain her senses, the bodyguard stationed on the other side of the sphere tackled her to the ground. Seconds later, two more arrived. They wrested the knife from her grip and pinned her down.

The rest was a haze to Margaret. A blink here and they were pushing her toward the museum building. A blink there and she saw guns aimed at the security guard. Her head lolled and the next thing greeting her eyes was the open door of a black SUV. They shoved her inside and slammed the door shut.

She stirred again and the SUV was bouncing along the bumpy access road. As hard as she tried, Margaret could not focus. She tried to lift up and steady herself. The movement was met by a crashing blow to the back of her head. All went black.

Indio Maiz Biological Reserve, Nicaragua

Pebbles stared blankly at Foucault and wobbled. She reached for Anlon to steady herself but missed. She pitched over and splashed into a small puddle. Crawling on all fours, she tried to stand while struggling to clear her mind. Foucault readied to clap his wrists together and shouted for her to sit. Anlon stood in front to shield her while Jennifer helped her up.

Pebbles leaned against Anlon, closed her eyes and recalled writhing on the cliff while Malinyah screamed. Pebbles howled and clutched at her stomach. From her mouth spewed Malinyah's rage: "Deceiver! Murderer! Betrayer!"

"Sit down, Mademoiselle!" Foucault commanded.

"F—— you!" yelled Pebbles, tears streaming down her face.

Anlon held up his hand toward Foucault. "Take it easy. She's upset. She didn't know. None of us did."

While Anlon consoled Pebbles, Cesar stood to join the others and cleared his throat. "How do you know this, Foucault? It is one thing to say Muran killed Malinyah's daughter, it is another to say Muran erased her mind and took her body."

"Because I have seen Alynioria's crypt, the final resting place of her body," Foucault said. "It is hidden on the slopes of Concepción, on Ometepe. Muran took her to spite Malinyah after she was defeated in the revolt."

"But, how can you know it's Alynioria? What proves Muran took her?" Cesar asked.

"The crypt of which I speak has many skeletons in it, Señor Perez. All young women. There is only one who is tall, with strands of golden hair.

"Tell me, have you ever wondered where the Aztecs and other Mesoamerican cultures arrived at the idea of human sacrifice?" Foucault asked. "Particularly, the sacrifice of young women? The academics will say they did it to appease the gods for good crops and other blessings. But, that's not the question. The question isn't why they did it, it is why they *thought* of doing it."

"I don't follow," Cesar said.

Foucault paced in front of them. "Muran ruled much of what is now Central America for many centuries, long after her countrymen perished of diseases in the post-Munirvo world. She was viewed as a goddess for the powers she commanded, for her unnaturally long life and her ability to change bodies — to take a young woman offered by the native tribes she conquered, lead her into the volcano, and emerge in the sacrificed body. They called her the Painted Lady. She could paint herself into the body of another.

"The culture that flourished on Ometepe and Zapatera—the people who made the statues—they have a long memory, as do many cultures around the world. We often miss the meaning of their legends and their works, applying our own ideas atop their art or stories."

"You're suggesting their memories are of Muran," Cesar said.

"I'm not suggesting, Señor. I know it for certain. The headdresses, for example," Foucault said. "The tribes on Ometepe imagined *transforming* themselves into eagles, jaguars and other animals. They believed the headdresses gave them the power to change from one thing to another. The headdresses were considered objects of power. Only great leaders were allowed to wear them. Now, where do you suppose these ideas came from?"

Cesar shook his head.

"A memory of the *Taellin*. The helmet used to transfer memories onto a *Sinethal* and vice versa. The fish head. They must have seen Muran use the *Taellin*. You see, the transfer cannot happen without assistance from at least one other person."

Foucault stopped pacing and leaned against a rock. As he slid down to sit, Anlon asked, "How was it done? Moving memories to the stone and back."

Foucault stared blankly at the Maerlif entrance. "Five pieces were required. A *Taellin, Sinethal, Naetir, Sulataer . . .* and a *Tuliskaera.*"

"You said the *Taellin* was a helmet. Was it stone?" Anlon asked.

"There is stone in it, but there are also diamonds," Foucault said.

Anlon pondered . . . The *Taellin* was a helmet made of stone and diamonds. Why diamonds? He closed his eyes and tried to picture the fish-head statue. There were no jewels depicted on it, just the fish symbol on the back. Ah, the fish symbol! It wasn't a symbol, it was a *Sulataer.*

He imagined the helmet placed on a person's head. In their hands, they held a *Sinethal* with the *Naetir* snapped in place. The *Sulataer* slotted into the back of the helmet. An electromagnetic pulse . . . from the *Tuliskaera?*

Yes, that made sense. A high-voltage jolt aimed at the gold coin. A pure gold coin. Pure gold isn't the best electrical conductor among metals, Anlon mused, but it's right up there.

Then what? The helmet, made of stone—almost certainly magnetic stone like the others—surrounded the head and created a contained magnetic field. The *Sulataer* conveyed the electric pulse into the helmet, creating a hypermagnetic environment, but not a very focused one. Something had to tap the hippocampus.

The diamonds, maybe? Were they inside the helmet? Yes, that might work. Diamonds used like styli. That would surely focus an electromagnetic pulse at the hippocampus. But damn, it would probably hurt. Anlon thought of the contorted face of the statue. "Remarkable," he mumbled. Turning to Foucault, he asked, "The diamonds are inside the helmet, aren't they? Stylus tips."

The dazed Foucault nodded. "There are thin diamond lines embedded in the stone that branch out from where the *Sulataer* is placed. The lines terminate into several tips that are positioned to target the central cortex."

"Incredible." Anlon stood and again began to pace. He turned suddenly and asked, "Why gold? Silver's a better conductor."

"Too intense," Foucault said. "There is a certain frequency, if you will, that is required to stimulate the brain just so. Silver, even copper, is too much."

"And the *Tuliskaera*, that's the key, isn't it? A small electric charge wouldn't work. Something was needed that could sustain a prolonged but controlled electromagnetic surge."

Foucault nodded. "The *Tuliskaera*, it is like your Cassiopeia, Dr. Cully. It takes life and it gives life."

During the exchange between Anlon and Foucault, Pebbles had quelled her emotions and now listened closely. "That's what Muran needs it for! To change bodies again." She paused and then said, "I can't believe Malinyah didn't tell me any of this."

"Do not be troubled, Mademoiselle," Foucault said. "I think her silence had less to do with hiding something from you and more to do with the pain she felt at the loss of her daughter. As to Muran, switching bodies is not the only reason she needs a *Tuliskaera*, but it is the most pressing reason."

"What do you mean? What other reason is there?" Jennifer asked.

In the distance, the sound of a helicopter approaching echoed through the treetops. Foucault looked skyward and then directed his attention to Jennifer. "Mademoiselle, if you would be so kind as to help Dr. Cully bring the *Tuliskaeras* outside. And one *Naetir*. Quickly please, no theatrics."

"You're taking them?" Pebbles asked.

"*Calme-toi, Mademoiselle.*"

Jennifer and Anlon entered the Maerlif as Foucault had requested. Once inside, Jennifer whispered, "What should we do?"

"Do as he says," Anlon whispered back. "I don't think he intends to hurt us. He could have killed us already if he wanted. Let him take the damn things, I don't care. We'll live to fight another day."

While Anlon and Jennifer gathered the three *Tuliskaeras* and a *Naetir*, Henri landed the helicopter in the center of the clearing and silenced the engine.

Foucault then instructed Henri to inspect the Maerlif to ensure no *Tuliskaeras* were left. When he reemerged, Henri confirmed no *Tuliskaeras* remained. He also reported that one of the cases was full of *Sulataers*. Foucault had Henri and the others remove the *Sulataer* case from the Maerlif and load it onto the helicopter, saying, "Recompense for my losses on Dominica."

With the helicopter loaded, Foucault stood before the group and held up a *Tuliskaera*. "The source of all our trouble. It was meant to be a stone cutter, but like all the *Tyls*, its polarity ebbs between positive and negative, reflecting the energy of the user. In the hands of Mereau and his captains, it helped rebuild the world after Munirvo, until disease took them, too.

"In the hands of Muran, it destroyed what was left of Munuoria, and for centuries after afflicted all who crossed her path. It is beautiful and sleek. Its power, awesome and seductive. And it can never fall into her hands again!"

Foucault slowly began to rub the *Tuliskaera* against the *Naetir*. As the Stones heated up, the snake on the *Tuliskaera* began to glow a dull orange. He increased the circling rhythm until the Stone made a hissing sound. The snake throbbed beneath his fingers and smoke rose from his hand. Pulling back the *Naetir*, he tapped the bottom of the *Tuliskaera's* cone. A spark leapt from the cone's tip.

Foucault raised the *Naetir* and with a stabbing motion, slammed it against the glowing snake. The *Tuliskaera* sparked brightly and a loud crack echoed off the Maerlif wall. Foucault opened his hand to reveal the *Tuliskaera* had disintegrated into shards of glowing rock that fell to the ground. He repeated the exercise with the other two serpent-tooth Stones, leaving only a pile of pulsing embers as memories of their existence.

The sun was low enough in the sky now that an orange glow coated the wall. Atop the hillside, the ceiba tree's waxy bark glimmered a dark bronze, and the jungle canopy cast a long shadow across the clearing.

"It is done," he said, his hands bleeding and charred. "Henri, *enjyia, s'il vous plaît.*"

Foucault turned his back on the group and walked to the open door of the helicopter with his hands outstretched before him. Confused looks passed between Anlon and the others as Foucault idly chatted with Henri while the pilot administered first aid, Munuorian-style. Anlon stepped forward and said, "What now?"

Foucault looked up. "That is up to you, Dr. Cully. I have accomplished what I came to do. The *Tuliskaeras* are destroyed."

Anlon's face turned a deep red. "That's it? Why the hell did you attack us?"

"It was vital to destroy the *Tuliskaeras* as quickly as possible. I could not risk the possibility of the Stones falling into Navarro's or Muran's hands."

Anlon was dissatisfied with the answer. "You still think we're helping Muran."

"*Non.* I have learned enough from our conversations to believe *you* are not aligned with Muran. But, I fear your uncle may have been. I warn you, she will come looking for Malinyah's *Sinethal.* She will seek Devlin's map and look for more *Tuliskaeras.* Until she is dead, the *Tyls* will not be safe in your hands."

Pebbles appeared alongside Anlon and said, "You said earlier that she was desperate, that she was running out of options. What did you mean?"

"Her time is coming to an end; *enjyia* only sustains life for so long, as I myself am learning. It is what pushed her to seek Devlin's help." Foucault paused while Henri finished wrapping his hands, then said to Anlon, "I don't know if your uncle intended to help her, or if he was duped into it, but he did help her."

"How?" Pebbles asked.

"She gave him Malinyah's *Sinethal*," said Foucault. "And your uncle used it to make a map."

"How can you be so sure?" asked Anlon.

"Because I know Muran stole Malinyah's *Sinethal* from her Maerlif," Foucault said. "She pulled the *Sinethal* and *Naetir* from her hands and left two things in their place: Alynioria's tunic, and a lock of her hair."

"Oh, my God!" said Pebbles, covering her mouth. "Malinyah knows, doesn't she?"

"I presume she does," Foucault said. "Muran would not have resisted the opportunity to inflict one final injury . . . one she knew would never leave Malinyah's memory."

"Right," said Jennifer. "And she screwed herself when she did that, didn't she? There was probably no chance Malinyah was going to show her the map anyway, but after flaunting her daughter's death? Hell, no!"

"So, she needed someone else to get the map for her," said Pebbles.

"*Précisément*," Foucault said with a nod. "When Devlin wrote to me looking for a *Naetir*, it shook me. I called him. Asked him why he was looking for such a common-looking stone. He wouldn't tell me. Instead, he asked me about my Waterland paper. That's when I began to suspect Muran was behind his inquiry."

Cesar interrupted, "When we discussed Ometepe, and we mentioned Devlin's interest in the statue and volcanos, you said it *confirmed* Muran lives. Why?"

"It told me one of two things, señor. Either Devlin was searching for a *Taellin*, another ingredient Muran lacks, or he discovered he was being used and went in search of the truth. I like to believe the latter," Foucault said.

Anlon concurred. "I want to believe it, too. Devlin was a rascal, but he was a good man. I can't believe he willingly helped a murderer."

"Nor can I, Dr. Cully," said Foucault. "Now, if you will excuse me, I have another urgent matter to attend to, and I must check on Christian. I offer you one final piece of advice. Leave the Painted Lady to me. I have laid a trap for her, and without a *Tuliskaera*, the scent will soon be too strong for her to ignore."

"We better get a move on, too, Anlon. Navarro, remember?" Jennifer tugged on Anlon's arm.

"I would not worry about Klaus Navarro, Mademoiselle. I don't think he will bother you again." Foucault turned and instructed Henri to start up the helicopter.

"You know him?" asked Pebbles.

"I make it my business to know everyone interested in the *Lifintyls*," Foucault shouted over the helicopter's waking engine. Leaning forward, he removed the gold medallion and gave it to Pebbles. "This belongs with Malinyah. Please tell her Mereau says, '*Aeh el sulous*.' She will understand the meaning."

As the helicopter began to rise, with Foucault seated comfortably inside, he cupped his bandaged hands around his mouth and shouted, "Dr. Cully, about the Galápagos . . . Isabela. Wolf. One thousand feet up. North side. With a clear view of Cassiopeia."

Route 34, Jaco, Costa Rica

When the gush of cold water splashed over her head, Margaret twitched and yelped.

"Again," a voice called out.

Another icy blast plastered her face and chest. This time, water shot into her nose and open mouth. She rocked back and forth on the floor, heaving and coughing.

"Wake up, Warrior Princess," mocked the voice.

The familiar words echoed in her ears as she tried unsuccessfully to move her arms and legs. While rolling on the floor, she coaxed her eyes open. Immediately, she cringed and quickly squeezed her lids shut.

"Are you a ghost?" asked the voice. "Or maybe a zombie?"

Shivering, Margaret tried to twist away from the puddle surrounding her. She raised her head from the floor and was greeted by throbbing pain from the knot on the back of her skull. As the pain awoke her other senses, a flurry of snippets from Finca 6 filled her mind.

"You tried to kill me, you little bitch!"

Cracking open one eyelid, Margaret craned her neck and squinted in the direction of the voice, but her vision was too hazy to make out anything but a white blob in the dimly lit room. She lowered her head back to the concrete floor and sighed.

"Pick her up!" Navarro said.

Rough hands gripped her arms and yanked her torso off the floor. While her legs dragged behind, they guided her to a chair and shoved her onto the seat. Woozy from the sudden movements, she teetered and started to slide from the chair. The hands dug into her shoulders and steadied her against the back of the chair. Head drooping forward, she felt another hand grip her soaked hair and yank it up.

She opened her eyes once more and came face to face with her tormentor: tan shirt, white slacks and a panama hat draped over his knee.

"You tricked me," she mumbled.

The observation drew a gruff sneer. "If only your brain was as big as your mouth." Turning away from Margaret, Navarro beckoned one of his men. "Bring the phone to me."

A prick of anger raced through Margaret, and she lurched forward to escape the hands clutching her shoulders. The beefy mitts slammed her back into place with little effort, but the brief struggle sent a rush of blood to her head. Shaking away the last of the grogginess, Margaret took stock of her surroundings while Navarro awaited the delivery of her cell phone.

The cinderblock room appeared abandoned at first, but as her eyes adjusted to the low light, she could see disorderly piles of tires against the far wall and two closed bays to her right. Her view to the left was blocked by one of the guayabera quartet, who stepped forward to hand over the phone.

Navarro snatched it and demanded the password from Margaret.

"Go f——— yourself."

A hand pulled from her shoulder and slapped her across the face. Navarro pressed again for the password; Margaret clenched her teeth and awaited another blow. When it came, she spat at Navarro and cursed again.

He shook his head and said, "We both know how this will end, Margaret. You will fight, and I will hurt you. You will fight harder, and I will hurt you more. It will go on and on like this until you either tell me what I want to know or you die."

She said, "You'll kill me whether I talk or not."

He waved off the suggestion. "Who put you up to this?"

"What? Trying to kill you?" she laughed. "You have the balls to ask me that after what you did to me?"

Navarro slid his ponytail over his shoulder and stroked it. "You received help. Who was the man on the phone?"

Margaret didn't budge. Holding up Foucault's treasured blade, Navarro probed, "Whose knife is this? Does it belong to whoever found you in the Amazon? Did you double-cross me, Margaret? Did you tip someone? Did they follow us?"

She didn't answer. Admiring the cleaned weapon, Navarro said, "This is ancient, you know. I've never seen anything like it. The blade was made from a meteorite, that I can tell. But it wasn't pounded like flint or other rocks. No, this one was forged. Who gave it to you?

"No answer? You know, Drummond found the site. But when we blew it open, it was empty inside."

"What's your point?"

"Your accomplice found the Flash Stone in the Amazon, didn't he? The one in the picture used to bait me here?"

"You're delusional," Margaret said.

"Am I? We'll see. Sooner or later, your friend will try to reach you, and then we'll see. At least I know now the map is genuine. I will find the Stone eventually, with or without your help. And I will bury your friend next to you." Navarro raised himself out of the chair, knife clutched in his hand.

A hand came off one shoulder and yanked her head back. As Navarro approached, Margaret flailed to free herself, then suddenly relaxed. She spat one last time at Navarro and laughed. "You'll never see him coming. You won't stand a chance."

Epilogue

Juan Santamaría International Airport
San Jose, Costa Rica
September 8

Sunlight streamed through the arching glass panels onto the concourse below. The rays bounced off the polished marble floors and splashed prisms of color in every direction. Every surface seemed to glitter with color: glass walls, chrome fittings and even the suitcases of queued passengers.

Tucked away in a corner, far from the swarm of tourists and business travelers, stood Cesar Perez. Engrossed in a phone call, he began to pace back and forth, nodding while he listened and gesturing while he talked. With bags checked, Anlon, Pebbles and Jennifer sat nearby and waited to say farewell to Cesar. When his call ended, he smiled. "It is all arranged. I will start next week."

The others stood and Anlon said, "Great, I can't thank you enough, Cesar. For everything."

"It was my pleasure, Anlon. I admired your uncle greatly. I'm proud to help you bring his discovery into the sunlight." Cesar motioned at the glittering surroundings. "And I thank *you* for agreeing to help me with my own little mystery."

"Huh? What mystery?" asked Pebbles.

"Uh . . . I'll tell you about it later," Anlon said. "We need to go, security line's getting pretty long. Cesar, be well, my friend. I'll call and touch base next week."

Hugs and handshakes were exchanged, and then the trio headed for their flight.

After Jacques Foucault departed Indio Maiz, Anlon had asked Pebbles to seal the Maerlif with the remaining Munuorian *Tyls* inside. In the fading sunlight, Pebbles had raised the *Breylofte* and summoned her howler choir. No longer afraid of the tree dwellers, Pebbles pushed the entry slab back in place, then climbed the hill to serenade the monkeys good night.

Trekking through the jungle with flashlights and machetes, they returned to the zodiac boat and slipped down the misty Cano Negro on their way to Greytown. After long showers and a hot dinner, the crew relaxed in the lodge's cantina. Aided by a late-night bottle of tequila, they rehashed the day's eventful discoveries long into the night.

Although Pebbles was sad at first, she was also relieved to finally know the source of Malinyah's anguish. The Munuorian's painful memories still found their way into Pebbles' mind in quiet moments, but they were softened by memories spurred by the gold medallion gifted by Foucault. The physical reminder of Malinyah's warm spirit felt at home dangling over her chest.

The following afternoon, the four explorers had embarked once more for Indio Maiz. Declaring he'd had his fill of river guides for one trip, Anlon chartered a helicopter for the return visit. Once there, Pebbles sat beneath the ceiba, Malinyah's gold medallion around her neck, and coached Jennifer through the steps to reopen the Maerlif. As Jennifer hummed on the Stone, the howlers returned to the tree. Most perched on branches, but several of the crooning monkeys sat alongside Pebbles.

While Anlon and Cesar waited patiently for Jennifer to wedge open the entry stone, Anlon wandered to the charred remains of the *Tuliskaeras*. Attracted by a bright glitter in the stack of rubble, he bent down for a closer look. Pushing away blackened chunks of olivine, he found twelve oblong diamonds scattered on the ground. Anlon examined them briefly and then slid all but one into his pocket. The last he presented to Cesar. "This, my friend, is the source of the *Tuliskaera's* power."

Inside the Maerlif, they had catalogued the contents of each chest, withdrawn a sampling of the *Tyls* to take with them and replaced the chest lids. All the while, Pebbles stood vigil with a *Breylofte* in case Navarro showed up. Despite Foucault's assurance, Pebbles wasn't about to let her guard down. False confidence had cost them more than once in the past.

Before leaving Indio Maiz, Anlon and Cesar had discussed plans for the site. Cesar agreed to do a formal survey of the Maerlif and its artifacts and claim the discovery on Anlon's behalf with the Nicaraguan Bureau of Cultural Affairs. Cesar suggested Anlon consider founding a private museum in Greytown to house the *Tyls*. He said an investment in the local economy would go over well with the bureau and lessen pressure to relinquish all the discovered artifacts.

Anlon embraced the idea on the spot and within days had formed the Alynioria Foundation. Its charter—to preserve and protect the art and technology of the forgotten Munuorian civilization. The Greytown-based museum would be the first of several museums dedicated to the memory of Devlin Allen Wilson and his rediscovery of the ancient star watchers.

Over a candlelit dinner the night before departing Costa Rica, Anlon had shared the plan with Pebbles and he asked her to lead the foundation and oversee the construction of the museum. It would mean giving up bartending at Sydney's and a fair bit of travel, he had said, but he couldn't think of a better person for the job.

"No one understands and cares for the Munuorians more than you," he told her.

Pebbles accepted the position with a high-pitched squeal and exuberant embrace that nearly toppled them into a couple seated nearby. Mistaking the impromptu public display as an engagement proposal, the restaurant's maître d' had stopped by with a bottle of champagne for the happy couple. With confused looks they stared at the maître d' until realizing the impetus for the restaurateur's gesture. Blushing deep red, they tried to dispel the impression implied by their embrace, but the maître d' just winked and uncorked the bottle anyway.

They toasted to Malinyah, Alynioria, Mereau and Devlin. Afterward, while strolling hand in hand back to their hotel, they laughed about the maître d's misinterpretation. Anlon jokingly asked her if she could imagine such a thing. Pebbles replied with a kiss, "I can think of worse ideas."

The morning of their departure, Pebbles performed her first act as the newly minted leader of the Alynioria Foundation. She convinced Jennifer Stevens to come aboard. The job offer, hatched over coffee and bagels in the hotel lobby, was met with puzzlement.

"What do I know about museums?" asked Jennifer.

"Hello! Bartender here! We'll figure it out."

"Geez, I don't know . . ."

"Come on, what's not to like? You get to stay in Tahoe . . . I'm sure Griffin will like that."

"Hmmm . . ."

"You'll get to use all your detective skills hunting for more *Tyls*, and God knows I'll need your help managing the museum construction."

"I guess . . ."

"It'll be fun! We'll make our own *enjyia*, I'll kick your butt with the *Breylofte*. Ooh, we can learn to zap each other with *Dreylaeks*, too!"

"Uh . . ."

"Look, Anlon said I have a blank check for anything and everything I need . . . and I need you. So, I'll give you one of those blank checks, you write in how much you want, and let's get to it! Easy peasy!"

"It sounds lovely, except the zapping part," said Jennifer. "What's Anlon going to do?"

"Oh, he's all 'mad scientist.' He said he's going to try and figure out how each of the Stones was made and try to recreate them. He's already emailed Antonio, and this guy Dylan who works with Antonio, to help him out." Pebbles said. "I'm sure he'll help us out when we need it, but he said it was my show to run."

There was much to like about the offer, Jennifer thought, especially given her current circumstances. While the Nicaraguan police decided against pressing any charges, news of her involvement in the Indio Maiz confrontation had quickly reached the Massachusetts district attorney—the same man who levied Jennifer's current suspension.

It didn't matter to the D.A. that Christian Hunte mysteriously disappeared before giving a statement. The mere *potential* of a scandal involving the shooting of an unarmed man by one of Massachusetts' finest was enough for the D.A. to press for Jennifer's termination. Though the police union and Captain Gambelli vowed to fight the demand, Jennifer knew it would be a nasty fight. And for what? Lawfully defending herself and friends?

As much as Jennifer enjoyed her profession and the close-knit group of detectives with whom she worked, it wasn't worth the hassle, or the overhang that would follow her if she was exonerated.

Plus, Tahoe had grown on Jennifer, much as it had with Pebbles. After less than two months staying with Anlon and Pebbles, she'd come to think of it as home. The perception was fostered by the friendship shared with the trio and by the not-so-subtle wooing of Griffin Taylor.

"Okay, I'm in!" said Jennifer. "On one condition."

Pebbles shared the news with Anlon while the four were on the way to the airport. Anlon was ecstatic and congratulated Jennifer.

Pebbles said, "There is one caveat, though."

"What's that?" asked Anlon.

"She's going to move out and get her own place. She thinks you and I need 'alone time.'"

Throughout the days and nights between Indio Maiz and their return to the States, there had been much discussion among Anlon and the others about Muran and Devlin. The conversation was most uncomfortable when discussing Muran, because the implications were too hard to believe.

As the group slogged through the long security line, Jennifer asked, "What should we do about Anabel?"

"You really think she's Muran?" asked Pebbles.

"It fits, don't you think?"

"Sweet, little Anabel?" Pebbles asked again.

"Look, she lied about her knowledge of the *Tyls* and the map. She lied about the statue. She was with Devlin at Zapatera. She gave me freakin' *enjyia* to drink. And she had one of these on her kitchen counter," Jennifer said, holding up one of the egg-shaped *Terusaels*. "Not to mention her trying to lift the *Naetir* at Stillwater."

Anlon had formulated similar suspicions, but he found it as hard to believe as Pebbles. Thinking back to the day he visited Anabel in Bennington, he realized how much she had shaped his early view of the map. She was the one who suggested the connection with the Egyptian Duat map. She was the one who told Anlon the map was "for finding more of the Life Stones." In so doing, she implied that was Devlin's primary interest in the map.

Nowhere else in Devlin's notes or writings did such suggestions appear. Yes, there was a draft of the map on his computer, but other than that, there was nothing to indicate Devlin was searching for more of the Stones.

In retrospect, even the Dominica expedition proved to have nothing to do with an archaeological interest in finding an undisturbed cache of Stones. Devlin went there looking for something specific. *Need to find one fast. Running out of options.* He went looking for a burial Maerlif, presumably to find a *Tuliskaera* or *Taellin*. When he couldn't find a way in, he directed his search elsewhere.

That curious action should have tipped Anlon earlier. The archaeologist in Devlin wouldn't have walked away from Dominica once he found the Maerlif beacon. If his primary interest had been archaeological, to find an undisturbed Munuorian site, Devlin would have marked the location and sought permission to excavate. Hell, the man would have moved to Dominica for as long as it took to locate the hidden chamber!

The unanswered question was, why? Why had Devlin pursued the *Tuliskaera* or *Taellin*? Was it to help or foil Muran? It would remain a mystery unless some new information came to light. That, at a minimum, argued in favor of revisiting Anabel.

"I'm struggling believing Anabel is Muran, too," Anlon said to Jennifer. "But, I think you're right, she definitely knows more than she told us. I think we should go talk to her again."

"But, A.C., if she is Muran, holy crap! That would be like going to visit the Devil for tea," said Pebbles.

"Yeah, doesn't seem like a smart idea, does it?" Anlon said.

Pebbles floated an idea. "What if we got her on neutral turf, and then one of us searched her home. Maybe something there will give us the proof we need, one way or another?"

"It's a thought," Anlon said. "Before we stoop to breaking and entering, let's see if we can drum up proof in Devlin's research. We didn't know what we were looking for before; now we do. That might cause something to pop out."

While the trio waited to board the first leg of the journey back to Tahoe, their conversation shifted to the topic of the *Tyls* and Foucault. They all professed amazement at Foucault's skill wielding the *Breylofte*, *Dreylaeks* and *Tuliskaera*. This led to a discussion of the man himself.

"I can't imagine living for four hundred years," Jennifer said.

"Crazy, right?" agreed Pebbles.

"To me, his loyalty to Mereau is more remarkable," said Anlon. "To do another man's bidding for four hundred years? And he was so passionate about stopping Muran. It was like Muran had done something to him personally."

Pebbles shook her head. "It's hard to understand, but I get why he felt that way. Malinyah's memories feel like my memories. It's your hippocampus-thing-e-o. You said they wanted to make sure their most important memories were never forgotten. What better way than making a person's brain store Munuorian memories like they were their own?"

"Couldn't have said it better myself," Anlon said.

"What do you think Foucault meant when he said Muran wanted the *Tuliskaera* for more than just switching bodies?" Jennifer asked.

"Yes, that was curious, wasn't it?" Anlon said. "Maybe Malinyah can tell us."

"Let's hold off on that for a while," Pebbles said. "I'm not sure I can handle any more rave-outs anytime soon."

"Fair enough," said Jennifer. "What should we do with the map?"

"I kinda feel like we should let that lie for a little while, too. We've got a bunch of the Stones now. I think we should concentrate on figuring out what to do with them before we go looking for any more," said Anlon.

"What do you mean?" asked Pebbles.

"Well, we've got some pretty sizeable ethical dilemmas on our hands," Anlon explained. "It's one thing to tell the world we found artifacts that prove the existence of a lost civilization. It's another thing entirely to show the *Tyls* are more than pieces of art.

"Imagine if we take one of the *Terusaels* and tell everybody that it could help them live five hundred years? What would happen? The word 'stampede' comes to mind. On the other hand, should we keep it a secret? Should we even use it ourselves?

"I've come to believe that's why Devlin never announced his discovery. Beyond any intrigue with Muran, I think he struggled with those kinds of questions."

Pebbles nodded. "I see what you mean. A lot of people would go crazy for the *Tyls*. And, we know already they can cause people to do bad things. Those without strong *gensae*, that is."

"Yeah, think about all the bad stuff that's happened since Devlin first put the puzzle pieces together," said Jennifer.

"Right. Think of what it did to the Munuorians themselves, after Munirvo. If they couldn't control them in a moment of crisis, what chance do we have?" Anlon said. "It's the reason I'd like to study them, figure out how they work. Learn the technology behind them. Test them. Experiment with them. We might ultimately find a way to reintroduce the Munuorians' technology without the downsides."

Midflight between Phoenix and Reno-Tahoe, Anlon awoke to find Pebbles staring out the window while caressing the medallion's black stone with her thumb. Anlon touched her hand and said hello. Pebbles didn't notice.

Nudging her shoulder, he tried again. "Hey there, you okay?"

Pebbles stirred from her thoughts and smiled.

"Whatcha thinking about?" asked Anlon.

"Do you think she's on Isabela?"

"Uh . . ." Anlon squirmed in his seat.

Pebbles leaned forward and gripped his hand. "Malinyah. Is that what Foucault meant?"

"I don't know, could be, then aga—"

"I want to go there. I want to see her." She squeezed his hand.

"Okay, sure," said Anlon. "It might take a little time to find her, but we can give it a try."

Pressing her hand against the medallion, she said, "I want to take the *Sinethal* with us. I want Malinyah to be there with us."

Wolf Volcano, Isabela Island
Galápagos Islands
September 15

Only half the sun was visible on the horizon when Pebbles entered the crypt. Outside, Anlon sat by the entrance and watched the sun sink into the Waterland. To his right, a full Moon was already visible in the eastern sky.

Looking upward and to his left, Anlon waited for the stars of Cassiopeia to appear. First would be Schedar, the brightest star in the constellation. Forming the bottom point of the second *V* of the astral butterfly's *W* shape, Schedar sits 1.4 quadrillion miles from Earth.

Next to appear would be Caph, the closest of the constellation's stars. Positioned fifty-four light-years away, an asteroid traveling at the whopping speed of one hundred thousand miles per hour would have taken more than three hundred thousand years to reach Earth.

Depending on its size and speed, a naked-eye observer might have spotted an asteroid streaking toward Earth from the direction of Caph thousands of years in advance, or a mere matter of months.

At first Anlon found it hard to believe a planet-killing asteroid could go undetected until only months away from striking the planet. But then he changed his mind after reading about the Chicxulub crater bordering the Yucatán peninsula. The massive depression that formed the Gulf of Mexico was believed to have been carved by a six-mile-diameter asteroid. The direct hit by the tiny asteroid was credited with wiping out seventy-five percent of all species on Earth, including the planet's dinosaur population.

Ceres, the largest asteroid in the Earth's solar system, has a mass equal to one percent of the Moon, but it is ninety-five times larger than the Chicxulub asteroid. At its current distance from Earth, Anlon calculated it would take a non-orbital asteroid of similar size around one hundred eighty days to reach Earth at an average-to-high asteroid speed of sixty thousand miles per hour. Despite the fact Ceres has orbited the solar system for millions of years, the first confirmed observation of Ceres didn't occur until 1801.

With these facts in mind, Anlon wondered what combination of asteroid mass, speed and distance might cause the Earth to flip as it zoomed past. Might tiny Ceres, passing between the Earth and Moon at sixty thousand miles per hour, be enough?

From Pebbles' first step inside the Maerlif, she trembled with emotion. Carrying Malinyah's *Sinethal* in one hand and a small lantern in the other, she moved into the dark and dusty tomb.

Fallen chunks of volcanic rock littered the chamber floor, some as large as footlockers. Pebbles stepped around the smallish boulders and aimed the lantern at the crypt's deepest point. There, under an arch carved into the ceiling above, lay Malinyah atop a rectangular slab.

Her skeleton was robed in shimmering crimson and gold. Surprised any fabric could withstand ten thousand years, Pebbles felt its edge. It was metallic, not cloth. A thin, beaded metallic cloak. With the lantern held close, the beads glittered like diamonds.

Across her chest were the dusky remains of Alynioria's tunic. Pebbles recognized the speckles of blue and gold smeared across Malinyah's crimson cloak. In the bones of her left hand was a trail of dust, the last remnants of Alynioria's golden hair.

Pebbles knelt beside Malinyah's skeleton and lowered her head. The medallion swung free and dangled like a pendulum. After a moment's silence, she reached into her jacket pocket and withdrew a *Naetir*. With a heavy sigh, she guided it close to the *Sinethal* . . .

When she arrived in the vision, the marble hall was empty. To her left, through the sheer drapes between columns, Pebbles spied Malinyah in the field of deep-blue Alynioria flowers. Walking toward her, Pebbles looked down to find herself dressed in a tunic of gold and white. Reaching for her hair, she found it tightly cropped in her current style. Holding up her left wrist, she saw her huddled angel tattoo and the scars beneath it.

Malinyah heard her approach and turned to face Pebbles. She smiled brightly and opened her arms. Pebbles did the same and they embraced. When they separated, Pebbles looked deeply into Malinyah's eyes and said, "I know. About Alynioria. What really happened to her. I'm so sorry."

The Munuorian mother teetered slightly and stiffened her jaw. Reaching out, she wrapped her fingers through Pebbles' and squeezed tightly. Without a word, she led Pebbles down into the field of flowers. In the middle of the field, Malinyah turned to Pebbles and reached for her other hand.

A new vision appeared. It was the same blue carpet of flowers, but across the field danced a small child with golden hair. Dressed in white, she frolicked and laughed among the full blossoms. Trailing behind was a flock of butterflies.

As she circled the field, Alynioria chattered with the butterflies. She waved her hand to the left and the flock followed. She ducked low and butterflies dipped in response. Finally, Alynioria stood up tall with arms outstretched and commanded the butterflies to descend. When they landed, Alynioria was covered with tiny golden wings from fingertip to fingertip. She closed her eyes and fell backward into the flowers, scattering the butterflies like fireworks.

Malinyah laughed, her voice full of joy. *"Aeh el sulous, Alynioria!"*

You are sunlight, Alynioria!

≈

BENNINGTON WOMAN'S DEATH PUZZLES AUTHORITIES
Woman found dead in garden, police suspect foul play

BENNINGTON–September 15–An unidentified Bennington woman was discovered dead in her flower garden yesterday afternoon by Bennington Police responding to a call from a concerned neighbor. The dead woman has yet to be identified, pending notification of family members.

According to officers responding to the call, a neighbor's dog wandered into the dead woman's yard around 1 p.m. yesterday afternoon and began wailing loudly.

The dog's owner, who requested her name be withheld from this report, indicated the animal's excited behavior was uncharacteristic. The neighbor entered the dead woman's yard to retrieve the dog and discovered the body. She immediately called rescue personnel and the police.

An unnamed police official with knowledge of the incident said the circumstances surrounding the woman's death indicated foul play. According to the official, the woman had been electrocuted.

As there was no source of electricity in the immediate vicinity, police suspect the woman was killed elsewhere and placed in the garden. The official also indicated robbery as a possible motive. Officers entering the home discovered evidence of a break-in. The official described the crime scene as "chaotic."

The Anlon Cully Chronicles series continues with *Curse of the Painted Lady*. And the adventure doesn't stop there! The fourth installment in the series will be released in 2019 and will feature a new archaeological mystery for Anlon and friends to solve.

To receive updates regarding the series' fourth installment as they emerge, including the expected publish date, follow K. Patrick Donoghue - Novelist on Facebook, or join the author's email subscriber list by visiting kpatrickdonoghue.com and clicking on the registration link toward the bottom of the home page.

Also, look for *Skywave*, the first installment of a new science-fiction thriller series from K. Patrick Donoghue, in the fall of 2018.

Illustration: Sinethal Etching

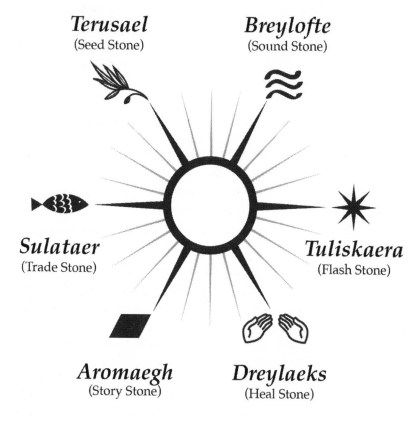

Sinethal Etching

Glossary of Munuorian Terms

Andaers–(*and-airs*)–the council of Munuorian elders/leaders. Malinyah was one of the Andaers.

Breylif–(*bray-liff*)–the Munuorian word for butterfly and the name the Munuorians attached to the constellation known today as Cassiopeia.

Enjyia–(*n-gee-yah*)–a drink produced from flowers of plants whose seeds were altered by a *Terusael* (described below). *Enjyia* tastes like a sweetened herbal tea and has a translucent, pinkish appearance. In *Race for the Flash Stone*, the Nerium Oleander is the primary poisonous plant whose seeds are transformed to create *enjyia*. Munuorians who consistently imbibed *enjyia* could live to the ripe old age of five hundred.

Fandis–(*fawn-dees*)–the council of Munuorian astronomers who kept watch over the approaching asteroid named Munirvo.

Gensae–(*jen-say*)–the word used to describe the Munuorian's magnetic sixth-sense.

Kaeto–(*kay-toe*)–the Munuorian word for "thank you."

Lifintyls–(*liff-in-tills*)–Munuorian translation: survival tools. Called Life Stones by Devlin Wilson, the name refers to the set of six Munuorian tools/stones depicted on a *Sinethal* (Master Stone). The *Lifintyls* are magnetized devices forged by the Munuorian civilization. Except for *Sulataers* (described below), the composition of each *Tyl* (tool) is a combination of three magnetic stone-types: olivine basalt, kimberlite and pure diamond. The *Tyls'* different powers are dictated by the relative concentration of the three magnetic stone-types and their unique shaping. The six *Tyls* are described below:

> **Aromaegh–(*air-uh-may*)**–Munuorian translation: teacher, helper. Called a Story Stone by Devlin Wilson, an *Aromaegh* is a square/rectangular tile that houses virtual-reality-like recordings (sights, sounds, aromas, touch and taste). A *Sinethal* (Master Stone) is one type of *Aromaegh*. *Aromaeghs* were created to store the

collective memories, skills, accomplishments of the Munuorian civilization. They were used to transfer knowledge from one generation to the next, to teach specific skills and to retain important cultural events and memories.

Breylofte–(*bray-loft*)–Munuorian translation: air mover. Called a Sound Stone by Devlin Wilson, a *Breylofte* is a bowl-shaped stone that amplifies sound waves to levitate and move objects. Devised as a building tool, *Breyloftes* helped Munuorians place or remove large, heavy objects. It was also used as a medium-range weapon.

Dreylaek–(*dray-lock*)–Munuorian translation: healer, defender. No name was established for this *Tyl* in *Shadows of the Stone Benders*, but in *Race for the Flash Stone*, Anlon calls it the Heal Stone. A *Dreylaek* is a cookie-shaped & sized stone. Two of them are needed to create their desired effects. By rubbing two *Dreylaeks* together, or slapping one against the other, different powers are generated. The Munuorians primarily used *Dreylaeks* to treat injuries. *Dreylaeks* also served as deadly short-range weapons.

Sulataer–(*soo-la-tare*)–Munuorian translation: stone melter. A *Sulataer* is a token/coin made of pure, 24K gold. *Sulataers* are embossed with a fish symbol on each side. The coins were used by the Munuorians to trade with foreign nations/tribes. However, *Sulataers* have specific purpose/value beyond serving as a currency, a purpose which is revealed in *Race for the Flash Stone*.

Terusael–(*tare-uh-sail*)–Munuorian translation: the refresher. Called a Seed Stone by Devlin Wilson, a *Terusael* is an egg-shaped stone, used in conjunction with a *Breylofte*, to alter the chemistry of the seeds from poisonous flowers (such as oleander) into seeds that produce life-extending flowers. The altered flowers are crushed into a tincture called *enjyia*. The enzymes in *enjyia* attack diseased cells in the body, which slows down the aging process, thereby extending life. *Terusaels* have a countervailing power not described in either *Shadows of the Stone Benders* or *Race for the Flash Stone* (one that will be explored in the third installment of The Anlon Cully Chronicles).

Tuliskaera–(*tool-uh-scare-uh*)–Munuorian translation: fire cutter. Called a Flash Stone by Devlin Wilson, a *Tuliskaera* is a cone-shaped stone that produces a powerful laser when used in conjunction with a *Naetir* (described below). *Tuliskaeras* were used by the Munuorians to cut and shape objects (mostly stone objects). *Tuliskaeras* were also used as long-range weapons against structures and people. They also possess a special power known only to the Munuorian elders (Andaers) . . . a purpose revealed in *Race for the Flash Stone*.

Maerlif–(*mare-liff*)–the name of the vaults/chambers where the *Lifintyls* were stored prior to the Munirvo catastrophe. Maerlifs were also used for another purpose . . . a purpose revealed in *Race for the Flash Stone*.

Manā–(*mahn-yah*)–the Munuorian word for the Moon.

Munirvo–(*moon-ear-voh*)–the Munuorian name for the passing asteroid that nearly wiped out all life on Earth ten thousand years ago. The name in their language means "star washer."

Munuoria–(*moon-war-E-uh*)–the name of the Munuorian homeland.

Munuorians–(*moon-war-E-uns*)–the name of the lost civilization. In their language, the name means "star watchers."

Naetir–(*neigh-teer*)–Munuorian translation: spark. Called a Port Stone by Devlin Wilson, a *Naetir* is a hockey-puck-shaped/sized stone that serves as a catalyst to operate *Tuliskaeras, Dreylaeks* and *Aromaeghs* (including the *Sinethal*). As Anlon learned in *Shadows of the Stone Benders*, a *Naetir* can also disrupt sound waves generated by a *Breylofte*.

Rosa–(*rose-uh*)–the Munuorian word for the planet Mars.

Seybalrosa–(*say-ball-rose-uh*)–the name of a Munuorian shrine featured in *Race for the Flash Stone*. The cliff-side shrine features a massive ceiba tree surrounded by a garden of saguaro cacti.

Sinethal–(*cinn-uh-thawl*)–Munuorian translation: mind keeper. Called a Master Stone by Devlin Wilson, a *Sinethal* is a specific type of *Aromaegh* that houses the memories and partial consciousness of select Munuorians, including Malinyah. Unlike other *Aromaeghs* (which are static presentations/tutorials), *Sinethals* are interactive. A user can ask questions of, and receive answers from, the Munuorian whose memories and consciousness are stored on a *Sinethal*. Not only does a *Sinethal* interactively share sensory experiences (sights, sounds, aromas, touch and taste), it also shares emotions associated with memories.

Sulā–(*sool-yah*)–the Munuorian word for the Sun.

About the Author

Kevin Patrick Donoghue is the author of the mystery thriller series The Anlon Cully Chronicles and the science-fiction thriller series The Rorschach Explorer Missions. He lives in the northern Virginia suburbs of Washington, D.C., with his wife and two sons. His books include:

Shadows of the Stone Benders, book 1 of The Anlon Cully Chronicles
Race for the Flash Stone, book 2 of The Anlon Cully Chronicles
Curse of the Painted Lady, book 3 of The Anlon Cully Chronicles

UMO, a novella prequel to The Rorschach Explorer Missions
Skywave, book 1 of The Rorschach Explorer Missions

Ways to stay in touch with the author:

Follow K.Patrick Donoghue - Novelist on Facebook

Join the author's email subscriber list by visiting www. kpatrickdonoghue.com and clicking on the email signup link on the main navigation bar.

Made in the USA
Columbia, SC
12 May 2019